Rooted in Evil

Natalie Joy Andrews

Copyright © 2016 Natalie Joy Andrews
All rights reserved
First Edition

PAGE PUBLISHING, INC.
New York, NY

First originally published by Page Publishing, Inc. 2016

ISBN 978-1-68348-185-0 (paperback)
ISBN 978-1-68348-186-7 (digital)

Printed in the United States of America

*"Evil enters like a needle
and spreads like an oak tree."*

—An Ethiopian Proverb

Prologue

The warm wind danced around me, whispering promises of love and freedom. The two things I desired most in this world. My soul longed to be a part of this beautiful nothing that held me in its arms, but I couldn't let myself surrender. My heart was painfully yanked in another direction. A thick heavy fog rose up from the earth. Dark and enticing whispers swirled within its vapor. It wasn't safe and free like the wind, but it made my heart race. I felt alive. Promises of knowledge and power slithered around my feet as the mist settled to the ground.

The wind was now swirling around me, attempting to draw my attention. "Find me, Addy. Follow me. Run to me. Dance with me!" The whisper was full of love and desperation as though I were choosing life or death rather than a little jog or tango. I wasn't sure why, but shame filled me for not accepting this loving offer. A game of tug-of-war, and I was the rope.

My heart softened. I curtseyed to the warm air and picked up my foot to twirl in the promise of life, but the fog tightened around my ankles and tugged. My knees fell hard against the large roots of a single tree. A perfect red apple bounced down the tree and tumbled into my lap.

"I can offer more than life," hissed a voice that made my blood stir. "All that you can imagine, Addy, just taste it. One little bite."

I picked up the plump, juicy apple and examined it. My mouth watered, and I was overcome with hunger. Hunger for power, or simply food, I wasn't sure. I sank my teeth into the blood-red fruit. The sweet juices tickled my tongue before the crisp bite turned to ash in my mouth.

The comforting wind whooshed passed me and oxygen escaped my lungs. I fell to the ground, gasping for air as something slithered up my arm and circled my neck.

I cried out just before the hissing darkness hooked its teeth deep into my throat. "No!"

1

Mailbox

"Whoa! Adelaide, wake up, sweetie. It's just a dream."

My mom's voice brought me through the darkness. I rubbed my eyes and struggled to open them. Fear raced through my veins. My scream must have broken past the walls of my dream world and into reality. But what was I yelling about anyway?

I squinted as I tried to remember the nightmare that faded into the abyss of my mind. I swallowed hard. My throat throbbed with pain. My fingers grasped at something pressed tight against my neck. I must have slipped down in my seat. I loosened the slack of the seat belt and swallowed hard. Rubbing the raw spot on my throat, I straightened and looked out the window.

It had been two hours since we had passed a town, if you can call five houses and a gas station a town. My mom's description of our new home was no exaggeration. The middle of nowhere, Ledo, Oregon.

I figure we have reached nowhere and are now racing along at my mother's speedy pace of forty to find the middle of it. She, obviously, was in no hurry; but I, on the other hand, had recently drank two bottles of water and an iced tea and desperately needed a restroom. And *no* I would not settle for the side of the road as my mom had suggested.

There was nothing but forest for miles. Big *green* trees spread out over thick *green* moss and surrounded by an assortment of leafy *green* bushes. It looked as though the land had been washed over with buckets of *green* paint.

I have lived my entire uneventful life in the big city of West Valley, Utah; in fact, I had hardly even traveled more than one hundred miles from my home. I had seen more in the last seventeen hours than I had in my whole seventeen years.

"Lee-doh," I rolled the name around on my tongue as if trying to decide if I could swallow it. I wouldn't say I loved Utah, but it is all I have known. We probably lived in twelve different apartments while living there, so I was used to the packing part. I consider myself a pro at it now. Perhaps it will be my *plan B* in case college doesn't work out next year.

Moving to a new school my senior year isn't exactly ideal but supposedly necessary. My mother suddenly lost her nursing job at St. Peter's hospital about a month ago. And, praise be to whomever, she found an opening at this hole-in-the-wall medical center in Oregon of all places. The name of it escapes me, probably because as she was telling me the news, back in our living room, I had placed two lime green throw pillows to my ears while oh-so-maturely humming our national anthem. Not the proudest of moments for me, I will admit. But I am not used to big changes. Even good changes scare me. I cannot stand that mysterious, inevitable happening that we refer to as *the unknown*. If I had it my way, I would have the gift of foresight so as not be caught off guard by any of those sneaky alterations. Unlike the easygoing carrottop next to me, I am *not* an adaptable person.

My mother wore a big, goofy smile across her face. What on earth is she so excited about? She reached over and turned the AC to high, causing her wavy red hair to swirl over the tops of her shoulders. Everything about my mom is beautiful, even the freckles that are splattered across her button nose and high cheekbones. I think she could have been a little more generous to me in the looks department. She passed along her pale skin and freckles but kept her magnificent green eyes and fiery red hair all to herself and let my father take over from there. I received his plain dark brown hair that would not hold a single curl no matter how much hair spray I unload on it. My eyes match my hair perfectly; dark and plain. I am bland compared to my mother, like a dandelion in the shade of a rose. She does her best to make me feel beautiful though. She likes to retell her account of my first day home from the hospital. She said, "'The sun descended for just a moment, peered through the nursery window, and left a soft kiss upon your precious lips'" Of course this left behind a sprinkle of freckles, but according to her, my smile can light up any room. It was a fun thought as a child, but she said it about every other day now, probably hoping it will make me smile more often. *Fat chance.*

    I turned my attention to the road in front of me trying to see anything worthwhile that might change the hopeless and doomed picture I have of my senior year. I felt overwhelmed by the thick trees that hugged both sides of the road. I watched as a squirrel climbed a sign up ahead, but in order to read it, I had to peer around my potted yellow orchids. I have been clutching on to the delicate beauties the whole drive in hopes to save their fragile existence from being crushed. I felt somehow connected with these flowers. Like they understood what it is like to be so easily broken. If only my mother could understand, could have seen that this move was going to crush me. In two weeks time, I would be a little yellow flower trampled underfoot, withered and dying.

"Welcome to Ledo, home of 948 happy people and one old sore head," my mother read the sign as we passed, now at a speed of twenty-five although the last speed limit sign showed forty. "Addy, I just know you are going to love this place as much as I did."

    My mouth fell open, and I slowly turned to see her face. "Excuse me? You have *been* here *before*? Why don't you ever tell me *anything*?"

    "Well, sweetie, maybe if you don't wear throw pillows for earrings you would hear what I tell you." She spoke to me as if I was a five-year-old, but I could see the little smile hiding at the corner of her lips. I opened my mouth to give a smart-aleck rebuttal, but I was too curious to postpone the answer.

"Oh, Mother, please do explain what I neglected to hear earlier." Fake innocence dribbled off every word I spoke.

She gave me a look that only mothers can give but thankfully proceeded to tell me the story for the second time. "This is where I was born, honey. In the same hospital I will be working in actually. I was seventeen when I, uh"—she frowned and I could see she was remembering back—"when I moved away. Anyway, this is where your grandpa lives. I can't tell you how excited he is that we are coming. Dad says he can hear this place calling your name." She chuckled silently at her last words, but it sent a shiver down my spine, or maybe it was that darn air conditioning she insists on blasting.

"Grandpa?" I whispered. I was five years old the last time he came to see us. It was Christmas day. I got to help my mom pass out the apple cider. I remember wanting Grandpa's to be extra special. I found a piece of cinnamon stick and dropped it into his cup. I didn't know he was so allergic. He never came back to visit after that trip. I was getting nervous thinking about seeing him again so I tried to distract myself.

"So is this the place in your paintings, Mom?" My mother loved to paint. It was like therapy for her.

She grinned. "Yeah, I'm sure you will love it."

"We'll see." My words were thickly coated with skepticism.

"Yes, we will, won't we?" Her confidence tugged at my nerves, but I stayed quiet and looked out the window.

We had already passed some old historical looking homes and were now driving down Main Street in the heart of Ledo. To my right, a barber shop, a post office, a jewelry store, and a very unique combination of an art studio/drug store/quilt shop. Looking over my left shoulder, there is some sort of café that I didn't catch the name of, next to that is Tom's General Store, a dress boutique, and a Laundromat. Each person we passed smiled and waved as if they have known us for years.

Everything looked so small and friendly. Quaint. Not at all like the city. After passing some more shops and a little park, we came upon a gorgeous old mansion that, according to the sign out front, was turned into the local library.

Time seemingly slowed as we turned the corner and passed the mansion. I gazed at its impressive details; the intricately carved columns on either side of the doorway, all thirteen windows adorning its face, and the evidence of time climbing its ancient green fingers up the well preserved brick walls. I watched through my passenger window like I was watching an old sepia film. The scene was historic. My eyes followed along the well-manicured lawn to a picnic table. My little movie focused in to reveal five teenagers leaning around the distressed wood table. Surprisingly, this didn't break the authenticity of the show. They were well dressed, to say the least, looking very studious with their armfuls of various books. It reminded me of some chic, scholarly scene out of *Vogue Magazine*.

Please don't tell me ALL the teens around here have such good fashion sense. I thought of my wardrobe full of worn blue jeans and my mother's hand-me-down shirts. The shopaholic ball of fashion next to me sucked in an excited breath. "You want to go shopping with me on Sunday?" That wasn't at all what I wanted. "Oh, could be fun, but we got a lot of unpacking before school on Monday." I hoped I didn't hurt her feelings too badly. She had to be used to my rejections by now. "Party pooper." She slipped the words out under her breath.

After a few minutes of meandering through neighborhoods I saw it. Big, blue, and magnificent. The ocean. Mesmerized by its beauty, mystery, and hidden dangers, it was love at first sight. The waves gracefully rolled up and down the beach like they were beckoning me to into its embrace. The trees obstructed my view of the cerulean ocean as we drove up a winding road to a cluster of houses that sat on a little cliff above the beach.

We had passed three homes when we saw the little pale blue house with the moving van parked in the driveway. It's thrilling we would have a view of the sea.

"Ah! Here we are, 232 Fjord Lane. We will be renting this house from Dad. He owns a couple of the houses around town. What do you think, honey? We actually have a yard. Oh, and look, our very own mailbox."

I shot a quick glance to the blue mailbox with a sea horse painted on the side and rolled my eyes. It's true that this would be the first time we would have our own separate mailbox. To most, it wasn't a big deal, but I grew up watching people on movies with a personalized mailbox in front of their home. I felt that, to have a complete and normal family, you need a mailbox. A silly notion, but it was a small childhood fantasy just realized. But of course I had to maintain my skeptical attitude due to my innate stubbornness. I couldn't deny—but I would to my mother—that it is lovely little house with a picturesque background. My opinion is top secret information of course. I had to stick to my guns. I had already told her—yelled actually—that this move was ruining my life. I'm not going to give in so easily.

Having temporarily forgotten about my need for a restroom, I stepped out of our silver Chevy Traverse and watched my overly excited mother come around the car and dance up the stone walkway to the front door. She had a big smile on her face as she greeted the movers who unloaded the last few boxes from their van. I stayed, leaning against the passenger door holding my green flower pot and trying to suppress the feelings of hope that was bubbling inside.

It was then that I saw him for the first time, eyes more breathtakingly blue than the crashing waves behind him. He looked rather close to my age. I couldn't help gawking at him. His slightly overgrown sandy brown hair danced back and forth with the light breeze as he turned and smiled at me. I am not one to stare with obvious admiration like an idiot, but I figure it won't really matter. In less than an hour he will be in the moving van and headed back to Utah. I managed to shut my mouth and narrow my eyes just a little as he approached. He smiled at me and stretched out his right arm. *Did he want to shake my hand?*

Before I made a fool of myself I realized he must be reaching for my flowers. He was a mover after all and that's what he does—move things. *"Nothing special, Adelaide, he's just doing his job,"* I whispered through clenched teeth trying to hold my composure.

When he was close enough that I feared he could hear my heart pounding, I held my pot out with both hands.

"There you go." I tried so hard to keep the emotion out of my voice that instead of sounding impartial I sounded like a snob. The man, or boy I suppose, looked at me with confusion for a moment before a huge grin spread over his face and he looked very amused with the situation. Maybe I was gawking again. I mentally checked my facial expression. Nope, seemed straight and indifferent to me.

The guy just stood there, making me feel awkward, so I tried to get him back to his work. "You can put that somewhere inside where it won't get knocked over and then come back. We have a lot more bags and..." I had to stop and swallow, my mouth was going dry. "And boxes in the car." I could barely finish my sentence.

He tried suppressing his grin as he stood up strait and said in an overly serious voice, "Yes, ma'am."

I toured the house and tried to ignore the blue-eyed worker as he carried the remainder of our things inside. He smiled at me every time he set a box down. I even heard him laugh once. I felt uncomfortable and decided I would go wait in the bathroom until he was gone.

I was on my way down the hall to put this plan into action when he set his hand on my shoulder. "All done, ma'am." His last word fell out in a chuckle, and I frowned to show him that I was not amused with his behavior.

"Thanks for helping!" my mom yelled from one of the bedrooms.

"Okay, well—uh, thanks."

He just stood there staring at me, with no smile on his face now, and I wondered if he could see straight through me with those deep blue eyes. It was silly to think that he could, but despite logic, I panicked. I didn't wear my heart on my sleeve. It was not even open for the viewing of my mother, and it absolutely was not available for a stranger. He gave me a look of sympathy, but before I could tell him to back off, he broke the silence between us.

"I like your house. The paint job looks especially nice, I think." He smiled as he proudly looked around the room and before I could respond he was speaking again. "Well, I better get going then." He walked toward the open door and without turning around he said, "Looks like you're going to want to unpack all your candles first." Then he walked out into what is no longer a light breeze but a roaring wind. Before he shut the door, I caught a glimpse of the dark clouds that rolled eerily over the sun. I wondered if we were going to get some rain. West Valley never saw much rain so this idea excited me.

* * *

My mother and I sat on the hardwood floor in the living room, unpacking by candlelight. The storm had knocked the electricity out and left us digging blindly through boxes to find our candles.

"I think we should save our unpacking for a day when we can actually see what we're doing." I chuckled as I looked at my mom with her whole head stuck into a box trying to discover its contents.

She was squinting as she backed out of the cardboard. "That is a very rational decision." She pulled a few packing peanuts from her hair. "Why don't you go shower while I find some blankets for the beds. I have to get up early for an orientation meeting at the hospital tomorrow. I'll be gone most of the day so you should go explore the town."

"Sure, sounds like loads of fun." My voice was purposefully unconvincing as I walked down the hall with a shampoo bottle in my hand.

"Don't stay out too late. We will be having dinner with Gramps tomorrow. Oh, and your new friend will be there too."

I sucked in my breath and stopped wide eyed with my hand on the bathroom doorknob.

"W-h-a-t f-r-i-e-n-d?"

2

Fresh Meat

"I can't breathe!" I giggled through my grandpa's short white beard. He was hugging me so tightly I felt as though he had squeezed every hurt and fear right out of me. In that moment I was completely safe—except for the high possibility of a broken rib. There was something so wonderful and warm about my grandpa. The moment I saw him waiting on his front porch I forgot all about the cinnamon accident that had separated us many years ago. He loosened his flannel-covered arms and ushered us inside to his dining room.

Sitting around the thick, hand carved cedar table was, to my relief, three unfamiliar faces. I was unaware that I was holding in my breath until it seeped out the side of my mouth.

"Kate," an older man welcomed my mother, excitedly, "it's been so long."

My mom responded back happily, greeting him as the old friend that he was. Apparently the two of them had attended high school together, here, in Ledo. He had married my mom's best friend. He even knew my father. This was what my mother explained to me on the drive over.

I didn't pay attention to their conversation as his grown children were already talking to me.

"You must be Adelaide! I love your name…It's German, right? Ooh, don't sit there. Sit here, next to me." An adorable, petite girl with dishwater blond hair patted the seat next to her.

"Don't scare her off *too* soon, Ollie." A muscular man about twenty-three with short cropped hair nudged what I assumed to be his little sister. "I'm Calvin, and if you don't want your ear chewed off by Olivia here, I suggest you sit next to me." He laid his arm across the chair to his right and gave me a big smile. I was overwhelmed by the warm invitations and large smiles.

My mom had already taken her seat and was deep in conversation with her friend who was sporting a thick head of light brown hair and a speckled gray goatee.

Panic washed over me as I carefully observed each empty chair. I didn't want to offend anyone. Why would they put me in such a position? They weren't making a very good first impression, but then again, what could they think of mine—confused eyes, awkward smile. I had yet to speak a word. I had to think of something quick.

"I need to use the restroom," I blurted out and clumsily whirled myself around.

"Oh, excuse me, *ma'am*." I ran right into a solid mass of gray cotton but quickly slipped around it, like oil around water, and headed down the hall without looking up. I didn't need to look up. The way he laughed as he addressed me as "ma'am," I knew exactly who it was.

When I stepped out of the bathroom, five short minutes later, I was composed and ready for battle. My brilliant plan had worked just as I hoped. Everyone was now seated, leaving one empty chair.

"I saved it for you!" Olivia whispered to me as I sat down. "Ben wanted to sit next to you, but I blackmailed him so he backed off." She looked across the table at one of her blue-eyed brothers and smirked.

I stared hard at my plate wondering why he would want to sit next to *me*. Humiliation was the best conclusion I could come up with. He must have found our meeting yesterday very amusing. In fact, I'm sure he did; I could hear it in his voice. The way he grinned when he looked at me, the way he could hardly keep from laughing when he spoke. He probably wanted a chance to rub it in my face, to humiliate me.

Olivia was rambling on about what she brought for dessert. I was thankful I didn't have to worry about keeping up a conversation with her next to me. I could feel Ben watching me, and I knew I had to face him or he would add *coward* to my, already long, list of cons. I lifted my head with dignity and met his imploring gaze.

The look he gave me was not belittling, it was more bashful actually. He almost appeared to be blushing with a look of question on his face. I was taken aback by his actions. I wasn't sure what to think. This was the look I should be giving him. I should be the one with uncertainty smeared all over my face. What was it doing over there looking back at me?

I strategically lowered one eyebrow and mouthed the word *what*.

My grandfather's excited, rasping voice interrupted my hope for an answer "All right, let's pray. Jack, would you?"

Jack, the man with the goatee, gave a long prayer, which I didn't catch a single word of. My mind had other oceans to swim through. I didn't need to listen to a stranger babble on to an empty void.

I partook of meatloaf and potatoes just as everyone else but didn't take a bite off any of the friendly conversations unless directly fed a question. It wasn't that I wanted to be merely an observer; I just couldn't seem to make any words come out of my mouth. I marveled at the men around the table, laughing and telling their favorite stories. Besides the occasional disappointing and short-lived boyfriends, the male species were not included in my estrogen-ruled world. It was me, my mother, and no others. There were times throughout the meal that I had to consciously keep the smiles from sprouting across my face as those four men burst out in unrestrained belly laughter. I felt happy and safe, but I had been fooled by men like this before. I had to stay guarded. I would learn to adapt to this new life for the sake of my mother's happiness, but I wasn't going to be trampled over while doing it.

With a full stomach and a new resolve to (cautiously) participate in whatever Oregon wanted to throw at me, I found a seat on the front porch swing. To my disappointment, the dumb state was already pitching me a curve ball. My view of the thick forest was replaced by, the admittedly lovelier, view of Benjamin. He sat himself upon the porch railing and tentatively smiled at me. As I stared into the face of flawless human architecture, I wasn't so sure how easy this participating thing was really going to be. The stones of my heart fell to pieces with a single look from that blue eyed boy.

I slowly filled my lungs with the thickly oxygenated air. Here we go…one…two…three…

"Hey. It's Ben, right?" The smile came to my face before I could mentally tell my muscles to play along.

"Yes it is. And you are…Adelaide?"

"Yeah, Addy is fine though."

"Your grandpa has told us a lot about you."

"Oh good." My tone was sarcastic. What could he say, she tried to kill me with cinnamon once?

"He asked me to come welcome you guys and help with the heavy lifting yesterday. But I really wanted to apologize for not explaining myself."

"Yeah, I didn't exactly give you the opportunity though, did I? Shoving flowers in your face before you got out a single word. So, let's just call it even."

"Sounds good." He grinned. "I suppose it would be nice for you to know a couple people when you start school."

"Oh, so we will be going to the same school, then?" I asked, curiously.

"Unless you plan on homeschooling. There is only one high school in the area, so we *all* go to the same school."

I could have guessed that one.

For the next fifteen minutes, we passed conversations back and forth like children swapping baseball cards. I couldn't believe how easily we could just talk. I never actually talked to my friends. Not of anything substantial, that is, but they weren't really substantial friends. I was just about to ask why his mom didn't come to dinner when the screen door burst open and out came my panicked grandfather. "RED! Where are ya boy? Come on now!" He followed up his call with a wet whistle. "Just calm down there, Allen." Calvin was right on his heels. "I'm sure he's not far." Ben jumped off his perch and stood at attention like a soldier awaiting orders. "How can I help?"

The remainder of our dinner guests squeezed their way onto the porch to join us.

"Well, Dad, he definitely isn't hiding in the house, but I found some pretty vicious-looking dust bunnies that—" Her voice was drowned out by my grandpa's hysterics

"If one hair on his head is hurt…I'll…well…they won't get away with this…"

Ben had his hand on Grandpa's shoulder, trying to reason with him. "Hey, it has been a long time since…" He shot a quick glance at me. "Well, you know…since that kind of thing has happened. So don't get yourself all worked up."

My grandfather's face became smooth and his voice was now slow and quiet. "That's exactly what I'm worried about, Ben. It's like the calm before the storm."

His words sent tingles up and down the back of my neck, and I noticed that Calvin and Ben were now nodding very seriously. What exactly were they talking about? My mind wasn't picking up on their conversation very well. Should I be understanding this, too? Maybe there was going to be a storm coming. I hoped it wouldn't be a daily thing; all this rain.

"How about it, Addy?" Calvin asked as everyone looked to me.

I had wondered off in my own field of thoughts and missed the discussion.

"Uh, yes?" I asked. It was a question, not a statement. I have found that 70 percent of the time, when you don't know the question asked or an answer to give, a *yes* will usually suffice.

"Thanks, sweetie. You guys be careful." My grandpa spoke as he was led back in to the house by Jack and my mom.

Two minutes later, I was climbing into Calvin's truck. I had been assigned to a dog-finding posse.

* * *

As the grey clouds let out their farewell tears to the descending sun, my eyes followed the methodical movements of the windshield wipers. They swished back and forth, back and forth, clearing off the splatters of rain and wrapping me in its trance. My mind wandered to and fro, contemplating all the wrong things for a girl my age. There had to be more to life than windshield wipers; more than the monotony of school, phony friendships, and pointlessly perfect grades. What was the significance in all this? Was there any real meaning in it? In me? And just how often was it going to rain in this little town, anyway? I tried to turn my attention back to my current purpose and point of being—finding grandpa's old hound dog.

I was tightly situated in the grey Toyota Tacoma. Calvin, being the oldest, took his place behind the wheel with me on his right. Ollie, the little chatterbox, was switched to *on* and nestled securely in between me and Ben. All eyes stared intently around the neighborhoods, alleys, and forest roads.

"So, what was your old school like, Addy?" the question came from Ollie, as most the questions did.

"Oh, the usual I suppose. So big that you never really know your way around, metal detectors always holding people up, drugs sold behind the bleachers, and a gang fight at least once a week. I really never enjoyed it much."

Cal lifted an eyebrow. "Are we talking about school or prison?"

Olivia giggled but continued on with her quest for conversation. "No, I mean like the people and activities. Fun stuff, you know. Will you miss your friends? I bet you had tons of them."

I thought about that for a moment. I badly wanted to say yes, and I wondered if I was a bad person for not having a second thought about leaving them. I didn't even have plans to call. "Yeah, I suppose I will miss some of them," I lied, not wanting to sound cold. "What is the school like here?"

"Oh, it sounds nothing like what you are used too, but I think you will like it a lot more. I'm so excited! Everyone is going to want to get to know you—being as you are fresh meat and all." She winked at me. "But Ben and I will be there to keep all your adoring fans at bay."

Fresh meat? It hadn't occurred to me that the people in this little town might find me to be someone of interest. Someone new and unique with exciting things to offer. It made me a little nervous knowing they would soon be disappointed when they discovered I was nothing but a hopeless empty shell. I had nothing to contribute. Not beauty, adventure, skills, nor wisdom. I wondered how long I could keep up such a charade.

Ben could see I was distressed. "Don't look so worried, Ollie is exaggerating- a little. You will be just fine. Take it one day at a—"

"Did you see that?!" Calvin interrupted as he pulled the truck over where the forest met the sandy beach. "I think Red just sprinted across the road."

"Well, where on earth is he going?" Ben asked, staring hard into the drenched, luscious greenery.

Cal gave his orders as he got out of the cab. "You girls stay here. We shouldn't be long."

Olivia grabbed my hand and started scooting her way out of the truck. "No, I don't think so. We want to go to too." Her lips formed a childish pout as she gave my hand a squeeze, her wordless way of asking if I was in agreement. I squeezed back and gave a supporting pout. My heart gave a quick flutter of realization; I already considered this girl a friend. She wasn't like the friends I had back home—self-centered and heartless. She was genuine, kind, and friendly. I didn't know they still made girls like that.

Ben smiled and I could tell he was on our side. "All right, come on, but you're going to get soaked."

We trudged, single file, into the thick brush calling out for the hound. The rain had ceased but the forest was dripping of the evidence and, after five minutes, so were our clothes. I could hear the waves of the ocean rolling on the shore and the occasional car passing so I knew we weren't too deep into the woods.

"There you are, boy. Geez, you wondered off far." Cal bent down to slip the leash over Red's neck as the dog bounded up to us. The hound's incessant barking brought to our attention something else coming down the trail. It was a young man in a stylish wool coat and a dog chain dangling in one hand. I immediately recognized him from the group I saw at the library yesterday.

We had a good excuse to be out in the slopping wet wilderness, but I couldn't think of any other reasons for such a soggy escapade. This made me wonder about our fellow hiker, and I could see that my friends were even more wary than I.

"Well, well, what a wonderfully pleasant surprise. I always enjoy running into the Tucker clan." The newcomer spoke with more confidence than warmth.

"And why exactly are we running into you *out here*, Charles?" Ben took a few purposeful steps to position himself in front of me and Olivia.

The tension between the men was thicker than the mossy carpet below us. I wondered what this boy could have done to make someone as friendly as Ben be so harsh and unwelcoming. There was no question that they disliked each other.

He brushed his messy brown hair out of his eyes. "Just enjoying an evening stroll, Benjamin. I saw Allen's old dog running around out here. I'm relieved to see that you found him unharmed." I couldn't tell if he was being sincere, but he was unquestionably more cordial than the two brothers.

Cal eyed the chain suspiciously. "We will be going back to the truck then. You keep on with your walk." His voice was thick with warning.

"I will be…" Charles faded out his thought. He took in a long deep breath and cocked his head to the side as he looked at me for the first time. He examined my pathetic appearance without any attempt at discretion. I was suddenly self-conscious; not about the hair plastered to my wet face or my unstylish clothing that was clinging to my body. I was self-conscious about what he might see inside me, my heart, my spirit, my desires and thoughts. I felt like a bodiless soul, completely exposed to his scrutiny. This made me really uneasy. Who does he think he is anyway? That is my soul, and I keep it hidden for a reason.

He took a step forward, eyes never leaving my face, and Ben mirrored his movements.

He understood Ben's offensive actions and didn't pursue further. "I guess I will be seeing you at school then. I wish you all a lovely evening." He slowly backed away before turning and heading back into the woods.

When Charles was gone, the boys gave each other a long look. Charles left me shaking in my muddy sandals. What irritated me the most was that I had no idea why.

Ollie broke the silence. "Okay, I'm soaked. Can we get back now?"

"Wait, what was up with all that?" I asked, hoping but not really expecting an honest answer.

All three of us turned to Ben as he spoke. "Just some bad history between us. One of those people you should avoid around school, trust me on that. They are nothing but trouble."

I assumed he was referring to the rest of the posse of *Vogue* models that I had seen with Charles. I didn't further pursue the topic. It was about all I expected from the mystery for today. We headed back to the truck in silence.

I went to bed that night dreading my first day of school. I didn't know what would be worse: being the new kid who didn't fit in anywhere or being pestered by everyone for my friendship. I stared at my ceiling for hours, trying to calm my nerves, the words *fresh meat* crawling around in my mind. I finally drifted off into a dark dream filled with tormenting whispers and the sound of a strong wind whirling around me. I woke up sweating and twisted in my sheets. It was a whole hour earlier than I needed to wake up, but I wasn't going to risk falling into that dream again. I broke free of my purple bedspread and stumbled into the hallway. I showered and threw on my newest pair of jeans and a white cotton blouse that my mother bought for me. I pointlessly stared in the bathroom mirror for ten minutes wishing the image would change. I soon decided to leave my face as it was and tied my hair into a single braid as I walked to the kitchen for breakfast.

I opened the pantry to get my Cheerios and was startled to find I was not alone. My mother was already awake and sitting at the table picking apart a piece of toast. She unsuccessfully tried to conceal her moist, puffy eyes as I sat down with my cereal. I hated when she cried. She was the one person in this cruel world that I truly cared about, and it was hard to see her in pain. The worst part was I always knew exactly who her tears were dedicated to; my tears fell for the same. It was hard to comfort her when all I wanted to do was cry with her. I gave a few hard blinks and bit my lip.

"Morning, Mom. I am looking forward to school today." I only lied because I knew it would make her happier than anything else I could say.

She looked up at me with surprise swimming in her eyes. "Really? That's great, sweetie. I bet you will fit in perfectly. Just promise me, you will be careful choosing your friends, okay?"

"Oh, don't worry, Mom. I will be meeting up with Olivia and her brother at lunch. I made them promise not to abandon me."

She was cheered up now, thoughts of my father seemingly vanished and replaced by a twinkle in her eye. "Speaking of her brother…"

I didn't want to have this conversation now so I cut her off and made my escape. "Yikes, look at the time…I better get walking. Wouldn't want to get lost or be late or anything like that. Have a good day at work, Mom. See you when you get off." I threw my backpack over my shoulder and was halfway out the door as my mom yelled her giggly farewell.

The walk to school took me about fifteen minutes. It wasn't raining but the ground was wet, which made me realize just how badly I needed my own car. As a senior in high school, I shouldn't have to walk or take the bus with the underclassmen. This wasn't fair; in fact, it was slightly embarrassing.

There were only a few cars in the parking lot when I arrived at the small two-story high school. It was probably better that I left early, this way I wouldn't have to shove through crowds to get my class schedule. I pushed open the double doors and was immediately greeted by the ladies at the front desk rather than metal detectors and security guards. I was warmly ushered into a small sitting area as they gathered my necessities—class schedules, locker number, and lunch card. I was soon set free to wander the halls and locate my first classroom.

I was joined in my English class by a flock of seniors I did not recognize and two that I did. Ben sat directly in front of me with Charles two seats to his left. Our teacher, Mr. Renaldi, was a very energetic, theatrical old man. He excitedly gave us our literature assignments for the semester and then proceeded to read an excerpt from *A Tale of Two Cities*.

Ben's head was slightly turned, and I could see a glare stiffening his face. I followed his gaze to see Charles and a wildly curly haired girl behind him, both staring at me. They met my eyes and gave me a curious but kind smile. I nervously smiled back. The girl was lovely with dark features. She was perfectly dressed, and I caught a twinge of jealousy shoot through me. I was overwhelmed with the need to distract Ben's attention off this beauty. It was childish and insecure, but I couldn't help myself. I quickly scribbled a note down and discreetly passed it up to him.

> What's the story
> with those people. They seem nice.
> I know it's probably not my business
> to be asking…
> And about lunch- PLEASE don't
> Forget about me.

He sighed and it took a very long five minutes before he passed me a torn piece of paper.

> Addy, you are too nosy for your own good.
> I was sorta friends with
> them, once. But they …
> …well they have weird ideas.
> And they aren't exactly happy that
> I turned down their friendship.
> Please just keep your distance. Okay??
> And OF COURSE I won't forget you…
> *No one would forget about you.*

A smile immediately popped onto my face when I read the end of his note, but I was not satisfied by his story. Was that really all? He didn't want to be friends and now they hated each other? I wasn't buying it. There had to be more, and Ben just wasn't ready to spill the beans. Maybe someday he would trust me with the answer but for now I had other worries.

Study hall and chemistry were filled with many of the same faces plus several new ones. I could feel eyes scanning over me throughout the lectures. During chemistry, I sat next to an attractive young man who was noticeably shorter than I. He smiled at me continuously until the bell rang.

"Hey, I'm Bryan Evans." We awkwardly shook hands as he waited for my reply.

"Nice to meet you. I'm Adelaide Dawson…Addy."

"Well, how are you liking school…*Adelaide*?" he tossed my name out like a foreign object, as most people did. "If you need someone to show you around or eat lunch with…" He let his words drift off.

"Oh, I already agreed to eat with someone. Thank you though… maybe next time." I hoped he would forget by "next time."

"Yeah, no problem. Just wanted to make sure you weren't all alone. See you in phys. ed." He picked up his books and walked out of the classroom leaving me with those haunting words. PE was my least favorite of all classes. It was truly a challenge of participation directly following the dreaded lunch break.

A few others managed an introduction as everyone flowed out of the classroom. I was like a fish in a strong current of ravenous teenagers; the rushing river led me straight to the cafeteria.

I got in the food line between a tall jock in a green letterman jacket, who stared incessantly, and a skinny brunette insisted on shoveling out her life story on me. When I had an apple and a slice of pizza on my tray, I turned to brave the forest of unfamiliar faces.

Like two oaks in a cluster of small pines, Ben and Ollie stood by their table waving me down. I said good-bye to the brunette and quickly worked my way passed the tables of watchful classmen. I stepped carefully, trying not to attract attention to myself. It would be just like me to trip and fall over someone's backpack.

I was just three tables away from safety when I was cut off by a truly gorgeous, dark featured young man. He was one of the five that I was warned to stay away from.

"Adelaide Dawson, it is a pleasure to finally speak with you." A hush slowly sank in through the cafeteria as eyes turned to witness the conversation. I sucked in my breath and shot a glance at the Tucker siblings. Ben's eyes were wide and his mouth was open. Olivia was grasping his arm as if to restrain him.

"Would you mind sitting with us for just a moment?" He gestured to the fashionable group sitting around the table beside us.

I fumbled over my words as I got lost in his dark inviting eyes. "Oh, uh, yeah, okay."

He pulled out a chair for me and took his own seat. "My name is James Roth and this is Charles, as you already know, and my sister, Sasha." He nodded to the lovely senior with wildly, dark curls. "And this is Rachael and Adam." He pointed at an adorable pixie-like junior and a surly looking freshman. "We just wanted to introduce ourselves to you and let you know that you are always welcome at our table."

I was completely baffled by their invitation. I could see Ben freaking out. I knew he was hating every moment I spent with them.

The short haired junior took my hand and spoke with excitement. "If you ever need someone to talk to or show you around town, we would be honored to assist you!"

I was speechless. I trusted Ben but these people were very considerate, and there was something about them. Something I couldn't quite point out, but it made my heart race.

I knew whatever I said was going to come out wrong, but it would be worse to just sit there like an idiot. "Well, that is very—uh, nice of you." I looked around and could see that nearly the whole school was watching me now. "I appreciate your...nice offer and... thank you." I had no clue what was coming out of my mouth. I was beginning to panic with all the attention, exactly what I was trying to avoid. When I was finally back on my feet and walking again, the crowd slowly averted their eyes.

My cheeks were flushed when I took my seat next to Ben and Olivia.

"That was amazing!" Olivia whispered excitedly. "They never talk to anyone unless they want something. That's almost kind of, well, creepy actually."

"Yeah, creepy," Ben murmured to himself.

"They were just being polite. Said they were around if I needed anything."

"This is ridiculous. Addy, please just leave them alone." The severity in Ben's voice sent shivers down my spine.

"Calm down, Benjamin. She's a smart girl. I'm sure she will be fine. Besides she's got us. Right, Addy?" She turned her big innocent eyes on me.

"Absolutely. I don't know what's got you all bothered, Ben, but I'm here with *you*...not them, so cheer up." The look on his face was ripping me apart inside. I had an unexplainably strong urge to make him smile. I wanted him to be the happy-go-lucky guy that I had quickly come to admire so much.

Against my better judgment, I softly placed my hand on top of his and said, "I like you guys better, anyway." He looked up at me, and I gave him my best reassuring smile.

I watched as his eyes brightened and the side of his lip curled up in an adorable little grin.

"Anyway, did you know we all have drama class together?" Ollie said, changing the subject and ignoring the awkward moment. "Ooh, you should see if your mom wants to help out with making costumes. We will be performing the *Wizard of Oz* this year. You *have* to try out. I'm super excited about it. I hope I get to be Dorothy."

"My mom isn't very good with sewing, but she always wants to be involved in everything I do so I'm sure she would be thrilled to do whatever she can. Will your mom be helping too?" I asked.

My heart dropped at the look that spread over both of their lovely faces. I recognized that look well. It was always there staring back at me in the mirror.

Olivia studied the ceiling and managed to push out words passed her quivering lips. "Oh shoot. I think I left a book in one of the classrooms. Sorry, I'll catch up with you later." She grabbed her backpack and was quickly off toward the bathroom.

I turned to Ben and quickly threw out the words "So sorry" as if it was the antidote to his pain.

He gave me the tiniest smile. "You're a sweetheart, you know that, Addy?"

No, I did not know that.

He slowly ran both hands through his perfect mess of hair and told me about how his mother had died of cancer not more than two years past. Since then, his father left his place as the youth pastor and Calvin stayed home instead of finishing his senior year in college. It was a dreadfully serious conversation but was cut short by the bell. We were off to PE.

3

Underground

Benjamin had a job assisting the only vet in town (his uncle Hank) and was able to get me some after-school time walking dogs and cleaning kennels. I had hopes of saving for my own car. Working three hours, three days a week wasn't going to get me very far, very fast, but it was a start.

It was a chilly November Friday, half an hour before closing when I unknowingly left the beaten path to blaze a whole new trail in my life.

The doctor was out on a house call and left Ben and I to close up. There wasn't much left to do so Ben decided to help me with the glorious job of cleaning out the dirtied cages.

"You know, honey, you are one of my best friends. I'm really glad you moved here." Honey was his annoying new nickname for me. It wasn't the typical pet name, it had meaning behind it. A few weeks back, Ollie and I made dinner for the Tucker family. Fresh biscuits were included in the main course, which is where the honey comes into play. I was standing tall on the tip of my toes reaching in a cupboard for the honey bear. The bear danced forward with the pull of my fingers and took a bow right off the shelf and strait at my head. Thanks to the loose lid, my hair was coated in golden goo. I turned around in shock with honey dripping down my face and that is when Ben chuckled and said, "Nice look, honey." He hasn't let it go since.

"I thought Mark and Cody were your *best* friends," I said teasingly to his last remark. Mark Johnson and Cody Moore were Ben's closest buddies who rarely ever left his side. Mark was debatably shorter than I with a hilarious sense of humor. Cody was a kind, tall, freckle-faced redhead. The two juniors were like brothers to me because I inadvertently spent heaps of my time with them seeing as they wouldn't leave Ben alone.

"Well, what I mean is…what I am trying to say is…Adelaide Dawson, will you…" He paused and waited for me to look at him.

This almost sounded like a pathetic attempt at a proposal. My heart skipped a few, panicked beats. Of course it wasn't, we hadn't even been on a date yet. But maybe that was going to be the question! Maybe he was attempting to ruin this perfect arrangement to ask me out. I turned to meet his blushing face with great hesitation.

"Will you be my date to the junior-senior prom? I know it isn't until May, but I would kick myself if I wasn't the first to ask." With his scrunched face and desperate eyes, he looked more like he was asking me to jump in front of a bus for him.

His question surprised me. Yes, it was a date, but just for a single event; was that excusable? Could I go on a date with him without actually dating him?

It was out of character, but the idea of prom really interested me. And if I were to go, there would be no one I would rather go with than Ben. I don't know why I was so excited about such a juvenile tradition, but I was very pleased that he had asked. I knew I wouldn't be able to tell him no, even if I wanted to…and, of course, I didn't want to.

So without too much contemplation on the matter, I agreed. "Okay, Ben. I would love to go with you."

A huge smile crossed his face. "You promise? You won't abandon me for any of your many other suitors?"

I hoped he was being sarcastic.

"Yes. Benjamin Tucker, I promise to go to prom with you and only you. I won't ditch you."

"And you won't forget about me?" He winked.

"No one would forget about you." I blushed as I quoted his note to me during my first day at school.

"Awesome. Hey, how would you like to go to a movie tomorrow night?" he turned to spray down the kennels.

Tomorrow? A movie…on a Saturday night? Now *that* sounded like a *real date*. You give a man an inch and he'll take a mile.

I often spent my afternoons at their house doing homework, playing games, rehearsing our play in which I had received the part of the Good Witch of the North. Sometimes I even got to tag along on their painting jobs. The three Tucker men had a small side business as painters. They had painted the inside of the house that Grandpa was letting us stay in. On occasions they even let Ollie and I help out. They treated me as part of their family, but despite our developing friendship, I still felt out of place.

I found that seeing Benjamin and Olivia was becoming a daily necessity. I adored everything about Ben yet I wouldn't let myself see him as a boyfriend. I was very thankful he hadn't yet pursued me in such a manner. Oh, he flirted and called me cute names but never more. Perhaps he knew what I knew, that he deserved better.

"I don't think that's a good idea."

"Why? Did you not finish your history essay yet?" He was oblivious.

"No, no…it's done. I just don't think that you and I should be…well, we are just such great friends."

"And I will always be your friend, but there is a good movie coming out tomorrow. You said you wanted to see it, remember? The one with ice caves or something."

He wasn't taking me seriously.

"Ben, we shouldn't date. We are really different you and I. I don't think that it is a good idea, okay?"

If it weren't for the shuffling of restless dogs, the room would have been deathly quiet.

I swallowed hard and hoped for his light hearted joking and oblivious comments again.

He stared at the concrete floor and shifted his weight three times before responding.

"What is it that you are so afraid of, Adelaide? I know you have a lot of...past hurts. I understand that it can be hard to put your faith in people, but it's okay to trust me. We do stuff together all the time, what's wrong with a movie. I just want to go to a movie with you, Addy." He thought for a moment and then his eyebrows rose. "But if you just don't like me like that...I totally get it...that's fine." He was suddenly very nervous again.

Of course I liked him. A girl would have to be a knucklehead not to like him. I was flattered that he reciprocated such warm feelings, but I dated boys who were more on my pathetic playing level. John, my last boyfriend, was a strong atheist with a bitter attitude and though he was loyal to his belief system (or lack thereof) he was not loyal to me. I hated myself every time that he begged me for a second, third, and fourth chance and I caved to his wishes. This was the kind of situation that I was comfortable in. Yes, it involved a lot of pain, but I wasn't sure how to function outside of dysfunction. But Ben, he had it all together. He was kind, confident, honest, and genuine. He knew who he was and always seemed content with life. I, on the other hand, was broken and lost. How could I explain this to him? He would just argue with me, and I'm sure as all our arguments went, he would win.

The mention of past hurts and the prospect of hurting my best friend's feelings made me an emotional wreck. Why did we ever have to have this conversation? I went through great efforts to avoid this talk.

I must have been taking too long to answer him because he quietly repeated his question. "What are you afraid of?"

I sighed. "Disappointment I guess."

"I would do my very best not to. Have I disappointed you so far?" He looked so sad and concerned, but I couldn't stop the short laugh that bounced in my throat. He completely misunderstood.

"No, *I* would disappoint *you*. I am so...confused with life. There is no doubt in my mind that at some point you would lose interest in me. You are right, about me having a lot of hurt and pain. You know my dad left me, but you have no idea how much that hurts!" My tone was unnecessarily harsh. "Do you want to know why he left us?"

His eyes were full of pity but he kept quiet.

"It's because of *me*, Ben. Me! I was about eight years old. I could hear him and my mom arguing in the next room. He was telling her that he had to leave. He said that he couldn't do it anymore. That life with us was torture and having *me* there was too much for him." I had tears streaming down my face now.

Ben stepped closer and enfolded me in his arms.

"I'm so sorry. That's awful. Really, really awful."

"Yeah, well, I am totally lost, Ben. You deserve someone as wonderful as you and that certainly isn't me." I blubbered like a little child into his shirt.

He gently kissed the top of my head and let me cry for a while.

Still holding me, Ben softly whispered, "You don't *have* to be lost, Addy. We are all lost sheep but there is a shepherd you can turn to. Jesus loves you and…"

"Don't start with your 'Christian theories,' Ben. I don't want to hear it. It's okay if you want to believe it, but don't try shoving it down my throat. I have heard enough of that from my mom and it isn't for me, okay?" I wiped the tears off my face with the back of my hand as I stepped away from him.

"But it is, honey. It is for *everyone*. It is exactly what you need in your life. And it's not a theory, its truth!"

"Shut up, Ben, I don't want to hear it. I'm going to go walk the dogs now. You can finish up inside."

A few minutes later I was outside with mascara-mixed tears streaking down my face and a black Labrador retriever on a leash.

Why did Ben have to bring all that up? I didn't know if I could face him now, but I knew I couldn't live without him either. I had no idea how to handle the situation, and I had no one to turn to for guidance. Everyone I cared about was on the "God" side of this battle.

I walked back behind the clinic, past the small barn, and into a field. I was absolutely furious, but it was nice to be outside. The cool air felt good on my wet cheeks. I tried to focus on nothing but the sound of dead leaves crunching below my feet. It was easier that way; just block out the pain and rebuild the shattered ruble around my wounded heart, if that was at all possible anymore.

The sun had set and darkness was falling over the tall grass that brushed against my legs as I walked. Off in the distance I could hear the sound of dead leaves crunching. The leash tightened as a low growl rumbled through the Labrador. My heart stopped. We were not alone.

I peered through the thickening darkness. There was nothing to see, but I knew I was being watched. The feeling was all too familiar; hungry eyes inspecting me, never letting me be, waiting for its wounded prey to make a fatal mistake. Perhaps I was overly suspicious as a result of my deep insecurities, but I knew this feeling was real. Someone or some presence was always there watching and waiting. An ever-present companion. Was it a loyal protector watching over me, or a hungry lion waiting to devour me? Was it watching with love or hate, kindness or evil?

A light breeze twirled around my waist and brought with it the faintest whispers. The words were indiscernible; all but one, that is—"Addy." Maybe Grandpa was serious when said that this place was calling my name.

Fear rose up inside of me as goose bumps swam up my legs. Was it time? Was I finally weak enough for the hunter to make its kill?

Not five feet to my left there was a sudden sound of flapping wings bursting out of the grass. I screamed and the leash slipped out of my hand as the dog took off. My walking buddy burst into a run after the fleeing crow. My heart was racing from the shock and I began to panic. I would be in so much trouble if I lost someone's dog. I ran after him across the meadow and into the trees. I was so worried about catching the runaway that I wasn't paying attention to where I was going.

When I had lost all signs of the dog, I stopped and took in the situation. Not only had I lost the dumb mutt, but I was lost as well.

The moon seeped through the tops of the trees, illuminating small areas of the forest floor. I desperately looked around hoping to see anything familiar. The trees moaned with laughter as they closed in around me. I was dizzy with fear and had forgotten how to breathe. The shrill screech of a crow brought me to my knees in horror. I had no understanding of forest inhabitants. Could there be some wild creature waiting to feast? I thought of Dorothy in the Wizard of Oz; lions and tigers and bears, oh my!—only I was completely alone. Where were my traveling companions to help me and my good witch to protect me?

There was a tightening deep in my gut; dread was curling its ugly fingers around my stomach. As each tree slightly swayed, the shafts of moonlight danced around me, taunting me. That old moon knew exactly where I was, but it wasn't going to tell.

My life was falling to pieces. I dug my hands into the thick moss, trying to hold the earth still. I was having a panic attack. I wondered how long it would take for someone to find me. How long could I survive as a debilitated bundle in the middle of the wilderness?

Every little noise echoed through my mind, haunting me with its eerie song. The faint sound of a twig snapping, wind rustling through the pine trees, it was the soundtrack to my demise. My final performance, my last concerto.

A new instrument in my death march awoke me from my despair. Dead leaves crackling underfoot.

The crunching came closer and closer until it was directly in front of me. I forced myself onto my feet as something warm slid past my leg. I quickly looked down to determine the source.

What luck! It was my lost Labrador. My excitement quickly faded. I wasn't out of the woods yet, literally and figuratively. There was someone else there with us. I followed the leash upwards to a hand.

"Is this a hobby of yours? Chasing dogs through the dark woods?" Relief washed over me. It was James. He must have been referring to my last forest outing to find Red.

"Is it a hobby for you guys to take *walks* through the dark woods to find lost dogs?" My voice cracked as I tried to regain my composure.

He smiled and handed the leash over to me. "Well, this is by far my favorite walk yet. We don't usually get to talk, do we?"

"No, I guess we don't." I discretely tried to wipe away the salty, black stains from my face.

"Is everything okay, Adelaide? You look troubled."

I had a fight with my best friend, lost a dog, and didn't know where I was. Yes, I was troubled.

I tried to think of a way to change the topic. Nothing came to mind, and as I looked into his eyes of endless darkness, I felt that I could be open with him. There were so many secrets behind those ebony windows. I didn't feel that I was beneath him. I didn't feel alone in my brokenness. Maybe he could understand me. Understand that my heart screamed with pain. Understand my searching eyes and wondering soul. Maybe he could understand because he knew.

"I'm all right. Benjamin Tucker and I just had a little fight. He can't get over his 'God' and how He is the answer to every problem. I don't know. I guess he is just trying to help, but I'm tired of hearing about it. Maybe it is the answer for Ben, but it isn't the answer for me."

"Ah, so what is your answer, Addy?"

I let out a deep sigh. "I don't know, James. I really don't know. Maybe there isn't one."

"There is an answer for everyone. You just need to keep looking."

"Oh really, and what is *your* answer?"

"I think I better get you back to work before they send out a search party."

"Are you purposefully ignoring my question?" I teased.

He gave me a wink and placed his hand lightly on my back to guide me through the forest.

James escorted me and the dog all the way to the back door of the veterinary clinic.

"Have a good night, Adelaide. Try not to let Benjamin bother you too much. You are too beautiful to be looking so sad. Most people like to think that they have the right answer and enjoy forcing it on others. But if he cares about you he will just drop it, and for your sake, I hope he does. You will find what you are looking for when the time is right." His words were kind and comforting. I could feel the blood filling my cheeks when he said the word *beautiful*. This was a surprising twist to my awful evening.

"Yeah, you're probably right, thanks."

Before he walked away, he left me with a tempting offer. "Sunday evening, we will be at the library. I would love for you to join us. We would all be honored to share with you the answer that we have found for our lives." He turned without waiting for my reply. I was actually sad to see him go.

I opened the door with a new hope and confidence in me. I was ready to face my friend.

Ben's face was smeared with concern as he ran up and hugged me.

"Are you okay?! I looked all over for you. I was almost ready to call the cops. You are supposed to take like a five-minute walk you know."

"Yeah, yeah, I know. I'm sorry I was gone so long, but this big guy got away from me and I had to chase him down." I nodded to the black Lab below me.

Ben still had me wrapped up close to him. "I'm so sorry I upset you. Please don't let this ruin our friendship. I want us to stay good friends if that's what you want. Please, honey."

"Well, maybe it would be easier if you didn't call me honey then," I teased and pushed my way out of his firm hold.

"That's asking quite a lot. How about a ride home instead?"

"Fine, I guess that will do for now." I smiled weakly at him. The flood of emotion had taken a lot out of me. I was more than ready for the weekend.

"You're still going to go to prom with me though, right?"

"Yes, I did promise you, but that's all, okay?"

"No problem. You are worth the wait."

"No. There is no wait, Benjamin Tucker."

He just grinned and didn't say any more.

* * *

Saturday went by easily. I decided to take a break from Ben and stay home with my mom. We spent most of the afternoon breaking down our empty boxes and decorating the house. By Sunday afternoon I was getting nervous. My mom was still at church, so I was left alone with my thoughts.

I needed to make up my mind about James's offer. Ben would be furious if I told him what was going on, but he was so hard to keep secrets from.

I knew that James was right; I needed to keep searching for my answer. I needed to get serious about pursuing my own happiness and not everyone else's. I had a pathetic excuse for a heart, and it was about time I did something about it. It was time to journey on, find the "all-powerful wizard of Oz" and ask him for a heart.

By four o'clock I had made up my mind to go to the library. There was a strong possibility that the missing component in my life was waiting there for me. Plus, I could hardly pass up the enticing idea of unearthing the secrets that Ben so badly wanted to keep hidden from me. And my mom would be going to work soon anyway. The timing was perfect.

I had just finished writing my mom a note to inform her of my whereabouts for the evening when the phone rang.

"Hello?"

"Hi, may I please speak with Adelaide Dawson?"

The female voice was familiar to me but I couldn't place it.

"This is she."

"Addy, this is Sasha Roth from school."

"Oh, hi. What's up?"

"I was just on my way to the library. James said you might need a ride."

Her call was extremely coincidental

"Actually, that would be great. Thank you." In this weather, I definitely preferred a short drive over a walk.

"Wonderful. See you in a minute."

She had hung up before I could give her my address. I stood by the phone waiting for a ring. I expected she would call back any second to ask directions. A minute later there was a ring, but not from the phone. It was the doorbell. She was here already. I guess she literally meant a minute.

As I reached for the doorknob, a phrase my mother always said jogged through my mind: "When one door closes another door opens." This was the start of a whole new opportunity for me. I was opening up a door full of unknown possibilities. I tried to hide my nervous excitement as we greeted each other and walked down the driveway.

I sunk into the bucket seats of her yellow Porsche with a handful of jealousy. It turned out that her father owned the local port, a large shipping company, and half of the stores in town. The Roths were one of the wealthiest families in Oregon.

"I am really glad you decided to join us tonight, Adelaide. But before we arrive, I need to ask that, whatever you see or hear, you keep it to yourself. Our way of life is…unique, but it is something that people like your mother and grandfather won't ever understand. We know you are meant to be a part of it, Addy, so try to keep an open mind."

She had my mind digging through ideas. What was their big secret?

"Can you agree to that?"

"Oh, yeah." Her voice pulled me out of my thoughtful excavating. "I'm good at keeping things to myself. No problem."

I had so many questions, but I held them in for our group meeting. Sasha purposefully kept the conversations light the rest of the way to the library.

We walked, side by side, through the towering, old doors of the mansion. The ceiling was covered with intricate white paneling, and the room was stuffed full of books with a staircase leading up to the second and third floor.

We made our way through rows of books, past the biographies and local history, and around a small reading area filled with suspicious glances and onto classic literature. Halfway down the poetry aisle, we were startled by the rasping voice of my grandpa.

"Adelaide, I missed you at church this morning. What are you up to today?"

"We are just, uh, getting a book for English class. We have to do a book report."

He glanced at Sasha with a disapproving look. "Ah, Miss Roth, I wasn't aware that the two of you were friends."

"Actually, Mr. Dawson, I asked your granddaughter to help me with the report. She does so well in school that I thought she could be useful. This is this first time we have had the opportunity to hang." Sasha spoke with full confidence that *I* almost believed her.

Grandpa reached across his body to scratch his left arm. "Well, then, I will let you girls get to it. You should come over for dinner tonight, Addy. Supper will be at 7:00." His face looked strangely pained.

"You know, that sounds really nice, Grandpa, but I'm not sure how long we will be here working."

"All right, sweetie. Just…be careful. I love you."

"Okay. I love you too, Grandpa. We'll have to do dinner another time." The look on his face shot straight to my heart. I would love to spend more time with him, but this was bad timing. This could be a life-changing night for me. This could be the missing piece to my life's puzzle. I couldn't just give that up for one dinner.

My heart pounded with excitement as we walked past the remainder of shelves to the back wall. It was like reading a thrilling mystery novel, and the case was about to be solved. We stopped in front of a single wooden door. What would be waiting behind it? Thoughts ran through my head as I waited for Sasha to open the mysterious portal. A closet? Bathroom? Old servant quarters perhaps?

The door creaked open to reveal a cold, dark staircase leading down to the basement. A dim light crept its way up the stone walls. I was relieved to know that there would be light at the end of this dark, downward tunnel. It wasn't an everyday activity for me to go waltzing in to the shadowy underground. The whole situation made me slightly uneasy. Were we even allowed through the door? I had never done anything to get in trouble. I never went to detention or got kicked out of stores. I always did my homework and never cheated on tests. I wasn't accustomed to this new thrill of danger.

I looked around for any curious librarians as we stepped into the darkness. The coast was clear. No one was there to catch us.

I looked to Sasha, who wasn't at all concerned about being seen. But when I took another step down, she grabbed my shoulder.

"Remember, Adelaide, this is a secret. This is beyond what you know life to be. This will change everything for you, but we only tell those who are chosen. Most people just won't understand this."

"I got it, Sasha, don't worry about me." I shrugged off her hand and smiled.

We made our way down the dark stairs and through a cracked door that was leaking streams of light. By this time my heart was racing and my mind was spinning. I had to consciously make my feet walk me into the room. I knew that I was on my way to the life that was calling me, but I was still scared out of my mind.

The room was dimly lit and did not contain a single window. It was decorated with scarves and blankets to disguise the cold foundation with pillows scattered over a large portion of the floor. In the corner I could see a pile of old books and several well-used candles standing in pools of dried wax.

The group was sitting crossed-legged in a circle and I noticed one unfamiliar face amongst the five that I knew. They welcomed Sasha and me to join them and we took our places on the available pillows.

Once seated, I was introduced to the new member of their secretive union. A boyishly cute sophomore, named Luke, with a very shy look clinging to his face.

"And Luke, this is Adelaide Dawson. The one we told you about. We have yet to share with her what you already learned last month. So tonight we are going to spend some time revealing our world to Miss Dawson." Charles looked at me as he spoke.

Every minute that passed felt like an hour. I just wanted to dive right in and skip all the introductions and explanations.

"Nice to meet you, Adelaide." Luke was slightly hesitant as he spoke. It was obvious that he was a very sweet boy. He reminded me of a younger, more timid version of Benjamin Tucker.

I smiled at the sophomore as I resituated myself on the large red floor pillow.

James was sitting directly to my left. He turned to me and placed his hand lightly on top of mine as he spoke.

"Are you ready for this?"

"Absolutely." That was a small exaggeration. I wasn't *absolutely* ready; I was *absolutely* uncertain, to be honest. Curiosity would always get the better of me though. So here I was, in the shadows of the cold underground, tentatively waiting for the unexplained mysteries to be revealed.

He lightly flicked a strand of dark hair off his face and grinned at me. For a moment I was distracted by his charming features, but his words quickly refocused my thoughts.

"First, Addy, we want to tell you the history of our…belief, religion, way of life, whatever you feel like calling it. It is the history of how we came to know the truth. The history of my ancestors. Somewhere around the third century AD, there was a Germanic tribe of people called the Chassuarii. They worshipped the god Donar, also referred to as Thor the Norse god of thunder. The Hessians were the descendants of the Chassuarii. In the year 723, many of the Hessians were being converted to Christianity and Catholicism. The religions were being forced upon them but many refused to accept the teachings of the church. They continued in secret to loyally worship Donar and to offer sacrifices to the trees and spirits. They performed incantations and practiced divination. They also continued their faith in auguries."

"Auguries?" I asked, never having even heard the word before.

"An augur's task is to interpret the will of the gods by studying birds," the energetic Rachel added.

James nodded and continued, "On the tribe's most sacred land stood an ancient tree called the Oak of Donar. There was a German missionary who decided to cut down the pagan tree. With the angered tribesman witnessing, he took one swing at the extraordinarily large oak leaving only a small notch. Suddenly the tree was shaken by a great wind, causing it to crash to the ground and separate into equal parts. The majority of onlookers believed it to be the will and work of the Christian God. They rejected Donar and began praising Yahweh, the supposed "one true God." Very few remained faithful to the gods and spirits that they knew to be real. The four shattered pieces of wood were taken to the church to be made into an oratory. But when the crowds had all gone, the loyal ones remained to salvage every remnant and sliver from their sacred tree. These few families came together, forming the Kinder von Donar, meaning children of Donar, later referred to as simply the Dons. This small tribe secretly practiced and passed on their knowledge for generation after generation. They slowly began to spread as the spirits chose more followers. Charles, Sasha, and I are direct descendants of the Dons. We have been brought up in their ways by our parents and their parents before them. The rest of the group here has been chosen just as you have been chosen, Adelaide, and as hundreds throughout history have been chosen.

"Many generations ago, several families moved to America. There are now an abundance of small clans around the States. Our parents moved here, to Ledo, when they were our age and have been the foundation for what you see here today. Someday, some of us will move on and begin another foundation for a new generation. To pass on and teach the sacred knowledge of ancient times. To help grow one more branch of our ever-growing tree of knowledge." James removed his hand from mine and leaned back, propping himself up with both arms locked behind him. He was taking in my excitement with obvious pleasure.

From across the circles, Charles continued with my education. "To fully understand and respect our teachings, you must forget about all the presuppositions of this culture. Forget about your mother's beliefs. Forget about the numerous religions and theories you have encountered. Forget about what you see when you walk to school, go to work, or sit on the beach. I want you to think of what you feel. What is in between all that other stuff. What you hear, sense, and dream. We live on the same earth, you and I, but we are in a totally different world. Your world is a physical, restricted world, but ours…ours is of the spiritual. Things you never thought possible…are. Things you have never seen before…you will see. This society has fed you lies. You are brainwashed by everyone else's myths and fairy tales.

"We are simply a select few who has had the curtain lifted. We have been opened up to the true reality of this world."

Deep curiosity was eating its way through my skin. I was dying to know more, to know what I was truly capable of. I was covered in goosed bumps. I had taken a small bite out of a hidden knowledge, and I was starving for more. It seemed so right to me. The world always felt like a big box that everyone lived on but never opened to determine its contents. This had to be what my soul was longing for. And to think that I was chosen, that I was special and desired. I couldn't wait to hear more.

"So what type of stuff do you do, exactly? What things are possible?" My voice was pitched with interest.

Charles laughed. "Well, Addy, everyone sees the physical of this world, but that is just the outer layer, the wrapping around the gift. The world is very spiritual, and we have learned to interact with it. We have—"

Charles was cut off by a sudden obnoxious ringing. I jumped at the sound but quickly realized that it was my cell phone. I pulled the annoying thing out of my jacket pocket while making apologies to the frowning onlookers.

I checked the number; it was my mom. I smiled nervously at Charles and said, "Sorry, go ahead."

"It's okay. So, as I was saying…what we do is—"

The ringing interrupted him once more.

James sighed. "You should answer it, Addy. It's pretty important."

I looked at him with worry and confusion grasping onto my face. With one last ring, I hesitantly flipped open my phone.

4

Fish

"Hello? Mom?" I spoke softly into the phone, hoping it would make the rude interruption a little less prominent in our evening.

"Sweetie, thank goodness you answered. You need to come to the hospital. Your grandfather has had a heart attack."

My heart dropped into the pit of my stomach, making me feel physically sick.

I thought of the look on my grandpa's face when he saw me with Sasha and when I refused his dinner invitation. We have had plenty of dinners together since our move, but it seems inevitable that at some point I'm going to put him in the hospital just as I did as a child.

I didn't know what to say except, "I'll be right there, Mom."

I hung up the phone and stared at the cracks in the old cement floor.

"It's going to be okay, Adelaide. Would you like me to take you to the hospital?" James spoke comfortingly as he helped me off the floor and onto my tingling feet.

Darkness accompanied us on the drive to Viktor Roth Medical Center. It was a comfortable ride in James's black Mercedes Benz. I sat upon heated leather seats and listened to the quiet hum of the engine. It was so warm and peaceful I could have easily fallen asleep. The threat of losing my grandpa was what kept me conscious.

"Please. Please. Please," I whispered over and over again. I wasn't sure who the question was directed to but I had to ask.

James reached over and took my hand. "It will be all right, Addy. I promise."

Relief trickled through my body. I wanted to believe him.

When the elevator opened to the second floor, James decided it would be best if he remained in the waiting area so I entered the hospital room alone. My grandpa was alive and smiling. My mother was sitting next to him on the bed, still in her nursing scrubs. A smile burst onto my face as I ran over to him and smothered him with hugs.

"Grandpa! Are you okay? I am so sorry!"

"Oh, I'm fit as a fiddle." He looked up at my mom who was shaking her head. "But I don't know what you're sorry about. It was a heart attack, not an Addy attack." He chuckled at himself.

I didn't want to argue with him but something kept whispering blame in my ear, "It's your fault."

I crawled up next to him on the other side of the bed and held his wrinkly, weathered hands.

"I was so worried. Thank goodness you're okay, Grandpa."

"No, honey, thank God." He gave me an almost tearful smile.

Not him too. I immediately tried to avoid the subject. "So, how about I make the three of us dinner tomorrow? Our house."

His eyes brightened. "Couldn't think of anything better. You don't have to work tomorrow night?"

"Nope, I only work Tuesdays, Wednesdays, and Fridays. I'll make lasagna."

My mom was assigned her part of buying groceries and picking me up from school while Grandpa was to rest all day with no exceptions. I played a few card games with my grandpa while waiting for my mom to finish her shift. To my great relief, their "God" was not spoken of again for the rest of the evening. The way people talked about Him made my insides twist, like he was it, the cat's meow, the secret to life. Their "loving savior" they call him. Well either he doesn't exist or they got his personality wrong. He obviously didn't *love* me enough to *save* me from the pain of my father abandoning me or the cruelty of this world. If they are worshipping "the one true God," I don't want to have anything to do with it. He is a liar who plays cruel jokes on innocent children.

Over the next few weeks, I spent every spare moment with my grandpa. We ate dinners together, read books, and watched TV. We played several easy card games, and he even taught me his favorite one: cribbage, which to me, is anything but easy.

I didn't see much of anyone until Christmas break. Ben had called, wanting to see me.

    I was invited bowling. To not make things awkward for me, he also invited Calvin and Olivia, and his two buddies, Mark and Cody. Bowling was one activity I was actually good at. For as long as I can remember, my mom and I bonded over a slick bowling lane and a pitcher of root beer. I had mentioned this to Ben months ago and here he was, strategically using the information to get his way. If he would have invited me to go ice skating, snowshoeing, or some other lame activity, I was likely to say no. I could never say no to bowling. It was one thing that made me feel good about myself. It annoyed me that Ben knew me so well.

    The Ledo Bowling Alley was much smaller than I was used to and was nearly empty when I arrived early on Sunday evening. Cody Mills was the only one who arrived before me. He was swiveling back and forth in his chair, already sporting clown-like bowling shoes.

    "Hey, Cody, how's it going?"

    He looked up from the spot on the floor that had him in deep concentration. "Oh, hey, Addy. I'm glad I'm not the only one here early. I got us a lane already." I noticed the computer on the table in front of him. Everyone's names were already entered in the machine and a single green bowling ball was patiently awaiting the game.

    "Well, I'm going to get my shoes. I'll join you in a minute." I made it half a step when Cody called me back.

"Wait! Can I ask you a question?" His anxiety had me concerned. Cody was so sweet and always happy. The most worried I had ever seen him was when the lunchroom served split pea soup with salad.

"Yeah, of course." I sat down and gave him my full attention.

"How come you don't like Ben, you know, more than just a friend?"

His question caught me by surprise.

"Well, I do, but…" I hesitated for a moment and Cody spoke up, allowing me to drop the explanation.

"I'm sorry, you don't have to answer that. I only ask because, well, I want to ask this girl out on a date. But I don't want to get the same answer that you gave Ben."

"Oh, well, I guess that depends on the girl. May I ask who?"

He leaned in and his voice crackled as he spoke, "It's Olivia. I just want to ask her to go to prom with me, you know, nothing serious. But every time I try, I get so nervous and I panic. What do you think?"

He quickly sat up and turned to the door. The rest of our party was walking in.

I swiveled my chair so I was facing the opposite wall and discreetly whispered, "Trust me, you should ask." I smiled to myself as I thought of how ecstatic Olivia would be. She had confided in me countless times on how she has adored Cody since the seventh grade. And of course, prom was right up her alley. Being that she was only in tenth grade, however, she couldn't attend without being asked. Despite the small hindrance, Ollie had already selected a dress from the boutique on Main Street. She had pointed it out to me back in October as we were walking to the coffee shop. It was a lavender Cinderella-looking ball gown that was displayed in the store window. She said the dress was her "Raison d'être" for her sophomore year, one way or another she would be wearing it to the junior-senior prom.

I could see the color filling Cody's cheeks as Olivia joyfully plopped down in the seat across from him.

Mark and Calvin stopped short of our table as they continued swimming in their pool of discussion. This left Ben standing five feet away from me, grinning, like a loyal puppy awaiting affection. It had been several weeks since I had seen him, and I had nearly forgotten what it felt like. The way I felt when I looked in those deep ocean-blue eyes. Such a wonderfully warm feeling of safety and love. Not the ooey-gooey type of love, but a something more. Something genuine and pure. Something I was not accustomed to. Although, we did have our ooey-gooey moments.

As always, a large smile decorated my face as I returned his excited gaze. Then his expression changed, he looked slightly more timid and bashful as Cody had looked just a minute ago. He stared at me for only but a moment, though that moment seemed like a hundred moments slowly passing in a silent breeze of adoration. Like some cheesy scene out of a romance film, everything faded away and left the two of us shyly staring into each other's eyes. He took a step closer, releasing a flutter of butterflies through my stomach.

"It's been way too long, Addy." I was glad to see we were on the same page with that.

I stared up at him from my chair, half expecting a huge bear hug to commence as usual. When he made no advance, I swiveled my chair and stood up.

"Well, let's get our shoes, and I'll show you how this game is played." I gave him a wink and walked to the front counter. I could tell that Ben was slightly withdrawn. I suspected he was guarding himself from being hurt just as I always did. I certainly didn't blame him, but I couldn't help but be disappointed. After all, I am only a girl, it would be nearly impossible to not be flattered by the pursuit of such a worthy man.

Within ten minutes, the group was equipped with shoes, bowling balls, and the necessary pitcher of root beer. We were separated into two teams of three: Ben, Mark, and I against Calvin, Cody, and Olivia.

Calvin and I were evenly matched and soon had surpassed our group in scores. Mark and Ben were ecstatic with my performance. I received giant hugs and cheers after every strike. I loved the whole experience. It wasn't often I was able to offer something to a group of people. Mark was decently skilled but Benjamin was adorably awful.

By 9:00 p.m. our team scores were neck and neck. Everyone was swept up in the suspense and hype of the moment. Ollie was screaming for Calvin as he took his last turn.

The ball struck and left two pins teetering back and forth. No one breathed as we watched the pins teasing us with every wobble.

"Come on!" Calvin urged.

THUMP. A single pin gave in to the pressure, leaving one standing to challenge Calvin to a rematch.

As our opponent took his ball once more and stepped up to the line, Ben and Mark each took my hand and squeezed tightly. I glanced at the both of them. They were absolutely adorable, wishing with all their might that Cal would miss the pin. In all my life I had never been as relaxed around men as I was right now. I sucked in my breath as I returned their tightening grip, hand for hand, and took in the beauty and excitement of this moment.

"SPARE! Yeah, beat that Addy," Ollie teased as she high-fived Cal and Cody.

The boys gave my hands one last squeeze before they released me to execute the ten pins that awaited their fate.

As I stood, with my toes behind the mark, I could feel the pressure weighing me down. Suddenly, my purple, number eight bowling ball that dangled at my side felt like it weighed fifty pounds.

"No pressure, honey," Ben whispered from right behind me. I jumped at his unexpectedly close proximity. He smiled at me and winked and then stepped back to give me room. The butterflies took flight, leaving no room for the heavy weight of anxiety.

I shot my purple canon ball right at the heart of the pins. Silence spread over each of my friends as all eyes followed the last seconds of the game.

"STRIKE!" Mark yelled as my bowling ball smashed loudly into the rows of pins awarding our team the winner!

My enthusiastic cheerleaders rewarded me with a short march through the building atop of their bulky shoulders. Laughter bubbled out of me at the awkwardness of my high throne. Mark was quite a bit shorter than Ben, leaving me lopsided and gripping their provided hands and with all my strength.

Eventually I found myself back on my own two feet. When Mark was sure I was securely grounded, he let me go and wandered over to our table to have some root beer. Calvin, Cody, and Olivia were already seated and looking very unimpressed by our grand display of triumph. I started to make my way to the group when I realized I had, unknowingly, let the steel fortress around my heart fall down. I was no longer being cautious and careful.

Ben was still holding on to my hand as we walked. I stopped in my tracks and looked at him. I hoped he couldn't read the panic that was written all over my face.

"I'm going to get us all some more root beer. Meet you at the table." My fingers spread and let his hand fall away as I rerouted my path. I didn't look back to see if my sudden actions had fazed him. I needed to be more careful, not just for my sake, but for his as well.

I stepped up to the concession counter and looked into an unexpected face. Adam, the young freshmen who spent his time with my more controversial group of friends, was not at all welcoming toward me. He had dark features and dark clothing to match his dark manner. He was the only one of his bizarre group that set me on edge.

"Hello, Dawson. Do you need something?" His voice was low and even.

"Hey, Adam. Can I get a pitcher of root beer and a platter of nachos?"

"Will that be all?" His eyes seemed to widen the longer he stared at me. There was an unpredictable wildness about him, like a hungry wolf sniffing at a cottontail bunny.

"Yeah, that's all." I quickly threw the words out, hoping he would get to work and stop staring at me. I was cautious and slightly frightened being left alone with him, as though he might, at any moment, leap over the counter and take a bite out of my throbbing neck. Why did he stare at me like that? I just wanted to get my order and take my place next to Ben.

A few minutes later, the root beer and nachos were set on the counter.

I reached for the twenty dollar bill that had I tucked into the pocket of my worn blue jeans. A loud gasp slipped out of my mouth as Adam leaned over the counter and grabbed my wrist. My heart pounded as my mind plotted an escape route.

"Leave it, Adelaide. It's already covered." He was so close now that I could feel his breath on my face.

My mind was so scattered that I wasn't sure what to make of his words. I just stared at him with question-coated horror saying what my mouth couldn't.

He slowly loosened his grip on me and said, "Do you know who Viktor Roth is?"

Viktor was James's and Sasha's father. I knew, but I couldn't say, so I nodded.

"Well, he owns the bowling alley. James said that if you were to come in, I was to tell you that anything you want is on the house. So keep your money and take your food." He slid the pitcher toward me. Still no smile.

Slight relief washed over me, but my heart was still pounding, I wasn't safe yet.

I took my things and started backing away as I spoke, "That is very generous. Tell James I said thank you."

Now, he smiled. A disturbingly dangerous-looking smile.

I took another step backwards and was stopped by strong hands around both my shoulders. I was once again startled, spilling a bit of root beer on my grey, long-sleeve tee.

"Or you could tell me yourself." James grinned as he smoothly slipped his hand under my tray of nachos and took the pitcher, unloading my burden. Despite his gentlemanly gesture I was still very unnerved.

My voice was shaking as I spoke, "Wow, you are always showing up when I least expect it."

"I like to keep you on your toes." His smile turned into slight concern. "But you don't look happy to see me."

My heart was slowing down now, and I was able to speak more clearly. "Oh, no, James, I was just startled. I always love seeing you, and thank you so much for the free food. That is pretty awesome that your dad owns this place."

"Glad to hear that. I hope Adam was nice enough. Can I carry these to your table for you?" He nodded down at the snacks.

"That would be great. Thanks." We started walking toward the table as the occupants stared with wide eyes and open mouths. "What is the deal with Adam, anyway?"

James shot a disapproving glance at the unfriendly freshman before he spoke. "Well, Adelaide, remember how we told you that you were chosen?" I nodded and then he lowered his voice. "*We* don't choose you, it is...Well, I think we are going to have to talk about this later. How about tomorrow night?"

We had reached the table so I just gave him another nod.

The nachos and root beer were not greeted with the enthusiasm I had hoped for. No one even looked at them. All eyes were on James. I hadn't considered how awkward this might be, especially for Benjamin.

James took in the stunned faces with a small trace of amusement.

"Well, I won't make this awkward for you. I was only assisting Miss Dawson here, she had a bit of trouble..." He nodded to the splatter across my abdomen.

Ben spoke in a surprisingly kind voice but his words were what really shocked me. "You are welcome to join us, James. Looks like Addy got us plenty of nachos."

James was obviously taken aback before he quickly regained his composure. "Very kind, Tucker, but I have some things to attend to. Next time perhaps."

"Anytime," Ben said.

I sat down and stared at Ben in disbelief as James wandered back to the concession stand.

"*Anytime?* I thought you hated those guys?" My voice was slightly rude due to my great confusion.

"Hate? No, no, Addy. I certainly don't hate them. I just disapprove of what they do. Actually, I feel really bad for them."

"You feel bad? For *them?* Why?" I couldn't see any reason to pity them. They were so full of confidence and purpose.

"They are very…misguided." Ben seemed truly sad about his statement.

Mark cut in the conversation with a much louder, less kind tone of voice. "What he means is…they are devil worshipers!"

"What!" the word just shot out of my mouth. I was shocked, is this why the Tuckers disliked them so much? Did they truly believe they worshipped the devil? I suddenly felt defensive as if this accusation was directed at me.

"They are deceived, Addy. The best thing we can do is pray for them. Like Ben said, we don't hate them, but they need help." Calvin grabbed some nachos as he spoke.

Mark smirked. "They need help all right. Like a padded room and buckets of holy water." Besides me, Mark was the only one in this group who didn't attend church, but it was apparent he was not on my side.

"Do you even have any idea what they do, or are you just jumping to conclusions? Maybe you shouldn't be so quick to judge." Silence followed my harsh statement.

After a very long, very quiet minute of me feeling very awkward, Ben grabbed my hand and said, "Let's talk about something else. Like the play. Did you know we get our costumes when we come back from Christmas break?"

There was another long silence until Ollie joined her brother's effort. "That will be fun, won't it? I'm actually getting a little nervous. I have a lot of lines to memorize."

Calvin nudged her ribs with his elbow. "You're the one who had to be Dorothy."

"Yes and it is worth it," she spoke indignantly as she lightly rubbed her assaulted ribs. "And speaking of which, I need to go home and practice."

Cody sat up strait and grinned. "Can I help?"

His eagerness earned him a few skeptic looks from the boys. In an attempt to regain his cool, he said, "It's just that I got nothing better to do, and I happen to be fond of that particular play." Cody cleared his throat and slouched back down in his chair.

"Oh, I thought we were going to watch *Braveheart* tonight. It starts at ten remember?" Mark gave a big satisfied smile.

I assumed that Cody kicked Mark under the table because Mark jumped in his seat and grunted.

"Wait, you know what, that is tomorrow at ten, isn't it? Never mind, Cody, it looks like you have nothing better to do after all." His lying was obvious to all but Ollie. She sat there grinning innocently, probably reciting "Follow the Yellow Brick Road" in her head.

Calvin stood up and pulled on his jacket. "All right, I'll give you both a ride. Anyone else coming with me, speak now."

"I got my truck," Ben said, his hand still gripping mine. I had yet to figure a polite way out of this situation. I didn't want to hurt his feelings, but I had a suspicion that he knew exactly what I was thinking and he just didn't care. He was probably getting a kick out of it.

"And my mom will be here any minute to pick me up. I told her about 9:30," Mark said.

"Good, then I guess we are off to see the wizard." Cal laughed and took his car keys out of his pocket.

Cody followed Calvin out the door as Ollie replaced her unfashionable bowling shoes with her boots. A moment later she bounced up, enfolding me in a tight hug and whispered in my ear. "I'm going to prom!"

Immediately following their departure, Mark's mother showed up, leaving Benjamin and I alone.

I quickly thought of a simple maneuver to free my hand. I gave a little shiver and reached for my hooded sweatshirt. As I pulled it over my head, I thought I heard a small chuckle. He may find this to be amusing, but it was very hard on me.

"Are you cold, Addy?"

"Yeah, a little," I lied as I rubbed my hands together, creating heat. I immediately dropped my hands at my side when I realized that the *cold hands* act could easily backfire on me.

"It is actually quite a bit warmer today than it has been." He had that annoying look of amusement on his face.

"Well, I get cold easy." That actually wasn't a lie.

Ben got out of his chair. "I'll ask them to turn the heat up for you."

I grabbed his arm to hold him back. "No, no, I'm okay now. The sweatshirt is all I needed."

He sat back down and scooped up my hand that was clinging to his forearm. "Okay then. So, are you guys doing anything fun for Christmas?"

Oh, he was good. One smooth movement, and we were back to where we started.

I sighed. "I don't know really. Mom works during most of my Christmas break, but we will probably spend what we can at Grandpa's."

"Addy, can I ask you something?" His tone was much more serious now.

"Ask away."

"Exactly how much do you know about the…about James's little coven?"

Coven was not a word I heard often, but when I did it was in reference to a group of witches. There he goes again, claiming that my friends are demonic little magicians or something. Why was everyone so negative? Just because they are secretive and unsocial doesn't mean they are boiling goat heads in a cauldron.

"If by coven, you mean his friends, well I don't know very much to be honest with you. Just that they see more to life than you or I do."

He frowned. "You shouldn't assume that I don't see more than this. As a Christian, I know that the spiritual world is very real, Addy, and that all this stuff"—he waved his free hand—"isn't what really matters."

"And you shouldn't assume that my friends are evil." I pulled my hand out of his, no longer caring if he noticed.

"So they are your friends now?" It was disappointment, not anger that came out in his words.

"Yes, Ben, they are. So if you want to talk about them, you need to be a little nicer." I tried to keep my voice even.

He hesitated and then said, "Okay, I'm sorry. I brought it up because, well, I want to tell you how I know so much about them."

Now things were getting interesting. I had been waiting for him to tell me this story since we first ran into Charles in the forest.

"All right Ben, I'm listening."

He took a drink of root beer and then stared into his cup as he spoke. "A few years ago, when my mom was dying, I was pretty angry. Angry at God for letting my mom get sick. I was raised in a Christian home. My mom loved Jesus with all her heart and my dad served as a youth pastor for most of my life. But I had yet to accept Christ personally. I was very lost. It was halfway through my sophomore year when Charles, James, and a few older classmen approached me. They told me I was chosen for a different life, and that if I wanted, they could heal my mother. I was confused but grabbed tightly on to the hope they held out for me. If there was any way to save my mom, I was going to try.

They showed me many things that were beyond anything I have ever seen. I was haunted by dreams and didn't know what to do. And when it came time to commit, I ran. I ran to my mother and told her that she could be healed. I explained to her what I had learned. I can remember that day so clearly; she kissed me on the forehead and asked for her Bible. She sat in her hospital bed reading passages to me for hours. And when we were done, we prayed. Two life changing things happened that day, God became real to me and my mom went to be with Him. Needless to say, my new friends were not happy about my decision."

"I am so sorry about your mother, Benjamin, but I don't understand why you chose not to...well, see her healed."

"Because, Addy, if they have a power that is not from God, then it is from the devil. No, ifs, ands, or buts. It is very black and white. And the last thing my mom would want is evil activity on her behalf. Besides that, she was quite ready to be in heaven."

I was glad that Ben wasn't remorseful about his decision, but I on the other hand, felt he had made an awful mistake. If he wasn't so blinded by the Christian theories, maybe his mother would still be alive and he could be a part of something much greater. Of course, I could not speak my mind on this matter, it was best to let him believe his mother was happy with his "God."

"So, I don't understand how you were 'chosen.' Do you know how that whole thing works?" I would be able to hear that answer from James tomorrow, but I wanted to know what Ben had to say about it.

"Sure, I know. But let me tell you what really happens. What they *won't* tell you. I believe that Satan, the deceiver, hunts down the insecure and broken-hearted, the lost and searching. And then he unleashes his hounds on them. He torments his followers into doing his will. The evil wants them, wants all of us, one way or another, dead or alive. He wants you to do his will on earth or suffer in hell.

But our God is the only protection. Darkness cannot dwell where the light is—"

"Okay, okay, I get it. Can we talk about something else now?" He was going overboard with this whole evil agenda thing.

He ignored me. "Research it. Look up the Dons on the Internet. They are witches, Addy. They are more lost than you are. It is just plain old witchcraft disguised with ancient stories and beliefs. They are so lost and deceived by the devil. What they do is purely wicked. I know you don't like to hear this, but I need you to know. I can see how they watch you, the way they look at you. They want you, Addy, and nothing will get in their way. Nothing but—"

"Don't say 'God'! Seriously, Benjamin, I put up with your belief as much as I can, the least you can do is let me be. Let me figure things out for myself."

"I only tell you this because I care, honey. I don't want to upset you, but this is more important than anything I could ever tell you. Jesus is—"

"No, I'm done. I'm going home. We can talk again when you aren't in such a righteous mood."

"At least let me give you a ride home. I won't say another word the whole way there. Please." His eyes were pleading but I was fed up.

"Ben, just let me walk. I want to walk." I tossed my bowling shoes in the pile of discarded footwear.

"I'll take them all up to the counter, don't worry about it." Ben said, obviously not happy with me but I was glad he wasn't insisting on the ride. I just couldn't seem to spend time with him without hurting his feelings. I didn't enjoy walking in the cold, but I would rather have ten shivering minutes over five minutes of Benjamin's holy torture.

"Thanks. I'll see you later." I got out of my chair and turned away.

"Not for about a week," he muttered.

I whirled around and faced him. "Really?" Despite Ben's preaching, I craved his company. A whole week without him was not my idea of a good Christmas present.

"We are visiting some family in Montana for Christmas. That's kind of why I wanted all of us to hang out today. We will be leaving tomorrow afternoon, and well, I'm really going to miss you.

He was pulling me back in again. Why was it so hard to just walk away?

"Sounds like fun," I said without looking him in the eye. "I might miss you too, but I'm still walking home tonight."

"It's chilly out. And dark. I don't feel right about letting you walk. What if it snows?"

"Come on, I walk all over town. It is my main mode of transportation these days. I really just want the fresh air." His eyes lightened, and I could see an idea pop into his head so I added, "Alone, Benjamin."

"All right, if that's really what you want." He got out of his chair and relocated the pile of shoes from the ground to the table.

"Have a good trip, Ben." I turned around and hoped to make it outside before I caved under those marvelous blue eyes.

"Wait."

Of course. I stopped and gave him a look that said, "What now?" He stepped over to me and took my hand. But instead of holding it as he had annoyingly been doing all night, he slipped something small inside. "Merry Christmas" was all he said as he curled my fingers around the gift. And with that he loaded the shoes in his arms and walked away.

Without looking in my hand, I walked right outside and into the cold winter air.

When I was a good three minutes away from the bowling alley, I stopped under a streetlight across from the city park. Winter was biting at my face and just a few overstuffed snowflakes could be seen falling in my chosen spotlight. I sat down on the curb and slowly opened my hand.

How beautiful, was my first thought. But then I looked closer. I didn't understand. He had hand carved a tiny piece of wood into the shape of a fish. It was dangling on a thin strip of leather. No man had ever given me jewelry before, let alone something uniquely handmade. But why a fish? I could feel a few tears welling up inside of me, and I tried to shove them back down. How ridiculous of me to cry over a piece of wood I didn't even understand the meaning of. It just goes to show how fragile and desperate my heart is. I held the little fish between my fingers and squinted. Something was engraved along the belly. It was almost too dark to read. From what I was able to tell, it read: *PSA* on one side and *91:9–16* on the other. What the heck was that? A little fish with random letters and numbers on it. He must have meant for some explanation to this. Or perhaps it was a riddle, something for me to figure out.

I wiped a rogue tear off my cheek and squinted even harder, wondering if I had read it wrong, when a wave of spices and dirt washed over me. I scrunched my nose and just as I lifted my head, a brown, solid mass of legs had knocked me to the ground. My fish went flying out of my hand and my head plopped on the cold cement.

"Ouch!" I yelled but my mind quickly switched gears. My fish! I couldn't lose that necklace.

I was lying halfway on the sidewalk staring up into a dirty yellow light. I knew the fish had swam off behind me somewhere so I rolled my body over to search the ground.

I could see it, peeking out of cement crack. But something was blocking my reach. My eyes focused onto the obstacle not ten inches from my face; filthy brown shoes connected to raggedy brown pants, and somewhere up there was a face staring down at me.

5

Wicked

A leathery hand with dirt-lined fingernails reached down into my face.

"Sorry" was all the voice said.

I looked to my necklace waiting in the crack of the sidewalk and looked back to the man's grimy hand. I wasn't going to leave my fish down here alone. I decided to go for it.

I made a quick lunge around his worn pant leg and reached for my new gift. Just as my fingertips touched the wooden carving, a heap of black feathers swooped down. The crow landed so close that I could feel its silky wing caress my hand as it screeched at me. I was so startled that I pulled my hand away and pushed myself up to a kneeling position.

The dirty hand was in my face again as his other hand shooed away the bird. This time I took it and was helped onto my feet.

"You okay?" The man didn't sound overly concerned.

I gripped my hair as the ground swayed below me. I had hit my head harder than I thought. I fingers found a small gash above my ear giving way to a tiny trickle of blood.

"Huh? I don't know, actually." I was a little dizzy and extremely startled by the moronic bird.

The man kept his arm out for me to steady myself on.

"I didn't see you sitting there." The man explained as his eyes wandered the sky. A thought suddenly popped into my head that this middle-aged ball of dirt next to me might be a mentally unstable homeless man. I thought it best if I got my necklace and went on my way as quickly as possible.

I looked down and saw only sidewalk.

"That dumb crow took my fish!" I yelled, releasing the man's arm.

For the first time the dark brown eyes of the dirt-covered man met my gaze. His forehead wrinkled as his eyebrows lifted.

"Whh-why?" he stuttered out the word in fear.

This guy was creeping me out. He could crack at any moment.

"Umm, I'm not sure why. Birds are dumb like that I guess. But I need to go now." I took a step back.

He put his hand on my shoulder and shook his head in disbelief.

"Why?" he repeated in a whisper. Then his face changed from confusion to anger.

I swallowed hard as he stared at me, his eyes fierce. I was just about to make a run for it when, to my great relief, he backed away. He didn't take his eyes off me as he took a few unsteady, backward steps, which was not a good idea in his clumsy and angered state. He tripped over the light post before picking himself up and running down the alley yelling, "Liar!" to the night air.

My heart was pounding as I turned in the opposite direction and sprinted across the street to cut through the park.

When I passed the picnic table, merry-go-round, and the swings, I slowed my pace. Once I made it across the park I only had two blocks more until I reached my house. There were no lights around, leaving me on a lonely path of darkness.

I wandered down the lovely scenic trail, which at nighttime, was not so lovely. In fact, it reminded me of the haunted forest from Disney's *Snow White*. Trees coming to life, moaning and grabbing at the innocent girl's dress.

I kept my eyes on the ground as I quickened my steps. A small whisper found its way to my ear. It sounded so real. "Addy."

I was hearing it again, something calling my name. Could I be imagining it? I looked around and the voice persisted.

"Addy." Maybe it was just the branches creaking in the wind. Although there was no wind, it was a perfectly still night. Still, but not quiet.

"Addy." The voice slithered through the air.

"What!" I stopped walking and threw up my arms. "What do you want?!" Now I was yelling at nothing. That old bum wasn't anymore crazy than I.

"Addy" was the answer. I swallowed hard and the hair on the back of my neck stood up.

I was close enough I could see the paved road ahead of me. A few good strides and I could be out of this nightmare and onto a nicely lit street.

The next whisper haunted me with a whole sentence.

"You can't run from me, Addy."

I gasped and looked around. Someone must be watching me; this had to be some kind of cruel trick.

I stared hard into the trees. "Leave me alone!" I demanded.

"Addy!" This time the voice was so loud that it made me scream.

"Whoa there, Adelaide! It's just me. Are you okay?" In my madness I hadn't seen Ben approach.

I was so overwhelmed and relieved that I collapsed to my knees and started sobbing. Not the kind of reaction I would be proud of tomorrow, but for now I didn't care.

Ben knelt down next to me and put an arm around my shoulders.

"Why did you do that Ben!" I was wishfully accusing him of being the cruel whisperer.

"What are you talking about, honey?" He was annoyingly innocent.

I started sobbing even harder. I couldn't make it stop. The tears were just gushing out. All the times I had been holding back were now catching up with me.

I think Ben was really shocked by my pathetic display of emotion. He was quiet for a minute until he lifted my chin up to see my dripping face.

"Addy, what happened?" He was truly concerned as he carefully wiped the blood that had dripped down the side of my face.

It took me a moment to quiet down before I could respond. I managed to squeak out two words. "I fell."

"You fell?" he asked in disbelief.

"No."

"No?" He was very confused.

"I was sitting on the curb and someone knocked me over." I sniffled.

"Wow, are you all right?" He was kneeling in front of me, gently holding my face in his hands.

My words were stuck in my throat as I remembered how I had lost his necklace. Every time I opened my mouth to give him an answer nothing came out. Salty tears silently streamed down my face as I stared at him.

"It's okay, Adelaide. I gotcha." He scooped me up in his arms like a white knight rescuing his damsel in distress.

My typical stubborn reaction would have been to jump out of his cradle and walk by myself, but I was tired. Tired of being scared, tired of hiding my sorrow, tired of being lost. But in that moment I was mostly just tired. I let him carry me to his old blue 1969 Chevy pickup and carefully set me inside.

Ben went around the truck and hopped in the driver's side.

"I'm taking you to the hospital," he said as he started up the loud engine.

I looked up at him and shook my head, trying to convey that it wouldn't be necessary.

"It isn't up for discussion. Your mom will be there, and I'm sure she would be upset with me if I just dropped you off at home. You look pretty messed up, Addy."

"Okay." I leaned my head on his shoulder and asked, "Ben, why were you at the park?"

"You didn't think I would actually let you walk home in the dark without making sure you made it home safely, did you?"

I shrugged, closed my eyes, and said, "Thank you."

I awoke as Ben carried me through the large double doors of the hospital. My mother would freak if she saw me like this.

"Put me down. I can walk now…please." I squirmed in his arms until he lightly set me on my feet.

"Are you sure?" He kept one arm around me as we walked to the elevator.

"Yeah, I'm all right."

As expected, my mother made a huge fuss over the scrape on my head. They cleaned, bandaged, and checked me for a concussion before I was released back into Ben's custody. My mom had twenty minutes left on her shift so it was back to the old Chevy. Ben drove me home and waited with me until my mother arrived. For me it was a very short wait because, within three minutes, I was asleep on the couch.

It was past noon when I finally awoke the next day, still on the living room sofa. Ben was probably packed and on the road by now. I pictured him, with his family, laughing and having fun. I should be happier for him, but I couldn't get passed my own selfishness. I wouldn't see him or Olivia for a whole week. What would I do with myself?

It was Monday, the first day of Christmas break. I had no school, no homework, and no plans.

My mom was already at work when I wandered to the kitchen for my afternoon breakfast. We were out of Cheerios so I had to go with, the not so favorite, Corn Flakes—already a bad start to my day.

I watched some television as I ate my bowl of cereal and then meandered back to my bedroom. I grabbed the *Wizard of Oz* script off my desk and plopped down on my bed. After ten minutes of rehearsing my part as the Good Witch of the North, I was bored. I walked over to my desk and slid into the chair. I stared down at the laptop that was once my mother's, wondering if it held anything of interest for me. When no better plans came to mind, I flipped it open and awakened the beast.

My e-mail inbox was full of spam and unwanted messages, so with disappointment, I redirected my search back to Google. I lightly tapped my fingers on the keyboard, knowing what I wanted to research, but hesitant about digging deeper. I wasn't sure what was holding me back, really. Maybe it was because Ben actually wanted me to do this. That concerned me.

I stopped my drumming and let my fingers fall heavily on the keys to spell out the words *Kinder Von Donar*.

I was offered several history and encyclopedia sites. I clicked on one and read.

The first paragraph was strictly boring information on the tribe and its forest location in the hills of Germany. It was the second paragraph that caught my attention.

The tribe referred to themselves as the children of Donar but their surrounding German neighbors had another name for them, Die Schlechten, meaning the wicked. The people complained about their evil practices, saying that they performed spells and practiced divination. Villagers told stories of how the Wicked ones communicated with birds and walked around in their spirits, leaving their bodies empty. Those with farmland would fear for their crops when the Dons performed rituals in their sacred meadow. It is said that when they danced around praising Donar, the god of thunder, that a dark storm would spread and the sky was filled with evil spirits as thunder and lightning echoed across the land, setting fire to anything they wished.

The Dons kept mostly to themselves but those who knew them feared them. They feared "the devil inside of them."

A chill ran up my spine. Did I want to keep reading? It was like listening to Ben, which truly irritated me. I hated hearing about the devil and his evil demons. People just use that old story as a scapegoat. If I believed in the devil than I would have to believe in God; and that wasn't going to happen, at least not the loving god that everyone talks about. I wanted truth, not feel-good stories. I wanted evidence not theory. I wanted to know, not just hope.

I decide I was letting myself be brainwashed by the world's view and quickly closed my laptop. I would find the truth for myself.

"Wicked." I spit the word out like poison. People are afraid of what they don't understand, confusing unexplained power with so called "evil." I wasn't going to buy into that. I would have an open mind. Something had chosen me for a different life, and I wanted to find out what it was.

I got up from my desk and marched to the kitchen. After I finished the dishes, I cleaned the bathroom and did the laundry. I kept myself busy with chores until five o'clock. I was exhausted and still carrying around my blanket of boredom.

Bundled in an old pair of sweats, I curled up on my favorite chair next to the window, and watched snowflakes kiss the ground. It only took about fifteen minutes until I was dozing off.

A loud noise awakened me to darkness. The full moon was peering through our living room window, offering light to my mother as she walked through the front door. I silently watched as she hung up her coat and tossed the keys in our change bowl.

"Hey," I whispered as she flipped on the light switch.

She jumped with surprise. "Oh! Hey, cutie-pie. What are you doing in the dark?"

"I guess I fell asleep. How was work?" I glanced at the glowing numbers on the microwave clock. It was fifteen past eleven, which means she worked late.

She smiled. "It was good. Not much happened but somehow they manage to keep me busy. You know, all these extra hours means extra money. We'll have to go shopping and have some fun with it!" My mom could find the silver lining in any storm cloud, even if that storm caused her house to flood and left her homeless.

"Well, I'm going to crawl in bed before I sleep the whole night away out here."

"It worked for you last night. You must have been exhausted. I couldn't wake you up if my life depended on it. You had me worried that you hit your head harder than we thought." She teased. "Speaking of which, how's the wound?" She stepped closer to examine me.

I lightly touched the side of my head. It hurt. "Much better, Mom. Just a little bruised."

"A little bruise around a *deep gash*," she scoffed. "Who would knock over a little girl and run away without helping? That's outrageous! If I ever find out who did that…" She took a deep breath and frowned at me. "Let me clean it for you."

"No, no. Maybe tomorrow. I would fall asleep before you even get out the hydrogen peroxide."

"Okay, okay. Well, good night, sweetie. I love you." She gave in easily, very aware of the extent of my stubbornness.

"Love you too," I mumbled as I trudged down the hallway to my bedroom.

Within three minutes I was wandering in darkness. With arms outstretched I took slow, careful steps. A breeze rustled through my hair, bringing with it powerful words.

"Find me, Addy." The voice was soft yet fierce.

I looked around the thick black void in obedience to the command. I had turned in every direction, nearly giving up when I saw the tiniest twinkle of light.

"Follow me." The whisper flowed over me in another passing of warm air. I stumbled my way closer as the light grew bigger. The closer I got, the larger it became, growing into the shape of a large, shining cross.

"Run to me!" The voice became louder with loving desperation. I had to lean forward to push myself through the now, roaring wind. It took all my strength to move forward but with every step, joy was building up in my heart.

"Dance with me, Addy." I was nearly laughing when the blazing figure was just a few steps away. I reached out with both arms but instead of embracing the light I found myself facedown before it. I had tripped over a root of a giant oak. I pushed myself to my feet and looked upward into the beautiful tree. It was so intricate and lovely. I ran my fingers up and down the thick, deeply textured bark. Suddenly I remembered the flaming cross. It was pulling at my heart, whispering to my soul. I turned to see if it was still there when something slick fell from the tree and slipped down my back. I looked down but saw nothing. Something else hit my shoulder and fell away. I looked up into the entangled branches of the large tree. They appeared to be moving so I looked more closely. The branches were crawling with snakes. I screamed and attempted to run but was roughly brought to my knees by the roots grasping at my legs. I desperately tried to pull myself away as snakes rained down on me, slithering around my waist and twisting through my hair. No matter how hard I squirmed and struggled I couldn't break free. I was being buried alive under a steady river of slimy reptiles. A hissing snake was tightening its grip as it circled my forearm. I let out a bloodcurdling scream as the snake struck, sinking its teeth deep into my wrist.

I opened my eyes to find myself entangled in the silky lavender sheets. Still squirming from the horror, I realized something was tightly gripping my wrist. I pulled and struggled in the darkness with no success.

"Shhhh. Hey, hey, little dreamer, you're safe now." It was a quiet male voice.

"Who are you?" I asked groggily, still trying to free my wrist with a pathetic strength.

"It's James. Are you always so hard to wake up?" He lightly caressed my wrist with his thumb as he kept a firm grip with the remainder of his fingers.

My eyes adjusted as my mind finally started comprehending. "Oh, you scared me."

"Not just me, you were freaking out long before *I* woke you up. What were you dreaming about?"

It was an awful nightmare, I thought, trying to recall the distant memory. "I...I can't really remember it anymore. But I have been haunted by awful dreams ever since I moved to this...this place." Wasn't it something to do with a light? I just couldn't remember. A thought suddenly occurred to me.

"Wait, why are you in my bedroom? And how did you get in my bedroom?" I whispered, not wanting my mom to wake up and find a strange boy next to my bed.

James let go of my wrist and stood up. "I entered through your window. I hope you don't mind. I'm here to see if you want to accompany me to a very special ceremony. I told you yesterday that tomorrow, being today, we could talk more and answer some of your questions."

By the time I went to bed, I figured he had forgotten about me. "Right now?" I sat up in bed, freeing my legs from the tangled sheets. "What kind of ceremony?"

"It's for Luke. This is his final show of commitment. After tonight, he will be fully claimed by Donar and accepted into our clan. I would really love if you joined me." He held out his hand to assist me out of my bed.

I stared at him with skepticism before finding my courage and taking his hand. When I was on my feet, he led me out of my room, but I held him back.

"Wait, what about my clothes?" Light grey sweat pants and a University of Utah T-shirt wasn't exactly my ideal outfit for a special occasion.

He scanned my attire and said, "Just put on some shoes."

"But…"

"Trust me, you'll be fine."

I pulled on my fuzzy brown boots and desperately patted down my frizzy hair as we silently walked out the front door.

Once we were both resting on the warm leather seats, James gave me the opportunity I had been waiting for.

"All right, Adelaide, what do you want to know?" He kept his eyes on the dark road.

"Well, let's start with the 'chosen' thing. I don't understand that."

"Oh, right, I started to tell you about that last night. First, you have to understand that, underneath the physical exterior of the world, there is a very active spiritual world. Our ancestors discovered this truth and have kept the knowledge alive for generations. They discovered how to communicate and interact with the spirits. These are spirits of the earth. Spirits of the sky, the ocean, the trees. Spirits that have great power and control over our lives. And to those who understand and respect this, are given power as well. Through them we can make things happen, Adelaide. Amazing and wonderful things."

His words were shocking yet exciting. I believed him but my imagination could not yet make it reality.

"Like what sort of things?" I whispered.

"You'll be able to witness it all for yourself if you chose. We can open your eyes to whole new life. A life of power, a life of belonging, purpose, and adventure. You would be bonded to a loyal and supportive group. A family. We will always be there for you. And it's not just the six of us. There are many, many others. We are just one branch of the tree.

"So Addy, is this something you want to be a part of?"

Of course it was. It was everything my heart craved and had nothing to do with the religion that tore my family apart. But I still had one question.

"Well, you still haven't explained how I was selected for this."

He smiled. "Oh, right. Donar chooses who he wants to walk in the spirit world, Addy. He knows who is ready and who can contribute. When someone is chosen, Donar communicates this to the spirits by striking the earth with lightening. Do you remember the storm on your first night in town?" I nodded, uncomprehending that there could be a storm on my behalf. "Well, the spirits, then, whisper your name to us, over and over until they have what they want. It is almost a little annoying at times. Like a craving. It is all we can think about. Does that make any sense?"

I remembered how Benjamin described it as being tormented by the devil, seeking out the weak. I liked James's version better. Even though it all sounded a little strange I couldn't contain the thrill of being wanted. I was specifically picked out of the patch of weeds to bloom into a beautiful flower amongst a select few.

"Yeah, I think I get it. Will I learn more tonight?" I asked.

"Yes you will. So, I guess that means you accept our invitation?"

"To belong to your family and learn the secrets of your…your tribe?" I asked, still unsure of the right terminology.

He nodded and without hesitation I said, "Wholeheartedly."

"Wonderful." He let out a deep sigh as if he had just completed a difficult task. "We have a whole week of no school. That will give us plenty of time. It will take several months before we can truly make you part of our family though. When it is time, we will have a ceremony for you, just like Luke's, to prove your loyalty and commitment. It's like a final initiation."

"Sounds perfect. I just wish I could have put some nicer clothes on," I said as I attempted to smooth out the wrinkles in my sweat pants.

He glanced at me from the corner of his eye and grinned. "Are you kidding me? I've never seen sweats look so good." Surely this was sarcasm, but I had to turn to hide my blushing face.

A few large yawns escaped my lips as I watched the motionless neighborhoods pass by. Shadows and slips of silvery moonlight had embraced the sleeping town, creating a whole new world. Everything looks so different in darkness. It's remarkable how light so drastically changes the world it rests upon. Light? Light! Bits of my dream were trickling back into my mind before it was abruptly shut off by James's voice.

"Are you tired? I know last night was pretty rough on you. But trust me, you won't want to miss this."

I didn't even want to ask what he knew about my wretched night. How do you tell someone you were running from voices in your head without sounding insane? "I'm all right, thanks."

We took a right turn past the high school, toward the forest which led us to a large iron gate with the name Roth forged into the metal. Passed the gate was a long stretch of dirt road surrounded by endless forest.

James did not baby his car as we drove down the pot-hole-covered road. His complete disregard for his beautiful and expensive vehicle stirred up feelings of jealousy within me. Here I was, unable to afford even a lemon of a car and he was thrashing his perfect cherry Benz, knowing he can get another if it happens to break down.

About three minutes into the frost-covered trees we came upon a few other vehicles parked and unoccupied. James pulled up behind Sasha's yellow Porsche and turned off the car.

"We walk from here." He twisted around and pulled something out of the backseat before exiting the car.

I followed his move and stepped out into the cold winter embrace. He came around the Mercedes and handed me the bundle that he pulled from the backseat. It was a heavy, full length white coat with white fur lining the edges. It was remarkable; I couldn't believe he was letting me use something so obviously expensive.

"Oh, James, I can't wear this. I'll get it dirty. It is so beautiful. I really don't want to ruin it."

He grinned at me and winked. "It's yours to keep, so it doesn't matter if you ruin it."

I was stunned. What could I say?

"Wow, that's so…thank you, James!" I said, sincerely, as I cloaked myself in heated comfort, running my fingers across the subtle red embroidery.

I stood, admiring my new coat as if it were gold. James laughed and took my hand, leading me into dark forest, holding a lantern in his other hand.

I was overwhelmed and speechless by his generosity. It was a very extravagant gift that I probably shouldn't have accepted so easily, but I couldn't make myself argue with him.

The deeper we ventured into the woods, the faster my heart was pounding. Soon, I could see light flickering through the thick trees and hear voices overtaking the eerie silence.

James tugged on my hand as he led me into a small clearing. I immediately realized that I was completely unprepared for what lay before us.

6

Voices

The meadow did not just hold the five faces that I knew, but nearly twenty strangers as well. The crowd was dressed in various white clothing that softly glowed in the light of the full moon. I noticed, for the first time, that James was also wearing all white, yet, still very stylish clothing. We stepped farther into the meadow, passing a few contained fires that lined the whole outer perimeter of the gathering.

Heads turned and locked their gaze on me; many faces wore the same wild look that Adam often sported.

I suddenly felt like a mouse dropped into a nest of poisonous vipers. I clung tightly to James's right arm, not even caring about the pleased look on his face.

"It's all right, Adelaide. These people are from the few other covens throughout Oregon." There was that term again, *coven*. His words did not fill me with comfort.

"We were wondering if you two were going to make it." A very tall and muscular blond smiled as he approached us. He was wearing a white linen shirt, tucked into a pair of light khaki pants. He was near twenty years old with strong facial features and pure blue eyes.

James gave the young man a strong handshake and looked down at me, who was still wrapped around his arm.

"Derek Adler, this is Adelaide Dawson."

I peeled an arm from safety to shake the man's hand.

James continued without letting us speak. "Derek is also from one of the original families that made up the tribe of Dons." I easily could have guessed at that one—he looked like the very definition of German.

"It's a pleasure," I said, trying to muster up enough courage to enjoy this night.

"The pleasure is all mine, Adelaide." I could almost hear the evidence of his heritage through his voice.

He looked back to James and said, "Is she, you know, Ven—" His words were immediately cut off by Rachel who had just approached.

"You two can't hog her all night. Come on Addy, I'll introduce you to everyone." She took my hand and led me away, leaving Derek looking slightly confused.

Now I had no one to hide behind, I was completely vulnerable and quite unhappy about it. I quickly decided that my best chance of survival was to assimilate into the camp of white shadows. I tried to open my heart and set free the hidden smiles.

One by one, Rachel slowly introduced me to her *"extended family,"* as she liked to call them. Each person was thrilled to meet me, some treating me as an honored guest, while others treated me like their main course of dinner, boring into my soul with their hungry eyes.

Rachel's energy and enthusiasm helped calm my nerves and uncover my excitement for this unexpected experience. The magnificent coat also helped. Not only did it keep me feeling warm and safe but I felt like royalty waltzing around in my moonlit courtyard. I was thankful that no one knew what lay underneath this exquisite façade—baggy pajamas and a desperate soul.

"All right, gather up everybody. It's time," an anonymous deep voice echoed through the crowd.

Clouds of white floated around, forming themselves into a large circle. Rachel took my hand and pulled me into the loop as James squeezed his way in, positioning himself on my right.

The ring united itself by linking hands, revealing to me a dreadful sight.

A young calf lay, struggling in its restraints, atop a large flat stone. The moonlight pierced through the clouds like a spotlight for the gods to view this bizarre ceremony. A few things were said by Luke, but I was unable to concentrate; my mind absorbed in the horror of the little cow.

Derek and Charles stood, next to the stone, on either side of the pale-faced sophomore. Luke was holding a small round bowl in his shaking hands, listening to his instructions. After a moment he rose up his wooden cup and shouted, "I am a child of Donar! I offer myself to him." He lowered his hands and hesitantly drank the mysterious elixir. Luke turned to the calf and lifted a dagger off the grey stone. "This is my sacrifice and show of loyalty." He raised the shimmering knife as a loud gasp snuck passed my lips. It suddenly occurred to me what he was about to do.

James tightened his grip on my sweaty palms and whispered in my ear.

"It's okay, kiddo. Nearly every religion known to man has practiced animal sacrifice. Besides, it wouldn't be a good example of commitment if it was easy, right?"

I silently nodded and closed my eyes as the innocent cow let out its death cry. I took a few deep breaths before forcing open my eyelids.

Derek and Charles removed the motionless offering and joined the circle of white. In one unified movement, excluding my clumsy imitation, the crowd was seated. Luke was now lying on his back across the bloody rock with his eyes closed and arms crossed.

I excused the terror that was shaking through my body and forced myself to keep an open mind. Normally, this is the kind of moment where your mind tells your legs to get up and run, but there was something irresistibly alluring about the power, excitement, and unity found here. Completely opposite of the dull, unhappy Sunday churchgoers who never experience anything real when they beg their god for help.

Every eye was closed, so after one, stomach churning glance at the crimson red pools of blood I did the same.

"And we are your witnesses," the circle muttered in unison. "Walk with us in spirit, in soul." A chant built up, overtaking the still song of the night. The sound pounded against my chest like a loud drum as my mind was sucked into the trance of the unfamiliar words.

I wasn't sure how much time had gone by when a voice broke through the powerful mantra.

"Silence now" was all the voice said but no one obeyed. The chanting did stop, but I could hear talking and whispering and other strange noises. I curiously opened my eyes to see why there was such open disobedience.

To my great shock and horror, every eye and mouth was shut; in fact, each person appeared to be lifeless. As voices slithered around the broken gears of my mind, I stared hard at James's face, hoping to find some sign that his body was still occupied. It was obvious that something was happening around me, I just couldn't see it. I studied each person in anxious desperation. Was I really the only conscious person in their sacred clearing? Had their minds abandoned me? How long would this last?

The sound of hard flapping wings broke my concentration. I looked around for the fowl culprit. The only sign of movement came from the small, subtle twitches of Luke's bloodied body. The faint movements were turning into convulsions. My fear and concern was now for Luke. I was just about to break the ring and go over to him when a high-pitched screech stiffened every fiber of my body. Simultaneously, the single fires that bordered the meadow rose up, the flames reaching nearly eight feet. Chills crawled up and down my spine, torturing me as if it were a deadly spider looking for a tender place to bite.

My mind scrambled to make realistic conclusions. A pressure in my chest diverted my fearful thoughts for just a moment, reminding me to breathe again. I opened my mouth and swallowed the air, hoping to recover, not just oxygen, but my mental sanity as well.

I didn't know whether I should panic and run or stay and observe. What was it like on the unseen side of this disturbing ordeal?

There was obviously great power involved. I couldn't let my fears overcome me and deprive me of this opportunity. This is what I had been waiting for—evidence. Proof of the power and reality of their god. Unlike so many other people, I couldn't believe simply because an old book says it's true. I had found what I was looking for, searching for all these years.

Despite my horror, I was going to remain where I was, no matter what. I lightly closed my eyes and tried to distinguish the words that were echoing through my soul. One voice stood out from the others like day from night. It said, "Run, Addy. Run to me."

I want to. I thought to the concerned voice. Perhaps the voice was simply a verbal manifestation of my instinctive apprehension. I looked around, considering the soft command. My eyes immediately fell on Luke, seemingly by force. His body slumped across the cold stone, as still as an ancient corpse.

I stared at him unwillingly as his head slowly turned toward me and his eyes opened. *Thank goodness!* I thought, relieved that I was no longer alone. Someone else was conscious with me!

"Don't run away, Addy." The words tumbled out of Luke's mouth as if they didn't belong to him.

My jaw dropped, and I nodded in obedience. Luke turned his head back, closed his eyes, and gasped for air like he was coming out of water.

He was still once more, leaving me alone with the voices.

"This is your destiny," a voice hissed in my ear.

"You cannot run from this," crackled another.

I closed my eyes as I listened more intently.

"Take a bite out of the forbidden knowledge, Adelaide." These words were clearer.

"Sink your teeth into its power!" screeched the final command before losing me between earth and air. I couldn't figure out how to lift my eyelids anymore. I didn't even know which way was up and which was down.

I could hear the crackling of the blazing fires and even feel the smoke swirl around my body. The faint odor of blood filled my nostrils until I was overwhelmed by the stench of death. The smell, the smoke, and the darkness had me spinning in nausea. My mind was fading as I felt my world leave me altogether.

When my eyes finally opened, I was on my back, staring at an ocean of white bumps and creases. I tilted my head to examine my new scenery; a floor lamp, a cluttered desk with an orchid, and a wicker waste basket. I sat up, pushing off the lavender sheets. That was *my* desk, *my* lamp, and *my* popcorn ceiling. I was back in my bedroom!

What had happened? Did I pass out? Was it all a dream? I slumped down on my bed, my mind whirling. Recent memories started seeping into the cracks of my mind as I sat, unblinking and uncomfortable, like a distorted statue. I tried to find evidence for the reality of last night's happenings; and there it was, hanging nicely from a hook in the corner of my bedroom—the white coat, even lovelier in the daylight. This settled the verdict; I was not delusional. I remembered the smoke and the overwhelming smell of blood. I had fainted. How embarrassing.

At that moment of realization, my mother cracked open my door and popped her head in.

"Oh good, you're awake." She walked into my room carrying a brown bottle and fresh bandages, completely oblivious of my outing.

I hopped off my bed. "Let's do that in the bathroom…if you insist it must be done at all." I pulled on her arm, turning her around and back toward the door. I didn't have any good alibis to explain away the expensive coat. The creative part of my brain didn't usually kick in until at least eleven o'clock.

My mom probed me with questions as she carefully placed on the new bandage.

"So, how are you liking Ledo, Addy? You haven't said much about it."

I grabbed a brush and ran it through my long, tangled hair. "You know, I think it's growing on me."

"I'm glad. You seem a lot happier the last couple months. It is great to see you making some *real* friends." I assumed she was referring to the Tuckers. I doubt she would approve of my newfound "coven."

I smiled so she continued, "I really like that Benjamin kid. I think he likes you."

My attempt to play it cool was overruled by the blood filling my cheeks. "Well, he did ask me to go to prom with him."

Her green eyes brightened. "And what did you say!" She took the brush from my hand and took over my grooming.

I tried to downplay it. "Well, it's not like we're dating or anything. But I did say…yes." My voice broke on the last word.

I stared in the mirror and watched as she peeked around the back of my head, an excited motherly smile consuming her face. "Oh my gosh! That is so wonderful, sweetie. I never went to my prom, and I always wished that I had been able to. I can't wait to see what dress you pick out! Don't worry about the money, I will…" She stopped and sniffed the air. "Do you smell that?"

"What?" I asked.

"Something smells like…smoke." She inhaled deeply through her nose.

I discreetly sniffed at my hair as panic rushed through me. My dark brown hair was thickly coated with that unmistakable "campfire smell."

"Maybe there is a forest fire." I shrugged as I turned to face her. Sure, Addy, wildfire spread over the snow-covered trees—good one.

She frowned so I tried to divert her attention. "Hey, do you want to take a walk on the beach with me?"

"I would love that, but I think it will have to wait till tomorrow. I got called into work again."

"They really keep you busy down there, don't they?" I asked, proud that I had successfully avoided the difficulty of explaining why I woke up smelling like burnt log.

"Yeah they do. But I promise tomorrow we will spend some time together. Okay?"

"Okay. You don't have to work on Christmas, do you?"

"Definitely not, sweetie."

My mom gave me a tight hug and walked out the bathroom door. I stayed put, not wanting to spread my betraying odor. I picked up a handful of my hair and sniffed it. My nose wrinkled in disgust, I had to be more careful. It would break my mom's heart if she knew what I was up to.

After I heard the jingle of the keys and shutting of the front door, I let out a deep sigh. Even after that hug she hadn't realized the source for the smoky smell. I was in the clear but still had no plans for my day. I wasn't sure how to get a hold of the Roths, but I figured they would contact me when they wanted.

I formed my hair into two braids and threw on my jogging pants, a sweater, and a beanie. I hadn't been down to the ocean in while and I missed it. I craved my walks by the ocean and even treasured my short strolls to our little blue mailbox out front.
 A quick walk through my backyard, and I was standing on the edge of the cliff, staring at the stormy ocean below. I had recently discovered a shortcut down to the beach. Rather than taking the winding, paved road down to the sand, I had found a small trail that zigzagged down a sloping part of the cliff.

I slowly made my way along the trail, gripping frost-covered bushes for support. I had made this trip several times over the last few months, but never had the path been so icy. My fingers grasped hard around available branches as my feet continuously slipped out from under me, leaving me with cold, numb hands, and a wet bottom.
 I sat, for the third time, on the ice-covered rocks, frowning down at my sandy destination. I looked back up to see how far my traction-lacking tennis shoes had carried me. Snowflakes harshly bit my face as I thought about my position; halfway between a blue house and white sand. The idea of climbing back up the slope seemed nearly impossible, so I choose to continue my course downwards.

I carefully maneuvered over the last steep drop off, my fingers clasping tightly to the sturdy roots that hung out of the side of the cliff. With two more side steps to safety and twenty-three feet of empty air below me, I lifted my foot for another risky move when a haunting laugh reverberated off the rocky wall. I was so startled that my foot slipped, causing a scream to burst out of me as I pulled myself back.

Following the deep laugh was a familiar voice that was colder than the winter air.

"What's the point, Adelaide. What do you have to live for, anyway?" The words were frightening but rang true, like they were pulled straight out of my heart.

"I…I have a new family now," I argued, thinking of my exciting friends who cared about me.

"You have nothing but hope. And hope is exactly what keeps people like you from doing the things you really want. Nothing but hope…" The frosty voice shook the rocks around me.

I thought about that depressing statement for a moment. What is it that I *really wanted* to do? I stood there on the ledge contemplating my disappointing life and my uncertain hope.

"Let go, Adelaide. Release the pain and let go," the voice tempted.

Freedom. That was what I wanted. To just let go and be free of the pain. Was this my escape? I clutched tightly onto the tree roots as I reviewed my life and debated my options. I had no idea what I wanted. Why did life have to be so hard?

A wisp of air warmed my frigid hands, hinting quiet words of hope. "…He brought me up out of a horrible pit, out of the miry clay, and set my feet upon a rock, and established my goings." This sounded like something my mother had muttered through my childhood. Perhaps that was all it was, echoes of my past.

"Hold tight, Addy." The soft words gave one more try before my debate was settled for me.

Three black crows soared above me, squawking viciously until they landed on the branches and roots adjacent to my little, red fingers. Their evil black eyes bore into my soul, frightening me more than my thin, frosty ledge.

The murderous laugh quivered through my arms as I released one hand to swat at the dark creatures.

"Stupid birds. Go away...shoo!"

They flapped their silky, black wings and pecked mercilessly at my fingers, causing me to involuntarily release my hold and soar backward into the empty void.

As the cliff fell swiftly away, my mind was filled with regret. Regret that I was always holding back in life. Regret that I never had the courage to trust and let go. Regret that I never knew the right choice. Regret that I went for a walk today!

I didn't know what I wanted, but I knew this wasn't it. Panic rushed through me and opened way to a bloodcurdling scream.

"Help me!" I shrieked. I knew there was no hope of human interception, and I wasn't asking for it. I was pleading with insanity, begging the mysterious voices for my life. I was uncertain of whom I was communicating with, but I was desperate.

I frantically flailed my arms and legs, twisting and crying in fear. "Please, please!" The words were falling out of me as freely as my body was falling through the air. "Oh god, oh god! Help me!"

A strong current of wind whooshed up from underneath me like a geyser of air, slowing my pace, immensely.

"...I will establish your goings..."

My body hit hard against the sand, knocking the wind out of me but, thankfully, not my life. It was as if I had fallen from three feet rather than twenty-three.

I lay, sprawled across my golden carpet of sand, like an abused ragdoll. Staring at the fluffy, grey sky above me, I mentally checked my physical status. I was alive, to be sure, but to what functional sacrifice? I wiggled my toes, bent my knees, and stretched my back. This wasn't right; something had to be injured. I slowly pushed myself up to a sitting position as I regained the ability to expand my lungs. Amazing! I was perfectly mobile and intact.

Still in shock from my miracle, I got up to my feet and stared at the rocky ledge above. My hair tickled the side of my face as it lightly floated in the ocean breeze, bringing a tiny smile to my lips.

"Thank you," I whispered softly to the sky. I was more confused than ever in my life. I wasn't sure if I was losing my mind or discovering a new reality, but I was thankful to be alive. Thankful that someone, something...had spared me.

"Who are you talking to?" James was standing beside me, staring into the sky as I had been.

"How do you always do that?" I asked startled and annoyed, remembering all the many times that he had shown up without warning like a sudden case of the hiccups.

"Do what now, little Miss Dawson?" He smiled down at me.

"Sneak up on me all the time! And I'm not little." I discreetly stood up on my tip toes to meet his eye line. "I'm nearly as tall as you are," I said defiantly.

"Well, I'm pleased to see you are feeling better." He chuckled. "Sasha and Rachel have twenty bucks that it was the blood that got to you."

"What blood?" The words came out just as I remembered last night's bovine offering.

"The girls think you fainted at the sight of blood. Derek's betting it was the spirits, but I have twenty on fear..." He glanced at me sheepishly. "Don't be mad. It is understandable. Those things can be pretty overwhelming at first."

I glared at him obstinately, angry that they were making bets at my expense.

"Well, you all lose." I folded my arms and turned toward the ocean. I, myself, was not certain why I blacked out, but he didn't need to know that. I had considered telling my mother, the nurse, about my loss of consciousness, but it seemed too impossible to explain without getting grounded or lectured.

"My goodness you are a firecracker, aren't you!" He shook his head and turned his attention back to the sky.

"I think you bring it out in me. You always catch me off guard. I'm not good with change."

"So I've noticed." He winked at me. "How about I take you to dinner tonight? That way you have a couple hours to prepare for seeing me."

"Well, I'm not sure, James. I'm a bit uncertain of everything right now."

"All the more reason then. You can ask me anything you want. And have a chance to experience more of what we have to offer. I promise it will be enlightening. No strings, no pressure."

"All right, I do want to talk to you about something that happened to me today, just now, actually. Something I don't quite understand."

"Perfect. I'll pick you up at six." He turned to walk back toward the road.

"Wait, James. Why are you here, anyway?"

His black leather shoes took a few slow steps through the sand until we met toe to toe. His dark eyes had locked me in a spell as he took my hand and softly kissed it.

"I'm here to ask you on a date, Adelaide." His voice was gentle yet unwavering.

My mind was blank as I watched him walk away and get into his newly washed Mercedes.

It took a few moments before I realized what had just happened. It had been quite a strange day for me. I survived what could easily have been my death and a few minutes later I had a date with a dangerously handsome young man. Oh my goodness! And I had nothing decent to wear.

I took the long, but comfortingly flat road back to my house, the whole way taking a mental inventory of my boring wardrobe. James is always so nicely dressed and put together, he makes me feel, well, rather homely.

I walked into my bedroom, regretting that I had not accepted my mom's many offers for a shopping spree. I dug through my closet, dresser, and even my over-flowing hamper with little hope of finding a worthy outfit. Frustrated and angry, I ran for my mother's boudoir. She had an overabundance of stylish clothes. Going into her closet was as good as shopping in a department store.

I slowly ran my fingers across the great mixture of fabrics draped so elegantly on their hangers. It didn't take me long to narrow it down and make a choice. It didn't really matter what I picked, it was all so beautiful.

I took my new clothes and laid them nicely across my bed. My excitement was beginning to build. There was a good chance of looking good for my date. It would be my first date in a whole year. But one thing had to be done first; wash away the smoke, sand, and sweat that clothed my body!

I undid my hair, undressed, and slipped into my bathrobe. The clock on my night stand read 3:50, giving me two hours and ten minutes to get ready. That should be just right.

I turned the shower to hot and gave it a minute to warm up when a phone rang. I ran to the living room, but it wasn't our house phone so I bolted to my bedroom to find my cell phone. Quickly reaching into my purse, I hoped it wasn't James calling to cancel.

I flipped open my cell and gave a very breathy, "Hello!"

"Addy? Is that you?" My heart leapt; it was Benjamin! The sound of his voice had my heart beating faster than the quick jog I just took through the house.

"Yeah, it's me!" I said, still panting a little.

"I know it has only been a couple of days but, man, I miss you!" he said cheerfully.

"Feels more like weeks. How's your trip so far?"

"Oh, fun. It's really cold up here though! I have like five layers of clothes on." We both chuckled before he went on. "I don't think you could make it two hours in this weather," he teased.

"You're probably right. It is cold enough over here. I'll probably be nothing but an ice cube by the time you return." It was so hard not to tell him about my crazy night with Don's.

"Oh, I sure hope not. That would be a shame. How am I supposed to take a block of ice to the prom?"

"Don't worry, I should be thawed out by the time May rolls around."

"Good. Hey How is your break going?"

It is going better than I thought it would, but I couldn't tell him that. I couldn't tell him anything I was doing, and I hated that I couldn't.

"It's all right. Haven't done much so far. Wish you guys were here to hang out with me."

"Well, don't sit at home all week. You should get out and have some fun. I'm sure Cody and Mark would hang out with you…or Krissy from English class. You guys get along well. You should call her and see what she's doing."

"Yeah, maybe." Krissy was always willing to start a conversation with me, but by the direction of most of her questions, I suspected she was only interested in why Charles and James would talk to me and not her.

"Just…" He paused. "Uh, be careful and…" He trailed off.

"And what, Ben?" I figured he wanted to go off about the dark and dangerous ways of the coven.

"…And don't forget about your best friend." It wounded more like an afterthought, but it was still sweet. He was my best friend. Probably the best friend I ever had.

"Who would that be?" I teased, trying to keep the conversation lighthearted. I felt that I could cry any second as I let myself think of the possibility of losing him. I can't keep my new life and new family a secret forever and when he finds out, well…who knows.

"Hey! That strikes deep, honey." The false pain in his voice was overly dramatic.

"I'm sorry, who is this? Is this a telemarketer?"

"Ha, ha, very funny. But seriously, Addy, I can't wait to come back and give you a big hug. I am actually looking forward to school just so I can see you every day."

"I don't hug telemarketers. You better try another number." My face was almost sore from smiling nonstop.

The conversation continued like this for another thirty minutes or so as I lay on my bed, laughing, smiling, and tracing the purple embroidered flowers on my bedspread. I jumped right up when I glanced over at my clock that now read 4:46.

"Oh no! I have to go! Oh shoot and I left the shower on this whole time!" I blurted out in panic.

Through laughter, Ben responded, "I bet all your hot water is gone."

"Hey, that's not funny! I'm sorry, Ben, I'm really glad that you called but I'm going to be late if I don't go get ready right *now*."

"Where are you going?"

I had said too much. The last thing I wanted to tell Benjamin was that I was going on a date with his least favorite person. *Lie Addy! You have to lie to him, you have no choice.* My mind was switching to autopilot, instinctively coming up with an alibi.

I hated to do it. "I'm going over to play cribbage with my grandpa. My mom has to work late so I thought I would bring him dinner. But I have to shower because I…I went jogging. But he is expecting me very soon. I would hate to keep him waiting." The words fell quickly out of my mouth, one right after another. I was surprised at how easily the excuses came to me. It shouldn't be that easy.

"All right, get going then. Tell Allen I said hello. I miss you, honey."

"I miss you too, Ben. Thanks for calling, and again, I'm sorry."

"No problem kiddo, but feel free to give me a call. I would love to talk to you more."

"Sure thing…Bye!" I threw my phone down on my bed and ran for the bathroom.

I stuck my hand under the faucet. The water was barely lukewarm. I frowned, disrobed, and jumped in. I was highly motivated to clean up quickly and was soon back in my bedroom shivering as cold water dripped from my hair and ran down my arms.

I slipped into my nicest dark wash jeans and the chocolate-colored Georgette blouse that I took from my mom's closet. Then it was back to the bathroom to blow-dry my hair, straight of course, there was no time to even attempt a curl. I just finished applying some eyeliner when the doorbell rang.

On my sprint to the door I grabbed my mom's brown boots and her deep red wool coat. I grabbed the doorknob and took a slow deep breath before turning it.

I was greeted by…no one! The porch was empty. Where was James? My first suspicion was a neighborhood child playing a joke, ding-dong ditch perhaps, but then I spotted it! A tiny velvet box was waiting in the middle of our welcome mat.

7

Classy

I slowly lifted the lid to the mysterious little box and gasped at its contents. Diamond earrings! They were extravagantly beautiful, but they couldn't possibly be real and certainly not meant for me. Possibilities ran through my head as I held the box in both hands and ambled down our walkway to peer around the garage. Whoever rang the doorbell couldn't be far.

"Good evening Miss Dawson. Wow, don't you look stunning." James was leaning against the hood of his car that he had parked in front of our garage.

"I think you mean…I look *stunned*," I said, still wide-eyed and uncertain of what I was holding.

"Do you like them?" He questioned as he walked over to the passenger door and held it open for me.

"Are they…"

"For you? Yes." James finished my sentence with a big smile on his face. I could tell he was very pleased with my astonishment.

"And are they…" I trailed off, not knowing if I wanted to actually ask the question, but again James finished it for me.

"Real? Yes, they are."

I wasn't sure how to say thanks to such an expensive gift. "Wow, James, I… really, this is… most boys just bring flowers."

"You're welcome, Addy. Now, let's get going. I made reservations."

I slid into my seat and silently stared down at my earrings as we drove away, but I wasn't thinking about diamonds. I was reminded of the necklace that Ben had given me. The little carved fish was nothing in comparison to this, but, somehow, I wished I could trade it for what was in my hands. Stupid bird.

"Well, are you going to wear them or just stare at them all night?" James asked.

"Oh, yes, of course." I took them out of the case and carefully put them on. I pushed the clasp on uncomfortably tight. My ears were now worth more than anything I owned. Losing things was all too common for me—exhibit A: Ben's necklace. The idea of diamonds falling off my ears was enough to keep me stiff and paranoid all evening.

The thick clouds had been holding the sun hostage all day and now they let loose with its aquatic artillery. It was a downpour like I had never seen. The raindrops pounded against the windshield as James counterattacked by turning his wipers to the highest speed. We raced down the highway at unlawful speeds, his headlights displaying unchartered territory.

"Where are we going, James?" I had automatically assumed that dinner would be at one of the very few restaurants in Ledo.

"To the city. It's only about a forty-five-minute drive. I wanted to take you somewhere nice." I was very thankful that he didn't remove his eyes from the road as he spoke. Despite the heat emanating from my leather seat, I was very stressed out and uncomfortable. A sudden realization made everything ten times worse.

"Oh no! James, we have to go back!" I clutched both hands to my seat belt, half expecting him to pull a sudden U-turn.

He frowned but didn't seem concerned. "And why would that be?"

"I didn't leave my mom a note. She has no idea that I'm going out…and I didn't even bring my purse and cell phone! She's gonna freak."

"Don't worry about it, Adelaide, I promise you everything will work out." His lack of disregard to my crisis was annoying me.

"That's easy for you to say, you aren't the one who will be grounded for the next six months!" I bored into the side of his head with a look that I hoped was expressing something along the lines of, "If you want to live, you will turn this car around right now!"

Fortunately for him, his eyes did not stray from the wet asphalt ahead.

"She will never know. I guarantee it. Okay?"

I said nothing.

"You are making this awfully hard to have an enjoyable evening with you. How am I supposed to romance you when you're angry with me?" He grinned and slid his hand over to hold mine.

My angry red face turned into a nervous red face. I held his hand, and my breath, and nodded silently.

"My dad's name happens to be on that hospital, and I happen to know that your mom will be working late tonight. Really late, so try to relax and have some fun.

"I'll try. It'll be cool going to the city. I haven't been out of town once since we moved here."

"I thought you would enjoy the change. Ledo can be a little stifling if you don't get out once in a while."

"Yeah it's nothing like Utah," I mumbled.

"I've never been there. Tell me about it." James didn't seem all too interested in what I had to say, but he kept me busy answering one meaningless question after the other and before I knew it we were walking into a restaurant as a valet parked the Benz.

"Oh wow, this is really fancy, James," I whispered to him as our hostess seated us at a candlelit, corner table for two.

"It's my favorite. I come here all the time, but never with such lovely company."

"That's sweet, but really, it's my pleasure, I have *never* eaten at a restaurant this...nice before. My dates usually consist of a boring action movie and if I'm lucky some buttered popcorn," I said this jokingly but it made me feel slightly embarrassed. I stared down at the cloth napkin I was fidgeting with, hoping that I didn't look as out of place as I felt.

"Well, as fun as buttered popcorn can be, I'm glad I can treat you to something nicer. You deserve it. You are a wonderful girl with a lot of heart."

A lot of heart'? This was probably his way of saying stubborn and unstable. He had been complimenting me all evening, and he obviously wasn't done. At some point, though, he would run out of things to say about me. Really, what else is there?

"Wonderful?" I questioned skeptically, choosing the light-hearted response to his suave remarks. "You obviously don't know me very well yet."

James raised an eyebrow but before he was able to reply our waitress approached the table.

"Welcome to *Château D'argentes*," our waitress greeted in a classy French accent. "My name is Tess. What can I serve you today?" Tess was a tall blonde who had her blue eyes glued to my handsome date. She spoke to him without even acknowledging me. I glowered at her as James ordered for us. He gave our order without any polite smiles or small talk. My quick moment of jealousy vanished when I remembered how passive the coven was to the rest of the world. They didn't even speak to other people in school. It was so easy to forget because they gave me so much undeserved attention. I almost wondered if James would even have liked me if I wasn't "chosen" or whatever.

When blondie was gone, James turned his gaze back on me. "Hope you don't mind me ordering for you."

"Not at all. I can't pronounce half the things on their menu anyway." I actually did mind. I hated when people ordered for me. I *am* capable of making my own decisions, and I happen to be quite opinionated. On this occasion, however, I didn't feel that I was in a position to complain. In fact, I was beginning to feel indebted to him. Was he trying to buy my adoration? I looked at his dark eyes and decided that maybe I think too much. *Just have fun, Addy*, I told myself. That is exactly what Benjamin was telling me to do, anyway. Ben always had good advice.

Ben.

My mind had completely derailed as I imagined what Ben was doing at that moment.

Ben...Maybe the Tuckers will decide to come back early. Maybe Olivia won't be able to handle the cold and Ben will suggest cutting the vacation short. Maybe...

"Adelaide?" James interrupted my hopeful thoughts.

"Huh?" I eloquently responded as his face came back into focus.

"You have been staring off for a few minutes now. Is something on your mind?" His curiosity was genuine.

"Oh, sorry, I was thinking about...about Christmas."

He looked at me doubtfully and then leaned in closer. "You know, we don't observe Christmas. It is a Christian ritual, celebrating the day that their so-called savior was born. It means nothing to us. We don't like to condemn other religions and practices...but Christians..." He scowled, looking around the dining room as if picking out the guilty ones. "Followers of Jesus Christ, they insist that our beliefs are 'demonic.' They insist that their way is the only way. That church, in Ledo, that the Tuckers go to, they are always trying to reach out to us with such pity and 'compassion.' Like we are pathetic and needy. Like we need to be saved from ourselves or something. They think we are going to hell. How arrogant is that?" He laughed and lowered his voice. "They are the hated enemy of our god Donar. Their ideas are dangerous, Addy. *They* are dangerous. It is best not to associate with them or participate in their ways." He leaned back now and his face softened. "But of course, we don't expect you to bail out on your family for this year's winter holidays. We don't want to cause any unnecessary concern."

I always loved Christmas, but I suppose it wasn't necessary. My life had new meaning now and that was worth a few sacrifices. Every word he spoke drew me in deeper. My heart had become like the energizer bunny with the consistent beating of the drum. The excitement I had experienced since our move to Oregon was more thrilling than anything I thought was within my grasp. A small corner of my mind told me to be cautious, to just touch my toe in the waters rather than a full on leap. But all my life I had restrained myself, and it hadn't brought me any happiness. I would probably be better off doing the opposite of my instincts.

"My mom would flip if I didn't show up for Christmas." I grinned, thinking of how my mother would react if I went MIA for the holidays.

"Hey, wasn't there something you wanted to ask me about?" James said lightly, after taking a sip of his water.

I can't believe I had nearly forgotten about my near-death experience today! I was very forgetful when I was in James's company. He could easily sidetrack me into any conversation.

"Right." I shoved my jacket off and leaned in to whisper. "Something really freaky happened to me today." I paused, debating whether or not I should include *all* the details. Would James believe me or cut our date short due to my undisclosed psychotic issues? "I took the shortcut to the beach this morning. You know, down the trail behind our house."

James opened his mouth to speak but I cut him off. "I know, I know. Not a wise decision this time of year. Trust me, I won't make that mistake again."

He just nodded, trying not to smile, so I continued, "Well, I stupidly ended up…uh, hanging from some roots on a very icy ridge." I watched James's eyes widen, but he didn't speak. "You might think this sounds crazy, but I'm not lying. I heard laughter and…and crows began pecking at my hands!" I lowered my voice again, realizing that I had the attention of a few neighboring tables. "I also heard voices, and then…I fell. I think it was about twenty feet. I begged for my life. I'm not sure who answered my request…but obviously someone did. I mean, I'm totally fine. Do you think I'm crazy? *Am* I crazy?!"

I sat back and waited for his response.

James smiled softly and then reached over to gently brush my hair away from my face. "You don't have to be afraid of telling me things like that, Adelaide. I won't criticize you or force my ideas on you." He lowered his hand to mine but had to pull it back as our food was set before us.

"Will there be anything else, sir?" the pretty blonde waitress asked, ignoring my existence once again.

"No," James replied, waving her off.

"Well, if you need anything, anything at all, you let me know," she said with a tantalizing smile.

James didn't even acknowledge her as he continued our conversation. "Anyway, beautiful, I don't think you're crazy at all." I watched the waitress's eyes widen in horror as she turned and stormed off. I, shamefully, found enjoyment in her disappointment. After all, she had been ignoring me.

James picked up his utensils and cut into his chicken. "Actually, I think you are very privileged. The spirits communicate with you freely, without you even having to summon them. The spiritual world has taken interest in you. Don't ever think you are crazy just because you are hearing voices."

"Really? But, well, the voices usually seem a bit…threatening," I said timidly.

"Not all spirits are good. If you find favor with the gods and learn to interact with the spirits, it will be a whole new world for you. There are so many things we have to teach you. Let me start with something very basic. Our god Donar created this earth, Adelaide. There was a time when gods and spirits drifted through the universe. Just a large ocean of stars, the largest—being the sun—is the resting place of the gods. Donar was angry with the spirits around him. They roamed about with no purpose or reason, causing mischief. So Donar gathered them up in his hands and threw them forcefully, creating the first lightning bolt. The lightning shot through the vast emptiness until it struck a star and exploded, forming this earth and trapping the spirits. But this also gave the spirits purpose, and we are able to communicate with them, you just have to learn to listen. They are kind of like the go-betweens for the gods. Some of course, are just troublemakers. So I'm guessing that those dark spirits were threatened by you, perhaps wanting you dead. Most likely sent by the god, Yahweh." He scowled at the thought. "Anyway, when you cried out for help, I'm sure that Donar heard you and protected you. And I'm so glad that he did."

I gave this some consideration. It sounded plausible. Actually, it made sense; Yahweh was Ben's god, my mother's god. My father only left us after she brought that god into our life.

I suddenly had a horrifying thought. "What if he really does want me dead?!"

"Well, he won't succeed, Addy. I will do everything in my power to keep you safe, but the spiritual battle is up to you. I guarantee that if you devote yourself to Donar, he will preserve you. But you must also stay away from the enemy."

"I can do that...how do I do that?" I asked.

"It can be harder than you think. You must stay away from those who worship him and invite him to 'live in their hearts' as they call it. In the case of your mother and grandfather, this will be hard. But there are others in your life that you can avoid. Remember, inviting the people in your life, invites their god in."

"People like Ben?" I asked with sadness, knowing the answer.

"Yes, Benjamin, and all the Tuckers. Also, your friend Cody, and even our history teacher."

I frowned as I thought of how difficult this would actually be.

James took notice of my concern. "Don't worry. You stick with us whenever possible. We'll be there to look out for you."

"Thanks," I muttered as I poked at the broccoli on my plate.

"Hey, cheer up. We aren't all that bad." He winked at me.

James had me cheered up in no time and we spent the next hour eating, talking, and laughing. He made for a very pleasant date and a flattering companion. By the time we left our seats, James had me feeling like the Queen of Sheba.

"Here, let me help you." James perceived my brief struggle with the red wool coat and assisted me in slipping it on.

"Thanks. You are quite the gentleman, James."

He walked around to face me. "If you want to wait for me in the lounge, I'll get our bill taken care of and be right with you."

"All right, but are you sure I can't pitch in? At least let me get the tip."

"You are so kind, but for the third time...no. It is my treat."

I smiled in appreciation and turned to go but James grabbed my hand.

Our eyes met as he stepped closer, causing my heart to flutter with concern. He wouldn't try to kiss me would he? It was a good date, but I wasn't ready for that.

My eyes darted from side to side, avoiding his gaze as I mumbled, "Ummm, ummm!..."

"Will you take the valet ticket and have them pull the car around?" James asked as he stuck a piece of paper in the hand that he was holding.

I sighed and nodded my head. I think my relief was plainly obvious because James smiled with amusement. Perhaps he did that on purpose, to see my response. Was he toying with me?

I turned and walked away without a word.

The valet politely took my ticket and walked out into the pouring rain. I sat down and waited on the elegant, white sofa next to the fireplace that was located near the door.

"Hi, Addy." The voice did not sound pleased to see me.

I lifted my head and saw Mark sitting in an armchair across from me.

"Hi, Mark! What are you doing here?" I asked, trying to disguise my concern. Mark was sure to tell Benjamin that he saw me here, and with James Roth of all people!

"My uncle owns this place. He lets me bus tables on occasion to make some extra money. What are *you* doing here?" he asked with harsh accusation.

I glanced down and saw a dirty apron in his lap. "I am here...to eat," I said as innocently as possible.

"Ah, I see. And who are you here eating with?"

He knew! He must have seen me and James together already. There was no point in denying it.

"Well, James Roth from school brought me," I said as though I had no idea how despised my date was.

There was great concern in Mark's eyes. "Addy, why?" He got up and joined me on the sofa. "I thought we talked about this." He lowered his voice and put a hand on my shoulder. "Devil worshipping, spell casting, creepo! Remember?"

"Oh, right. Well, I think you guys are totally wrong about him. He is very nice and generous." I instinctively pulled a hand up to my ear to feel if the diamonds were still in place.

"Nice?" he snorted. "James is anything but nice. Does Ben know about this?"

"What does Ben have to do with this?" I knew the answer, but Mark was starting to annoy me. "I am capable of taking care of myself. Besides, Ben said I should get out and have some fun."

Mark rolled his eyes. "Yeah, and I'm sure this is exactly what he meant," he said sarcastically.

"Oh back off, Mark. It's just a date." I pushed his hand off my shoulder.

"Ask anyone at school, Addy, James and his cult are…scary. The only people that they talk to and actually hang out with either become a part of the group or…or…"

"Or what? They turn into toads?" I scoffed.

"Or they go missing. It's happened a few times before." He shuddered.

"So they probably coincidentally moved away and your superstitious mind has a field day."

"Whatever, Addy. I want you to know that I don't approve of this." Spoken like a protective big brother. "But if you need me to come pick you up or anything, let me know."

"Okay, Mark, if they ask me to sign my life over to Lucifer, I'll be sure to give you a call." He didn't reply. He was silently staring up at James.

The two boys glared daggers at each other until they were interrupted by our sopping wet valet.

"Right out front, sir," the young valet said as he wiped his wet hair away from his eyes.

"Come on, Adelaide, I have a very special surprise for you." James nodded to the dripping driver and held his hand out to me.

"Okay." I took his hand and gave Mark an apologetic look. "Bye, Mark."

"Good-bye, Addy. I'll make sure to tell Ben that you said hello." Ouch. Mark's words cut deep. Ben didn't deserve to be hurt. He was so better off without me in his life.

James pulled me along; my feet didn't seem to know where they wanted to go. Or maybe they did…well, I did. North. To the freezing temperatures of Montana. To Benjamin. I wanted to give him a big hug and tell him I was sorry. The thought of him sad was nearly too much to bear. Why was that? Well, it didn't matter. It *couldn't* matter. I had made my decision, and that decision was now taking me to see a "special surprise."

"I didn't know we had more plans for tonight," I said as we drove down a dimly lit road.

"That's what makes it a surprise," James replied plainly.

We had only been driving a few minutes before we slowly turned down a dark alley and came to a stop. I looked around with concern and doubt. I could see a rusty dumpster, brick walls on either side of us, and a flickering street lamp behind us. Just what kind of "surprise" was awaiting me?

"What are we doing here, James?" I asked with obvious skepticism.

He unbuckled his seat belt and turned toward me. "What's the matter, Adelaide? You look a little worried." The look in his eyes frightened me; I think he enjoyed seeing me afraid.

"Well, this place just looks a little sketchy. What's the surprise?" I tried to keep calm and not let my imagination get carried away.

James leaned over and unclasped my seat belt. His face was uncomfortably close to mine as he whispered, "Come on. I'll show you." He leaned back, winked at me, and then got out of the car.

This is dangerous, Addy! You shouldn't follow him. My heart was screaming warnings at me, but I proceeded to open my door and step out.

We walked side by side down the alley, sharing the cover of his black umbrella. The only sounds to be heard were the thudding of raindrops, the pounding of my heart, and the clicking of my high heels against the cement. There were no cars driving by, no buzz of the city nightlife. I felt as though I had stepped into a horror film. I was the naive girl that I used to yell at in the predictable horror films who finds herself alone in a dark alley with a psychopath. *How stupid is she?* I would think, but here I was living it out, well, except I had not yet determined if James was indeed the psychopath.

"Don't look so freaked out. You're almost starting to offend me. I kind of thought you trusted me by now," James stated calmly as we turned the corner.

"It's not you, James. I'm not good with surprises, remember?" I tried to give him a convincing smile.

"Right. Well, try to cheer up a little. This is gonna be fun." We stopped walking and James escorted me in through a rusty metal door.

The inside of the building matched the outside—dark and creepy. The windows had been boarded up, and there were several holes in the dark wood floor. The place was rundown to say the least and appeared to be abandoned.

We walked in farther around an old staircase into a large, open area that was lit with candles and smelled of…something…dirt and ginger perhaps. To my great relief, we were not alone. Rachael and Sasha greeted me with a hug, and Charles put a hand on my shoulder. Luke met my eyes across the room. There was a trace of fear in his look. I smiled back at him, thankful to have someone there that wasn't so "Captain Courageous" as all the others seemed to be. Adam was also there, as well as six others from the night in the field. Derek's coven no doubt. They were the closest group to us.

I hoped no one expected me to remember their names.

"We have been waiting for you, James," Derek said as he walked over to us.

"My apologies. Are we ready to begin?" James replied.

"Sure, unless you want to tell me about your date first." He winked at me. "Did you two have fun?"

James slid an arm around my waist and pulled me to his side. It felt as though he was claiming his property. "We certainly did," he reported with a smile.

"Ah, that's unfortunate," Derek said, taking my hand and giving it a light kiss, "for me, that is." I could tell that his words weren't truly sincere. He was just certifiably charming and yet I giggled like a little girl anyway. I didn't mean for that to come out but fortunately it was quickly overlooked.

"So, Miss Dawson, have they taught you much since we last met?"

"Somewhat. I'm sure there is still a ton I don't know."

"But I'm sure Charles has told you the big secret by now." Derek raised his eyebrows with a mixture of curiosity and excitement.

"What do you mean?" I asked seriously as I glanced at Charles who looked suddenly alarmed.

Derek shifted his weight and answered. "You know, about how Charles—"

Charles quickly cut him off. "That's enough, Derek." His voice was deathly serious.

Derek gave a small chuckle as he took a step backward. "I don't know what you are waiting for. We all think it's time she knows. Come on, this is exciting. We have been waiting…how many years for—"

"Derek! I said that's enough. I'll tell her when the time is right. I'm listening to the spirits' direction on this, so don't tell me when it should be done," Charles barked.

My curiosity was bubbling over. "What are you talking about?!" I asked, looking back and forth between the two men.

Charles sighed. "Adelaide, you have to trust me, it isn't time for you to know yet. But soon. Can you have patience and trust me?"

Me? Patience? This would drive me insane! He had no idea the torture this would put me through. Waiting was not my strong suite.

I bit my lip and paused for a moment, in hopes that he might change his mind. "I guess I don't have a choice."

"No, you don't," Charles said flatly, slicking his hair back with both hands.

"I'm sorry, Charles. You are absolutely right." Derek lowered his eyes, displaying honest shame.

"Well, now that Derek is done causing mischief, I think we should get on with our night," James added.

I glanced behind Derek and noticed that everyone had been observing our strange discussion. James reached down and slipped his hand into mine. "Come on, Addy," he whispered as he led me toward the group.

As everyone shuffled around, finding a place to sit, I noticed something unusual on the ground.

In the flickering candlelight I could see some sort of red substance smeared across the floorboards. A large circle was drawn with several connecting, smaller, circles weaved around the outer edge. I could see symbols inside of the outer circles but before I was able to take a closer look, James had pulled me into the large ring and sat me down.

I followed the others example and crossed my legs. We all sat knee to knee with a small ring of candles in the middle. There was a man directly across the circle from me that everyone had turned their attention to. I could vaguely remember meeting him but couldn't recall his name. Billy or Braun or Baxter…some B name. He was a few years older than me, probably around Calvin's age.

"Let us form the bond before our gods and the spirits of this world." He took a dagger and laid the blade across his left palm. In one quick movement, his hand was dripping crimson droplets into a goblet that sat on the floor.

I grimaced, but this time I was more prepared and was able to keep myself from gasping. From the corner of my eye I could see James watching me; no doubt expecting a more open display of my churning stomach. I was proud of my control. I was maturing in my blood endurance, at least I thought I was, until the B guy sipped from the cup! He actually drank the blood and whatever else was in there.

My stomach tightened as I concentrated on my breathing. I had to get used to this. It's just…blood. Just blood. That idea wasn't at all helpful. Okay, It's just…grape juice. Yeah, just passing around some grape juice. Wait, passing?

8

Possession

The goblet and dagger were being passed around the circle, one person at a time performing the same gruesome ritual. Cut, drip, and drink. I guess this is how we formed the bond. I wasn't going to embarrass myself by fainting again. I had to do it. I was going to be strong and do just as everyone else was doing.

It seemed only seconds had passed before James was handing me the dagger and placing the cup in front of me. I held the knife tightly in my right hand and could feel the pull to my flesh. Faint whispers of power and knowledge echoed in my mind. I was being pushed in the direction I did not know but at the same time my free hand was cringing away, pulling me in the direction of safety and understanding. My heart was twisted in too many directions.

It was characteristic of me to take the safe road, but tonight, the push was stronger than the pull.

I slowly curled my hand around the sharp blade and pulled the handle down. The flesh of my palm slit open easily. I cringed at the stinging pain, but it was bearable; in fact, it was slightly exhilarating. I made a fist with my hand and watched my blood mix with the others. I set the knife down and took up the goblet with both hands and drank. The smell and the warm thick texture didn't have the repulsive effect on me that I thought it would. It was as though I had just swallowed my destiny, tasting life for the first time.

When the union was complete, we joined together our wounded hands and offered up promises and requests to our god Donar. It was a chant, said in unison, so I closed my eyes and repeated the words silently in my head.

"We give you our blood, we give you our life. We belong to you and shall never stray. We come together, united as one, to ask of your voice. Teach us your ways and tell us your bidding. Send us a spirit. We open our minds. We offer our bodies." I had to peek to see what I was supposed to be doing. We released each other's bloodied hands and placed them both, palm down, on the floor in front of us.

James leaned over and whispered in my ear. "We can't be touching for a spirit to speak through us."

I nodded and closed my eyes as the chant…prayer…invocation…whatever it was, continued.

"We call upon the spirits. Come, come and instruct us. We call upon the spirits of the earth. We call upon the spirits of the moon and sky. We are your willing servants. Whatever you ask shall be done."

"Stop!" I jerked my head up to see Rachael's face, contorted with anger. A look I didn't think was possible for her. Every head was lifted and waited for her to continue.

"There are seeds of doubt among you," Rachael went on in a voice not her own. "These seeds will turn into weeds and will destroy you!" She flew her arms in the air as she spoke. Her eyes locked with mine and sent a stabbing pain in my gut. She couldn't just be talking about me. I had no doubts this was real. Or did I? Luke had doubts; I could see it in his brown, fearful eyes.

Charles spoke up for us. "What can we do? What does Donar ask of us?"

Rachael's voice crackled as she commanded us. "Go to the root of the problem. Your little town," She slowly extended her arm and pointed a finger at Charles. "It holds a dangerous man, a man who spreads deceitful words and steals souls of the innocent, all in the name of…" She screeched in pain and clawed viciously down her neck and throat as she spoke the name. "Jesus!"

"What man is this and what shall we do with such an enemy?" Sasha asked passionately.

"You know of whom I speak!" Rachael hissed at us. "Morris is his name. Teach him who is god! Show him who has the power! Make him see the error of his ways. His god is nothing and his preaching is destructive! Stifle his lies. Let his voice be heard no more." She dropped her head like dead weight before looking at us all sheepishly with the soft face I was used to seeing. Whatever had been talking to us had left her body. She ran her fingers through her short brown hair, fluffing it out and trying to overcome her obvious exhaustion.

I inconspicuously rubbed my arms, erasing the backstabbing goose bumps that revealed my fright. Fear is linked with doubt, and apparently that wasn't acceptable.

"Thank you, Rachael," Derek said calmly as he leaned over and kissed her forehead.

Rachael stumbled over her response. "It's an honor…for… to be…used by…" She sighed, her eyes lifeless as her long fingers lightly traced her self-inflicted scratches down her throat.

Derek turned to the group. "Let's discuss what must be done about Morris."

James was the first to speak up. "Well, he's in our town, so let us take care of it."

"Yes, we can do it tomorrow night. Christmas eve, it's perfect," Charles added.

"Excellent," Derek replied. "The rest of us will gather at midnight for the next eight nights and perform candle rituals and communicate with the spirits to support your activities against the enemy." Derek looked at me and added. "Are you sure Ms. Dawson is ready for this?"

I looked around anxiously at the group. I hated being the newbie.

James was first to speak up. "Of course she is ready. She is already conversing with the spirits more freely than most here. I know she can handle it." He looked over at me, and I smiled gratefully to him.

"This is her life now, she needs to be involved," Sasha supported.

"All right, I trust your judgment." Derek nodded toward James and turned to wink at Sasha, who blushed.

Charles chimed in with the best comment of all. "Perhaps we should ask her opinion on this matter."

Every eye was on me, as I pushed down my fears and responded, "I believe what you guys have been telling me, and if I am lucky enough to be a part of this, then I want to embrace it and give it my all. You don't need to leave me out, I'm ready for this." I gave a confident smile.

"I believe her. Let her come," Rachael said absentmindedly, still caressing her neck.

I was pleased by the positive support but was really taken aback when Adam also spoke in my favor.

"Miss Dawson," he hissed in his usual bizarre manner, "needs to understand who we are and be fully aware of what we do. No point in keeping her from it. Donar may have chosen her, but she still must choose for herself...and if not—"

James cut him off. "Well, now that that is settled, I better get you home, Adelaide. Need to get you back before your mom gets off work."

"Oh." I hadn't even thought of the time. "I guess so. Thanks, James." He assisted me up to my feet and we said our good-byes.

James took a lot longer to get back to town. I suspect he was hoping for some extra quality time with me, but to his dismay, I was half asleep when we arrived at my house—my dark, empty house.

"Well, good night. Thanks again for dinner," I said through a good deep yawn.

"Actually, Addy, would you mind if I come in for a while?"

I hadn't expected that. I blinked a few times before responding, "But my mom..."

"She won't be off work for another forty-five minutes. We have time."

I wasn't sure how he knew my mom's schedule or what exactly we needed time for. I just looked at him silently. After a few awkward minutes I managed to get out an, "Um..." Out of nowhere, James started laughing. "No, no, Addy. I only want to come in to help you with your problem."

"What problem?" I asked confused but relieved.

"Well, last time I was in your room, you told me that you have a lot of bad dreams. Remember?" He reached in the backseat and grabbed a small black bag.

"Yeah, I don't remember them much, but it seems like every night I'm waking up all freaked out about something," I said as we both got out of the car and walked to the porch.

"Yeah, well I thought you might like if we did something about that." He gave me his dangerous smile that made my heart race and lose all recollection of how to unlock my front door.

"That would be…I mean, that's, uh, very thoughtful of you. What can we do?" I glared at the door. Something seemed to be wrong with my key.

James grinned and took the key from me. "I'll show you." He had the door unlocked and open in less than three seconds. I guess the key wasn't the problem.

Once in my room, which, by the way, was slightly awkward being alone in my dark bedroom with him, he had me sitting on my floor holding a white candle.

With the lights remaining off, James lit a few candles around my room and the one in my hand before sitting down in front of me.

"Now, carve the name of our god into the candle, as you invite his presence in your mind," he whispered in a very calming voice.

With my fingernail I scratched *Donar* across the wax. Watching the white shavings fall into my carpet, I silently did as James said and invited our god.

When I had finished, James took a long, silver, velvet ribbon from his bag and tied it around the candle. "Good, now let yourself relax as you stare into the flame. Empty your mind, Addy. Release your fears and worries. Let your mind be free."

Everything in my room seemed to fade away as the flickering of the flame consumed my consciousness. After nearly five minutes, I was completely relaxed in a nearly hypnotic state.

"Now close your eyes, Adelaide," James whispered. "I want you to imagine a large open field full of your favorite flowers and tall grass, gently dancing in the breeze. Picture yourself resting peacefully in your bed amongst the flowing grass. Focus on that for a while. Meditate on that image." James placed both his hands over mine, as I continued to hold on to the candle, but his touch made my heart jump, breaking my calm trance.

I closed my eyes tight trying to get back to where I was in that field.

"Relax, Adelaide. You feel tense. You need to relax. We have plenty of time. Relax. Relax," James repeatedly whispered as his thumbs caressed my hands.

My heart was not slowing down. He was making it nearly impossible for me to "relax." I tried ignoring him, but he didn't make it easy.

James gave me a few more minutes to meditate before having me stand up and walk to my window at the end of my bed. He stood behind me, whispering in my ear.

"See the moon? Focus on it, just as you did the flame."

Still holding the candle, I looked out my window to find the luminous crescent. It was glowing brightly beside a shining cloud reflecting its glory. I tried to put my focus on it and it alone, but it was hard to ignore the reality of my situation. My mom had a strict "no boys in the bedroom" policy, and here I was, not only alone in my dark bedroom with a cute boy but alone in the house. I seemed to be developing a new bad habit of allowing myself to fall into uncomfortable situations that could be potentially life threatening, or worse, could get me grounded.

"Now repeat these words:
Donar, my god, I call upon thee
Bring forth good spirits to watch over me
By the moon and the stars that are shining so bright
Awaken their power to guard me this night
When I close my eyes, all that I find
Is good dreams, protection, and peace of mind
Donar, my god, I call upon thee
From these nightmares set me free."

Goosebumps ran up my arms as I methodically recited the words. This whole thing was quite a bit more frightening than my usual bedtime ritual of watching an *I Love Lucy* rerun with my mom before brushing my teeth. I could really feel things happening though. Like a presence was moving about my room. It was a slightly uneasy feeling but reassuring at the same time. I mean, that's what we were asking for, and I think it was working.

"You can do this a couple times a week if you need to. I'd be happy to come over whenever you need me," James said, in a slightly flirtatious tone as he set the still-burning candle on my nightstand.

"You'll want to wear this around your neck as you sleep, and even throughout your day," he said as he untied the ribbon that wrapped the candle. "It's part of the ritual to keep away bad dreams and bad spirits. You also need to keep something silver with you."

"Silver?" I repeated, wondering why the ribbon didn't count.

"Real silver. Do you have anything?" he asked, looking at my small jewelry box that was open on my dresser.

I thought for a moment. "I'm not really sure. Maybe." I made a move for the box but James stopped me.

"I got it," he said as he slipped off a silver band from his middle finger and let it slide down the ribbon.

"Oh, James, I can't…It's yours…," I stammered as my mind searched for words.

There was no point in arguing with him. He was already tying the ribbon around my neck. "Hey, don't worry about it. It's pure silver…just what you need. Besides, I'm only lending it to you."

"Well, okay. Thanks, James. You have given me so much today. I feel like I owe you."

"Nonsense. It's fun spoiling you. But I suppose if you really want to pay me back, I wouldn't refuse a kiss." He lightly brushed my cheek with the back of his hand, sending my already racing heart into warp speed.

With the amount of money he had spent on me in one evening, he certainly did deserve my gratitude, but a kiss? That felt, somehow…well, wrong. He may be charming, rich, and ridiculously handsome but my affection can't be bought. His suggestion gave me a slight, girl-in-short-skirt-on-a-dark-corner kind of a feeling. Not that he wasn't tempting, he certainly was, but I was too stubborn to give him that satisfaction. Guilt is a horrible reason for a first kiss.

I gave James a slight smile as he leaned closer. His dark eyes pulled me in, nearly losing me in his enticing scheme. But to his surprise, my lips met his cheek for one quick moment. Hopefully sending a clear message of "I'm not some tramp off the street you can buy with money."

James stepped back and frowned. I bit my lip, trying to suppress the grin that was forming. I was quite pleased with myself. James had been enjoying my surprise and confusion all day, now it was my turn to put the uncomprehending look on his face, though it only lasted a moment.

James worked up a smile and said, "Well, now we're even."

He was being a good sport and for the first time today I was running the show.

"I should get to bed now, James."

"Of course. I'll see you tomorrow. Big day."

"Okay."

James turned and walked away, whispering, "Sweet dreams, Miss Dawson," as he shut my door behind him.

My dreams weren't so sweet; in fact they were more terrifying than ever. I fell asleep clutching the silver ring around my neck while muttering what I could remember of the poetic-like ceremony.

"Adelaide…Aaa-delll-aaaide…," whispers beckoned me into the dream—kind, friendly whispers.

I was sitting on my bed in a field of wild flowers just like I had imagined in my trance. I could see Ben reaching his hand out to me and calling my name. I smiled at him, but he looked worried.

"Ben!" I said with excitement as I reached my hand out for his. Our hands didn't touch however. Benjamin was too far away and the distance was becoming greater and greater between us.

"Where are you going?!" I yelled at him.

"I'm still right here, Addy." I could hear his words as though they were right in my ear, but I could no longer make out his face. I watched with sadness as my friend faded into the distance.

I sobbed uncontrollably into my purple sheets. James was suddenly next to me, consoling me with gentle words that echoed through the field.

"It's all okay now...Donar has heard your plea. He wants you, Adelaide, and nothing can stop him." I looked up at James through watery eyes. He was still right next to me. He wasn't fading as Ben had. James spoke again, but this time it wasn't his voice. "Commit, give yourself to him, sacrifice. Your time is coming, little one. You can't escape!" James threw me down on the bed with painful force. "One way or another, Addy!" The voice screeched through James.

I screamed and instantly threw my hands up for protection. James didn't attack, in fact, nothing happened.

I stared up at my hands that were guarding my face. They were dripping with blood! Fresh, red blood. I threw them down in horror and felt a hard stone beneath me; it was also covered in blood. What had happened? I looked around and saw every face I had ever known staring back at me with blank faces. My fifth grade teacher, my friends from Utah, old boyfriends, Mr. Rinaldi from English class, and some girls from my new school.

Mr. Tucker was standing by my side shaking his head. "It's too late," he said plainly.

"No! No, it's not. This isn't my blood!" I yelled at them. My body was heavy, and I was unable to sit up but I could move enough for them to be able to see that I was alive. I turned my head and saw Calvin and Ollie next to my mom. "We did everything we could," Calvin said in an uncaring tone to my mother.

James, Sasha, and Adam were standing over my head looking down at me.

"Please help me. Help me up," I begged them.

Sasha leaned over and brushed the hair off my face and said quietly, "It's done."

I was overwhelmed with frustration. "What's done?! Can't you all see that—" I winced. A sudden sharp pain seared through my ribs. "Can't you see I'm…" I grabbed at my chest and unexpectedly bumped something hard. I lifted my head to see a dagger stuck deep into my heart. Suddenly the pain and reality, or what I thought was reality, hit me. I screamed and cried out for help but no one listened.

"Mom!" She ignored my plea. "Daddy!" I cried out in desperation to the faintly familiar face in the crowd. He turned and walked away from me. That was more painful than the steel that had pierced my most vital organ. Ignored and abandoned by my father once again.

I gasped for air as I stared into the sky. *This is it*, I thought, *the end*. Did it really matter? Wouldn't it be easy to just give in and stop fighting? "NO!" my heart screamed. I wanted life. I truly wanted to live. How had I even gotten to this point? I looked around the field; my friends, family and teachers had all gone and were replaced by the many covens that had come together for Luke. They all stared at me but no one moved. I slowly sucked in my breath expecting it to be my last. Surprisingly, I gasped once more from pure horror. As if my present circumstance wasn't awful enough, a blanket of snakes and smoke came out of the ground and slithered over my body pulling me down into the earth; to my everlasting grave. I tried to fight it, but there was nothing left in me.

"Please help me." I whispered. "I need…help."

Over the hissing of disgusting reptiles I was able hear a lamb bleating. I could feel the fleece rub against my side as it gently pushed against my body. This seemed to throw the snakes into a frenzy. They moved quickly every which way. Their smooth, overlapping scales slipped easily across my pale skin and over my clothes until finding their way upon the sheep.

With every snake gone, I quickly sat up to see if they were hurting the poor, innocent little lamb.

"Worthy is the lamb who was slain." The words seemed to float up from the earth. "He was led as a lamb to the slaughter…With the precious blood of Christ, as of a lamb without blemish and without spot…To Him who loved us and washed us from our sins in His own blood…By the blood of the Lamb."

My lungs filled with air and the pressure left my chest. I could feel my heart beating again. I felt alive.

The crowd had left me and all that remained was a single white lamb lying dead in the field. The dagger that had been in my heart was now sticking out of its side as blood gushed forth, staining the pure white wool.

I got up from the ground to examine the animal. Tears fell freely from my brown eyes as I lightly touched my bizarre little savior. The feeling of loss and sadness was overwhelming, but I couldn't understand why. I lay down and rested my head upon the blood-stained fleece as I wept.

When I opened my eyes, I felt my pillow, wet with tears, and sat up in my bed. I didn't feel like I had woken from a dream, more like I just stepped into a different room. The reality felt the same and the feelings of horror, confusion, and sadness still remained. This was the first time I was able to fully remember my nightmare; and I wished I hadn't. I didn't know what any of it meant.

I went straight to kitchen for breakfast and realized my mom must have come home and went back to work all before I woke up. We were supposed to spend the day together. Sadly, I wasn't too disappointed. Lately, I only felt nervous and slightly guilty around her. Not because I felt that what I was doing was wrong, but rather that she would see it as so.

I still felt the pain of my dream after my second bowl of cereal. I replayed the nightmare over and over as I went along with my day, wrapping the last few presents for my mom and grandpa, checking my e-mail, and doing laundry.

Nurse Redhead was finally off work and home by five o'clock. But for the first time this year, my mom wasn't happy to see me.

9

Grounded

I was sitting on the couch, channel surfing the TV when my mom came through the door.

She hung her coat with unnecessary force before turning to me. "How was your day yesterday, Adelaide?" She used my full name; I knew I was in trouble.

"Oh pretty boring, I guess. How was yours?" I held my breath as I kept my eyes glued to the television.

"And what did you do? Did you go out?" She walked over and stopped in front of the TV.

She couldn't possibly know what I was doing last night. "Well, I went for a short jog down to the beach but other than that I just stayed home. I talked to Benjamin on the phone for a while. That was fun." I tried to play it cool.

I saw the corner of her mouth twitch; never a good sign. "Yeah, I heard about that."

Uh-oh. "Wh-what do you mean?" I asked, trying not to panic.

"Well, Calvin called Dad to ask him if he could check their porch to make sure there weren't any packages getting wet from the weather. Calvin also said to tell you hi since you were supposedly eating dinner with Grandpa. He heard that from Ben. Did you tell Ben that?" She gave me a stern look, but I could see hope behind her eyes. She wanted me to have a good excuse, but I didn't.

"Yes, I told him that...but I...I changed my mind. I was just being lazy I guess." My eyes darted across the floor, to the kitchen, and back over to my mom's feet; anywhere but her eyes.

"I see. So you just decided to stay home? Simple as that?" She shifted her weight.

"Sure. I don't know why this is such a big deal." What else could I say? "Yeah, Mom, I went to the city alone with a boy that you don't know, called up some spirits, drank some blood, and then invited the boy into my bedroom while you were away." I didn't see that going over very well.

"Why are you lying to me, Adelaide?" Her face was nearly as red as her hair.

"I...I...what do you...I'm not lying." That didn't exactly shout innocent.

"I love that you are such a bad liar." Her face softened for just a moment before she continued. "But I *hate* that you are lying to me! Your grandpa was worried when he heard that you were supposed to be at his house, so he came over and you weren't here either. He looked around town for you. He was very worried. As was I, until I came home and found you sleeping. Do you have any idea what you put us through?" Typical mother tone, dripping with anger and love all at the same time.

"I'm sorry" was all I managed to squeak out.

"Oh, I bet you are. You better have a good explanation for me." She paused giving me a chance to respond. I had nothing so she went on. "You are grounded for three weeks. You go to school and you come home. You don't go anywhere unless it's with me! Do you understand?"

I swallowed hard. That wasn't going to work for me. I just nodded, got up, and headed for my bedroom.

"Where are you going?" she asked, her voice a little more calm.

"To my room?" I said, as if asking permission.

"We need to get ready to go. Christmas Eve at Grandpa's house and caroling, remember?" She finally smiled. "Just because you are grounded doesn't mean we aren't going to have a good Christmas together."

I just stared at her. She could never hold on to her anger very long. I wished I could be like that.

"Well, what are you going to wear? I have a beautiful, deep red, cashmere sweater that would look wonderful on you!"

"Really?" I said hesitantly, unsure if I was allowed to be happy yet.

"And I could do your hair up too!" she said excitedly.

"Cool." I gave only half a grin. This was like dancing on the devil's dance floor. One wrong move and I could be condemned to a much more hellish sentence.

As we got ready, I tried to have enough fun to make her happy, but not enough that she felt I hadn't been properly punished. An hour later we were festively dressed and loading our presents into the silver Traverse.

"You probably don't remember what Christmas Eve at Grandpa's is like. You were very young," she said fondly as if remembering back in time.

"Yeah, not really. Are other people invited too?" We pulled up to the old cabin and had to park on the street behind three other cars; two trucks and one jeep, actually.

Mom grinned while she checked her makeup in the rearview mirror. "Always, darling. That's what makes it so much fun."

Sure, for a social butterfly maybe. I sighed; this wasn't going to be the calm evening I had hoped for.

We each carried an armful of presents up the porch. The door swung wide open and two strangers greeted us with enthusiasm, escorting us into the crowded house.

I set my presents down next to the tree and looked around. It was like Christmas had exploded in my Grandpa's house; the smell of pine and ginger bread, the sound of jolly chatter and merry laughter, with red, green, and white covering every unfamiliar body.

"Adders!" Grandpa came up and gave me a big hug, rubbing his Santa-like beard in my face. "I am so glad to see you." I could tell he truly meant it. I felt slightly uncomfortable knowing he had caught me in a lie, and it had really worried him. I would hate to be responsible for another heart attack.

To my great relief, Grandpa never mentioned anything and was quickly back in the kitchen pulling out fresh molasses cookies from the oven.

From what I could tell there were two families with children, an elderly couple, and a man who looked to be in his thirties. I also spotted Mrs. Price, the receptionist from the veterinary clinic. She was widowed by the time she was twenty-eight and had never remarried. I had never met a sweeter or more joyful old lady. It made me smile just seeing her. I couldn't understand where she found so much happiness through such pain and loneliness. Her eyes just sparkled like a girl in love, as she poked around on the little piano in the corner, playing a beginner level "Walking in a Winter Wonder Land."

I drifted over, like a moth to a flame. Drawn by her radiance, I leaned against the wall and smiled at her.

"Oh, my favorite little brunette!" She jumped up from the bench and wrapped me in hug that smelled of peppermint. "How's Addy today?"

"All right."

"Oh, and you look so lovely tonight! I can see why you have been the talk of the town." She winked at me and went back to her song.

"You're too sweet, Mrs. Price. But you're the one who looks beautiful." It was true, though her youth was far gone, she was always glowing, always beautiful to me.

She giggled. "This old skin and bones? Oh no, honey, what you must be seeing is God's beauty reflecting off me." She laughed again, stumbling over a few keys.

What was that supposed to mean? I watched her for a few minutes before making my way to the table to find a sugar cookie.

"Isn't she adorable?" A friendly looking man holding a baby boy nodded toward our evening entertainment.

"Mrs. Price? Yeah, she is something," I said biting off the head of a frosted angel.

"She just learned to play a few months ago. Practices every day."

"I wish I could be like her when I'm her age. What is she always so happy about?" I asked, not expecting an answer.

"She's in love," the man said.

My jaw dropped. "Really? With who?"

"Jesus." He smiled as he watched her play. "She is so in love with Jesus. Has been for a long time too."

"Right." I rolled my eyes. What a stupid answer.

The man looked at me, adjusted the baby, and stuck out his hand. "My name is Nathaniel Morris."

I shook his hand, realizing that this was the name of the enemy: Morris. "I'm Adelaide. Do you…are you the pastor of…what's it called…Ledo Christian Fellowship?"

"That's me. You must be Kate's daughter. It's so nice to meet you!" He smiled a big, kind smile. How could anyone hate him? How would this guy have any enemies? He was so nice and—"Do you want to hold him?" He looked lovingly down at his baby boy.

I couldn't befriend him. I had to distance myself. This house was full of people I shouldn't be around. I was behind enemy lines now.

"No, no thanks. I have to, uh…" I turned and walked away. Making my way past the crowd of people, I grabbed my coat and made it safely to the porch. It was cold, and lightly snowing, outside but quiet. The noise and voices had all faded off.

"Cider?" Someone asked from behind me.

"Luke! What are you doing here?" I was so grateful not to be alone in this battle; I had a comrade in arms.

Luke handed me a plastic cup. "My family dragged me here. I'm so glad you came! It's hard…to be around all of them, you know?"

"Yeah, I know." I was really glad it was Luke here with me. We really connected. "Wait, your dad isn't the pastor, is he?"

"Thank goodness no!" He put up his hand to emphasize. "My dad is the dark-haired guy with the beard." I remembered seeing him. "My mom is the blonde sitting on the couch with three children pulling for her attention. Those are my younger siblings. I have another sister too, she is a twin actually and two older brothers. The oldest, William, he is in Europe."

My eyes widened. "Wow, I didn't know you had such a big family."

"Yeah, and I'm stuck right in the middle. Just the place where no one really notices you," he said in a slightly bitter, sad tone.

"Oh, I can imagine. I'm sorry. I bet that's hard." I took a drink of apple cider.

"Yeah well, it makes it easy on me. I mean, they don't really pay attention if I lose or succeed. They love me and all. They're just so busy all the time."

"What a bummer." I had just learned more about Luke in the last two minutes than I have over the months that I have known him. "I bet it is nice to have James and Charles and everyone," I said, trying to be optimistic.

"Yeah, I guess." He forced a smile.

"Well, doesn't it give you a purpose? You know, make you feel important and unique?"

"In a way, it does. It's just, well, I'm not sure that it's worth it." Luke was so young and timid, I felt like a big sister talking to her little brother.

"Why wouldn't it be worth it?" I asked with concern.

"Well, ever since they started talking to me for the first time…I have had really creepy nightmares and…" He glanced around.

"And what?" I was intrigued.

"It sounds stupid, but, I always feel scared like there is someone watching me…someone bad. I hate going to sleep at night…I'm even afraid to be alone in the dark now. Does that sound pathetic?" I was surprised that he opened up to me so much and even more surprised that I knew exactly how he felt.

I put a hand on his shoulder. "I feel that way too, Luke. And I have really bad nightmares all the time." I remembered once again the horror of last night's dream.

"Really? You do?"

"Yeah, but James explained to me that Yahweh will sometimes send bad spirits out to bother us and keep us in fear, you know. That's why we have bad dreams." I pulled out the silver ring from around my neck. "Did they teach you how to do dream—"

"Yeah, yeah, I have tried all that. Not to be a downer, but it doesn't work, Addy. At least not for me. We used to live Michigan before we moved here, did you know that?"

"No."

"I got involved in a little group that practiced a form of Wicca. Witchcraft. I was always looking for somewhere to belong, so when Charles approached me, I was thrilled. I thought this would be different but it's not."

"What do you mean?" We weren't supposed to be talking like this. Doubting. No one was around to hear, but it felt like someone was always listening.

"I mean, what I have now, with the Dons, it is just another form of witchcraft. It might be covered up with a few ribbons and bows, but it is downright, dirty, old, pagan witchcraft," he said sternly, gaining a little courage.

"But...but, Luke, I thought...You, you chose to..." I didn't know what to say. Could I get in trouble for listening to him talk like this?

"Don't worry, Addy, I'm not going anywhere. I can't. It's not like I'm against witchcraft, a lot of it makes sense. I just want to make sure that you know what you are getting into. You deserve to know. I think this spiritual world is all pretty new to you, and I want to make sure that *someone* is being honest with you about it. This isn't a game, this isn't a club, and it isn't what you think."

"But..." I thought for a moment. "It's...it's so real, Luke. I mean, the voices and the...the power. It has to be real."

He looked down at his feet while he spoke. "Yeah, it's real, Addy, that's for sure, and that's why it's so scary. This is serious business. I don't know exactly what's going on, but I think we are being misled. I don't know, I think maybe...maybe we are on the wrong side." His eyes shot up at me to see my response. I nervously rubbed my neck. "I guess that's possible, but...I just don't know, Luke. I thought for sure this is what I wanted. That I finally found my...reason for being... somewhere I fit in."

"Yeah, I don't know either. But I want you to see what I'm saying." I looked at him quietly so he continued. "When I practiced witchcraft before, I had this same feeling, scared and alone, a kind of…real heavy feeling. I thought this time would be better, that I would have more power and not be afraid anymore. It's all the same though, just a different god and different stories. I almost wonder if…" He faded off in his own thoughts.

"If what, Luke?" I whispered, as though what we were doing was illegal.

"I wonder if your friend Ben is right."

My face scrunched in confusion. "How do you know what Ben thinks about all this?"

"Oh, I used to hang out with him and Cody a little until…well, you know."

"Until he became the enemy?" I said, annoyed by the idea.

Luke nodded. "Have you ever considered that he might be right about us, about what we do? What if everyone in there"—he motioned toward the house—"knows the real truth? I mean, they don't seem to be afraid like we are. Why is that?"

I thought over the devil-worshipping accusations from my other friends. I didn't like the idea of a supposedly all-powerful, loving God and the evil devil. I looked at Luke and just shrugged. Why did life have to be so fuzzy?

Luke sighed. "Well, maybe we'll never really know. Maybe nobody knows." He frowned. "Gosh, I don't know! My parents used to be so unhappy all the time, and now, well supposedly they 'found god' and they're different now. They are happy and it's like they fell in love with each other again…and fell in love with life. I don't get it." His frustration was very apparent.

"Me neither."

"Thanks for listening to me. Do you understand what I'm saying about the Dons?"

It was very sweet. He was the young one, rather thin and not too muscular, yet he was looking out for me; trying to protect me.

"I think I get it, but I don't like it. I'm really lost. I want to be happy like your parents or Mrs. Price but the realness and power that Donar offers…I want that. You really got me mixed up now, Luke."

I grinned at him and he smiled back. "How come you don't get out if you don't like it anymore?" I asked.

Luke stared out at the falling snow; his breath visible in the cold air. "You can't tell *anyone* what I told you. Please." He took my hand and looked into my eyes with fear. "Promise me you won't tell anyone."

His fear was gripping its long fingers around my throat, causing a tight strain as I swallowed down my own questions ringing out in my mind like a high security alarm. "I promise. My lips are sealed." I patted his hand to reassure him. "We should probably go inside now."

"Right, presents." He said, unenthused, although I could see a glint of excitement in his eyes.

"And then, caroling." I said, matching his tone.

Once inside, everyone found a place to sit in the living room near the tree. The presents were passed to their owners, and rather than taking turns with all the people, we all opened them at the same time. Apparently, this was the Dawson family tradition. Joyous, loud, and disorderly. I liked it.

I was given the usual clothes, books, new purse, and the yearly framed painting from my mother. A pair of mud boots from Mrs. Price, which was very thoughtful. My poor little tennis shoes always wandered back inside covered in mud after walking the dogs at the clinic.

To my great shock and excitement, my grandpa had bought me a new laptop! It wasn't the best or the cutest, but it was *new* and all mine. I showered him with hugs and kisses, trying to overemphasize my gratitude.

"I'm glad you like it, Adders." He peeled my arm off from around his face so he could speak. "Here is one more present for you." He handed me a poorly wrapped gift. "It's from Mr. Tucker. He left it with me to give to you."

"Really? That is so nice." I sat back and tore off the green paper. A book, a heavy book. I looked up at Grandpa but he was already talking to Pastor Morris about his new fishing pole.

I traced my fingers across the beautiful leather cover. Down at the bottom right hand corner were the words *"Seek and ye shall find"* written in gold. Confused, I flipped through a few pages. I saw words like Jesus, sin, love, faith, and demons. I shut the book and frowned. Turning it to the side, the spine read "The Holy Bible."

I rolled my eyes but caught my mom's gaze halfway around. "You be sure to thank him for that," she said with wide smile across her face.

I nodded.

When everyone was done saying their thank-yous, we told a few stories and sang a few songs, most of which were about God. I was having more fun than I knew I should have. I was pleased to see Luke enjoying himself and singing along on the floor next to Red, grandpa's old hound dog. I didn't understand why he continued to be involved with the Dons if he had changed his mind about them, but his warning got me thinking. Maybe I don't understand what I am getting myself into. Maybe I'm making the wrong decision.

I looked around the room at all the happy, loving faces. How could these people possibly be so dangerous? I watched the pastor interacting with his wife and three children. I would love to have a dad like him. His adoration for his family was obvious, how was *this* man our enemy? How could Benjamin be my enemy?! My anger was bubbling up inside of me, but I was overwhelmed with distractions so I let my concerns be buried for the time being.

By eight o'clock I had a baby in my arms and a five-year-old girl on my knee as we listened to Pastor Morris telling about the life of Jesus with such animation that even I was captivated.

My grandpa bent over and whispered in my ear. "There's a boy on the phone asking to talk to his 'honey.'" He chuckled softly, trying not to interrupt the story.

I had been so caught up in the pastor's words that I hadn't even heard the phone ringing.

"Ben?" I asked excitedly. I looked at our storyteller and back at my grandpa. "But…I kind of wanted to…the story…" I felt like a little child asking to stay awake just a little longer. I knew it was wrong of me, but I was so intrigued by the man in the story, "the son of God," I had never heard his story told all the way through.

My grandpa smiled. "Don't worry, you will get to hear the rest of it tomorrow at church."

"Church?"

"Christmas tradition, sweetie pie, now hop on up." He gently took the sleeping baby from my arms. "The phone is in the kitchen."

10

Curse

"Happy Christmas Eve, Benjamin!" I said joyfully into the phone as I scooted backwards on the kitchen counter.

"Well, aren't you chipper today?"

"I suppose," I said and then remembered, "although I did get grounded for a few weeks." After I spoke the words I remembered that Mark would have told Ben about my date with James. I sucked in my breath, wishing with all my might that Ben wasn't hurt by what I did.

"What! What did you do to get grounded? Does this mean we can't hang out when I get back?"

"I don't know. I'll have to ask my mom. Maybe if you come to my house…" I was mentally scheming ways to convince my mom.

"So…" He paused, "What did you get in trouble for?"

Was it possible that Mark really hadn't ratted me out?

"Uhhh, well, I went out with some friends…like you suggested." I thought for a second, this wasn't really a lie, I just hoped he wouldn't ask me the details. "And I stayed out too late without telling my mom. I guess parents don't like that kind of thing." I forced out a laugh.

There was a moment of silence on the other end of the phone.

"Yeah, usually not the wisest choice." He was trying not to show it, but I could hear the questions behind his voice. "Well, as long as

I get to hang out with you I'm sure it won't be so bad. Maybe it will keep you out of trouble." I guessed he was thinking that it would keep me away from James and my other friends. It was a rational thought, but I knew it wouldn't keep James away from me. He would find a way.

"Actually," Ben continued, "I'm surprised that you're still allowed to talk to me."

"I'm grounded to the house. Mom never said anything about talking on phones. Besides, she likes you. I'm sure she wouldn't mind if—"

He cut me off. "I'm not talking about your mom."

Oh, right. I suppose I really shouldn't be talking to him; I shouldn't be talking to any of these Christians. I really hated that rule; the Tuckers were one of the best things in my life now. Maybe…I could feel my guts twisting and my heart racing as I even considered the idea…Maybe I should give the Tuckers, my mom, my grandpa, Christianity a chance. Maybe I should know my options before I commit.

I took a real deep breath in.

"Addy? I didn't mean to bring up—"

I interrupted him. "Actually, Ben, I was thinking, maybe… maybe I don't like that rule so much. Maybe I want to…to know my options."

I heard a faint gasp and could just picture the smile on Ben's face. I couldn't help but smile either. I felt strangely at peace with my decision.

"Are you serious? Oh, honey, that is…that is so…this is the best Christmas present ever!" He definitely wasn't trying to suppress his delight.

"All right, calm down. I'm not promising anything, I just…I just want to keep hanging out with you." Heat flooded my cheeks, and I was glad he couldn't see me.

"Addy, I really… you are…I…" He stumbled over every word and wasn't getting anywhere with them.

"I'm going to church tomorrow," I said, matter-of-factly, knowing he would like that.

"Really?"

I loved it when Ben was happy.

"Yup." I almost felt proud of myself. It had been many years since my mom had stopped forcing me into attending Sunday school at her church in Utah. "Oh, and will you tell your dad thanks for the gift. That was very nice of him."

"Yeah, I'll tell him."

"Ben?"

"Yeah, Addy?"

I lowered my voice. "I really can't wait for you to come home."

"I know, it has been so..." I couldn't hear the rest because a chatty group of people walked into the kitchen wearing their coats and gloves.

"Let's go caroling!" my mom said to me over the other excited voices.

"Ben, I'm sorry but I have to go now," I said loudly as I glared at the intruders.

"Okay, have fun tonight. Wish I was there to go with you."

I smiled. "Me too."

"All right, come on, we need our most talented vocals with us." My grandpa pulled me down off the counter.

"Bye!" I yelled into the phone as it was pulled away from me.

"Oh Come All Ye Faithful" was the song we sang through the first neighborhood. I walked beside my mother, singing my heart out; one thing I really enjoyed doing. Most of the houses were festively decorated with twinkly lights, snowmen, and nativity scenes. I would definitely miss caroling in the future...but then again... maybe that wouldn't be in my future.

Our next song was "Silent Night." I knew the words verbatim but never realized what the song was actually about until that night.

"Glories stream from heaven afar. Heavenly hosts sing Alleluia! Christ the Savior is Born. Christ the Savior is born." Goosebumps ran up and down my arms as I sang the words. But it wasn't fear that I was feeling. I didn't really know *what* I was feeling.

By the end of the song I felt a tug on the back of my coat.

"Slow down," Luke whispered in my ear.

I slowed my pace and we fell back behind the group as they walked up toward another home singing "Joy to the World."

"What's up, Luke?"

"They're waiting for us." Luke was staring down the road.

At the end of the street I could make out five silhouettes standing motionless in the dark.

"Come on. We'll go down the back alley so no one sees us. Let's just hope they don't notice we are gone," Luke said as he blew out the little candles we held and stuffed them in his pocket.

We walked across a thin layer of snow that rested atop the black pavement, leaving a perfect trail of footprints down the whole length of the alley way.

"Don't worry," Charles said when we joined them, walking together to another destination. "We'll have you back before they know you are gone."

"Where are we going?" I asked, not very excited for our endeavor.

"To a house" was all Charles said as we turned down another road.

"Are you having a fun evening?" James asked, finding his way next to me.

"Sure, it's been fine." I tried to play it down, knowing we're supposed to be anti-Christmas.

"I've been thinking about you today," he said quietly.

I forced out a smile. I had been doing my own thinking.

"Would you like to go out with me tomorrow night?" he asked confidently.

"Tomorrow is Christmas," I said under my breath.

"Tomorrow night? It's a Friday night, and I bet your mom will have to work?" he persisted.

I frowned, my mother wasn't scheduled to work but the way James said it I assumed he could it make it happen. I didn't appreciate that.

"James, I can't."

"Why?" He didn't look happy.

"I'm grounded," I whispered apologetically.

"Oh." He smiled. "I'm sure we can work something out."

I didn't know what to say so I quickly changed the subject. "So, what are we doing?" I asked loudly.

Rachael skipped up beside me, wrapping her arm around mine. "We are going to Morris's house…to stop the seeds of doubt, remember?"

I nodded.

"Don't sound so excited, Rachael. We don't take pleasure from cursing others, even our enemies. This is necessary and must be done. It's not right to let him spread his lies and deception to so many people. It is getting carried away so we need to step in."

Cursing? We were on our way to curse Pastor Morris? I didn't feel right about this. I liked him. I liked his family. It didn't seem fair.

I looked over my shoulder at Luke. His face was showing the same apprehension that I felt. He caught my eye and frowned.

"You okay, Addy?" James asked.

"Oh, yeah, just…taking it all in." That wasn't a very good excuse but apparently it was good enough.

"Good. Well, this is it." He pointed to a cute little house with a huge yard enclosed by a picket fence.

Charles opened the gate and we all followed down the walkway, stopping at the porch steps.

"Okay James and Sasha I want you to take the candles and begin the cursing at their front door. Rachael, Luke, and I will sprinkle powder across the yard. Adam, have Adelaide help you burry the bottle." Charles's voice was stern and commanding. "And remember, it is extremely important that no one sees us doing this, so be quiet and keep an eye out."

Rachael pulled me over to Sasha who had a black bag opened up and set on the lawn.

Everyone dug through the bag and spread out to do their assigned parts. Adam pulled out a large glass bottle and a hand shovel and walked back to the porch steps.

"Come on, Addy," Adam quietly called over for me. "Hold that."

He handed me the bottle, and we both knelt down in the snow.

"What is this stuff?" I asked, examining the contents of the bottle. It appeared to contain needles and nails and chunks of some type of root, along with a powdery substance and a small piece of fabric.

"Family recipe, you could say." He grinned as he pulled back a stepping stone and began digging.

I looked around at the house and the yard. "And what exactly are we all doing?"

There was a light muttering coming from James and Sasha on the porch. I could see the dark shapes of the others, lightly spreading a white substance across the lawn and walkway. Whatever it was blended perfectly with the light blanket of snow that covered the ground. Not only was I feeling regretful about hurting the Morris family, but I was also freaked out by the dark situation that I found myself in, not to mention I was probably breaking the law on top of all that.

"We're cursing the property, Miss Dawson, what do you think?" I didn't appreciate his condescending tone. Why did I get stuck with Adam? I preferred to keep my distance from him and his creepy, dark demeanor.

"Okay, but…what will it do?" I asked in a loud whisper.

"Ssshhh." Charles knelt down beside us. "We need to be quick and quiet about this. If a neighbor sees…" he looked toward the road. "Do you hear that?"

"Someone's coming," Adam responded.

I heard voices and obnoxious laughter. They were toward the end of the road but were slowly headed our way.

"Everyone finish up, quickly!" Charles whispered urgently.

Without a word, Adam stuck out his hand and I gave him the bottle. In less than a minute, the bottle was buried with the stone put back in its place. Everyone threw their items back in the bag and stood by the gate staring at Charles for direction. The voices were just a house away, and we couldn't just walk out into the street.

"Find a place to hide, quickly. Adam, you stay with me," Charles said, no longer worried about keeping his voice down.

James pulled me over behind the thick, snow-covered shrubbery that lined the fence. We both knelt down in the snow and quietly waited. I heard the clink of the gate and assumed that Charles and Adam had left the yard. Rachel and Sasha were also out of sight.

"Well, look who it is!" said a male voice from the other side of our hiding place. A few others laughed before Charles responded.

"Good evening Paul," he said calmly.

"Shouldn't you boys be off stirring your cauldron or something?" mocked a voice that seemed familiar to me. That comment stirred up a spring of laughter from the other boys.

Curious, I pushed aside some branches to get a look at the trouble makers. I recognized a few faces from school including Bryan Evans, from my chemistry class.

"And shouldn't you be off celebrating the holiday with your parents?" Adam fired back. The comment didn't seem that harsh to me, but I could see pain on Bryan's face.

James gently grabbed my hand and pulled it out of the bush. I looked at him, and he slowly shook his head at me. I frowned at him as I repositioned myself. The snow had soaked through my jeans, making me cold and uncomfortable.

I sat quietly, with my back to the bushes and listened.

"Maybe you should mind your own business kid!" The fence rattled.

"Take your hands off him, Bryan," Charles said, keeping his soothing tone.

"Or what?! You'll turn me into a frog?" Bryan laughed as did the others.

I noticed some lights come on in the little house next to us. They were disturbing the neighborhood. I shut my eyes tight. I just want to get out of here! What if the neighbors were to find us? I would be in so much trouble. I didn't like this one bit; I didn't like the cursing, the fear, the hiding. It was probably for the best if I spent less time with them. If the people that I loved the most hated what I was involved in, well, perhaps there was some reasoning to it.

My head lightly bumped the brush behind me and sent a tiny shower of snow down my jacket. I sucked in my breath, trying to suppress my desire to stand up and shake out the biting crystals of ice. By my third convulsing shiver, James put his arm around me and gave me a gentle, "Sshhh."

"Trust me, Bryan, you're going to regret this," Charles said in a more threatening manner.

"What are you two doing here anyway?" Came a different voice.

"Yeah, isn't this that pastor's house?" another boy chimed in.

Adam and Charles were silent.

"What are you doing in front of a pastor's house, boys? Were you hoping to confess your sins?" Bryan hissed at them.

"None of your business. You better just leave us alone now. Walk away, and we will forget this happened." I could hear Adam trying to suppress his anger.

"I don't like getting bossed around by freshmen." The fence rattled again.

"Get your hands off me!" Adam yelled. I could hear Bryan stumble as though Adam had pushed back.

This is no time for a fight! I looked to James as if he could do something about this. He put his finger up to his mouth.

There was a loud noise and then Adam groaned.

"Stay where you are, Charles. There is five of us and only two of you."

"It's rather immature to beat up on a freshmen, don't you think?" Charles growled.

"Like you're one to talk. You turned this freshman into your little cult follower. And Luke, he used to be a cool guy, until you got your hands on him. And poor Adelaide, it's obvious that you're brainwashing her into your devil worshipping family, too!" Bryan yelled.

"They are all making their own decisions. They are free to do what they want so—"

One of the other boys cut him off. "Oh yeah! My dad said that you freaks have an all-or-nothing policy. He said that if someone decides they don't want to be a part of what you do, then you…you make them disappear. He has witnessed it happen."

There was a loud thump and someone yelled in pain.

"You're going to seriously regret that, Adam!" someone yelled.

A short siren sounded as a car rolled up in front of the house.

"Cops! Get out of here!" one of the boys yelled.

I could hear them running off. Bryan yelled back. "This isn't over!"

James tightened his grip around me as a car door slammed. I could hear an older man talking quietly and the return mumbling of Adam and Charles. They talked for a few minutes, but I couldn't make out their words. *This is it*, I thought, *I'm grounded for life.*

"The neighbors must have called the cops," James whispered in my ear.

"My mom is going to kill me," I mumbled to myself as I pictured my mom bailing me out of jail.

The gate creaked open and a flashlight swept across the yard. I felt like I was sitting in a courtroom waiting for the judge to sentence me. Guilty was going to be the verdict.

I held my breath, watching the light flash across the bushes. I could see the man now. He was tall with short cropped dark hair, and I noticed that his shirt read "Sheriff" on it. He wasn't just a cop, we had the actual sheriff of Ledo here to arrest us!

My heart pounded as the beam of light splashed across my face.

11

Darkness

I held my hand in front of my eyes, guarding from the blindingly bright light that rested there. James pulled me up to my feet and walked forward.

"It's the sheriff!" he said as though speaking to an old friend.

"I heard the call come over the radio about kids being disruptive. A patrolman was on his way over, but when I heard it was at the Morris's house, I told him I would handle this one." The man paused for a moment. "You are supposed to be quiet about these things," he said a little more sternly.

James nodded as the light was lowered out of our faces.

"This must be the lovely Ms. Dawson." The sheriff looked me up and down like he was examining the authenticity of a piece of art.

"Adelaide," I offered hesitantly, still uncertain if I was going to jail or not.

"It's truly a pleasure, Adelaide." He stared into my eyes in a way that made all my muscles tighten defensively. There was something about his face, something so familiar.

"Have we met before?" I asked, sure that I knew this man from somewhere.

"No, my dear, this would be a first."

"Henri! You scared us!" Rachael yelled as she and Sasha appeared from the side of the house.

"Well, you still need to be quiet." Sheriff Henri smiled. "The neighbors expect me to take care of this."

"Oh, sorry," Rachael whispered and bit her lip.

"Charles." Henri motioned for him to come over. "I want you to come with me as we escort Mr. Sheppard and Ms. Dawson back to their little singing group." His voice was stern like he was punishing Charles for making him come out here.

Charles nodded as he turned and walked to the car.

Who was this man, and why was he helping us? Why did he look so familiar to me?

"James, will you make sure everyone else gets home without more problems?"

"Yes, sir." James replied as Adam walked over to us looking furious and it was obvious why; he had a black eye and blood was dripping down from his lip

"Oh, and try to clean up your footprints here." Henri motioned over the snowy yard.

James nodded and winked at me before I walked away.

Luke and I were uncomfortably sat in the hard backseat of the patrol car; behind the cage that separated the law breakers from the law enforcers. Charles sat quietly in the front seat like a guilty child, not something that I was accustomed to seeing from him.

"So, Adelaide," the sheriff said, watching me in his rearview mirror as he drove. "Did Charles tell you about me?"

"No, I don't think so," I said, my curiosity rising.

"Well, my name is Henri. I'm Charles's father."

"Oh, okay." That made sense. They did look slightly similar; I suppose that is why he seemed so familiar. "Sorry we have to meet under these circumstances," I apologized, feeling very guilty sitting in the back of a cop car.

"I don't blame you in the slightest." He shot a condemning look at his son. "I suppose the two of you will be going to church with your families tomorrow?"

Luke and I looked at each other and nodded.

"Well, you will be the first to see if tonight was successful for us. Keep an eye on Morris and see if there is any change. You know, if he feels any different." His voice hardened. "But be careful. You will be on dangerous ground with dangerous people. You shouldn't believe anything that is said during the service. They can be very deceptive people, remember that."

Luke and I nodded again, but I didn't take his warning to heart. I was capable of deciding for myself, and frankly, I wasn't sure who the real danger was.

It only took us a few minutes to find the street that our caroling buddies were on. To my great relief, we parked around the corner where we wouldn't be seen. My mother would have a fit if she were to see me riding in the back of a police car.

Henri had to walk around and open each of our doors; they seemed to be locked from the inside, no doubt to safely contain the criminals.

"If you go down the alley and cut across after the fourth house, you should come up right behind them," the sheriff said as he helped me out of my seat.

"Thanks for the ride," Luke said, coming around to my side of the car.

"Yeah, thank you," I added.

Henri put his hand on my shoulder. "Any time, sweetheart." My heart ran leaps and bounds as I looked into his brown eyes. The familiarity of them stunned me. I stood there staring stupidly at him as Luke tugged on my arm.

"Let's go, Addy. I really don't want them to realize we left." He said, pulling our candles out of his pocket.

"Okay," I said absently.

I caught a glimpse of Henri's name tag just as Luke pulled me around toward the alley.

Though my feet were moving, my body felt limp. I trudged along behind Luke guided only by the pull of his hand; my mind completely focused on that name. Every fiber of my being was numb, my breathing seemingly stopped, and my heart pounded against my ribcage.

I found myself inconspicuously mingled amongst the carolers, following like a soundless zombie. I don't know how much time passed or what was sang and discussed. Everything went by like a silent film on fast forward, and before I knew it, I was tucked in my bed staring at the ceiling. My mind couldn't focus on anything but the one word I read on the sheriff's shirt. The one name that flooded me with memories.

For three hours I stared at my popcorn ceiling wondering why the name Venhaus was on Henri's name tag. Could it be coincidental? And his eyes; I knew now why they looked so familiar.

After those three long hours of dumbfounded contemplation, I threw myself out of my bed, pulled on my hoodie and boots, and quietly pulled open my bedroom door.

There was no way I was getting any sleep tonight, at least not until I got some answers.

I had made it down the dark, silent roads to the old library before I realized just how cold it really was. Shivering, I walked up the steps to the front door. I knew I wasn't going to find anyone here, but I didn't know where else to look. I didn't have anyone's phone numbers or addresses and until now I hadn't needed them. The library was my best bet.

I sucked in my breath and slowly turned the doorknob.

It was locked. I walked around to the back door but there was no luck there, either. The snow was falling harder now; feeling like a hundred pounds on my shoulders as I desperately examined the building for a way in. I considered the windows, but *breaking and entering* would look pretty bad on my college résumé. But, if I did break in and was arrested, perhaps the sheriff would be there and— no, no that was a really bad plan. What else?

The school! They had everyone's addresses. Maybe, for some weird reason the doors would be unlocked or someone would still be there working, on Christmas, that could happen, right?

I shivered uncontrollably the whole way there but was determined not to give up. There was something I had to know and nothing would stop me.

I trudged through the snowy parking lot and flipped my hood over my mess of hair; remembering the one video camera over the front door. I kept my head down as I shook the doors. They wouldn't budge so I rattled them harder, tears formed in my eyes.

It was Christmas Eve, not to mention almost two o'clock in the morning, which I guess would technically make it Christmas day. No one would be in the school. I didn't know what else to do, where else to go. Why hadn't anyone given me a cell phone number or something!

I racked my brain trying to remember if anyone had ever spoken of what street they lived on; any kind of clue that would help me. I remembered the dirt road next to the school. Somewhere down that road was the Roth's property, well basically that whole piece of forest was their land. Their house had to be in there, somewhere!

* * *

Once I was so far down the dirt road that all I could see was trees, I had my first moment of sane reasoning all night. I was freezing and roaming into the woods, this could potentially be a huge mistake. The house could be miles away for all I knew. I had been wandering for what seemed like an hour, the falling snow was getting thicker, and there was still no sign of a home anywhere. This would be so much easier if I had a car. Although, now that I was thinking more clearly, it seemed strange that I wouldn't have just taken my mom's. I mean, I was already sneaking out of the house in the middle of the night while grounded, I might as well have taken the car too.

My only bit of light from the moon was momentarily blanketed by clouds leaving me in complete darkness; and not the kind of darkness you get when you turn off your bedroom light, this was thick, tangible, wild darkness.

I stood in the middle of the road and swallowed hard. What the heck was I doing out here? I turned around deciding if I should go back or continue on but it was so dark I couldn't even see the road on which I came. I whirled back around, squinting into the night looking for the road, trees, anything.

The snow swirled around me, whistling through the invisible trees.

"I have come into the world as a light." Faint words carried with the harsh breeze. "So that no one who believes in me should stay in darkness." The voice was kind and the words enticing but the fact that I was hearing voices again disturbed me.

"Not now!" I said to the crisp, winter air.

My heart was picked up speed and my chest felt tighter. I had to calm myself before I had a panic attack or something.

I remembered what James had told me about hearing spirits; some were good, some were bad. So who was talking to me?

I wrapped my arms around myself trying to steady my shivering body. "Who are you?" I asked into the darkness.

"I am the light of the world," came a gentle whisper. "Whoever follows me will never walk in darkness, but will have the light of life."

My question wasn't directly answered, but somehow I knew, this was Yahweh. To my mother this was the Prince of Peace but to me, he was…the enemy, or at least, that's what I had been told. His invitation was inviting. I understood it was probably not the literal darkness that he was referring to but the offer still tugged at my heart. Day or night, I always felt that I was living in darkness, feeling my way about, never knowing what is real and true.

I closed my eyes. "The light of life…," I repeated under my breath. How wonderful that sounds. Obviously this God was real, and he was speaking to me. I wasn't alone in this darkness; I had a companion. The question was he the enemy or the answer.

"Okay…." I said, feeling a little uncertain of my own sanity. "So, how do I follow you?"

For a moment I heard nothing but the breeze whirling around me. Did he go? Was he ever really there? Was I just hallucinating? Maybe I had hypothermia; that would explain…

"Everyone who calls on the name of the Lord will be saved." My answer softly floated down with the snowflakes that caked my eyelashes.

I pulled my hood farther over my face. The name of the lord, Yahweh. My mind was spinning. I could almost feel my heart being literally tugged in two directions. The love I felt at this moment fighting against my desire for knowledge; most urgently, the knowledge I was seeking when I left my bed a few hours ago. The name on a stranger's uniform…or…

"The name of the Lord…," urged the whispering voice.

I took a few teeth-chattering breaths in before testing the word out loud. "Yahweh."

I smiled. It felt freeing to say his name, although it was just a whisper.

"Believe in the Lord Jesus and you will be saved…" The words felt like they were coming from the voice I had been conversing with but they weren't. It was from my head, from a memory. Something my Sunday school teacher said at the end of every class, back when my mom forced me into going.

I prepared myself to try the name once more as the road before me flooded with light. The hair on my arms stood up. It was a beautiful bright light catching every snowflake and the outline of the trees.

I threw my hands up and watched the light dance around my fingers.

There was light! Literal and glorious light!

Smiling widely I said, "Yahweh I—"

My moment of excitement was quickly shot down by two startling honks from a car.

I turned around and squinted at the bright headlights that rested on me. My heart sank. I should have known. How did I let myself get carried away?

"Adelaide? Is that you?" James yelled as he leaned out the window of his Mercedes.

I pushed my hood back and nodded shamefully. I must have looked horribly pathetic.

"Well, what the heck are you doing?" I was asking myself that same question earlier. "Get in the car, it's freezing out there!" he hollered at me.

I slowly walked to the car and got in. James stared at me silently, waiting for an explanation.

"I was, uh, looking for your house," I said through chattering teeth.

James turned up the heat. "Why?" He looked me up and down.

"I needed to talk to you...well, Charles, actually. How come you haven't given me a stupid phone number yet?" I was upset but my voice was too shaky to convey the correct message.

James smiled. "Why don't we get you warmed up and back to my house and then you can tell me your crazy reason for taking a midnight hike in twenty-degree weather."

I was too cold and wet to argue. I leaned back in my heated leather seat and tried to organize my thoughts.

I needed to find Charles. I had to talk to his dad. I had to know...

"What happened?" I heard a deep voice ask.

I was hearing things again. More spirits?

"She was wandering around our forest. Silly girl, she can be a little too impulsive sometimes." That sounded like James's voice.

"Lay her down here and get some blankets. I'll start a fire."

This wasn't the usual spiritual conversation I was used to.

"What's Adelaide doing here? Is she okay?" I knew that voice. Was it...Sasha?

"I think she's fine, just needs to get warmed up. Let's keep it down though, your mother is still sleeping and if someone wakes her up...I'll be the one to hear about it." The deep voice again. What was he talking about? Was he talking to me? Was *my* mother sleeping?

"Whh...t?" I tried to ask but the word came out a little garbled.

"I think she's waking up." It sounded like James again.

"What was she thinking, coming out here on foot...at night... when the weather..."

"I know, I know, Dad. She said she had to find Charles. I guess she didn't know where else to look."

I opened my eyes...which was weird because I didn't know they were closed.

James was staring down at me with a smile. I turned my head a little and saw Sasha and an unfamiliar man sitting across from me on a couch.

"Are you feeling okay, Miss Dawson? Would you like me to drive you to the hospital?" The man, I assumed to be Viktor Roth, had curly brown hair, a very distinguished goatee and concern in his eyes.

The word *hospital* got the gears in my mind cranking again. "Nnn...no. No, I'm okay now, thank you," I assured him.

A faint whistle blew from the next room and Sasha bounced up to attend to the noise.

I pushed myself up to a sitting position, pulling a soft red blanket with me as I went. "Did I fall asleep?" I asked James.

"Yeah, you were out within a minute. Don't blame you either."

I noticed the room I was in—high ceilings, luxurious furniture, and crackling fire surrounded by beautiful slabs of dark marble. Exactly how I would have imagined the extravagant Roth home to be.

"I made you some hot tea," Sasha said as she walked back in the room, her wild curls bouncing with every step. "Chamomile." She held out a green mug, steam lightly rising from inside.

"Thanks Sasha." I smiled as I took the cup. "I'm sorry if I woke you guys up...I... I didn't mean for that to happen."

"Don't worry. I got home just a minute after James...and Dad, well, he's always up late," Sasha consoled me as she sank back into the couch.

"How did things go tonight anyway?" Viktor asked in a smooth voice, much like the one James often used.

"Pretty well," Sasha started but James took over.

"We did what we needed to do but there were a few issues at the end we will have to take care of later," James said seriously.

Viktor nodded but then his face wrinkled up. His wife came down the stairs in her robe and slippers.

"Did I miss the memo about a family meeting?" she asked sarcastically, rubbing her tired eyes.

Everyone looked at me, as though I was their good excuse for being noisy.

"Oh..." Mrs. Roth tied her robe and smoothed out her hair. "Who's this?" she asked, her tone more gentle now that she knew there was company.

"This is Adelaide, Mom," James responded quickly. "She, uh, came over to discuss something important. We didn't mean to wake you." I liked that he left out the part about me wandering around town and through the woods in a mild snow storm like a moron.

"That's fine, dear." She popped out a little smile. "I was wondering when I would get a chance to meet you," she said with a shadow of excitement on her words.

James's mom was not at all what I pictured. She was rather short and petite with long graying blonde hair, but a truly lovely face.

She plopped down next to me on the couch. "You have to tell me *all* about yourself. James said that you are from Utah. Do you miss it there?" Her eyes widened. I noticed a deep purple bruise on the side of her cheek. She must have seen me looking because she dipped her head down to let her hair fall across the side of her face.

I opened my mouth to respond to her question, but James was already talking.

"Not now, Mom. It's really late, and we have things to discuss before I take her home."

Her eyes dropped and her disappointment was obvious. "You're right. I'm sorry." She stood back up and looked at me. "Adelaide, please come over for dinner soon. You are welcome any time."

"Thank you, Mrs. Roth."

She smiled at me for a moment before turning to Sasha. "You should go get ready for bed now. It's very late. You kids never get enough sleep anymore." She trudged over to the stairs and looked at her husband. "Are you coming up soon?"

"I'll be right up," he mumbled and then chugged down the remainder of the amber liquid in his glass.

Sasha sighed as she pushed herself up to her feet. "Well, I guess I'm going to bed now. Good night, Addy."

I quickly swallowed the large gulp of hot tea in my mouth to hoarse out the words, "Night, Sasha."

"You're coming shopping with me and Rachael on Saturday, right?"

"I can't. I'm grounded." I rolled my eyes to display my displeasure on the matter.

"Oh, that's okay. I'll work it out. We are going to the city to shop...for you...so you have to come." She winked at me as she walked past.

"Good night, sugar," Viktor said as he struggled slightly to get to his feet. "James, I'm going to bed as well, you should take Miss Dawson home shortly." He looked at me. "That is...unless you need me." His eyes were startlingly dark like his son's; the family resemblance was blatantly obvious.

"No I don't, thank you though...and it was nice meeting you."

"The pleasure is most definitely mine, Adelaide. I have heard so many wonderful things." I could see where James got his charm. He got up and walked to the stairs. "Try to get to bed soon, James."

"Okay," James replied as he took my hand and looked at me. "Now, Addy, what is it that you need to talk to me about?"

"Well, I was hoping you could take me to Charles." I slipped my hand out of his and ran my fingers through my hair as a reason for the rejection. I wasn't at all interested in his affection right now.

"I think that it would be best if you waited until tomorrow... but if you want to talk to me..." He trailed off as he lightly set his hand on my soggy, sweatpants-covered knee.

I stared at him with noticeable annoyance in my eyes.

"It's just really late, Addy."

I quickly stood to my feet, letting his hand drop. "No, James, I really have to talk to Charles or his dad!" I said defiantly, feeling a flood of emotion as I remembered the reason for my quest.

"His dad?" He looked confused before sudden realization crossed over his face. "Oh, you...oh." His look turned to slight worry.

"You know why...don't you?!" I accused. James shook his head but I knew he was lying. "Please, James, tell me! I have to know."

"Addy, darling, I...I really don't know what you are talking about."

I could feel tears forming again. "Please! Why did Henri's name tag say Venhaus?" James just stared at me expressionless. "Do you know what that name means to me, James?" He gave the same blank stare so I continued. "It took me a long time to memorize that name when I was little, *Adelaide Venhaus* is quite a mouthful for a child." I tried to stop the tears but they kept coming. "That was my last name, James…" I choked out the words. "My father's name!"

12

Legacy

"You should probably go around back and through your window. It will be quieter that way," James said as we pulled up to my house despite my wishes.

"James I am really not happy with you." He hadn't shared one bit of information with me, and I wasn't against using guilt. "Just tell me where Charles lives, and I'll take care of it myself."

"Addy…you just have to wait." James was getting really frustrated with me. I hadn't stopped pestering him since we got in his car.

"So, there is something to this, right? It isn't just a coincidence that Charles and I have the same last name?"

James gripped the steering wheel and let out a long sigh. "You are the most stubborn person I have ever known."

"You have to give me something, James…please!" I grabbed both his hands and put on my best pouting face.

James rolled his eyes. "Okay. You and Charles…are…related."

I sat and waited for more but he was done; that was all he had to say.

"How? How are we related?" I asked excitedly. Even my mother admitted that she had never met any of my dad's family members.

"Do you remember that big argument we had with Derek?" I hoped he wasn't changing the subject.

"Yes…," I said impatiently.

"He thought you should know about...well, you know...but this is Charles's job. He has been waiting for the right time to talk to you, and believe me, he won't be happy if I just jump in and tell you everything. So please just be patient and talk to him tomorrow." James got out of the car and walked around to open my door.

"But, James! Do you have any idea how crazy this is for me to find out? How can I possibly go to sleep?"

James took my arm and led me to the back of the house where my bedroom window was located. "I know. Your dad was very important to you and this must be driving you crazy but...for my sake, Addy, wait for Charles to tell you."

"Fine!" I threw up my hands and gave him a look that I hoped displayed my sincere displeasure with him.

"Thank you." James turned to slide open my unlocked window. "In you go." He knelt down with one knee up to give me a step.

"Good night, James. Thanks for the ride." My words may have been kind but my tone said otherwise.

I stepped one snowy boot on top of his nice tan slacks and pushed off unnecessarily hard as I crawled into my window and plopped onto my bed.

The next four hours went by slowly as I lay wide awake, imagining all the possible ways that my dad was involved in this secret world and if my mom knew about all of this. I let my mind get carried away until finally my alarm went off, and I yawned for the first time in several hours.

I sat up and ran to the shower; the sooner we got on with the day, the sooner I could talk to Charles.

I was ready in forty minutes, not even bothering to take the time to get frustrated with my long, boring, uncooperative hair. My stomach was too full of butterflies to make any room for food, so I sat impatiently at the kitchen table waiting for my mom to finish sipping her coffee and nibbling at her toast.

"I figured I was going to have to drag your stubborn little butt out of bed this morning," my mom said, her hair sporting a nest of hot curlers. "Are you actually excited for church?"

"Uh, yeah, sure. It has been a long time since I went to church with you." That was a lie. Yesterday I may have been slightly interested, but not now, I could care less. "Shouldn't we get going soon?" I urged.

"Relax, Addy, we have plenty of time." She grinned at me. "Do you want me to do your hair up for you?"

"No, that's okay." I didn't care one bit about my hair today, I wasn't even quite aware of what clothes I had put on, just something I grabbed off the top of my hamper.

I breathed in slowly and tried to keep myself calm. "Mom?"

"Yeah, sweetie?"

"You said that you met Dad in this town…," I said the words carefully, closely examining her response to the subject.

"Umm, yes, that's right." She looked a little surprised, but willing to talk about it.

"Did he have any family here?" I tried to make it sound like the idea just came to me.

"No. Well, he had a brother, but he had gone off to college in some other state, I never met him. Why?"

"No reason, just…was wondering."

"Okay." She nodded, slightly suspicious.

"Can I ask you something else?" I blinked a few times, cutting off the tears before they developed. "Something I have never asked you before?"

My mom looked at me slightly concerned. "Sure, baby. What is it?"

"Why did Dad leave us?" The words came out in a whisper.

I saw her eyes widen, but she quickly looked down, coughed, and then took a long drink from her coffee.

"I'm sorry!" I quickly tried to cover up my stupid question.

"No, no…that's okay." She cleared her throat. "I suppose you are old enough to know more. As I have told you before, I met your dad when I was a senior in high school…your high school, actually. He was already graduated, but we immediately fell in love. What I haven't told you is that both my parents didn't approve of him because…well, your dad had some, uh, weird beliefs. He was always a little hesitant with me. I don't think he was allowed to marry outside his religion. I always felt a little uneasy with his way of thinking, but it was just the way he was raised. He never told me exactly what his religion involved. At that age, I didn't think it mattered that much, anyway. He was so handsome and charming, even a little mysterious." She sighed. "But when we found out that I was pregnant with you…well he was a little freaked out and also very thrilled, so we ran away together and got married. He really wanted to do the right thing for us. I was able to go to college while he worked hard every day." I saw a few tears run down her face. I felt horrible for asking, but I wanted to know everything.

"Everything was fine for a few years, but then…I started going to church and soon after I became a Christian. That's when things started happening. Your dad was tormented by nightmares and well he had serious issues with my new god and my new faith. Something about it really bothered him. We began arguing all the time. I could see how much he loved me…loved you…but it was like, like he physically couldn't be around us anymore…I still don't understand it, except I think that he was under demonic attack, and it was too much for him. He tried for a while but it was destroying him, so one day…he left."

I had more questions, but I couldn't bear to make her go on. "I'm sorry, Mom." It was obvious how much she still loved him.

She smiled softly. "I better take these curlers out of my hair now."

A half hour later, we were standing in a small sanctuary as the music began. I yawned just remembering how boring this used to be; slow, sleepy piano music and a preacher who seemed as excited about Jesus as I was about math.

"Worthy is the Lamb," a young man sang as an electric guitar strummed lightly.

I looked to my mom, wondering if she was as surprised as I was by the entertaining and moving song.

The drums picked up along with the piano. "Holy is the Lord God Almighty." Chills ran up my whole body.

My eyes widened as I looked around me. Never before had I seen people worship anything with such passion. I felt a wave of love come over me like I had in the darkness the night before.

"All creation sings. Holy are you!" The whole congregation belted out their praise in unison. It was a powerful sound that had my legs trembling beneath me.

I fell to my seat and tugged at the collar of my shirt; it felt like all the air was sucked out of the room. I looked up at my mother, her face coated in joy, was yelling out the words like a little child to her loving father. I was glad she wasn't witnessing my bizarre episode.

"Be careful...you shouldn't believe anything that is said." I remembered Henri warning us. His words hissed repeatedly through my mind as the room spun around me. I clutched onto my seat and tried to focus only on my breathing, but it was nearly impossible to ignore the potent lyrics sung all around me.

The song had ended providing me with a second of relief. But the torment picked right back up as the words "Light of this life, You break through the darkness..." were sung so beautifully and fervently.

A familiar pain shot through my gut that had me doubling over; the same pain I felt when Rachael looked at me from across the circle as she spoke of doubt. This church was certainly different than the gatherings we had involving candles, chanting, and blood.

"You are the God we worship, creator of the Heavens, a Light to all the Nations..."

I wanted to scream; scream at them all to stop!

"The pain that you have suffered, for the sake us, unworthy sinners. You died upon the cross so that way would not be lost." They repeated over and over again as though they were purposefully trying to torture me.

I had to get air...I had to get out of there!

I forced myself up, quickly whispered, "Bathroom," to my mom and ran down the aisle. Several faces stared at me as I forced my quaking legs to take me through the doors but I didn't care.

I pushed through the double doors, gasping for air and clenching my stomach. I ran straight for the lawn hoping to collapse with relief, but I could still hear the voices pushing through the walls of their brick church, "Shout praises to the King, all of the earth, let us sing. A day will come when every knee will bow at the mention of Your name, even the demons believe the same, they tremble at Your power. All glory be to the King of Kings. Shout praises, let us sing!"

I groaned in pain, "Stop!" I begged as I ran across the road, not even looking for oncoming cars. I heard someone honk at me, but I kept going until I couldn't hear the music anymore.

Silence. I fell to my knees in the overgrown, wet grass of an empty lot. The pain was subsiding and the weight was lifted off my chest.

What a horrible, horrible place, I thought as I looked back down the road.

I rolled onto my back and stared up at the sky. Sweat dripped off my pounding forehead. I felt perfectly content just lying there for the next few days; I was thoroughly exhausted and the day had just began.

I watched a few puffy clouds drift by before I started to nod off.

"You won't be sleeping long once that snow soaks through your clothes."

I opened my heavy eyelids and saw Charles standing over me. It only took me a few seconds to remember that he was the man I wanted to see.

"Charles!" I yelled up at him, causing him to step back. "Why didn't you tell me!" I got up to my feet.

He frowned. "Tell you what?"

"That our dads are brothers!"

There was a hint of surprise in his face. "James told me that you saw the name...but...how did you know they were brothers?"

"I figured it out," I said quickly not caring about the side topics. "When were you going to tell me? And what else should I know?"

"Let's go for a ride." Charles started walking to the curb where his father sat, waiting in his police car.

This time Charles let me take the front seat. I got in and buckled my seat belt, conscientious of the fact that I was sitting next to a sheriff.

"So, Adelaide, I guess you figured out that my name's not Henri," Charles's dad said seriously as we pulled into the street.

"It's not?" I asked confused. I hadn't figured that out.

"Nope, it's Uncle Henri now." He winked at me.

I gave a polite chuckle. "How come I'm just now finding this out?"

"Things work out better when you listen to the spirit's timing," Henri said lightly.

That was no good excuse, but I didn't want to waste time complaining about it.

"So...was my dad...did he..."

"Follow Donar as we do?" my uncle guessed.

I nodded.

"Yes he did...and he still does." He looked at me with the brown eyes of my father.

"Does, uh, do you talk to him? Do you know where he is? Does he—"

"Whoa, slow down there. He contacts me occasionally...but... only through the spirits," Henri said quietly, taking a left turn down Main Street.

"What do you mean? Why through...is he?" The words got caught in my throat.

"Yes, Adelaide...your father passed away quite a few years back." His forehead wrinkled with lines of sadness. "But don't cry. I know it must be hard to hear, but you have to remember that the world is a spiritual world...he really only left behind his physical body for a spiritual one."

Tears were falling freely down my face, but I was probably closer to my dad now than ever. I had actually assumed his fate for many years. It was the only good reason for not contacting me. Though the words, being said aloud, had dropped a huge weight into the pit of my stomach.

Maybe I could..."Can I talk to him?" Hope bubbled up inside of me.

Henri smiled. "Absolutely." My heart leapt. "He asks about you all the time. The last thing he asked of me was to make sure that you knew the truth…about life. That's why we had the hospital give your mom a job over here…"

"Really? You guys did that?" I had no idea.

"Yes, for your own good. Nothing would make your father happier than having you a part of his life…of his legacy. And someday soon we can contact him. But contacting the dead is…a special and rarely performed ritual. You will have to go through your commitment ceremony before that can happen…"

I nodded, as if to say "no problem." If I could talk to my dad, nothing would stand in my way.

"You know, Adelaide, you are a very unique young lady."

I wiped my fist across my wet face. "Why?"

"They explained to you how the spirits…well…pester us, basically, when they pick someone to know the truth…Well, that doesn't happen to those of us who are born into the families…but you…you are the first blood descendant to also be chosen by the spirits. Pretty cool, I think."

We had made a loop through the neighborhoods and were pulling up in front of the church.

"So how did Pastor Morris look today?" Charles asked from behind me.

"I haven't seen him yet. I left before the preaching started."

"That's the best time to leave." Henri winked at me. "You better get back in there though, your mom will get worried…and speaking of your mom, it is probably best you don't say anything about us…and about your dad. I'll answer all your questions later. But it's just best to say as little to your mom as you can manage for now. She wouldn't handle this well. She wouldn't have the connection with him that you will."

I thought for a moment. That was a huge secret to keep from my mom. How could I not tell her that dad was…dead. How could I not tell her I met his brother?

He must have noticed my hesitation. "It would be a lot harder on her, Adelaide. It would be for her own good."

"But shouldn't my mom know the truth?" I had quickly come to the conclusion that if my dad believed it, then it must be right. I wanted nothing more to follow in his footsteps, to make him proud, and to talk to him again someday.

"She will never understand, you need to accept that. She is so far gone in her Christian faith that she is blinded to reality. It's her God that drove your dad away, remember that. You wouldn't want the same thing to happen to you. This is your legacy, Adelaide, accept it, embrace it." He paused for a moment. "Now get on back in there."

I unbuckled my seat belt and looked back at him, hoping he would change his mind.

"You will be able to ask us anything you want…but later, Addy. You need to go now," Charles said.

"But…I hate it in there." I sounded like myself ten years ago when my mother was trying to bring me to church with her.

"You're going to be okay, I promise," Charles spoke softly from behind my chair.

I sighed and stepped out of the car; at least I had my answer.

"Adelaide!" Henri called out the window. I turned around and looked at him. "Merry Christmas."

I sat in the back pew listening to the last few minutes of Morris preach on the life of Jesus. I could see Luke sitting with his family a few rows in front of me. He appeared to be handling things better than I was.

The words were similar to the story that the pastor had told the night before, passionate and powerful, only this time something was off. He seemed to be struggling to speak and was continually stopping to take a drink of water. I felt guilty, as though I had directly injured him, but I knew it was for the best. He had to be stopped and now it was my responsibility to help, just as it had once been my fathers.

It wasn't long until everyone was piling out of the sanctuary onto the front lawn to mingle. I hurried out before the crowd and watched for my mother to come out, hoping she wouldn't be to upset with me for not sitting with her.

"Mom!" I stood on my tippy-toes and waved at her over a small group of ladies.

"There you are, sweetie. What happened?" she asked as she weaved her way over to me.

"Well, I went to the bathroom and decided to sit in the back so I wouldn't distract anyone. I hope that's okay."

"Oh, you could have come and sat with me…no one would have cared. But, that's okay. What did you think of the service?"

I answered honestly. "Well, the ending was kind of sad. I don't know why he had to go into such gruesome detail about his death."

My mom clutched her Bible to her chest. "I know, it is so hard to hear, but it's the beauty of his sacrifice…he did all that for you." A tear slid down her smiling face. "If you come back with me on Sunday you can hear the rest of the story…"

The rest? What else is there, the man is dead?

Just then Sasha and Rachael waltzed over to us.

"Adelaide! Wasn't that a great service?" Rachael said excitedly. If I didn't know better, I would have thought she meant it. I was very surprised to even see the two of them. I hadn't noticed them in the church, but I wasn't looking.

"Uh, yeah, it was," I said, not nearly as convincing.

"Is this your mom, Addy?" Sasha asked.

"Yeah. Mom, this is Sasha and Rachael. We go to school together."

My mom was always thrilled to be meeting my friends. "It is so nice to meet you! Are you girls having a Merry Christmas?"

"Yeah, it is such a lovely day," Rachael responded.

"Mrs. Dawson, I absolutely love your blouse! It is so cute," Sasha said sweetly.

I frowned at her, uncertain of what they were getting at but my mother grinned widely, oblivious to their underlying intentions.

"Thank you! It is one of my favorites."

"Speaking of clothes…," Rachael started.

"Yeah, are you still going shopping with us tomorrow?" Sasha finished.

"Tomorrow?" I glanced at my mom.

"Remember, you promised that you would go shopping in the city with us before we go back to school," Rachael lied, acting worried that I might say no.

"Oh, well, I can't, I'm—"

My mom cut in. "Hold on, Addy, do you actually want to go shopping?" She seemed surprised.

"Well, yeah, Mom, I was pretty excited about it…but…since I'm—"

She quickly cut in again. "Well, I think that would be really fun. You should go. As long as you come home at a reasonable time."

I wasn't particularly excited about the shopping, but it beat being stuck in the house.

"Really? That would be awesome!" I forced out a little enthusiasm.

"Remind me to stop at the bank on the way home and I'll get some cash for—"

"Oh that won't be necessary Mrs. Dawson," Sasha interrupted. "My dad is Viktor Roth. I'm sure you have seen his name all over town. He pays for me and a couple friends to go on a shopping spree every year as my Christmas present."

My mom looked like she just picked the winning lottery number. "Wow, that is so generous. If you…I …" She laughed, not really sure what to say. "That's great! I'm sure it will be tons of fun. Will you be picking Addy up?"

"Absolutely. How does ten a.m. sound?" Sasha gave a sweet little shrug of her shoulders, convincing my mother of her virtuous innocence.

"Perfect!"

"Oh, I'm so glad you're coming, Addy!" Rachael's bright eyes and wide smile created an immediate grin across my face.

We stood atop the frosted lawn and chatted for another ten minutes about stores and school and any questions my mother had for them. When Sasha and Rachael finally said their good-byes, my mom was completely unaware that she had just been conned. My two friends were nothing like she thought they were, and I hoped to keep it that way.

The rest of the day drug on as I unmindfully participated in lunch with my mom and grandpa at the local diner and then on to our house to open a few more presents and watch our traditional Holiday movie: *A White Christmas*. I don't know that I actually heard a single word from the show. How could I? With everything that was going on in my secret world, especially the news of my father, how could I possibly care about the fake, fantasy world that Hollywood had to offer?

When my grandpa had gone, I stood in my bedroom staring at a small crack in my wall. I don't know how long I stood there. It felt like hours, but I could still hear my mother in the bathroom starting her nightly de-beautifying routines.

A rhythmic tap at my window brought me out of my trance.

I dropped all the thoughts running threw my head when I saw James's dark figure waiting behind the dirty pane of glass.

13

Makeover

"What are you doing here, James?" I asked quietly as I carefully pushed open my bedroom window.

"It's Friday night," he said, as though that were enough explanation.

I stared at him for a second and then it came to me; we had discussed a date, but I thought I had rejected him.

James looked me up and down. "Are you ready?"

I hadn't yet put on my pajamas or washed my face, but my hair was very messy and I couldn't remember if I even put on makeup this morning.

I frowned at him. My mom was in the next room, and I'm pretty sure sneaking out my window on Christmas with a boy would be disobeying her whole "can't leave the house without me" rule that she had instituted.

"But my mom…" I jumped at the sound of my mother mumbling as she walked down the hall toward my room.

James put a finger up to his lips. "I'll be waiting in the car."

I quickly slid my curtain across the open window, thankful there was no wind.

"Sweetie." My mom knocked once on my door before pushing it open. "I just got called into work." She didn't look very happy about it.

"I'm sorry, Mom. That sucks," I sympathized.

"I'll just be like two minutes fixing this." She waved her hand at her partially washed face. "And then I got to go. I might be a few hours, so don't wait up."

"All right. I'm just going straight to bed anyway.

"Are you sure it won't bother you? It is Christmas after all. Maybe I could ask them to—"

"No, Mom. We had a good Christmas and now it's over. I can't miss you when I'm sleeping, anyway." I gave her a wink. "See you tomorrow." I was impressed at the convenience of it all.

While my mom got ready in the bathroom, I tried fixing my hair in front of my dresser mirror and applying a little eyeliner to help my eyes not look so dead.

When I heard the front door close, I slipped out my window and walked down the street where James's car sat.

When he saw me coming, he stepped out and held open his door for me.

"You want to drive?" he asked with a heart-skipping grin across his face.

A lot of things had changed since last night. I had almost made some serious mistakes. But now I knew the truth, I felt certain and I was ready to dive in. I wanted to trust in Donar. I wanted to go on a date with James. And, yes, I wanted to drive.

I smiled at James as I slid into the warm leather seat and started the engine.

"Where to?" I asked when he was settled in the passenger seat.

"I thought we could do something simple, like a movie."

I wasn't in the mood to sit through another pointless film, and although I agreed, I took my sweet time getting there, enjoying every passing second behind the jet-black steering wheel.

We didn't talk as I cruised through the town, feeling a sense of freedom and control. James probably would have preferred conversation over the loud, unfamiliar songs playing over the radio but I didn't care; for ten short minutes, I wasn't thinking of anyone but myself. I let myself get washed away in the flood of music and gentle rumble of the engine.

I probably would have driven forever if James hadn't kept pestering me to turn down Second Street. Apparently, we were now running late for the movie, so I succumbed to his wishes and found a parking spot.

James hurried me out of the car and pulled me along down the sidewalk to the theater entrance.

"Come on, Addy," James said, laughing at my snail-like pace.

"Okay, okay." I grinned at him. The wild and free feeling that I felt behind the wheel had not vanished. Was it the new knowledge I had gained that excited me? Was it the thrill of rebellion and disobedience that stirred my blood? Perhaps it was everything combined. My father had given me something to belong to; something dark and enticing. I felt new. Like my protective walls of inhibition were bulldozed over by a sudden revelation of truth. I saw the world differently. Saw myself differently.

James and I were both laughing as we halted our run before the small town cinema.

"Let me go in and get the tickets. I'll make sure there is no one in there that will recognize you. Don't need you getting in any more trouble than you already are." James winked at me and walked inside.

I peered through the window behind a poster advertisement of an animated cartoon about a squirrel. I hadn't seen any previews for the movie but the adorable little chubby cheeks on the rodent's frightened face made me laugh out loud.

My laugh echoed off the surrounding buildings. Eyebrows raised, I quickly glanced around, assuring myself of my solitude.

The street was vacant, so in my rush of freedom, I let out another laugh.

Smiling, I turned back to the window and saw James staring at me, tickets in hand. He looked confused by my actions as he nodded for me to join him.

"What were you laughing at?" James whispered as we took our choice of seats in the nearly empty theater.

"You're not the only one with secrets, Mr. Roth," I said flirtatiously, attempting to throw a little mystery into my small list of qualities.

James grinned. "Okay, well how about telling me what kind of soda you like?"

"Root beer."

James stood up and scooted past my legs, but I grabbed his hand and held him back. "Wait. What movie are we seeing?"

He grinned mischievously. "Well, apparently, a one Miss Dawson believes me to be full of secrets." He waved the tickets in front of me, taunting my curiosity. "I wouldn't want to disappoint." He slipped his hand from mine and made his way down the aisle into the darkness.

Five minutes later James returned with popcorn and a large soda. "There was no root beer so I got Diet Coke. It's *my* favorite, hope that's all right." He explained after I took a large gulp of expected goodness and nearly gagged.

I nodded to his question as I stuffed popcorn in my mouth to rid my traumatized taste buds of the repulsive taste of diet soda.

The music changed and words were flashing across the screen.

"Not all small towns are what they seem…"

The music thundered as big red dripping letters slid down the screen, *Blood Town*, and the show began.

I rolled my eyes. James was obviously unaware that I detested horror movies. There are a few entertaining ones, suspenseful ones, that I enjoyed, but blood and gore? Aren't my dreams bad enough without throwing late-night slasher movies into the mix?

Three people had been mysteriously murdered within the first five minutes of the movie, definitely a bad sign. I tried closing my eyes, but I had already seen too much, the images just flashed behind my eyelids, allowing me no escape.

I wasn't thrilled with James for picking such a disturbing movie for me to watch. The least he could have done was consult with me first.

I watched as a handsome young man desperately rummaged through his kitchen drawer searching for something to protect himself with.

"Crystal? Crystal is that you!" He shouted for his girlfriend as he held out a butcher knife toward the heavy footsteps that slowly came down his hallway.

Without realizing it, I had dug both hands into the edge of my seat cushion. Wide eyed, and hoping to see the lovely face of Crystal appear in the kitchen, I screamed at the sudden sight of steel-toed boots stepping onto the tile floor.

James chuckled at my outburst. "You okay, my dear?"

I didn't want to stick around for the death of Crystal's boyfriend. "Yeah, I have to go to the bathroom."

I got up and made my way through the darkness, ignoring the horrible screams.

The moment I pushed through the theater door, I was blanketed in light and the feeling of safety. I sighed and shook my head. "What a stupid movie," I mumbled as I headed for the bathroom.

"Well, well, if it isn't my favorite little chem partner," Bryan Evans chirped as he swayed over to me.

We were nice enough to each other at school; in fact, he usually flirted with me as he did all the other female students to walk his way, but I was uncertain of where I stood with him. Should I be concerned that I was alone in the small cinema lobby with him? Was I assumed guilty by association, thus hated and labeled as a witch?

I examined his knuckles. His right hand was darkly bruised, I assumed from his run-in with Adam and Charles the night before.

"Hi Bryan," I said sweetly, trying to avoid a confrontation.

"I've never run into you at the movies before." He threw me a charming smile.

"Well, this is my first time here."

"Seriously? What do you do every day?" He sounded baffled. "I'm here all the time. I seriously can't wait to get out of this little town, there is nothing to do."

"Really, have you picked a college?" I eyed the bathroom door only five feet behind him.

"Yeah right! Have you seen my grades? And my foster parents won't spit out a dime for my future." Bryan's big eyes shot down to seventies-style carpet for a moment before smiling and shrugging his shoulders. "Yeah, I don't know. I think I'm going to try law enforcement or security or something. My Uncle Kevin lives over in Boulder, Colorado, and he's a U.S. Marshal. I'll probably head over there as soon as we graduate. What about you, little Miss Honor roll?"

This was probably the first real conversation Bryan and I had ever had together. When he wasn't flirting or being obnoxious, he was actually quite likeable. He really only wanted attention, wanted to be liked, to belong. I could relate.

"I've applied to some schools around the country. Not sure where I'll be going yet…"

"Probably trying to get into the same school as Ben, aren't ya?" He raised one eyebrow.

"Ben?" I hadn't thought of Ben all day. "Why would I do that?" I asked coolly.

"I thought you guys were dating?" He seemed a little confused. "I mean, you are always together, you pass notes in class, hang out after school, and he only tried out for the *Wizard of Oz* because you did." He laughed. "I guess I assumed wrong."

I blushed and tried to push away the thoughts of Ben that wanted to consume my mind. "Yes, you did."

"So, who are you here with, then?" Bryan animatedly peered around the room searching for my date.

"A friend," I said grinning.

"Just a friend? Because now that I know you aren't with Benjamin, well, perhaps there is hope after all." I assumed by his joking manner that he was teasing me.

"Hope for what, Bryan?" I said skeptically.

"For you and me, baby." He swept up my hand and pressed it to his heart.

Laughter plopped right out of my mouth at his dramatic scene.

To my relief, Bryan smiled and dropped my hand. "You think about it," he said with a wink.

"Sure thing." I nodded, suppressing my smile.

"My movie's about to start. You came out of blood town, right?"

"Unfortunately," I said, allowing my face to display my dissatisfaction.

"Stupid movie," he agreed.

"Very."

"Wanna come see *Picnic Basket* with me?" He pointed to the squirrel poster to my left.

I laughed. I found humor in the situation, not the invitation. One night he gets in a fistfight and runs from the cops and the next he is watching animated cartoons at the movie theater.

"I'm sure it's better than mine, but I can't," I said honestly.

"Who's waiting for you?" he pried once more.

I opened my smiling mouth to respond with the same answer but my words were suddenly unnecessary.

James walked up beside me, holding his soda.

"I was coming out for a refill," James said to me without taking his eyes off Bryan.

Bryan looked at me with a mixture of disappointment and disgust. "Of course it's him."

"What's the matter, Bryan?" James sneered at him as he wrapped his fingers around mine, flaunting me like his possession.

I frowned at the both of them. "Let's go, James." I tugged him toward the concession stand.

"She's having a lot more fun standing here with me than she was with you." Bryan smiled widely at him.

I hated how they used me to their advantage in their twisted little conversation.

"Is that so?" James wrapped his arm around my waist and pulling me tight to his side.

Bryan laughed. "But let's be honest with ourselves, we both know she would rather be with Benjamin Tucker right now. Isn't that right, Addy?"

This seemed to make James angry. His face tightened as he glanced over at me.

"This is ridiculous!" I shook my head at them as I forced my way out of James' arm. "I don't appreciate you boys using me in your sick, childish game. James, if you want to continue our date, you better knock it off!"

"Go ahead, James. I'm done talking, but I want you to know that I'm keeping my eye on you. You think you can get away with whatever you want because your daddy is rich…Well, it's time you people were stopped. I'm not afraid of your so-called 'magic' and I'm certainly not afraid of you." Bryan looked at me. "Have a nice *date*, Adelaide." Then he walked into his 11:30 showing of *Picnic Basket*.

I looked over at James, expecting to see anger seeping from him but instead he was smiling. The strange, amused look on his face was almost more disturbing than the thought of returning to our gore-filled movie.

The remainder of our date was filled with tension. A word was barely spoken between us until we reached my house.

"Thanks for the date, James. Oh, and thanks for letting me drive your car earlier."

The movie was horrid and the soda grotesque, but the drive to the theater was bliss. I even had fun talking with Bryan until James showed up. All in all, it probably wasn't the best night of my life.

"You're welcome," James said without looking at me. I had a feeling it was the comment about Ben that had James acting so cold toward me.

"So," I said hesitantly. "Are we going to do this again…sometime?" I was suffocating my feelings toward Ben. It was pointless to indulge them. James was just better suited for me. My dad wouldn't have approved of Benjamin for me, I was certain of it.

"I'm sure," he said as though I were boring him. "I'll see you at school on Monday."

I glared at the side of his face. I took a few deep breaths of heated air and smiled.

"Well, okay then." I leaned over and kissed his cheek. "Good night, James!" I moved quickly out of my seat and shut the car door behind me.

In a matter of seconds, James was leaning over the roof of his car. "Hey, my mom would love if you came over for dinner next week. How about Wednesday?" He was smiling a little now.

That was better.

"Sure." I shrugged, pretending as though I didn't care either way.

"Would you like to do another candle ritual tonight? I suppose a horror movie isn't the most helpful in preventing nightmares." He grinned.

You think? I rolled my eyes. "That's all right, James. I'm rather tired." Now that I thought about it, I wasn't sure if I had gotten any sleep in the last forty hours.

"Are you still wearing my ring?" His question sounded very strange coming out of his mouth.

I hooked my finger around the silk ribbon around my neck and pulled out the ring to show him. "Yep."

"Good. You should light the candle next to your bed before you go to sleep," James said in caring and attentive manner.

"Okay, I will. See you Monday."

The candle did not prevent my dreams from being gruesomely horrible. My night was filled with dark creatures, fresh crimson blood dripping from my body, and the threat of death lingering over me like a crushing weight. It was a relief to wake and get on with my day. Luckily, I had an early rendezvous with Rachael and Sasha; this would leave me little time to contemplate on my nightmare.

It was nearly noon when the three of us stepped out of Sasha's yellow sports car and into unfamiliar territory. I had never been to this part of the city before and was excited to see what it held for us.

"Lunch first!" Rachael declared, eyeing a group of boys leaning against what appeared to be a brand-new Dodge pickup.

"Absolutely, but then we got to get busy," Sasha said, distracted by the five young men who were now whistling and hooting to us, or just as likely…to the deliciously yellow Ferrari—boys and their cars.

Although we all ordered salads and ice water, the meal was very expensive. I felt strange not offering to pitch in for the bill, but I knew it was completely unnecessary. I just followed Rachael's lead when it came time to pay up. We chatted and sounded our praise over the extravagant purchases as Sasha swiped her credit card without even twitching over the amount.

We had bought several outfits from designer stores I had never even heard of before. Sasha and Rachael chose outfits for me that I would normally never give a second glance. I cringed when they forced me to try each piece on and blushed each time they cooed over my appearance.

My first reaction was to reject each selection they made for me, but they wouldn't take no for an answer. They turned out to be pros at the whole fashion designer role. I looked stylish, grown-up, and nearly attractive enough to be beside my friends in a chic *Vogue* magazine article. With each new outfit I thought of my mom and how thrilled she would be about my new wardrobe. I also thought of Benjamin, wondering if he would find me attractive in this blouse or those pants. It was hard to escape the thought of him. He was like an elusive weed sprouting up in my cerebral garden. I didn't want him there. I didn't want to think of him, and I did my best to push him from my mind.

I enjoyed myself far more than I thought possible on a shopping trip but then came our three o'clock appointment. This was the part of the day I had been dreading.

"You have to trust us, Addy. I promise you'll love it!" Sasha pleaded as she tugged on the shopping bags that were looped on my forearm.

"She's not the only one who'll love it," Rachael mumbled teasingly.

I shot her a look that said, "What's that supposed to mean."

"You have a skin brightening facial first, and then Rachael and I will join you for a pedicure and manicure," Sasha explained as she pulled me farther into the posh beauty salon.

It turned out that the facial was surprisingly relaxing and did wonders to my skin. My fingernails were done with a clean and classy French tip while my toenails were polished in a deep red.

"Mine aren't quite dry yet," Rachael said, examining her toes.

We were reclined in leather chairs located in an oasis; well, technically it was the waiting room, but it was spectacular. A small fountain trickled amidst a sundry of plants and flowers throughout the overstuffed sofas and lounge chairs that filled the room.

"So, Adelaide, it's been kind of a crazy week for you," Sasha said.

I nodded in complete agreement. "Yes, it has."

"Were you excited to find out about your dad?" Rachael asked.

"It's hard to believe, you know. I loved him so much. All I ever wanted was to know why…he left." I avoided the tears and focused on the joy of finding my dad rather than the pain of losing him.

"I'm sorry we didn't tell you sooner, Adelaide," Sasha said.

"Yeah, it was really hard to keep that secret." Rachael looked at me and grinned. "It was especially difficult for James."

I could tell where this was going. I lightly blew across my fingernails ignoring her last statement.

Sasha rolled her eyes. "Well, I think I'm going to go see if they are ready for your hair appointment, Addy. I'll be right back."

I stared at the back of her head as she walked away. Hair? What were they going to do with my hair?

I didn't have time to dive into a full panic over the idea. Rachael was quickly back onto the topic of James.

"He really likes you, you know."

I looked up at her, and although she was smiling, I could see something hidden behind her grin—jealousy perhaps.

It suddenly occurred to me that I had possibly intruded upon Rachael and what could have been.

"Did you…were you and James ever…?" My words were apologetic but incomplete.

Her eyes widened. "Oh no, honey!" Honey, there was Ben again, popping up in unwanted soil. Rachael giggled. "Well, sure he is cute and …" She trailed off with a hint of bitterness. "But Derek and I actually have a little something."

"Oh really? That's cool. He seems...nice." I wasn't really sure *what* Derek was. Was he nice? Was he a decent person? The only thing I could say for sure was that he was a flirt.

"Yeah, but now you are avoiding the topic. We can all tell that James really likes you, but no one is certain just how much you like him."

Well it seemed we were all on the same page then.

I didn't speak up right away so Rachael continued, "I mean, James said that you had a thing with Benjamin Tucker. So..." She looked at me curiously, waiting for me to respond.

"No, not really. We were good friends, but that's kind of over now." The words came out before I put much thought into them. Was it over? Was this the end to our friendship? Rachael read the pain on my face. "I had to leave a few friends behind too, Addy. The best thing to do is just let them go altogether. Don't prolong it."

"Just quit cold turkey," I said, forcing out a grin.

Rachael laughed. "Exactly. It's better for everyone that way. You should learn from your father. It obviously didn't work out for him. I'm sure he wouldn't want you to go through that same pain."

She was right. I had the truth laid out before me, an opportunity for greatness. Why was it so hard to commit? The choice had to be made.

"So do you?" Rachael interrupted my thoughts.

"What?" I asked oblivious.

"Do you like James?"

"Well, yes. He is..." What is he? I thought for a moment. "Exciting..." Yes, he was always exciting, and... "And he is very charming, and handsome, and yeah, I like him." It sounded a little like I was convincing myself, but I wasn't...was I?

Rachael was ignorant to my uncertainty. "I thought so," she said smugly as Sasha called us out to the lobby.

"You want I should chop it all off?" A tall, French woman stood over me, examining my braided hair.

Sasha laughed. "No, no. It's really quite beautiful. It just needs... some help."

My face softened with relief.

"Very well." My foreign stylist frowned as she unbridled my hair.

I winced with every snip of the scissors and slice of her little razor blade. I tried to put my attention elsewhere as I watched my hair fall softly to the floor. Sasha and Rachael had gone to purchase makeup for me, apparently my one stick of eyeliner and tube of mascara didn't cut it.

So, I was left with only my stylist to converse with. This didn't exactly thrill me because I had absolutely no desire to speak with her. She was now on my list of least favorite people. Her face was straight and indifferent as she chopped what I assumed to be unnecessary amounts of precious hair from my head. I glared at her and she glared right back.

"Don't you trust?" she said in her snobbishly beautiful accent.

No, I don't trust.

"Sure," I said with a forced grin, not wanting to be on *her* bad list.

Dark brown strands of silk caressed my forehead, tickling the tips of my eyelashes. She had given me Bangs! This would be a first for me. I wasn't good at *firsts*. Change was not my cup of tea…or my forte, as mademoiselle hair destructor might say.

The blow drying had just finished when my friends returned for me.

"Oh wow, I love it!" Rachael exclaimed.

Skeptical, I gave the ground a little kick to twirl my chair, in search of the mirror.

"No, don't turn around yet." Sasha stopped me mid spin. "Rachael and I are going to do your makeup first."

As they skillfully applied my paint and powder, they explained to me the process with added tips and secrets of the trade. A long five minutes later, the new Addy was revealed. With a spin of the chair and a finger drum roll by Rachael, I was staring at a cute, long haired brunette with bangs.

A smile found its way onto my glossy lips.

"Wow," I whispered as I swished my hair back and forth, admiring the change.

"My thoughts exactly. Now please move along." The stylist was sweeping up my fallen locks around our feet.

Laughing, we loaded our arms with the day's purchases and headed out the door. Sasha had already paid for our luxurious pampering and beauty treatments. The only thing left to do before our travel home was to see our neighboring family. Rachael had been looking forward to it all day, and now I understood why; Derek had captured her heart, or at least her interest.

14

The Lion

"Addy, I can't get over how great you look," Rachael said, leaning forward from the backseat as we traveled down unfamiliar roads.

"Thanks, Rach. It's pretty drastic though. I'm kind of nervous about what people will think." I tilted my head forward and watched the bangs dangle in front of my eyes.

"They'll think it's great!" Rachael encouraged with enthusiasm.

"Yeah, don't even worry, Addy. You look fantastic. You *have* to promise to wear the makeup and clothes we got you! You can't chicken out on us."

After hesitating for a moment of suspense, I responded. "Okay, okay, I promise. Thanks again for doing all this for me. I know I was a little hesitant about everything, but I had a lot of fun and am very grateful."

"You are *too* hesitant about everything, Adelaide," Rachael commented as she sat back in her seat.

"I'm working on that." I glanced at Rachael in the rearview mirror.

"You don't always have to think things through so much, you know. Sometimes it's good to just let life carry you away, get caught up in the moment, follow your heart." Rachael used her arms to create dramatized gestures as she spoke.

"That's very dangerous advice, Rachael." Sasha remarked. "But I do agree, you could do a little less thinking and a little more doing sometimes, Addy."

I frowned. "What is this, pick on Addy time?" Despite my lighthearted come back, I knew they were right. I wished I could be more like them, more accepting and open to the possibilities of life. From now on I would try. Try to roll with the punches, try to be undoubtedly devoted to my new god and the power that he offers. Besides, what better way to discover the man that my father was than to step into his shoes?

A wooden sign hung above the door of the old brick building, *Familiar Grounds Bistro*. It was a cozy little coffee shop complete with comfy sofas and melodic New Age music playing in the background.

"Are we getting coffee?" I asked, slightly confused at our location.

Sasha shrugged. "If you want."

Rachael giggled. "We're going downstairs." She pointed toward the back wall.

I nodded and followed the girls to our destination. I expected it to be similar to our cold, slightly creepy basement below the library, but was surprised at what I found.

Similar to the upstairs, the room was filled with overstuffed couches and chairs, along with deep red draperies hanging across the brick walls. Lit candles were glowing all throughout the room, providing a flickering, calm ambiance. The back, undraped wall was home to several wooden shelves holding various canisters, bottles, and books. A thick wooden table stood adjacent to the shelved wall, displaying a mouthwatering variety of foods.

I recognized every face in the room and felt welcome by the smiles, hugs and slathering of compliments on my new look.

"I barely recognized you!" said a sweet brunette, whose name had escaped me. I had seen her several times, but we had only spoken briefly at the night of Luke's dedication ceremony in the meadow. Before I could get a word out to respond, Derek was in my face, hints of flirtatiousness on his words. This made me uncomfortable, seeing as Rachael was standing beside me.

"Miss Dawson! You look breathtaking." He unnecessarily examined my body from head to toe.

I nearly explained, "It's just the face and hair, buddy." But not wanting to draw Rachael's attention to his unbridled staring I said, "It's amazing what a little makeup can do."

Rachael laughed and started her own conversation with Derek. Sasha pulled me along into the room, searching for empty seats. We found two available, comfortable squares of sofa cushion to sink into.

The abundance of laughing and talking, drinking and eating suddenly brought me back to one of those high school parties I dreaded attending back in Utah. My friends, of course, pressured me into participating in the monthly my-parents-are-out-of-town house party. Occasionally I would dance, converse with strangers, and partake of the snacks, but never did I accept any beer or throw back some shots with my girlfriends. I never drank, simply because my mother disapproved. Well, that, and I feared being that oh-so-unattractive girl that spends the night throwing up in a stranger's toilet and sleeping on the bathroom floor after making a complete fool of herself howling *Delta Dawn* over the karaoke machine.

"He asked if you wanted a drink, Addy." Sasha nudged me with her elbow as she accepted a drink from the young man standing in front of us.

My initial reaction was hesitation and question. I had no idea what this drink was, but rather than asking and most likely refusing as I normally would, I smiled and accepted without a word.

I could see Sasha grinning at me as though she could see the inner struggle I was experiencing.

I took a big gulp of what I could only assume to be some type of homemade cider. The warm liquid slid down my throat in triumphant accomplishment. Yes, I was going with the flow from now on. I would welcome life into my arms like an old friend.

"Um Donar. Ehre und macht des Königs!" Derek shouted from across the room, in impressively perfect German.

"Um Donar. Ehre und macht des Königs!" the whole room repeated, holding the glasses up in a toast. I drank with them, confused by the foreign words being shouted with fierce enthusiasm.

"Um die Göttliche Mutter der Nacht!" Derek held his glass high as the room repeated after him. We drank again and this time Sasha leaned over and whispered, "We are toasting and giving honor to Donar and the Divine Mothers of the night. This is—"

Sasha was interrupted as the all the men stood up and shouted, "Müttern, um der Geber des Lebens, Frau!" This was followed by masculine hoots and hollers, hugging, and more drinking.

"I would be careful with that cider for your first time," Sasha said, observing my participation in the toasts.

First, I'm too careful and now I need to be more careful. What do they want from me?

Before I was able to ask her what was in my festive, spicy drink she began explaining the meaning of this celebration.

"We are celebrating Mōdraniht," Sasha said matter-of-factly, as though that were all the explanation I would be needing.

I gave her a look that said, "I have no idea what you are talking about," so she continued.

"Night of the Mothers. It's a very old celebration, observed by many people. It is special to Germanic heritage. It is a Yule celebration in honor of Idisi, warrior goddesses, fertility goddesses, personal guardians, dignified female spirits. Basically a celebration of woman and winter. The Divine Mothers are said to come out with the moon on these cold nights and bestow gifts upon us."

Rachael plopped down beside me, cheerfully repeating a saying as she bobbed her head back and forth.

> Once the Idisi sat, sat here and there,
> some bound fetters, some hampered the army,
> some untied fetters:
> Escape from the fetters, flee from the enemies.

She grinned at me and then took the drink out of my hand. "Don't drink too much of that."

"What's in it?" I asked, feeling like a child who had their cake taken away for eating too much sugar.

"Just what you need," Rachael said confidently. "But it's not fun if you overdo it."

I frowned and looked at Sasha.

"Just herbs and stuff, Addy. It helps you loosen up a little."

There was a lot of movement in the room, and I noticed that all the men were making their way up the stairs.

"Oh! It's almost time," Rachael exclaimed, setting my cup down on the coffee table.

"If you want food, you better get some now," Sasha suggested.

"Time for what?" I asked, completely ignoring Sasha's comment.

"You'll see. I just wish we could stay for the whole thing." Rachael sighed.

"Why can't we?" I wondered, knowing my mom would be at work until ten o'clock and it was only seven, maybe seven thirty.

"Well, I guess we could, if you think your mom would be okay with you *literally* partying until the sun comes up," Sasha teased and Rachael followed with a fit of giggles.

"This goes *all* night?" I asked surprised.

"Enough questions, let's go!" Rachael pulled me off the couch.

I estimated about ten of us girls walking up the stairway several flights, whispering and giggling the whole way.

We stopped before reaching a black door at the end of the staircase.

"Pick one!" a voice said behind me.

Hanging along the wall was an assortment of masks and white robes. I wasn't sure what they were for, but I was getting excited and slightly…slightly something…lightheaded? No, more…relaxed and care-free.

"Each mask is different. They represent different goddesses," Rachael spoke through her beautiful porcelain white mask.

"Mine is Nerthus, she was the primary goddess of the northern Germanic tribes." Someone spoke to me through a lovely green mask. "Here, take this one." The mystery woman handed me a golden bronze mask and I slipped it on. "That is Lorelei, a beautiful siren that lured sailors to their death with her songs." The green masked girl giggled.

I slipped on a robe and pulled the hood over my head as Rachael had done.

"We are going to be acting out traditional interpretations and dramatizations of our history. These are ancient rituals. It's really quite an honor to be a part of it, especially from the woman's side of it," Rachael whispered to me as the black door was opened, and we gracefully entered onto the candlelit rooftop.

Wir sind Göttin.
Wir sind Göttin.
Wir sind Göttin.

We slowly chanted over and over although I was left completely unaware of the meaning.

We circled around the row of men, on their knees, bowing before their goddesses. I followed, in turn, as each woman picked up a pine branch and dipped it into a large bowl.

I pulled my prickly branch from the darkened dish and watched the thick red blood slowly drip from its needles.

Each hooded female lightly brushed the branch across the face of the male before them, smearing blood over their skin. It was a strange experience. Actually, I was quite impressed with my own willingness to participate, though my stomach did tighten as I watched my velvet-dipped brush stain the face before me.

"Goddess of the night, goddess of the moon and sky, we summon thee to us this hour, we open our minds—fill us with your power. Goddess of the night, goddess of the moon and sky…" The men repeated slowly as they stood up and formed a circle with us. We linked arms and stared into the darkening sky.

The roof was swaying beneath my feet, and I suddenly noticed a hundred blurry faces surrounding me rather than the fifteen or twenty that were originally gathered. When did they show up? I stared groggily into the endless sea of dark faces and…"We cast our sacred circle before thee where no evil purpose or spirit be. Before Donar, our god of power and before the Goddesses with spiritual gifs upon us they shower. Surround us and guard us as we journey between the worlds. We align ourselves with the spirits and open our souls to your guidance." The circle chanted to the glowing moon. "Shower us with your gifts, Oh, Mother of the Night, give us your wisdom and all-knowing sight…"

Then suddenly all was silent. As I was still unfamiliar with this celebration, I was the last to fall to my knees. Arms were thrown heavenward toward a black, mysteriously vast blanket above us. I assumed this was the meditation slash worshipping portion of the night. Eyes closed and arms raised high, as though being pulled upward by marionette strings, I found it surprisingly easy to fall into a trance like state. I focused my attention on praising Donar and the other gods, goddesses and spirits. I invited them just as James had taught me to do when seeking a nightmare-free sleep. I didn't know if there was a specific protocol on my usage of words or direction of thoughts and to be honest, I wasn't too concerned about it. My mind had caught a current in the spiritual river of my soul and was sweeping me away. The feeling was exhilarating. Life altering. Like I had pushed my way through a crowd of people to find someone; pushed my way through chaos and fear and found serenity.

Silence. A peaceful, perpetual nothingness surrounded me. I had nearly lost myself completely when my forgotten, physical companions started speaking. Each taking turns throwing a sentence in, creating a beautiful call into the darkness.

"Our glorious moon, mistress of the night."

"Full of wisdom, full of power."

"Shining goddess in the sky" came a high-pitched voice next to me.

"You entice our seas and caress the shadows."

"By the power of Donar, shine for us a pathway of light." I recognized Sasha's voice.

"We call upon you, great moon, mother of us all."

"I invoke thee and call upon thee."

"Shower your gifts upon this circle."

"Love and wisdom, power and life, Descend to aid us, descend tonight."

"Teach us things that are yet unknown."

"Tell us your secrets, show us your power." Rachael's singsong voice was unmistakable.

"Bestow to us your strength this night."

"Come darkness, come shadows. They are willing. Partake. Fill their hungry souls." These words did not come from behind a porcelain mask but from one of the new arrivals. A dark figure standing inside our circle, crowded by hazy figures and unclear faces, spoke his command. A mirage of thick smoke weaved its way through the circle, disappearing and reappearing as though it only existed in one world as my mind swayed in between the realms.

The group fell silent again in meditation once more. "Addy?" whispered a voice next to me.

"Yeah?" I asked the blue mask beside me.

"Use this time to listen and except any gifts or revelation."

"Okay, thanks." I was glad someone recognized that I was new to this.

I closed my eyes and reentered my empty serenity. I could feel things moving about, brushing against me, like black waves swaying my weightless body to and fro in a dark, silent lullaby.

I focused on listening. Trying to hear anything; the sound of an ocean perhaps? Waves lapping against the shore? I could feel it but I couldn't hear it. Instead, I heard something similar to the faint sound of flapping wings and other noises that were unrecognizable to me. My stomach growled strongly in discomfort, likely due to excessive cider, but in the darkness before me flashed the sight of a fierce lion. Then, in response, my heart awakened in a startled panic.

"Who is it you fear?" spoke a muffled voice, almost as though it were under water.

I tried to open my eyes but I wasn't sure if I was successful. Rather than seeing the expected circle of friends in candlelight, I saw the lion once more, walking toward me. I pulled back in fear but had no concept of the location of my body in the physical sense.

"Your enemy, Adelaide?" the voice answered for me, carrying across a distance.

"What?" was the question I would have asked but it wasn't necessary.

"Your enemy prowls around like a roaring lion, seeking whom he may devour." The words were right in my ear. I could feel a cold breath tickling the side of my neck, but no one was there.

"My enemy," I repeated, thinking of Ben and his God. Why was it that *this* God was such a threat over all the others?

"He wants your soul, little one. But bow down and worship me and I will give you life!"

I could sense the lion circling me. With fear rising in me that he would attack at any moment, I shouted, "Yes! I will, I promise." With those words everything vanished, the dangerous predator, the darkness, the ocean that I was floating in, everything but the voice.

I looked around to see masked and bloodied faces, linking arms in our quiet sphere.

"This is your family, Adelaide." The voice echoed in the distance.

"Take the mark." These words floated in the cool air, leaving me confused by the meaning and even uncertain if I heard them at all.

One by one the circle became alive again. Derek and the boy who gave me the cider rose and passed around candles that sat in a shallow dish, one to each person as well as torn pieces of paper and small pencils.

When the two young men were seated again, Derek spoke to us. "Write down your negative traits, problems, or anything you wish to be rid of in your life." He gave us all a moment to accomplish this task.

I scribbled down things like: Fear, nightmares, shyness, apprehension, freckles, doubt, insecurity, lions, and cold weather.

"Now burn that paper as you call upon Donar and the spirits that surround us. Ask them to put these things right, to transform your negative thoughts, issues and pain."

I held my problems over the flame of the green candle and watched them burn away. I watched the ashes drift down into the silver dish below as I beseeched my god about the list.

"By banishing those negative things from your life, you have created a void, a void that needs to be filled. I want you all to close your eyes. Visualize light washing over you, filling you up with its warmth. Now, focus on a purely happy moment in your life, something that makes you smile, even laugh, and let that emotion come forth. I want to see you all smiling and laughing. Fill your mind with joy and let those thoughts and nothing else consume you for a moment," Derek instructed.

I racked my brain for a memory that would bring a smile to my face. A memory that didn't involve an enemy of mine. This ruled out my own mother, grandfather, and closest friends. I tried to think if James had ever made me laugh, truly laugh. Nothing came to mind. Christmas, I was happy at Christmas, especially when I got to talk to Benjamin on the phone. Ben always made me laugh. I smiled just thinking about him. I wasn't sure if it was against Derek's rules, but I let myself get lost in thoughts and memories of my best friend. I could feel myself grinning widely when I remembered him asking me to prom and when he kept trying to hold my hand that night at the bowling alley. I even smiled thinking of his amused face the day he helped us move in.

"Great. Now personally thank our god and the Divine Mother and any other spirits that assisted you in your requests." The drink boy commanded the laughing group. "We give thanks to the goddesses for guarding our circle this night. Hail and farewell."

"Hail and farewell," others repeated.

With that the circle was broken. People were standing up and sharing their experience with each other. I took this time to ask a question that had been gnawing at me. I just needed to find a free ear.

"Hi. I don't think we have been introduced yet." I slipped off my mask as I approached the young man who had supplied my wild cider. "My name is Adelaide."

"Oh, I definitely know who you are. I'm Danny. What did you think of your first Mōdraniht celebration so far?" He wasn't particularly handsome with his short brown hair and glasses, but he had a kind smile and a very friendly way about him.

"It was pretty incredible, actually. Certainly not a night I will soon forget." I paused for a second, debating if my question would make any sense. "Can I ask you something?"

"Yeah, of course. What's on your mind?" Danny said, pulling me to the corner of the rooftop, away from the noisy crowd. Speaking of which, I had just realized that the crowd had dwindled back down to its original size. I was curious of what I thought I had seen, it all was beginning to seem like a dream.

"Adelaide?" Danny asked, pulling my attention back to him.

"Oh, right. If I told you I wanted to 'take the mark,' would you know what I was talking about?"

Danny's eyebrows raised above his wide-rimmed glasses. Slowly he pulled the sleeve of his left arm up to his elbow. He held his arm, palm up, for me to examine. A scar, resembling the shape of a "T" adorned his upper forearm.

"It is the Hammer of Donar. The symbol of our high deity. It's his mark, we all have it. The ritual dates far back in your heritage. In fact, if your dad was here, he would be the one to give it to you. It is given right before the commitment ceremony unless otherwise commanded by the spirits, which, doesn't happen very often."

I couldn't imagine how I could have overlooked this shared mark upon all my friends. Cold weather and long sleeves do go hand in hand, I supposed.

"So, if I was told to take it...?"

"Well, then you better take it, Adelaide." Danny smiled.

"Tonight?" I whispered, developing some concern.

"Absolutely! Don't look so scared. This is an honor. It signifies your loyalty and displays your heritage and connection with the gods," Danny said, trying to encourage me.

I took a long, deep breath of winter air. "All right, let's do it." My heart was pounding but mostly due to excitement and wonder.

"Fantastic. There is a table over there." He pointed across the roof where the majority of people were mingling and conversing with each other. "Snacks and drinks. I suggest you get yourself some more cider. I'll get everything ready for you and inform every one of the good news." He rested an arm on my shoulder, as a proud parent would, and then walked off and made the announcement.

I was congratulated and hugged by everyone on my short journey to the required cider.

Rachael and Sasha visited with me for the next fifteen minutes, answering questions and reassuring me of my choice.

In no time at all, the group was gathered around me as I slipped off the robe and knelt on the ground. The drink had such a strong relaxing effect on me that I didn't even flinch at the sound of a torch heating the metal brand.

Derek stood over me asking me questions that I was unable to focus on. When I didn't answer his jumbled words, Sasha bent over and asked slowly, "Who would you like to do this for you, Addy?"

I reached over and took her hand. "You."

"Your father would be so proud of you," she whispered before walking away.

Derek spoke in an authoritative voice as he asked more questions, questions of loyalty and commitment, to which I responded with a wholehearted "yes." Danny and Rachael tightly held my arm as a glowing red symbol approached me.

"The pain is all a part the experience, Addy. Embrace it."

There was an annoying scream vibrating in my ears. It took me a moment before I realized the sound was coming from me. I stared down at my arm in horror. It felt like something had ripped into my flesh. Through moist eyes, I saw the lion maneuvering through the legs of my onlookers, blood dripping from its teeth.

I pointed to the creature and screamed again, certain it was him that took a bite out of me.

"It's okay now, Addy. It will sting pretty badly for a while, but Rachael is getting ice and bandages. It will be healed up in no time," Danny said, still clinging onto my arm.

The lion had disappeared in the forest of khaki pants and robes. I was hit with the reality of what had just happened.

I kept ice atop my white bandages the entire ride back to Ledo and was safely tucked away into my lavender sheets before my mom returned home from work. I stared off into space for several hours, replaying the events of the day, unaware of the time. It wasn't until 2:00 a.m. that I finally decided that I had to sleep. Unfortunately that decision meant nothing to my exhausted body as I lay, eyes wide open, until my 8:30 alarm went off. Not a wink of sleep.

I skipped out on church Sunday morning and spent half an hour playing with my new laptop, which was the most I accomplished with my day. Most of my gloomy hours were spent wrapped in blankets on the couch or in my bed. There was no sleep, but I rested, recuperated, and contemplated. My mother flipped out over my new haircut and insisted on seeing every purchase. She was absolutely in awe but by the end of the day I could sense her slight annoyance at my pensive and sluggish self. I didn't blame her.

When I lay down in bed that night, I was dying for sleep. Frightening images flashed in my mind every time I closed my eyes but at some point during that night I did fall asleep, though my energy would have argued otherwise. I arose from my blankets like a zombie arising from its grave—drained, stiff, and basically dead to the world.

I was very thankful that my mom was able to give me a ride to school, certain that my legs wouldn't have carried me that far.

When we pulled up to the school parking lot, my heart was pounding faster than the swishing windshield wipers. I would get to see Ben today. My excitement was nearly diluted with nervous concern. How was I supposed to treat him? Rachael had suggested the "cold turkey" approach to severing our relationship. Could I do that? Could I completely ignore him? I had developed a new strength in my decision and burning pain upon my forearm to remind me, but this would a challenge I wasn't sure I was capable of handling.

"Can you get a ride home today? I have to go to work at one." My mom spoke, turning the heater up to high.

"Yeah, I'll figure something out. Oh, actually I'm invited to Sasha's house for dinner tonight. Would that be all right? I know I'm still grounded, so I haven't given her an answer yet."

My mom looked at me for a second, debating if she should give in to her stern rules. "I suppose that would be all right. It was very nice of the Roths to pay for your shopping and makeover." She smiled and touched her finger to the tip of my nose. "You look absolutely gorgeous today by the way."

"For the twentieth time this morning, thank you." I laughed. "And thanks for helping put together an outfit. All those clothes were a little overwhelming." Thankfully in this cold weather there was nothing suspicious about me insisting on long sleeves. I was so paranoid about my mom discovering my mark that I kept one hand over it all morning despite the shirt and jacket that did the job for me.

"Oh, it was my pleasure. I wish I could have gone. I insist you let me go shopping with you for your prom dress!"

I nodded, wondering if I would even be going to prom. It didn't seem likely.

"You better get in there," my mother reminded me.

I bit my lip and exited the safety of the car.

15

Cold Turkey

James, Sasha, Rachael, Charles, Luke, and Adam all greeted me as I entered through the school doors amongst the crowd of late arrivers.

James was slightly discouraged to hear that he had missed my branding for the mark. Charles, on the other hand, was thrilled and almost proud of me. They had me explain in detail my experience of the celebration.

"It's a shame you couldn't stay for the whole night," Charles said, sympathetically.

"I know! It was an amazing evening," I said, the excitement rekindling inside of me.

"Does it still hurt?" Luke asked, reminiscently rubbing his own forearm.

"Yeah, it stings. I can't wait till it's all healed up."

I could see the disappointment on Luke's face. He probably felt like he was hiding behind enemy lines and had just lost his only comrade in arms. I really liked Luke and felt a twinge of guilt for abandoning him in his fearful doubt.

The bell rang as we walked down the hallway, each finding our respected classrooms.

Ben was already seated in English class as I walked in with Charles, James, and Sasha. I instinctively stopped breathing as my thoughts went to what he would think of my new look and then to the fear of hurting him, as I knew I would.

The classroom faded away as Benjamin turned his head and stared at me with obvious surprise and delight. A wide smile slowly covered his face as he took in my new appearance. He got up from his desk. I knew if I gave him the chance he would welcome me with a hug and make me lose any willpower I had to move on.

"*Cold turkey, cold turkey, cold turkey,*" I mumbled under my breath.

Sasha nudged me from behind to keep moving. With more harshness than I knew was in me, I looked away without a smile and followed James and Charles to our desks. This was the first time I hadn't sat with Benjamin. Charles even had to insist some girl move out of the desk in front of him so as to make room for me. This girl happened to be Krissy, someone I considered a friend. But the look she gave me as she scooped up her backpack told me otherwise. In fact, the whole classroom of seniors seemed to be having sympathetic pains for Krissy as they were all giving me that same look.

I couldn't bear to look at Ben. I knew the expression on his face would hurt most of all. I looked straight at Mr. Renaldi for the next hour without comprehending anything he attempted to teach us.

My next few classes were terrifying. I felt like a superstitious mob had unjustly labeled me as a witch and condemned me to hell.

My first day back at school was as close to hell as you can get in a high school, which I imagine is closer than people might think. Not one of my classmates would speak to me, not even Bryan Evans, my chemistry partner. A handful of my teachers even seemed to be sentencing me to the gallows with their silent, judgmental looks.

When the final bell rang, it was like Saint Peter had blown his horn. I was out of there. Through the crowd in drama class, down the halls, and out the front doors. Despite the biting snow, I chose to wait outside, away from my fellow students.

Some seniors passed by as they walked to their cars in the parking lot. I could hear them whispering and a few boys even felt it appropriate to call out some cutting words.

"Where's your broom, Adelaide?" shouted Jake, a classmate of mine.

"I saw it in her locker next to her bubbling cauldron and magic wand," Travis added.

"Looks like your friend drank the Kool-Aid, Mark," Nicholas remarked, as he elbowed his little brother Mark Johnson.

Mark pushed away his sibling's arm and kept silent as he walked to their car. I was fond of Mark for not telling Ben about my date with James, but I knew how he felt about my friends.

The boys in the group laughed as their girlfriends worriedly pulled them along.

"How much did you get for it?" Jake asked. I stared at him with a pleading look. "How much did you get for your soul when you sold it to the devil?"

This brought out a roar of laughter followed by a sudden silence as James walked over and took my hand. He stared at the little village of seniors with their torches and pitchforks.

Not another word was spoken from the group as they decided to move on and locate their vehicles.

"Are you okay?" James asked with residual anger on his lips.

"I guess so."

"What are you doing out here in the snow anyway?" James asked as he led me to his car.

"I didn't want to stay in there another second," I said.

"I guess it wasn't much better out here, was it?" James asked.

I shook my head, trying not to become emotional. So the whole school hated me, and I was ignoring the few people that still cared about me. I suppose Ben hated me now too. And no doubt Ollie wasn't too thrilled about me blowing her off when she tried to talk to me in drama class. So what if no one liked me anymore? So what?

"Are you crying?" James asked as we pulled up to my empty house.

"No." I blinked a few times and then exited the car. So maybe I cared a little.

Over the next couple of hours, James and I did homework together and discussed my college options and career possibilities. His family could buy me into any university I chose. A generous offer they granted to each of us in the coven. The world was at my feet, but I couldn't make a decision. I had no direction. James, however, had chosen to attend Princeton University and wanted to persuade me in such a direction.

Apparently, it was "recommended" that the Dons place themselves in influential positions to be more greatly used. Certainly not a loser type mentality, but the subject had me quickly stressed out and irritated.

"What do you have against Princeton?" James asked, obviously frustrated with me. I stared at him blankly so he continued. "Just think about it, Adelaide. You'll have to choose soon." He forcefully stuffed his books back into his bag.

I rolled my eyes as I stood up from the dining room table. "Isn't dinner going to be ready soon?" I intentionally changed the subject.

James checked his watch. "You're right. We better get going."

I ran to my bedroom and brushed through my hair, touched up my makeup with the new techniques that I learned, and searched my closet for warmer shoes. I pulled out my brown boots from under a dirty pair of jeans and noticed the beautiful white coat that James had given me, hanging elegantly against the wall. I hadn't worn it since the night he had given it to me so I pulled it on.

"Come on, Addy!" James called from the living room.

Relaxed in the comfort of a cloud, I walked down the hallway smiling, hoping for even the slightest reaction to my apparel. Nothing. James's behavior toward me seemed to be shifting slightly from pursuit to ownership. His reaction to my haircut was even more approval than delight.

I allowed my eyes to display my disappointment as I moved passed him and out the door.

The drive to his house involved more discussion about Princeton and our future, which ended when he pulled into their garage filled with three other foreign cars and one motorcycle.

"Why do you have to be so difficult about everything?" James said as he got out of the car and slammed the door.

I sat, still buckled into the warm leather seat, fidgeting with the cell phone in my pocket. How I wished to call Ben and talk to a sane person who wasn't upset with me. That thought was quickly shot down when my memory replayed the events that occurred in English class. I tried to shove it out of my mind and put on a smile that I would have to wear all evening.

"So, Adelaide, Sasha tells me that you have already been marked?" Viktor Roth inquired at the dinner table.

"Yes, sir, I have. And thank you so much for allowing me to go shopping with your daughter," I said, trying to be polite.

"You look absolutely lovely, Addy." James's mother smiled sweetly at me.

I smiled back, noticing another dark bruise resting beneath her makeup-covered cheekbone. "Thank you, Mrs. Roth."

"You can call me Lottie, dear," she said in her faint foreign accent, passing me a bowl of green beans.

I nodded and took the bowl.

"Addy is considering Princeton," James said lightly.

"Oh, really?" Lottie was excited by this.

I frowned at James from across the large table. He didn't notice.

"It's a very important decision to make," Viktor said, seriously. "However, I attended Princeton and would applaud you for making it a consideration. After dinner I can show you some information about the university, if you would like." He took a long drink from the crystal glass of amber liquid he never seemed to be without.

"Okay."

"When is your play, Addy?" Sasha asked, noticing the tension on my face.

"The second week of February," I replied.

"Addy is performing in *The Wizard of Oz* as the Good Witch."

"Oh I would love to see that." Lottie's eyes lit up. "I always loved the theater."

"Mom was an actress in the theaters of Germany before she met dad," Sasha explained.

"Wow, I bet that was amazing," I said with interest.

"It was fabulous." Lottie wandered off in thought.

"You should have tried out for the play, Sasha. I bet you are genetically gifted at acting," I said, thrilled that the subject had been changed.

"Yeah, I don't think so," she replied.

"It would have been so much fun to watch you act, Sasha. I think your friend is right, you would have made an amazing actress." Lottie giggled.

"She's laughing because she knows how ridiculous you would be on stage." James laughed.

Sasha glowered at her brother. "I guess we will all have to be satisfied with watching Addy perform."

James smiled at me. "That *will* be fun, won't it?"

I was suddenly nervous and embarrassed at the sudden smack of reality that my friends will be watching me act. I opened my mouth, but Mr. Roth interrupted my chance to speak.

"Sasha," Viktor called from the head of the table, rattling the ice cubes in his emptying glass.

Sasha stood up to refill his drink.

"Are you done eating, Adelaide?" Viktor asked.

I looked at my plate. "Yeah, I guess so."

"Good, come with me to my office," he demanded with a slur.

"Viktor, let her finish…," Lottie attempted to be a good hostess.

"She said she was done," Viktor argued and stood up from his throne-like chair.

I looked to James for any input, but he was busy scooping more mashed potatoes onto his plate.

I soon found myself alone in an office with my suspected drunken host. His office filled with dark cherrywood furniture, leather chairs, and books covering every wall.

"Come over here," Viktor said, motioning me to his desk. He was spreading pamphlets of the university in question.

"You know, Mr. Roth, I've really never had any interest in attending this school," I said bravely. Hoping he would appreciate my honesty.

He looked at me with glossy eyes. "Well, I suggest that you gain interest in it. This is a perfectly good school. In fact—"

"I didn't say it wasn't good, I just was stating that I am totally undecided." I felt guilty and pressured to do what any of the Roths wanted as they had spent so much money on me and was offering so much more. But I didn't want to be forced into anything I didn't want.

"Okay, well what school do you have interest in?"

"Well to be honest, I have no idea."

"Are you waiting to see what school Benjamin Tucker settles upon?"

"No, not at all," I said, surprised by his accusation.

Thoughts of what I had done to Ben earlier that day crept into my mind. Cold turkey!

"James told me that you were able to ignore him today, but he could see the pain that it caused you," Viktor said, breathing the smell of alcohol in my face.

"Ben is just a friend. I don't see what he has to do with anything."

What exactly does cold turkey mean anyway? Really, who came up with that?

"If he becomes a problem for us, we will have to deal with him," he said threateningly.

He had my attention now. "How would he be a problem?"

Viktor stared at me as though to say "you know how."

"There is no problem." My voice broke.

"You are your father's daughter," he said, throwing back the remainder of his drink and slamming the thick crystal class on his desk.

"What does that mean?" I asked, confused by the insulting tone.

"Don't give me that innocent look." He growled at me. "Your father was a failure. He betrayed us all! Leaving us for your no-good mother!" He was shouting now.

"Hey!" I intended to defend my family, but Viktor stepped closer, repeatedly shoving my shoulders as he spoke.

"I can see him in you. See the potential for betrayal!" He gave a final shove as my back hit the wall and the corner of a book shelf, knocking the contents onto the floor.

I grimaced in pain as he gave one final warning. "I hope you make wise decisions, Miss Dawson. I would hate for you to disappoint James or any of us." He smiled at me and then sat down in an overstuffed leather chair. "This isn't a game you're playing; I suggest you take it a little more seriously. And don't feel bad about your dad. He knew he made a mistake. Hopefully you will have the foresight to see the mistake before you make it."

I stood there in shock as James opened the office door. "It's getting a little late, Adelaide. I should take you back home now." He glanced down at the books on the floor, to the slanted shelf, and back to me.

Viktor leaned back in his chair and rubbed his temples. "Clean this up before you leave."

My eyes widened. Was he kidding? He threatened me, pushed me, and expected me to clean up his mess! I looked at James, hoping he would save me from this disturbing situation.

James walked in and fiddled with the wooden shelf. "Adelaide," he said sternly as he looked over at me and nodded down at the mess, silently commanding me to follow his father's wishes.

My mouth fell open in shock, but what choice did I have? I was certain that Viktor was capable of much worse; his wife was the unfortunate evidence of his disregard for limits. I knelt down and stacked the books as my mind stacked its concerns. Would they actually hurt Benjamin if I chose to let him in my life? Did James have his father's tendencies? Was I in any danger?

I considered all these possibilities as James drove me home in silence. I decided it would be best for everyone if I took Viktor's advice. It was true, my father had made a mistake and that mistake had cost him. I wondered how accepting the coven was when he returned to them. Charles said he had died in a car accident many years later. Was it truly an accident or the consequence of betrayal? I didn't want to jump to any outrageous conclusion. Donar was a powerful god, and it would be best for me to stay on his side.

I had let go of friends when I moved from Utah, I should be able to do it again. It bothered me that Ben had made his way past the walls of my heart and had sunk in his roots; roots so deep it was painful to rip them out.

I was able to summon the courage to be committed to my beliefs and decisions for the next several weeks though it was undoubtedly a major drag.

My classmates lost interest in my harassment but continued to ignore me. I spent the majority of my free time with the group, learning ancient Germanic spells, how to summon the help of spirits, and learning a little about the skills of an Augur and their connection with birds. James was usually at my house whenever my mom was away; I was rarely ever left alone. The vet had called me and told me he wouldn't be needing me for a while and would let me know when things changed. I wondered if Ben had anything to do with that.

It was the third week of January when my mother finally "ungrounded" me, though it made little difference. My mother on the other hand was increasingly concerned at the absence of any Tuckers in my life. She was fond of Benjamin and adored Olivia and Calvin. She also found great amusement whenever Mark, Cody, and Ben were together in one room. The three boys never failed to bring about laughter. It had been nearly a month since I had spoken of any friends other than Sasha and Rachael. They were my excuse for everything, and my mother was growing tired of their influence. She could see the dark circles permanently forming under my eyes and depleted interest in my usual activities. I had become slightly withdrawn and lost in my own world.

I had overheard one of her conversations with grandpa asking him to be praying for me. It saddened me that she was genuinely convinced that her God loved her, if she only knew. I had almost attempted to explain the truth to her on several occasions, but I could see my words only brought her grief. She looked at me, as though I was a stranger, a lost and lonely stranger to be pitied. If she was praying to her god on my behalf, I think he heard her. The intensity of my dreams only heightened as did the unseen but spiritually tangible presence that surrounded me, bringing with it a constant fear and paranoia. The emotions in my nightmares followed me throughout each day. I had learned to use the candles by myself and continued to wear James's ring around my neck but this brought no relief. I lost much sleep and was beginning to think that I had forgotten how to laugh.

Diving headfirst into dark waters without a flotation device wasn't the safest idea I had ever had. Ben had kept me afloat all these months and now he was gone. I didn't just let him slowly drift away either. No, I dropped him like dead weight to the ocean floor. Some bright idea Rachael had about frozen poultry.

I was like a druggie trying to quit my beautiful addiction, forced to watch him go through life every day without taking a hit. No one knew the intensity of my withdrawals. I craved his friendship. Dying for a bite of my forbidden fruit. I was jonesing.

16

Uninvited

It was a Monday after school. My mom hadn't left for work yet, so I had a rare, short period of time to be alone with my thoughts. James was certain to show up as soon as my mother had gone.

I was not aware of my surroundings or of the watchful eyes that waited in my doorway. I lay wide-eyed and motionless atop my bed, listening to the radio lost in the hypnotic, angelic voice of my favorite artist singing, *Uninvited*. I had been staring up at my ceiling for the last twenty minutes, not quite aware of what thoughts were passing through my head.

I don't know how long he had been standing there, but I nearly screamed when his voice announced his unwelcome and uninvited presence.

"Addy?" Ben asked hesitantly.

I sat straight up, stifling my shock.

"What are you doing here?!" My voice was laced with delight and horror.

"They really got to you, didn't they?" He looked at me, his face smothered in sympathy.

If he was referring to the threats to not speak to him, then yes, they had gotten to me. But I assumed he was implying that they had "deceived" me into worshiping the devil or something stupid like that. "There is a lot you don't know, Benjamin. You didn't have to come all the way over here to condemn me. You can just join the mob at school tomorrow. Safety in numbers, I guess."

Ben walked right in and stood in front of my bed. "Explain it to me, then. What is it that I don't know?" He appeared to be sincere. I was secretly glad he was here. I tried to deny it, but his very proximity to me seemed to lift my heavy spirit.

"Ben, you need to go." I was nervous for him. My god was watching me, and he was capable of communicating with us. Could I really hide *anything* from the coven?

"What are you so worried about, honey?" He touched my arm as a comforting gesture but my heart melted and began scheming against my mind. Would anyone really have to know if Ben and I were friends?

"Ben, you shouldn't be here." My mind attempted one last battle against my soggy heart, truly hoping he wouldn't heed my warning.

"Well, we all do things we shouldn't, don't we?" He smiled.

Benjamin was smiling at me! I felt like I could finally breathe again.

I offered him no words in response so he continued. "There is no way I'm letting you walk out of my life that easily, Addy. Ollie is going crazy without you, and Calvin and Dad whine every day about not having you around making us those delicious dinners anymore. We all miss you, honey. You have no idea…how badly…" I couldn't bear it anymore, so I cut him off with a suffocating hug and smothered him in apologies.

"I'm so sorry, Ben! I never wanted to do it. I didn't want to hurt anyone! I thought it was for the best. Please forgive me! You have to forgive me. It was killing me to see you so sad, honest. It was awful, just awful! I am such a bad friend."

"Adelaide, honey, it's okay. I forgave you a long time ago." He hugged me tighter. "We all have, we just want you back."

I nodded, fighting the salty tears that wished to burst forth.

Ben released me and sat down in my desk chair.

"I really missed you." His tone was very serious.

"I missed you too, Ben, a lot."

"So, how are you?" I could tell he was concerned for me.

That was a difficult question to answer. In many ways I felt I had purpose and a connection with my father, but in other ways I felt like every day was a battle and it was wearing me down.

"I'm okay, I suppose. How about you, how have you been?"

Ben looked at me hesitantly, as though he saw right through me. "Well, not very good without my best friend." His mouth curved in a smile. "Although, my grades have gone up a little now that I have a lot of extra time on my hands. And I think I finally got all my lines memorized for the play."

"Oh, the Great Wizard has learned his lines. Good for you. Maybe you *are* better off without me," I said, teasingly.

"Yeah, I think not. Maybe we should just make more time for homework when we hang out."

Despite his grinning face, these words brought disappointment. I realized it wouldn't be easy to spend time with him. How could I, when I was constantly surrounded by disapproving eyes. There was no time for Ben in my life, even if he wasn't a "mistake I would regret."

"Ben, I don't think we can spend a lot of time together." And by not "a lot" I meant basically none.

Ben frowned. "You still haven't filled me in about the things in your life that I'm not aware of." He was attempting to avoid that conversation.

I plopped my head down on my pillow and spoke to the ceiling. "This is where I belong, I'm sure of it. I have learned a lot of things that have brought meaning to my life. Please don't try to ruin that for me." I didn't look up to see his face. "Ben, did you know that my dad was a part of this? Charles's dad is my uncle. Isn't that amazing? My dad loved me, and he wanted this life for me. He never wanted to leave me. He was really committed to Donar, and so am I."

"Was?" Ben whispered.

I couldn't bring myself to say the words. I don't know why I did it, perhaps my subconscious knew I couldn't handle talking about my father's death right now, so I lied.

"Well, *does*, I just don't know where he is right now."

"Does your mom know?"

I shook my head.

Ben contemplated this for a moment before responding. "Well, I'm happy for you. I mean, it must be almost life altering to think of seeing him again. To be a part of his life. I can understand you would probably do almost anything to see him again, to be connected to him." His face displayed a mixture of feelings. He looked sad and far off in his thoughts yet he was trying to smile.

"So, you can see how desperately I want this? Please don't try talking me out of it anymore."

"Okay."

That was too easy. "Okay?"

"Yeah. I will do my best to not try to talk you out of it, but you know I have my own beliefs, and I'm not going to pretend otherwise."

"That's fair, I suppose."

There was a moment of silence until Ben lightened the mood. "You'll never guess who asked me for permission to take Ollie to prom!"

"Cody," I said knowingly, ruining his mystery.

His eyebrows rose. "How did you know that?" He sounded disappointed.

"He told me he wanted to, back before Christmas break. Has he asked her yet?"

"No, Mark and I have been making fun of him for weeks. He is so nervous about it." Ben laughed.

"He better not wait too long."

"Yeah, I think he decided to ask her on Valentine's Day."

"That's sweet." I smiled, thinking how ecstatic Olivia would be. "It will give her a little extra boost of confidence before the play."

"Yeah, like she needs more confidence." Ben rolled his eyes.

"Well, if she has any to spare, I could sure use some."

Ben stared at me with a weird look on his face.

"What?" Curiosity dripped from my one worded question.

"Oh, nothing. Hey, are you still going to prom with me?"

"It was a promise, wasn't it?" I had no idea how I would be keeping that promise, but for now it was fun to dream.

A big smile plopped onto Ben's face. "Awesome."

"It certainly is good to see you smiling again, sugar pie." My mom poked her head into my room. "I'm off to work now. Ben, you stay as long as you like, and help yourself to any food if you get hungry."

"Thank you, Mrs. Dawson. Have a good evening at work. See you later." Ben never failed to be respectful and kind.

"Bye, Mom. I'll see you tonight...or in the morning."

"Oh, I almost forgot. Can you get a ride to school in the morning? Susan from work wants me to go to her Tuesday morning Bible study at the coffee house. But I won't go unless you have a ride. It's too cold for you to be walking this time of year." She was looking at Ben instead of me as she spoke.

"I'm sure I can work something out," I assured her.

"Okay. Love you."

"Love you too, Mom," I said as she slipped out of the doorway.

Ben was smiling at me. "I have room."

"For what?"

"To bring you to school."

"It's out of your way."

"Barely. And besides, I can stand a couple extra minutes alone with my sister if it means spending a couple extra minutes with you."

I smiled at his sweetness, but it was way too risky. I would walk if I had to. "Sorry, Ben, but that just isn't a good idea." I heard the front door shut as my mom left the house. James could be here any minute. "And I think you better go now."

"Why?" he seemed confused.

"You can't be seen with me, Ben, I'm serious."

"I'm not afraid of them, Addy," Ben said, as though it were no big deal.

"Well, do it for me then. So that I don't have to suffer the consequences." Ben was my biggest concern. I really wasn't sure of their limits and what might happen to Ben if I didn't stay away from him. I knew he didn't care enough about that but he cared enough about me.

"Are you expecting someone?"

"Yes." I felt guilty at this admittance.

"It's James, isn't it?"

I bit my lip and gave him a nod. Why did I not want him to know this?

Ben looked horrified for a moment. "Are you and James…" He faded his thought, probably debating if he wanted to know the answer.

"Are we what?" I asked, knowing the question but wondering what my answer would be.

"Never mind." He chose to dismiss the idea.

"Please leave, Ben."

"Okay. For you. But we will talk again soon, okay?" He looked concerned that I would abandon him again.

"How?" I was rather hopeless on the matter.

"We can slip notes into each other's lockers when no one is looking, and you can call me whenever you have the chance to. It will be our secret. Just don't avoid me again, please." His pleading eyes were irresistible.

"Our secret," I said in agreement. "Now get lost," I teased.

He laughed. "Fine. I'm leaving." He winked at me. "I love your haircut, by the way." He turned and walked out of my bedroom.

"Tell Ollie I said I'm sorry!" I yelled out after him.

James did show up soon after Benjamin left my house. We spent the evening at his home, doing homework with Sasha. Despite being around his father, I was happier than usual. My joy, however, was covered with an extra coat of nervousness that someone would discover my secret. It seemed to go unnoticed and the night passed without confrontation.

When the morning came, I realized I had forgotten to ask James for a ride to school. I didn't feel like disappointing my mother, so I told her it was arranged. I would brave the harsh air that mother nature provided and walk to school.

I sat at the table, eating my bowl of Cheerios as my mom wandered around the house gathering her jacket, keys, and Bible.

"What's this?" she asked, finding the Bible that Mr. Tucker had given me, still tucked away in its partially wrapped box atop the book shelf where I had set it. She opened the box and gave me a stern look. "This was a gift, Addy. Have you even opened it since Christmas Eve?"

"Well, no, but…it's a Bible, Mom." I'm not sure what made me think that would be a sufficient response.

She tucked the Bible into my backpack that was lounging across the living room sofa beside the lime green throw pillow. "Bring it to school. Read something from it. Please, baby. Just see what it has to say." She was being overly dramatic, as though this were a life or death decision.

"Sure, Mom." I smiled at her, cutting off the argument before it began.

"See you after school." She pulled her arms through her coat and walked out the door.

I dressed for the occasion with my long johns, a hooded sweater, and snow boots. I slung my backpack over a thick wool jacket and flattened my bangs with an old beanie. It had been easy to make the decision to walk when I sat in the comforting warmth of my home. I may have chosen otherwise if I had been aware of winter's cold heart and crying eyes. Tears of ice fell upon a frozen sidewalk. A thick blanket of snow had been laid across the dead earth during the night. The scenery was breathtakingly beautiful, like crushed diamonds sprinkled across the town, whiting out the existence of color. But it was also just plain breathtaking. It was so cold it hurt to breath. I carefully waddled down the dangerous sidewalk, holding my jacket around my mouth.

I was in front of the city park when my feet made one wrong move. I landed on my hands and knees, surviving with only a few inevitable bruises but my backpack had slipped off my shoulder and sent books sliding across the frozen ground.

"Great," I muttered.

Did life *ever* get any easier?

I was stuffing the books back into my backpack when a police car pulled up. "Want a ride, Adelaide?" It was the sheriff, my uncle Henri.

"Yeah thanks," I yelled back, relieved, as I picked up the last book that had slid under a bench. It was the Bible. I turned my back to Henri and stared at the book. This was dangerous. I had to get rid of it.

"Are you coming?" Henri stuck his head out over the top of his foggy window.

"Yes!" I discreetly dropped it onto the park bench. When I looked back up, I was startled to see the homeless man who had knocked me over last month. He was nearly thirty yards away from me and walking closer. He didn't look so disheveled, from what I could tell, but the memory of him screaming at the air as he ran away frightened me. I quickly turned around and walked to the car.

"You should watch out for people like him." Henri nodded sideways as we pulled out into the road.

"Homeless people?" I asked.

"Yeah, homeless people." He almost sounded amused by my description. "Did you find all of your books?"

Had he noticed that I left one behind? "Yes, I did." Technically, I did find them all, that wasn't a lie.

"Good." Henri reached over and turned up the heat. "Why are you walking in this weather?"

"I forget to get a ride. I didn't think it would be that cold out today." I rubbed my stiff, red hands together in front of the vent.

"I see. Is your mom working?" he asked.

"No, she is at a Bible study."

"Ah, that's no good."

"No." It suddenly occurred to me that I had never heard Charles mention his own mother. "Does… Is…I've never heard anyone mention your wife." I wasn't sure how to phrase my question.

"Not my wife. Charles's mom died soon after he was born," he said, hiding his sorrow well if there was any to be hidden.

"I'm so sorry, Henri."

"It's okay. She's around, watching over Charles, I'm sure."

I nodded. It would have been fun to have an aunt.

"How's your arm doing?" I was glad he didn't leave us in silence too long.

I touched my forearm. "It's still a little sensitive. A lot better though."

"Charles and I are proud of you."

I remembered what Viktor had said about my father being a failure. "Henri?"

"Yes?"

"Was my dad a disappointment to everyone?"

"Not beating around the bush on that one, are you?" He chuckled. "No, Adelaide. He was a very great man. There may have been some hurt feelings and he was disappointed in himself for making the decisions that he did. But he did what was right in the end. I'm sure he would just want you to learn from his past and not repeat his mistakes."

"Okay. Thank you for your honesty."

"Anytime." He pulled up in front of the double doors of our school. "Tell Charles to behave." He smiled at me as I got out of the car.

It hadn't occurred to me that stepping out of a cop car might give the wrong impression to some until the comments began.

"Did devil worshipping finally become a crime?" It was Mark's brother, Nicholas. A crowd laughed as I walked passed them.

"Keep it to yourself, Nick," Benjamin called from behind me.

I smiled but didn't turn around.

I walked straight to my locker and scribbled a quick note: "Thanks." I dropped the folded piece of paper through a slit in Benjamin's locker on my way to English class. Though we didn't speak, we caught each other's eye several times throughout the day, which painted a smile across my face that I was forced to suppress.

It was almost fun keeping our secret. It made school bearable again.

Drama class was my favorite part of the day. I was able to talk openly with Ben and Ollie.

"I'm so sorry about everything, Ollie," I whispered to her as our teacher explained the details of the stage sets.

"No problem, Addy. You had me really worried," she whispered back.

"Miss Olivia, did you have something to add?" our teacher interrupted.

"Well, I was just thinking. Maybe the brick road should be blue," Olivia responded in a serious tone.

"You mean the *yellow brick road*?" the teacher asked, unimpressed.

"Yes, ma'am." Ollie giggled as did the rest of the class.

Mrs. Buchannon rolled her eyes and continued with her descriptions.

Ben was paying close attention because he and Calvin had volunteered to paint several of the props.

"Are you coming over after school?" Ollie's big eyes were filled with hope.

"Sshh. I missed what she said." Ben glared at his sister.

"I don't think I can. Not today," I whispered back, ignoring Benjamin's request.

Ben turned his gaze on me. I offered him a big innocent smile. He smiled back and shook his head.

"Okay. Well whatever you do, you should try to go to bed early," Ollie whispered as she stared up at the teacher, appearing to pay attention.

I looked at her, confused by the recommendation. She glanced at me and grinned. "You look like you literally haven't slept in a month."

"Oh thanks a lot," I said, feigning emotional injury.

She laughed. "Don't get me wrong, you look gorgeous with your new haircut. You just got this...I don't know, *Night of the Living Dead* kind of look going on. You look exhausted. I'm worried for you."

I laughed out loud at her comparison, immediately stifling the sound when Mrs. Buchannon shot me a warning glance. "I'm just not sleeping well, lately. I'm fine. Thanks for the ego boost."

"When are we going shopping for your prom dress?" Olivia asked after a moment of pretending to listen to our informative lecture.

I could see Ben watching me from the corner of his eye.

"Soon, I hope. I'll try to make time one of these Saturdays. My mom insists on going too. I hope that's okay."

"Of course! I love your mom." Her affection was sincere. She had latched on to my mom since the first day they met. Ollie was like a lost puppy searching for someone to offer her love. She had plenty of friends and several wishful boys, but she wanted a mother and my mom was more than happy to fill in.

When the bell rang, I walked out of the classroom alone, wiping the telltale smile from my face. James greeted me in the hallway. "How was class?" I could tell he had other things on his mind.

"Lots of boring stuff about props today." I laughed as I shared with him Ollie's opinion. "Someone suggested we paint the brick road *blue*."

"Huh." He excused it without even an upward twitch of his lips. "Do you have plans tonight?"

I thought this was a silly question. When did I ever have plans that didn't involve him? "No, nothing as of yet. Why?"

"We are going to the library tonight. We have to take care of some unfinished business." He spoke in a hushed voice as we flowed down the hallway, intermixed into the rush of teenagers.

"What business?"

"It's time Bryan Evans learned his place." His tone sent shivers up my spine.

I frowned at him. I happened to be fond of Bryan.

"Christmas Eve, remember," he explained himself. "We gave him a chance to back off, and he didn't."

I stopped and looked at him. "Is it really necessary, James? I mean, can't we just let it slide this time?"

He looked very displeased with me. "We have let it slide before."

"But what if I don't want to...to do whatever we are going to do?" I stepped backwards from him.

"What do you mean, *if you don't want to?*" He growled at me. "We are all in this together, Adelaide. Bonded by blood, united as one. We are a family. Someone hurts one of us, we are all there to make things right. Please don't be difficult about this. "

I took another step back, pleading with him. "James, I don't want to abandon anyone, I just don't feel right about—"

He grabbed my arm and forcefully pulled me closer to him. "You don't *feel* right? Are you kidding me?!" he yelled, gathering the attention of those passing by.

"Let go of her arm, James." The uninvited and unwelcome enemy that had found his way back into my life was now standing up for me. Benjamin pushed through the crowd to face James.

"Ah, Mr. Tucker comes to the rescue. What exactly do you think is going to happen, here? I let her go and she comes running into your arms?" James mocked.

"I said, let her go, James." Ben stepped closer, his words more forceful than before. The hallway had filled up with onlookers all hoping for a fight. I had no doubt they were all wishing to see James sprawled on the floor in pain.

James released my arm. "She isn't yours to worry about, Benjamin."

"And you think she is yours?" I noticed that Mark and Cody had found their way to Ben's side. His loyal friends were there to back him up. Only problem was James's friends had also made their way through the crowd to stand beside us.

"She *does* wear my ring around her neck every day. What does that say to you, Ben?" James hooked his finger around the ribbon that encircled my neck and pulled out his silver ring.

I glared at James. This was very deceiving of him. It looked bad on my part.

I looked at Ben, wanting him to understand. "It isn't what…" I saw the look James was giving me. Here I was, standing at a crossroads. Would I blow everything to protect Ben's feelings? What would happen to Ben if I did? "It isn't any of your business, Benjamin." I changed the direction of my sentence, hoping to protect him.

Ben's eyes turned to me but the expression on his face remained the same.

James smiled. "That's right. I suggest you mind your own business before someone ends up hurt."

"Don't be stupid here, Benjamin. Your God can't protect you from everything," Charles warned.

"You guys think you can do whatever you want, don't you? You think you are better than all of us?" Mark yelled at them, receiving a few hoots and hollers from the crowd.

Charles smiled. "Yes." He was calm and collected, speaking his simple answer as though it were a fact.

"If you hurt her in any way...," Ben said.

"What, Benjamin? What would you do, pray about it to your pitiful god? Go to church and have 'faith' that she will be okay, that justice will come upon us?" James laughed.

Ben's fist slammed hard into James's face. James fell backwards into the lockers and moaned in pain. "You hurt her, I'll hurt you, understand?" Ben muttered to James, barely loud enough for anyone else to hear.

Charles and Adam were quickly on Benjamin. Charles struck Ben's face from the side. I winced. Adam took a few hard swings to his stomach. In a matter of seconds, Mark and Cody were in on the action with teachers now pulling and shoving the boys away from each other. I was appalled at this sudden outcome. I could have prevented this whole fiasco had I more quickly succumbed to James's request.

The uninvolved student body was warned to move along and the remainder of us were sent to the principal's office. This was a first for me. We sat, quietly in a row of chairs, each of us being called in, one at a time, to accept our punishment.

Ben exited the office. There was a small smile hidden on his bloody lip as he walked past me. I wondered at what his consequences were to be. Ben, Cody, Mark, James, Charles, and Adam, all being punished for my choices.

My head hung low with guilt as I was summoned to the ruler of this juvenile kingdom: Mr. Phillips.

"Adelaide Dawson." He acknowledged me as I took a seat. "I expected more from you."

I hated that phrase.

"I'm really sorry, sir. I didn't mean for that to happen." I stared down at my knees.

"Seeing as this is a first mark any of you have received on your records, I have given your friends two weeks of detention, every day after school. I considered suspension, but I am convinced this will be an isolated incident."

I nodded.

"Graduation is almost here. Can you behave yourself until then?" Mr. Phillips leaned forward, elbows resting on his desk.

"Yes, sir."

"Because the punishment will be much worse if you show up in here again, do you understand me?"

"Yes. It won't happen again."

"Since you were not involved in the actual fighting, only a provoker, you will receive one week of detention."

Provoker? I wasn't trying to provoke anyone. But seeing the blood and bruises on the faces of my friends, I felt I deserved every bit, if not more, of my punishment.

"You are all free to go home today. I will be calling each of your parents and discuss the situation. Detention will start tomorrow in room 14."

Great. I had just finished serving time without parole and was likely to face another grounding.

17

House Visit

"Would you like a ride?" James was waiting for me in the school parking lot after I left the principal's office.

I looked at him for a minute, examining the dark bruise that had formed around his eye. James was human like the rest of us, and he had no right to push me around. He bled, like any other human would. This thought gave me courage. Courage to stand up for myself.

"To the library?" I crossed my arms and planted my feet.

"Is that where you want to go?" His attitude had drastically changed, as though he literally had some sense knocked into him.

"I would rather go home and sleep. I don't feel very well." I carefully spoke these words, examining his reaction to my defiance.

"Then home, it is." He gave me a small smile before getting into his car.

Surprised, I walked around to the passenger side and got in. "What about family and unity?"

He gave me a look I hadn't seen in several months, an exciting and mischievous look. "Well, technically, you aren't a committed member yet. So the choice is yours."

"Huh. Okay." I found this hard to believe after that unfortunate alpha-male show of masculinity that had just taken place.

James drove me home as he said he would. He even walked me up to my door.

"I'm really sorry for the way I've been acting lately."

"That's okay. I'm sorry about your eye," I said, sympathetically.

"It wasn't the first and it probably won't be the last," he said with a smile.

This reminded me of the fight he had been in on Christmas Eve. And now they were going to make Bryan pay for his actions. Would the same thing happen to Benjamin? Would they take their own revenge on my friend?

"Thanks for the ride." I stepped inside my house, trying to keep the concern out of my voice.

"I would love to give you a ride in the morning. I would hate for you to have walk in this weather." His tone was sweet, almost erasing my memory of his past offenses.

"That would be nice, James, thank you."

"No problem. If you ever need a ride anywhere, just say the word."

"I will. Thank you, James." It disturbed me how his smile was still capable of sending my heart into a full on sprint.

"Rest well." His voice was husky as he leaned over and softly kissed my forehead.

My blood stirred and my heart screamed: danger, danger!

"Good-bye." I quickly shut the door before losing myself in the depths of his dark eyes.

I had no plans for resting. Truthfully, I did want to rest as I had told James earlier, but I had to go see Ben. I felt responsible for the beating he took, and I needed to apologize. I had a rare opportunity of freedom without the watchful eyes of the coven. I had to take advantage of it.

After a chilling walk through town, I knocked three times on the Tuckers' front door before Olivia answered. When she saw me her eyes widened and she gave me a big hug.

"Hi!" she whispered excitedly.

"Hi." My voice was normal but slightly confused by her hushed voice.

"They are praying. We have to be quiet." She motioned to the living room where a group was gathered. "Let's go to my room." She grabbed my hand and pulled me inside.

"Okay, now we can talk." Ollie plopped down on her green bean bag.

I sat down on the edge of her bed, comforted by the familiarity of her room.

"I can't believe you came over." There was a hint of curiosity in her voice.

"I wanted to hang out." I shrugged my shoulders as though it were no big deal.

Ollie was never one to sugarcoat things, and she felt that everything *was* her business. "I just thought that, well, I didn't think you were allowed."

I found that statement irritating. "I can do whatever I want."

Ollie eyed me and waited for the truth to come out.

"Okay, not whatever. We have certain rules, that's all. It's not like I have no choice in the matter."

"Ben said you weren't allowed to come over." Question marks dripped off the end of every word.

"How is Ben doing?"

"He's got some pretty bad bruises across his ribcage and a cut on his lip but otherwise he's just dandy." I was relieved by her lack of concern but the description plagued me with guilt.

"I feel awful about that whole thing," I said honestly, scooting back, farther onto the bed to lean against the wall.

"Yeah, but it's kinda cool, don't you think?" Ollie's eyes lit up.

"Cool?" That was the last word I would have used to describe the event.

"Well, I've never had boys get into a fist fight over me." She giggled with delight.

I thought about that. I guess that did kind of make me feel good. Deep down, underneath the horror and guilt, I was slightly flattered.

"I hadn't thought of it like that. It was very sweet of Ben to stand up for me, wasn't it? I never expected him to actually hit James."

"I know! None of us did. Ben has never been in a fight before." She leaned forward and lowered her voice. "He's never acted like this over a girl before, either."

Heat poured into my face. "Well, that's...nice." I tried to act cool.

"Yeah, *nice*." She mocked at my choice of words.

"Where is Ben, anyway?"

"Oh, he's in the living room. Dad started this prayer meeting last month. Every Tuesday and Friday afternoon."

"What do they pray about?" I could hear the judgment weighing down my voice.

Ollie shifted in her bean bag. "People. Just, uh, certain people." She glanced over to her door.

"I thought you weren't coming over today!" Ben's hushed voice was entangled with excitement as he gently shut Olivia's bedroom door behind him.

I quickly pushed myself from the bed and rushed over to him. "I had to come see if you were okay! Oh, look at your lip. Do you hurt pretty badly?"

Ben was amused by my attentive concern. "I'm all right. I'm glad you came to check on me, though." He smiled down at me, sending another rush of blood into my cheeks.

"Did you get grounded? I just feel so bad. I'm sure I could explain to your dad--"

"No need. He understands. He thinks two weeks of detention is more than enough punishment. I suppose he should be a little more upset, but I think the whole town finds me justified in what I did."

I frowned at him, wondering if he was about to give me a speech on my bad choice of friends.

"I probably could have handled it a little differently," he admitted, responding to my apprehensive look. "I hope you aren't upset with me."

"Me? Upset with you? No." I glanced down at Ollie. "I'm actually a little flattered."

"Someone has to look out for you," he said sheepishly.

I returned to my spot on the grassy green bedspread. "How about Mark and Cody? How are they doing?"

"Cody has a black eye!" Ollie said, jumping back into the conversation.

"Mark took quite a beating too, but it was probably the best day of his junior year. He's been dying to…well, he's always got my back. Always up for a fight, too. You should have seen his big bloodied-tooth grin when we left school." He laughed. "They've always got your back too, Addy. Mark might be acting a little cold toward you but I promise, if you ever need them, they'll be there for you."

"Thanks." It still surprised me that Mark had come through for me and not told Ben about my date with James.

"How about you? Are you grounded again?" Ben asked.

"I don't know. My mom is still at work," I said through a yawn.

"Man, Addy, you look so tired," Ollie commented.

"Yeah, you've mentioned that."

"She's right, do you sleep anymore?" Ben sat down on the other end of the bed.

I looked at both of their concerned faces and slid down to rest my head on the bed. "Sometimes," I said through another yawn.

Ollie squeaked out a yawn as well. "Stop that." She yawned once more.

Ben laughed at us.

"You laugh now, but it will get you too!" Ollie forced out more contagious yawns his way.

Unmoved by her assault, Ben looked down at my sleep deprived eyes. "What's keeping you up?"

"Nightmares," I muttered the word under my breath as though speaking was enough to curse my night's sleep.

Ben's finger brushed across my neck, causing my intake of oxygen to cease. He picked up the ribbon-laced ring that had slid to the side of my neck when I lay down. "Is that why you wear his ring?" He spoke softly without a trace of accusation.

I easily forgot that Ben knew much more about our untold world than most. Though only for a short time, he had stepped into the powerful truth that now illuminated my life.

I released my breath and nodded. "It's supposed to help."

Without a word, Ben gently untied the ribbon and set my silver adornment on Olivia's nightstand.

I stared up at him, thinking I should object, but I felt so safe under the watch of his astonishing blue eyes. It wasn't just him, either. His family, his home; I was wrapped up in the trusting warmth of his life.

"We could pray for you, Addy," Ollie whispered as she knelt down beside the bed.

I scrunched up my face and slowly shook my head. That wasn't at all what I wanted. Drawing more attention from their god was the last thing that I needed.

Ben brushed a strand of hair from my face. "Well, you don't really have a say in the matter."

I couldn't work up the energy to argue. I was so relaxed and already fading away into another level of consciousness.

When I awoke from my unexpected nap, I found that I was alone in Olivia's bedroom, covered by a fuzzy, pink blanket. I slowly inhaled a deep breath as I cherished the feeling of perfect rest. Blinking the sleep from my eyes, I took in the details of her bedroom. Bright pink and green dominated her decor. The walls were also a shade of green with pink words painted across the border, just below the ceiling: *Love, Joy, Peace, Patience, Kindness, Goodness, Faithfulness, Gentleness, and Self-control.* I faintly recognized this from Sunday school, but I was confused by the small letters and numbers that rested at the end, Gal. 5:22–23. It was similar to that bizarre code that was written on my little wooden fish. A mystery I had left unsolved due to the crazy man and that demented bird.

Wiping away that unfortunate memory, a smile spread across my face as I slowly sat up and stretched.

The house was quiet except for the faint sound of a masculine voice. Curious, I wandered down the hallway and peered into the living room.

Mr. Tucker was reading distantly familiar words from his Bible as the group listened intently. To his right sat the dear old Mrs. Price. Seeing her kind face brought a smile to my lips. I also recognized Mr. Morris, the pastor of my mother's church. Seeing him quickly wiped the smile *from* my face. Facing away from me was another male. His dark brown and gray speckled hair didn't pull any memory out of my facial recognition department but what sat resting on the arm of his chair set off a few bells. A familiar book. It was big and black with the words "Seek and you shall find" written in gold letters at the bottom corner. It was the Bible Mr. Tucker had given me! How did it end up here? My gut twisted with concern. Was Mr. Tucker aware that I ditched his book on a snowy bench?I tried to get a better look at the man who brought the revealing evidence but was unable to see his face without revealing my presence to the group. How dare he bring that book into this house?!

"Sleep good?" I jumped at the sound of Calvin's voice. He was brewing coffee in the kitchen behind me.

"Actually, I slept amazing," I admitted as I quietly entered the kitchen. "I really needed that."

"I guess so." He laughed as he eyed the state of my undoubtedly disheveled hair.

Maybe I felt too at home here; I hadn't even glanced at a mirror after my afternoon snooze.

I tried to comb through the tangles as I braved my confession. "Calvin, I have to tell you something."

He poured himself a cup of coffee and turned to give me his full attention. "What is it, kiddo?"

"Well, I noticed a certain Bible in there. It's the one your dad gave me. I feel awful, I probably hurt his feelings. It's just…" I trailed off trying to come up with good explanation.

"Yeah, I know. But my dad isn't mad. He thinks it's rather special."

Special? Who thinks it's special to have someone throw out a gift they gave them? My lack of comprehension was evident so Calvin continued with his explanation.

"This is his first time here. He said that a sweet young lady gave him a Bible this morning when he was at the park."

Wow, that guy *was* crazy. I did no such thing, but I was thrilled by the kind tale.

"I saw him walking down the street this afternoon when I went out to get the mail. I saw his Bible and invited him to come in for our prayer group. The cool part is he said he never would have had the courage to come if you hadn't given him that Bible earlier." Calvin was radiating joy as he told the story.

Oh, good. I inadvertently convinced someone to pursue a life of lies and deceit.

I glanced around the corner to the living room. "So, that's the homeless guy?"

Calvin laughed. "He's not exactly homeless, just…"

"Just weird?" I offered.

"Something like that. He's had a fascinating life though. You should talk to him." Calvin took another sip from his coffee.

Or not. "Maybe next time." I smiled at him and walked farther into the kitchen. I could hear people up and walking around.

"I better go say good-bye to everybody." He set down his cup and walked to the next room.

I waited until everyone had left before saying my own good-byes.

Ben handed me the silver ring. "This isn't mine to keep."

I smiled at him. "It isn't mine either." I took it and shoved it into the pocket of my jeans.

He was obviously pleased by this gesture.

"I hope your nightmares go away," Ben whispered as he helped me into my coat.

"Me too."

"Good luck with your mom." Ben's face reflected my own concerns.

"Thanks, Ben. I'll see you in class tomorrow."

"I look forward to it, but this time try not to be so obvious about our secret friendship," he teased.

"Me? Obvious? You're the one throwing punches for me." I playfully poked his chest.

"Ouch!" Ben clutched his faded blue T-shirt and bent over, moaning in pain.

"Ben! I'm so sorry. Are you okay?" I wrapped my arm around his back to comfort him.

His whining was beginning to sound more like laughter. "Benjamin Tucker, are you laughing?"

He straightened out with a goofy grin slapped across his face.

I pushed him backwards with fake outrage. "Not funny."

"You're right, I'm sorry."

"Why don't I believe you?" I stepped over to the door.

Mr. Tucker walked out of the kitchen and saw us standing in the entry way. "You're still here? We said good-bye like twenty minutes ago." He laughed. "Instead of standing there talking you should give her a ride home, Ben. It's starting to snow again."

"Good idea, Dad." He looked back at me. "Can I?" Ben grabbed his coat off a hook and slipped it on without waiting for my response.

How could I possibly keep this a secret when I was so careless? We were bound to be discovered. "I guess so."

"I'll be right back," Ben said to his dad.

"Bye, Mr. Tucker."

"Good-bye, *again*, Adelaide." He grinned and walked down the hallway.

Ben reached around my neck and pulled the hood of my jacket over my head. "Don't worry, honey, no one will see you."

The two of us talked and laughed the whole way to my house. Despite the darkening sky and dreary weather I felt rejuvenated and uplifted; warmed from the inside out like I had spent the afternoon lounging in a beam of sunlight.

To my relief-filled satisfaction, my mother chose not to ground me. She found the story highly entertaining and had the wisdom to understand that I didn't wish for anyone to get hurt.

"I bet you didn't know that I went to school with your principal," my mom said as she popped a bag of popcorn into the microwave and sat back down in front of her painting in progress.

"Mr. Phillips?"

"Yeah. We even went on a date once before I met your dad." She smiled, artistically caressing her canvas with a golden-dipped paintbrush.

Her reminiscent conversation must have distracted her from focusing on my behavior. Thank you, Mr. Phillips.

"Wow, I didn't know that." I saw my cell phone sitting on the counter. I hadn't realized that I left and wondered if James had tried to call me. I walked over and flipped it open. No calls. "Mom, did anyone call for me?"

"No. We're you expecting a call?"

"No, just wondering." Good.

I was glad to not be a part of whatever took place in the library basement that afternoon. I returned James's ring the next day without any question on his part. He was the exciting man that I knew him to be; full of complements, mystery, and intrigue. He gave me a ride to school nearly every morning, and I found myself growing fond of him again. Detention, however, was not so pleasant. My two worlds pushed into one classroom for an hour every day of awkward silence. It was torturous knowing that I was the reason behind their punishment. No one complained, in fact not a word was ever spoken about it. It was like an alternate reality; an afterschool vortex that sucked us into a realm of silence, our existence lost between time and space.

Detention aside, I had the faintest hint of fulfillment. I was undeservingly getting the best of both worlds. Ben and Olivia were able to secretly remain my close friends, I was developing a deep connection with the coven, and I had James's adoration.

I knew things couldn't go on like this forever, but I couldn't bear to think about letting any part of it go. There would come a day when I would have to make a choice. I knew what my decision must be, and I hated myself for it. Ben and Ollie deserved better.

ROOTED IN EVIL

The dreaded day was coming sooner than I hoped. My self-destructive, downward spiral took off just a few days before our debut of the Wizard of Oz. I had stretched my devotions too far, and it hadn't gone unnoticed. It would have been just an average day of school, like any other. A simple Thursday in February. But this particular day fell onto a pile of hearts and arrows, a day labeled Valentine's Day.

18

Witch

Cupid had smeared his mark on every wall of the school. Red and pink paper hearts, streamers, and balloons filled our halls and classrooms. Whispers and giggles echoed through the building.

Cards, chocolates, and flowers were allowed to be delivered throughout the day, causing unnecessary hype and chaos.

I couldn't help but roll my eyes as I walked down the decorated hallway and entered my first class of the day.

Mr. Renaldi regaled us with the history of Saint Valentine while Dixie cups of hot chocolate and pink marshmallows were distributed. "In ancient Rome, February the fourteenth was a holiday to honor Juno, the goddess of women and marriage…" His voice faded into the background as James leaned forward in his desk to talk to me.

"Can I take you on a date tonight?"

I turned my head to look at James and caught Benjamin's eye. He smiled at me and for a quick moment I forget James was there, sitting patiently behind me.

"Okay, what time?" I whispered, keeping an eye on our teacher.

"I'll drop you off after school and pick you back up around six."

"We are rehearsing and setting up for our play after school. We won't be done until around 5:30. Want to just pick me up then?"

"That works for me. When is the play?" James delicately played with a strand of hair that was resting on my arm.

"Saturday at 7:00. Will you be there?" The light brush of his hand against my arm sent shivers up my spine. I could see Ben watching us, and James was aware of it too.

"We will all be there, Addy. Wouldn't miss it."

Before I had a chance to respond, Zach, the sophomore office aid, was standing at my desk. "Adelaide Dawson?" He read from his clipboard.

"Yes?"

"For you." He handed me a long stemmed red rose.

Zach had already moved on passing out a few cards and a box of chocolates without giving me the chance to ask of its origin.

James was my first thought until he leaned forward and whispered, "Who's it from?" His words were buried in jealous curiosity.

"I'm not sure." I stared down and admired the beautiful simplicity of the rose. A small white petal stood out amongst its bed of velvet crimson. I carefully pulled the small slip of paper out of the soft petals that sweetly embraced it.

Will

The name baffled me. Did I know a Will? It didn't make any sense to me until I received an identical rose during history. The note read: *You*. Another lovely red message carrier also showed up in chemistry reading: *Be*. By then I was getting an idea where this was going. I could only assume who... "Who's the secret admirer?" Bryan Evans asked during chemistry.

"You mean it isn't you?" I teased.

"It could be." He winked. I was surprised he was talking with me again, let alone winking. "I bet it's Ben." He glanced over his shoulder at his suspect. He gave him that distinctive nod that men give each other and turned back to me. "Are you two going out yet?"

"No." I carefully tucked my little notes into the pocket of my wool coat that draped across the back of my chair.

"You're still going out with James, aren't you?" Bryan raised one eyebrow.

"Yeah." No point in lying. I hoped this wasn't the end of our sudden returned friendship.

"What's he like? I mean, besides a jerk to the rest of us."

"He's not a jerk to me, if that's what you're asking." I pretended to read over our assigned chapter.

"The girls seem to think he's hot stuff. It doesn't make sense to me, but I'm pretty positive that's why most of the girls hate you now, they're jealous. They like to blame it on the witch thing though," Bryan said, lightly. He had no idea the insult he just struck.

"I'm not a witch!" My voice rose above the soft chatter that filled the room.

Eyes turned to look at me. I lowered my voice. "I'm not a witch, Bryan."

"I guess I'm misinformed."

"I guess so," I agreed.

Bryan leaned closer as he talked. "You see, I was under the impression that you worship other gods and spirits." He paused.

My eyes wandered from my book up to his face. I guess you can't live in a town this small and not expect some truth to trickle onto the gossip vine.

"And perform spells and curses and freaky rituals," he continued. "Maybe even do a little talking with the dead?"

His accusations were spot on and he knew it. With surprise lathered all over my face, there was no hope for denying his shockingly accurate statement.

"You tell me that's not true and I'll admit you aren't a witch." His voice was cocky. He knew he had just won the battle.

He was right. Like Luke had told me, it was plain old witchcraft blanketed with ancient history and exciting secrets. That didn't make it a lie though. That didn't change anything, really. It was more real than life itself; I just never expected to wear that title. Witch.

I stared down at the open textbook before me. Witch? Really?

When I didn't respond, Bryan put a hand on my forearm that rested across words on page 94. "You're still okay in my book, Adelaide."

PE went by without a delivery but a fourth rose was brought to me in Study Hall. *My* was the predictable new word. I couldn't help but smile by the mystery and thoughtfulness of it all. James, however, seemed quite displeased. He was sweet and talkative throughout class, but he frowned with every glance at my growing bouquet. I'm sure that he could guess at who my mysterious admirer was. I tried not to consider how this might upset James.

My fifth and final rose waited upon my blue plastic seat in drama class. *Secret Valentine?* read my last paper petal.

Ben plopped down in his usual seat beside me. Without a word, he waited for my response.

My secret friend wished me to be his secret Valentine.

I smiled at him, and he held a single finger up to his lips, warning me to retain our secret status.

I picked a pen out of my bag and pulled his hand over to rest on my leg. Palm up, I wrote in big red letters: *YES.*

He slid his hand back over to read my answer. His dimpled joy that spread from cheek to cheek made me smile so big I felt I had to look away.

Ollie was staring back at my flushed face when I turned to my right.

"Whatcha doin'?" she asked, amused.

"Uh…" I looked down at the roses in my lap.

"Never mind." She laughed. "I already know. But guess who asked me to prom!" She was bouncing up and down in her seat, unable to contain her excitement.

I glanced at the heart-shaped box of chocolates she was holding. *Prom?* was scribbled in marker across the lid.

"Mark?" I faked ignorance.

"No!" Her eyes widened in horror.

"Kyle Tomlin? Matthew? Chris?" She shook her head, annoyed by each of my guesses. "Oh, let's see. Taylor? Nathan Rochester? Josh—"

"You're no good at this. It's Cody!"

I laughed. "I know."

Her jaw dropped, and she smacked my shoulder. "How did you know? Why didn't you tell me? We have to go dress shopping tomorrow after school! Can we? Will your mom be off work? Oh, I'm so excited! I can't believe Cody Moore wants *me* to go to prom with him!"

The teacher interrupted with instructions for the long afternoon ahead of us, postponing our conversation until later. We had much to do and tension was high.

We spent the duration of the class period setting out props, preparing the stage, and dressing for our final rehearsal. Every red, upholstered theater seat in the auditorium was empty, leaving us with a false sense of security. How could we possibly prepare ourselves for the critical audience that would sit in silent observation before us? I tried not to think about it, not to let my nerves get out of hand, as we performed our play to near perfection. Olivia was fantastic as Dorothy, as though she were born for the part. Ben was highly amusing as the Great Wizard of Oz, and I was pleased with my own witchy performance as well.

Mrs. Buchannon worked us hard, only offering a ten-minute break when Calvin showed up with snacks and drinks. The class of teenage boys and girls quickly turned into a pack of hungry coyotes ravaging through the bags of junk food. The fresh crackle of soda cans being opened and the crunching of chips and cookies was all that was heard for several minutes as we refueled our hungry stomachs.

We went through the play one more time, this time with Calvin as our audience. Five o'clock came upon us more quickly than expected, and it was time to get dressed and clear the stage.

"Oh my goodness, I'm so nervous! Are you nervous, Addy? I bet you're not, you're so good," Ollie chattered on from behind a curtain.

"Are you kidding? I'm terrified. You're the one who shouldn't be nervous." I wiggled back into my jeans and walked out of our little dressing area. "I'm gonna go help with props."

"Okay. Be out in a minute!" I could hear her questioning the other girls as I left. "Are you nervous, Michelle? I've got these wild butterflies in my stomach. I don't know if I will be able to sleep! What if I forget my lines, or lose my voice during a song or…!"

"Need help with that?" Calvin was attempting to tighten a few screws on a leaning, painted tree.

"That would be great. If you could just hold this up like that. Yeah, thanks." He directed me and began repairing our prop. "You were great out there, Addy, I'm impressed."

"Really? You think so?" I was glad to have an outsider's opinion.

"Yeah, pretty good, Adelaide," Jake, our talented Tin Man had overheard our conversation. He finished tying his shoe and then stood up to look at me. "But, remember, there's no such thing as a good *witch*." He smiled and walked backstage. I stared off after him. Was he attempting an insult or just trying to be helpful in his own awkward sort of way. The way Benjamin sometimes tried "helping" me to see the truth.

I looked back at Calvin who had stopped twisting his screwdriver to watch me. "He is right, you know," Calvin said his words cautiously but with no malice behind them.

"I'd have to disagree on that." I stared up into the fake leaves and hoped this wasn't the beginning of a lecture. "I'm sure many of them have really good hearts." I thought of my dad and the sweet, young Luke. Excluding Adam, my entire coven was well intentioned. Besides, if a witch was what I truly was, for those who insist on labels, then I would consider myself a good witch. I was certainly no Wicked Witch of the North.

Calvin adjusted his position on his knees. "You're probably right, Addy. They might mean well but witchcraft is *never* good. But the truth is, none of us are really good." My eyes widened by his statement. This was new; I thought all Christians claimed to be the "good" people of the world. Calvin looked back down at his work. "We are all sinners, Addy. We all deserve death. The difference is God. God is good. And no, He is not one of many. He is the one and only, the Alpha and Omega. He is our creator, our savior. Through Him we gain our strength, through Him we can be good, we can know how to love and what it truly means to *be* loved."

His words had almost sucked me into their poetic, deceptive theory but I knew better. He couldn't be the only God. Donar was so real, more real than that Christian god ever was to me. "What about Morris?" I asked, defending my side.

Calvin's eyes shot up at me and locked into mine. "What about him?"

"Well, if your god is so powerful and awesome like you say, then how do you explain what happened to Morris? If there aren't other gods than how do you explain the power, the voices, the—"

"What happened to Morris?" Calvin cut me off, his words stained with doubt and confusion.

I leaned in and whispered, "Haven't you noticed how he can barely talk, how he has lost his voice?"

Calvin nodded slowly, probably wondering where I was going with this.

"Well, we did that, we cursed him. *Our* god told us to. He actually speaks to us and helps us," I snarled at him. "So, Calvin, if our god isn't real, then how is it that he can overcome your pastor, a man of the church?"

With the look that covered Calvin's face, you would have thought I just told him I only had six months to live. Some bizarre, twisted mixture of love and pity. "I want you to listen closely, Addy. I'm not at all saying that what you are experiencing isn't real, that the power isn't real. The spirit world is more real than most of us realize, but the thing is…There is God and his angels, and then the devil and his demons. No spirits and gods and goddesses. If you seek power from anywhere but the one true God than that power will come in some nicely disguised package from Satan. And the thing with Pastor Morris, well that was months ago, Addy. He's fine now, he was not 'overcome.'"

"He is?" This caught me off guard. I thought we were meant to make him stop preaching, to stifle his voice.

"Satan is powerful and he can affect our lives, especially if we aren't guarding ourselves with the armor of God. But Jesus is so much more powerful than that. Morris loves God. He spends his time pursuing a relationship with the Lord, reading and praying at home, at church, and throughout his day. That's one tough barrier for the devil to worm his way through. But he finds cracks. That's what he does, he finds our weaknesses. That's why God tells us in the Bible to be watchful because our enemy, the devil, prowls about like a roaring lion seeking whom he may devour."

His words disturbed me to my very core. A lion. How terrifyingly familiar this was to me.

"I'm sure more was intended for our pastor than a short voiceless week. And what Satan intends for evil God can turn to good. He didn't think he would be able to manage a sermon for the following week so he asked if my dad would preach. God really did a lot of healing in my dad that week. It was the first sermon he gave since my mom died. It was amazing, Addy." Calvin's eyes were glossy with emotion. It was obvious how much he loved his father and was happy to see him healing. "It even gave him the strength and determination to start the Bible study and prayer group we are having at the house. And you know what else? That guy you gave your bible to asked Christ to come into his life this week, at our bible study...if you hadn't given him that Bible, if my dad hadn't started this Bible study, he might still be a lost man, miserable and lonely. His story is amazing, Addy. I know he would love for you to hear it. God works in mysterious ways!"

I was speechless and strangely aware of my breathing. It was like the first time you're told that Santa Clause isn't real. I didn't want to believe anything that he had told me, and I didn't know what to make of it or how to process it.

I just stood, silently, supporting the false tree as Calvin tightened the last screw.

"There is so much I want to tell you. So many wonderful things that God has done. Having Him in my life is...well, He's the greatest thing in my life!" Calvin pushed himself up, alight with passion. "Sometimes I don't know how I would survive without Him to help me through my day. With Him, there is no need for fear, Addy. No need to fear this life or the next. Darkness cannot dwell where the light is. Jesus lives in my heart and someday I will live with Him in heaven." Calvin paused and put a strong, brotherly hand on my shoulder. "He can live in your heart too, Addy."

"That's another thing I just don't get. Why would you worship a dead man?" This was something I had wondered about for a long time. It just made no sense.

"Dead? Jesus isn't dead," he said softly.

"Oh come on, Calvin. I heard the story. He was gruesomely beaten and nailed to a cross. Are you telling me that he didn't die?"

"No, he did." He smiled. "But the incredible part is that he arose from his grave, conquering death three whole days later. Has no one ever told you that before?" His forehead scrunched for a moment before he continued his little sermon. "Hundreds were there to witness his resurrection. He is the Son of God, He is God. He came to earth to die for our sins, to die for you, Addy. And that isn't the end of the story…He is coming back one day. A day will come when each and every one of us will have to face judgment."

I had to speak up, I had my beliefs, and I was going to hold on to them and hold on strong. "Is that so? And what will my judgment be? Am I going to hell? Is everyone who doesn't accept your Jesus condemned to eternal torment? Is that what you think?!"

He let his hand fall from my shoulder, sadness filling his annoyingly sincere eyes. "I want you to know that I don't take any pleasure in saying this, but I wouldn't be doing you any favors by lying or sugarcoating it. Jesus said that no man shall come to the father except through Him. He is the way, the truth, and the life. The way to heaven is straight and narrow, Adelaide, so yes, not 'religion' but a relationship with Jesus is the only way, all others lead to hell, no matter how 'good' or 'well intentioned' they may be."

I was furious. What right did he have to make such an outrageous statement? I put my hands on my hips and stood up straight. "What about my dad? You think he is in hell? Is that what you are telling me, Calvin? Well, is it?! He's dead and you want me to believe he is burning in hell?" For the first time over the course of our conversation, I let my eyes wander. We had a small audience, including the two other Tucker siblings, all pretending not to be paying attention as my eyes brushed past them.

"Who told you that?!" Calvin was stunned. "How did you—"

The clanging of the theater door broke the tension and ended our heated discussion.

"James!" I was so thrilled to have a friend among all my foes that I ran down the stage stairs and fell into his arms with a welcoming hug. I didn't care what everyone was thinking; I was safe now.

James held me close for a minute before pulling back to see my face. "Is everything okay, Adelaide?" He read my face like the answer was scribbled into my pale skin. "Did they do something?" He glared up at the crowd on stage.

"It's okay. I just want to go." I tried to pull him toward the door.

"Are you sure? I could—"

"No, let's just leave, please."

"Okay." James took my hand and led me down the aisle. "Are you still up for our date, my lovely Valentine?" he asked.

"Yes." I didn't want to go home and replay the conversation in my mind. For the first time in months I didn't want time to myself. I didn't want the time to allow doubt and uncertainty into my thoughts. I wanted to be distracted, and James was the perfect man for the job.

The date went just as I had hoped. James took me to the nicest restaurant in Ledo, which truly wasn't that extravagant but quaint and romantic just the same. Thoughts of Ben were inevitable, but I forcefully shoved them away. I couldn't think of Ben without thinking of church, God, and all my friends and family with annoying preaching habits.

We talked and laughed over a small flickering candle, keeping me satisfyingly distracted. Whenever a moment of silence came, my mind was quick to betray all my efforts of forgetting Calvin's unsettling words. I tried to keep the voids filled with excessive talking or asking James questions about himself so that I could focus in on him.

The more James talked, the more I envied him. If only I could have his convictions; his strong, unwavering faith. He couldn't be swayed; unaffected by the world. I was like a reed swaying side to side whenever a wind came by. Sure, I ultimately was able to keep my roots planted, but I was too easily affected by the breeze of doubt; fear and concern my constant companions.

I didn't even want to talk to James about what Calvin had discussed with me. I wanted to erase it from my mind. I wanted to get swept up into the choices that I had made for myself; get lost in the excitement of power and knowledge, get lost in the world where my father lived on, waiting to speak to me again. I wanted to get lost in the dark, enticing eyes that stared at me from across the table.

James kept my thoughts occupied until we pulled up in front of my house and he said good-bye. I instinctively panicked, knowing that I would be left alone in my room with unwanted thoughts and the high possibility of another nightmare.

"Is everything okay?" James pulled me out of my inner panic. "I was saying good night and you just zoned out."

"Oh, sorry."

"No, problem. You seem kind of bothered about something tonight." He turned sideways to face me, resting an arm across the steering wheel. "Is it me?"

"You? No, not at all. It's just…people." I didn't want to explain in detail.

"Yeah, I know. People are uncomfortable by what they don't understand. You can't let them get to you though."

"How do you do it, James? How do you not let anything phase you?"

He chuckled. "You just over think everything too much. You need to let go, Addy. You can't be in control of everything. Sometimes you try too hard to take life by the horns and you just need to let yourself get scooped up and enjoy the ride. Don't try to make sense of every ones personal opinions. Just stick to your own. Follow your heart. Focus on the truth rather than analyzing all the lies that come your way."

I offered an interested smile as I soaked up his words of wisdom.

"Your smile is incredible." James lowered his voice to a husky whisper.

I stared back at him in an intense moment of silence before he leaned in so close that I could feel his breath against my blushing cheeks.

"Your lips are amazing." He lightly put his hand against my cheek.

My heart was racing from his touch. Not a thought of unwanted memories passed through my mind.

James leaned in until his lips were pressed to mine. A kiss from my Valentine; this was the ultimate distraction.

19

Fish, Lion and Serpent

My mind was blank for the short duration of time that James and I kissed in the darkness of his Mercedes Benz.

"You probably need to get to bed now," James suggested as he sat back and smiled at me.

I didn't want to go. I didn't want to be alone.

"I really don't want to go to sleep," I whined.

"Nightmares again?"

"Yeah." A dangerous thought came to my mind that I chose not to over think. "Would you come in and try the candle magic with me again?"

The side of James's mouth curved up in a smile. "Are you sure?"

"Yeah, I don't want to be alone."

Before James was able to answer, my cell phone beeped twice—text message. I reached in my pocket and flipped open my phone.

"My mom," I explained.

"Almost home," the text read, sending my mind back into a reasonable thought process.

"I have to go!" I screamed, jumping out of the car and running down the walkway.

"Talk to you tomorrow!" James yelled after me.

My mother returned from the Valentine's Day party that she had attended at Grandpa's house just as I made it into my bedroom.

I had told her that I would be hanging out with friends throughout the evening, which she was fine with as long as I was home before ten. My clock now read ten forty-five! Thank goodness for her technological warning.

I had just slipped into my pajamas when my mother gently tapped on my door.

"Come in." I crawled under my covers.

"Hi, sweetie. How was your evening?" She walked over to my bed.

"Oh, pretty good. The rehearsal went pretty late."

"I wish you would have come to the party. It was fun. Grandpa missed you." She started to walk away.

"Wait, Mom! Are you working tomorrow afternoon?"

"I get off at about two. Why, what's up?"

"Cody asked Ollie to prom, and she wants the three of us to go dress shopping tomorrow. Can we?"

"Well, that would be wonderful. I would love that."

No big surprise there. "Thanks, Mom. Good night."

"Good night." She reached into the pocket of her red wool coat as she turned to leave. "Oh, I almost forgot." She walked back to my bed and handed me a small box. "I found this on the porch earlier. Looks like you have a secret admirer." She wiggled her eyebrows up and down.

"Cool," I said casually but was overwhelmed with curiosity. "Good night."

"Okay, good night." She smiled, taking the hint. "Love you."

When my mom had left, I examined the little white box that was tied with a tiny pink ribbon. A small tag was attached to the ribbon with my name written across it.

I excitedly untied the ribbon and lifted the lid. Not at all what I was expecting, but I was thrilled to see it; my tiny hand-carved wooden fish that Benjamin had given me for Christmas! What a relief.

As I tied it around my neck, I concluded that the not-so-homeless homeless guy must have returned it to me. I was glad to have it back. I had so much guilt over losing it.

I lay in bed that night rifling through the mess of words that Calvin had heaped upon me, exactly what I didn't want to do. I tried to focus on other things as I drifted off to sleep clenching tightly onto my long lost fish, wondering at its meaning, something which I was soon to find out.

* * *

"I hope they still have my dress!" Ollie announced as we walked into the small boutique with my mother the next day.

School was the same old same old that Friday. I ignored Ben and Ollie until it was safe to do otherwise, but I soon had to admit to James that my mother wanted to take Olivia and me shopping. He gracefully smiled, but I could see the hatred burning in his eyes. James wasn't fond of any Christians, but he despised the Tuckers most of all. I was just glad that he didn't make a problem of it.

My mother picked us up after school beaming with excitement and an excessive buildup of chatter that had been waiting for Ollie's eager ears. The two talked back and forth nonstop until we reached our destination.

The store held a sundry of beautiful gowns, shoes, and accessories. Ollie ran straight to a rack and found her, already selected, prom dress. She had been waiting all year for this day.

"They have it!" she squealed.

"Is it the right size?" My mom examined her selection.

"Yes! I'm going to set up a dressing room, Addy, and then I'll come back and help you pick one out."

It took us about fifteen minutes of slow, hard searching before we found three lovely dresses for me to try on.

"Wow!" I could hear my mom exclaim as Ollie showed off her dress.

I grinned at their enthusiasm, slipping the straps of my first dress over my shoulders.

"Come out, Addy!" Ollie called.

"Okay." I pushed back the curtain of my dressing room and walked out onto the large round platform that was half surrounded by mirrors.

Olivia was twirling back and forth critiquing her reflection. "Oh, Ollie I love it!" I watched her swoosh her beautiful lavender ball gown back and forth.

Ollie stopped her movement and stared back at me. "Oh my gosh, you look incredible!"

"Sweetie! You look fantastic! So grown up...too grown up. Oh, I love it. What do you think?" My mom was literally sitting on the edge of her seat.

I turned to see myself in the mirror. The dress was amazing, exactly what I wanted. It was a dark blue satin with a black lace overlay and sprinkled with stone studded embroidery. It looked like starry diamonds in the midnight blue sky. The bodice hugged my slender figure with a sweetheart neckline and crisscross straps that laced up my bare back. The dress flowed all the way to the floor with the smooth, graceful movements of pouring water.

"It's absolutely perfect," I said confidently.

"I think so too," my mom said. "But are you sure you don't want to try on the others?"

"I'm sure."

"Good. Let me go find you two some heels!" My mom got up from her chair and skipped off to the other side of the store.

I was admiring my dress in the mirror when I noticed Ollie staring at me awkwardly.

"What's up, Ollie?" I turned to meet her gaze.

She walked over to me and grabbed my arm. "What's this?" She was examining the branded scar upon my forearm.

"Nothing!" I pulled my arm away. How did I forget about the mark? I could only hope my mom had not noticed it.

"Hey, calm down. I love you no matter what. You don't have to lie about it." Her big blue eyes were filled with love and understanding.

I sighed. "You're such a good friend, Ollie. I don't deserve it." I lifted the bottom of my dress and sat down on the edge of the platform.

Ollie walked over and carefully sat down next to me, surrounded by the poof of her gown. Like a wide-eyed baby bird peeking out of her lavender nest, she stared expectantly at me.

"It's the mark of Donar," I said, wondering at the hint of shame in my voice.

"Oh. Does that mean...are you like, fully sworn in, or whatever it is you do?"

"No, not fully. Not yet."

Olivia forced out a smile. "Well, looks like it hurt."

"It really did." I laughed. "What am I going to do though?"

"What do you mean?"

"I can't let my mom see this, and I really don't want Ben to be haunted by it during the dance either."

"Yeah that is a problem. Guess you better get one of those long sleeve, pilgrim-type dresses." She giggled.

"Not funny! I'm seriously worried about this now."

Ollie grinned at me. "Wait here." She hopped up and disappeared amongst the racks of hanging formal wear.

It only took her a minute to come hopping back with my solution. "Here" She handed me a pair of black satin, elbow-length gloves.

"Ollie, you're brilliant!" I stood up and threw my arms around her.

She laughed. "Don't suffocate me before I get a chance to go to prom!"

I released her and slipped on the smooth gloves.

"Do they fit?" she questioned.

"Like a glove." I smiled gratefully at her.

"I got some too, so no one gets suspicious." She winked at me. "You better be more careful though, if you don't want your mom to see it."

My mom soon returned with a pair of silver high heels for Ollie and black satin heels for me. It was all so perfect, and Olivia's excitement for prom was rubbing off on me.

"Oh, May is so far away!" Ollie complained as we made our purchases. "I wish prom was tomorrow!"

"It gives us something to look forward to," I tried to console her. "Besides, our play is tomorrow."

"Ah! Don't mention it. I'm so nervous I'm trying to pretend that it's a long way away so I don't have to be freaking out yet." She laughed at herself and thanked the lady for having the dress in her size.

"Olivia Tucker, you have nothing to freak out about. I've heard you two practicing and you are both incredible. Don't let fear ruin the experience for you. Jesus offers peace that passes our understanding. Just ask him, sweetie, and let him calm your heart." My mom smiled at Ollie and brushed the blond waves of hair from her face.

"You're so right, Ms. Dawson. Thank you!" Olivia hugged my mother and despite the mention of their god, I had to smile. Ollie was starving for a mother's influence; hungry for that tender love and kindness that only mothers seemed to have perfected. Even though it was through my mom, I felt that my life had something to offer my sweet, young friend; something more precious than a million fancy ball gowns hanging in the closet.

"Are you nervous too, Addy?" My mom glanced at me over the top of the light head of hair.

"A bit."

"We could all go to the house and pray about it together," she spoke softly as Ollie released her hold.

"Oh, that's okay. I'm fine really." I tried not to show how repulsed I was by her suggestion.

My mom looked at me with a funny smile. "Honey, is that a fish hanging from your neck?"

My hand instinctively touched the wooden figure. "Yeah, it was a gift from Ben."

Ollie smiled. "And he thought you never wore it."

I glanced away nervously.

"And you're okay with it?" My mom seemed surprised.

"Yeah," I said hesitantly. "Ben and I are really close, and we *are* going to prom together. Should I not be okay with it?" I was confused by her question.

"No, I think it's great. That's very special and meaningful." She held the fish between her fingers and examined it with a smile.

Yeah, what was that meaning anyway? For the life of me I couldn't figure out what a fish meant to either one of us.

"Have you looked it up?" my mom asked, with a glimmer of excitement in her green eyes. "The verses, Psalm 91:9–16," she read and let my fish fall back against my skin.

Of course it was from the Bible! I should have known.

"No, I haven't looked it up yet," I admitted.

"Aren't you curious?" My mom asked as we scooped up our belongings and walked out of the store together.

"I guess."

Ollie and I scooted into the backseat of our Chevy Traverse. "I can't believe you haven't looked it up after all this time," Ollie stated, buckling her seat belt while still clutching onto the garment bag that held her new dress.

Give me a break. I had no idea what it meant until just a minute ago, although saying that now would make me feel rather lame. But still, a fish?

"Why a fish, Ollie?" I whispered to her as my mom started the engine.

"It's a symbol to recognize Christians." She lowered her voice even more. "Kind of like that hammer on your arm."

Oh shoot! My arm bore the mark of Donar and around my neck was bound the sign of Christ and the scribbling of His word. This was hypocrisy if I ever saw it.

"I love those verses," Ollie stated, raising her voice to normal.

"Really, can you remember them?" my mom asked hopefully.

"I think so. Dad had us memorize it last year. Let's see if I can remember." Ollie stared hard at the back of the seat and cleared her throat. "If you say, 'The LORD is my refuge,' and you make the Most High your dwelling, no harm will overtake you, no disaster will come near your tent." She paused and bit her lip in contemplation. "For he will command his angels concerning you, to guard you in all your ways; they will lift you up in their hands, so that you will not strike your foot against a stone. You will tread on the lion and the cobra; you will trample the great lion and the serpent. 'Because he loves me,' says the LORD, 'I will rescue him; I will protect him, for he acknowledges my name.'" Ollie smiled and took a deep breath. "'He will call on me, and I will answer him; I will be with him in trouble, I will deliver him and honor him. With long life I will satisfy him and show him my salvation.'"

My mother applauded her memory as I sat in horrified silence. Why was it that whenever someone quoted the Bible to me, it was as though the words were sharply written to pierce through my heart. Each word she spoke branded itself upon my mind. *"Trample the great lion and the serpent"*? What a strange statement. These two creatures were a common theme that tormented my subconscious through nightmares and visions. How I would like to tread upon them and trample over them, to be loved and protected. What deliciously, deceptive words their god offered.

The fish hung heavy around my neck throughout the next day, pulling with it perfectly verbatim words from my head; words I didn't want echoing in my thoughts. I don't know why I didn't just take it off. I told myself that Ben had to see me wearing it at least once before I removed the enemy's hold around my throat.

I arrived at the school around five o'clock, anxious and ready for the play to begin. Mr. Tucker, Calvin, and Benjamin were moving props about the stage, following the orders of Mrs. Buchannan.

"Hey, it's Addy!" Calvin spotted me as I wandered down an aisle.

I frowned and waved politely, hoping to avoid Calvin as much as possible. Ben and his dad greeted me just as enthusiastically as I walked up the steps and joined them on the stage.

"You're here a little early, Miss Dawson," Mrs. Buchannan observed.

"I thought you might need some help." I avoided eye contact with the three working men next to me. I think I would have cracked if I had to hear one more sermon from any of them.

Our teacher adjusted the red glasses that rested atop her small nose. "That's wonderful of you, Adelaide. What I really need is to get a hold of Bryan. Ben has tried calling his cell phone and his house. He should have been here..." She paused in her stressful venting as we all turned at the sound of a slamming door. "Oh thank goodness. Bryan Evans! I was beginning to think you were going to bail on us. Meet me up at the sound booth. We have so much to go over!" She scurried away behind the curtain.

I could understand her concern. Bryan was our sound technician, and without sound effects, the play would be like a bad soap opera that only airs past midnight. He was critical to our success.

"Hey, Bryan," I greeted him as his legs sluggishly pulled him to the stage.

"Umm," he grunted at me, forcefully rubbing his temples.

"Everything okay there, Bryan?" Ben walked over to us.

"I haven't been feeling too good lately. I have had this awful headache, a week straight now, and I can't get any sleep. Sometimes the pain is so unbearable I want to…ugh, I just can't stand it." Bryan scrunched his face while grasping his head in both hands.

"That's horrible, man. Have you taken something for the pain?"

Bryan nodded. I reached out to touch his shoulder, but he jerked away from me.

I shot my eyes down and examined the tiny cracks in the wooden floor, feeling uncomfortable at the awkward moment. Ben reached over and touched the back of my hand to comfort me.

"You really had the boss freaking out on you. Glad you made it though." Ben was referring to Mrs. Buchannon. Most of the boys in the class had come to give her this name during the last month of chaos and commands.

"I completely forgot." Bryan's bloodshot eyes were half closed in a tight, wrinkled look of fear and concern with a light coating of exhaustion brushed across his face.

"Forgot what?" I asked.

Bryan didn't look at me but talked straight to Benjamin. "I forgot I was supposed to be here. I've been forgetting a lot of stuff." Now he chose to shoot a glance at me, throwing daggers along with it.

Ben looked at me too. What was this? Did they think that I somehow had something to do with his issues?

My mouth parted slightly as I slowly realized that perhaps I was, in some way, inadvertently, involved by association. Maybe these symptoms that he was experiencing was a form of justice upon him; his curse for his bullying actions.

"I'm really sorry, Bryan. What do you think is wrong?" Ben's face displayed genuine concern.

Bryan avoided eye contact with me as he opened his mouth to speak but was interrupted by the loud frantic yelling of our teacher.

"Bryan! I thought you were coming! Stop chatting and get up here!" Her voice echoed in the auditorium like a bird screeching through a canyon.

Bryan grimaced and trudged away.

Benjamin suddenly smiled. "Nice necklace."

"Thank you. A wonderful friend made it for me." I slipped out of my jacket, sheepishly avoiding eye contact.

"Do you know what it means?" Ben stepped closer to me to examine his handy work.

Oh, now he wants to fill me in on the puzzle. A little too late, buddy. "Lions and serpents," I repeated the two words that rested heavily upon my mind.

Ben chuckled. "Yeah."

Excitement was high when the play began at our scheduled time of 7:00 p.m. My mother, along with what seemed to be half the town of Ledo, was attending our performance.

Everything was moving along beautifully. Ollie sang "Somewhere Over the Rainbow" with a moving passion, her house was dramatically swept up in a tornado, and the munchkins joyfully sang "Ding Dong the Witch Is Dead."

20

Bloody Debut

I stood on that stage proudly adorned in a giant pink ball gown, wand in hand, pretending as though my audience was nonexistent. "What a smell of sulfur! I'm afraid you've made rather a bad enemy of the Wicked Witch of the West. The sooner you get out of Oz, the safer you'll sleep, my dear."

Ollie clenched her fists and stood on the tips of her ruby slippers as she spoke. "Oh, I'd give anything to get out of Oz altogether—but which is the way back to Kansas? I can't go the…"

Dorothy went silent as a burst of noise overpowered the entire room. Wind and thunder howled and boomed as the lights flashed with an imitation of lightening. It was as though we were suddenly dropped in the dark eye of a storm. We all stared in confusion, murmurs trickling through our windless tornado. Something had gone wrong, very wrong. Bryan, our sound technician had either seriously messed up…or—my eyes widened as I remembered his unusual behavior earlier. Maybe he passed out onto the sound board… or worse!

Before any of us could make a decision for action, Bryan stumbled onto the stage, clutching his head in both hands, and yelling into the ferocious sound effects, "Make it stop! Please, stop!"

The cast was frozen in place—horrified, confused, and concerned—as Bryan wandered across the stage, now grasping his hair in his fists and crying in pain. He bumped into several munchkins and the green-faced wicked witch before he tripped and landed with a loud crash into our fake fountain.

The fountain had been Mrs. Buchannon's favorite prop of Munchkinland. Beautifully done with thick cardboard painted to look like built up stones and mirror fragments to reflect the crisp clarity of water. Bryan's splash was a rather painful shattering of glass. He moaned as he bent over on his knees, surrounded by the shimmering shards of water. Tears fell onto his own broken reflection as a shriek of pain burst out of him.

"I can't take it anymore. Make it stop! Make it stop!" he whimpered as I awoke from my shock and took a few steps in his direction, hoping to comfort him in his misery, but I hadn't moved quickly enough.

I gasped, as did others when a flash of lightning shimmered off the seven years of bad luck grasped tightly in his raised hand. Thunder cracked and roared as he desperately pulled the sharp edge of glass down into his gut.

"Stop!" I screamed, reaching his side as he pulled the bloodied weapon from his abdomen, intending to strike again. Instinctively, I grabbed the dripping mirror in my own hand, hoping to stop his suicidal act of desperation. Not the wisest method of choice, but I was successful.

Bryan cried out in pain, now clutching onto his stomach as he curled up on the floor. My own whimpers were intermixed amongst the tempest sounds as I slowly loosened my grip on the glass, allowing it to fall hard onto the wooden floor; my own hand now gushing with blood.

I knew that some gears were off track in my overly productive imagination but the next clap of thunder sounded like a deep throaty laugh rolling in above our heads and despite the darkness and crowded stage, I felt I was under the close watch of an audience. Something that surpassed merely the lacking condition of light surrounded Bryan, a darkness that would remain even if he were drenched in a high-powered spotlight. I wondered if I was the only one who noticed this thick, heavy presence.

I struggled against my own pain, pushing past the pink overflow of my dress to stop the bleeding from Bryan's self-inflicted wound. With my good hand, I pressed hard against his stomach as I unthinkingly was screaming out for Benjamin.

Every member of the play seemed to be standing around us, but Ben quickly twisted through the crowd to kneel at our side and begin yelling out orders.

"Ollie, go get Addy's mom up here! Jake, call an ambulance, and somebody stop this storm!" He hollered, competing with the unwanted sound effects and blood-chilling screams from Bryan.

My mom was up on stage in less than a minute, dishing out her own commands as she took my place across his crimson-stained abdomen. Blood was pooling beside him and soaking into my extravagant costume; the sight and smell suddenly smacking me with a wave of nausea.

I sat, unmoving amongst the chaos, until the paramedics demanded everyone make room. My mind was whirling but my body, seemingly frozen as Benjamin slid his arms around my waist and pulled me to my feet.

"Come on. There is nothing you can do for him now." Ben held my good hand and pulled passed the velvet curtain and didn't stop until we reached a sink.

"Does it hurt?" Ben gently rinsed away the blood from the sliced flesh of my palm.

His question forced my mind to return to its regularly scheduled program of interaction and logical thinking.

I winced at the sting of warm water flowing over my exposed muscles. "Yes," I whined.

Ben ducked under the sink and started digging through the cupboard for a first aid kit. "That was very brave of you."

I looked down at the back of his head. "I wish I would have known…sooner…before…" A tear slid down my cheek. The images in my mind were unforgettable.

Ben stood up and opened the lid of a red metal box. "Hey, you couldn't have known. No one had any clue what was going on. He's lucky that you stopped him, you might have saved his life, Addy."

"What would cause him to do that?"

Ben stopped applying ointment to my hand and looked straight into my eyes. "You're really not sure, are you?"

I couldn't hold his gaze. Unexpected guilt washed over me. Bryan had been cursed. I couldn't be sure of the details, but I was certain this was his undeserving punishment that he was warned about.

His persistent headache had become extreme; the pain so unbearable he could think of only one escape. There was no way I could have prevented this, no reason for me to beat myself up over it, but the heavy weight of guilt was there nonetheless.

I studied my friend's face as he carefully wrapped a bandage around my hand. This would be his outcome as well, if I were not more careful.

"I'm glad your mom was here tonight," Benjamin commented as we rejoined the crowded auditorium.

I nodded and looked around. "Where is she?"

"She left with the paramedics. She asked me to give you a ride home."

Behind Ben stood six critical members of my own personal audience. They were watching me closely, waiting for me. "No," I said, staring straight at James. I walked right past Benjamin and summoned the strength to face my unregretful mistake. I had interfered with their work, but I was certainly not sorry for it.

"Are you okay?" Charles asked, examining my bloodstained body and bandaged hand.

"I suppose." I stared unblinkingly back at their unhappy faces.

My eyes rested upon James who stared past me, no doubt at Ben who was likely watching me in confusion and hurt, a look I didn't care to see.

"We need to discuss some things." James still did not meet my eyes.

"First off, Adelaide, it was not our intention to ruin your play," Charles said. "But you should not have intervened."

"You not only have gone against us but you have been spreading your devotions, stretching the limits," Adam chimed in, his voice hissed with accusation. "Don't think we haven't noticed. Your loyalties are not where they should be."

"Your ceremony is not for a couple months, but we don't like what we see. It needs to stop. We need you to make a choice," Sasha spoke softly but firmly.

James looked at me now. "This is the life you want, isn't it, Addy? The power, the knowledge, the unity, purpose and meaning, not to mention the chance to communicate with your father. Are you willing to give all that up to be trapped in a meaningless, monotonous life? Isn't this what you want? You can't have both worlds. It just isn't that simple. A choice must be made. Are you sure you want to accept your legacy? Is this really what you want, Adelaide? Because I'm not so sure anymore. Isn't this life better than what you had before you ever met us? Isn't this what you want?" He lightly ran his finger down my arm, leaving behind a trail of goose bumps.

It was true, I wanted that life. I couldn't imagine giving it all up. How could I return to my sad and empty existence? My own desires were a factor, but it was the fear for my friends that overruled any doubt. "Yes. Yes it is. I'm sorry for not seeing the damage that I was causing."

My gaze locked with Luke's. A strange glimmer of hope seemed to distinguish as I gave my answer. He stuffed his hands in the pockets of his khaki pants and let his eyes slowly drift away from mine.

"You see, all we had to do was ask," Rachael chirped, happily.

I had an uneasy feeling, but this was the choice I wanted to make, the choice I knew was coming, the choice that hurt me deeply.

Without a glance at Benjamin, we all walked out of the school, everyone seemingly happy with our discussion. James gave me a ride home, risking the filth of my dress upon his leather seat. I was thankful that he didn't keep me any longer than was necessary to reach my house, allowing me to get right to business.

I used up every last drop of hot water, standing under the splash of cleansing comfort. It was disturbing to watch the water wash across my arms and intermix with the dried blood, turning the water red. Images of Bryan's desperation flashed through my mind, leaving me with a feeling of unease.

Blood had somehow managed to crust into my hair as well. It took several soapy washes before I felt worthy of crawling into my flannel pajamas and drifting into my world of nightmares. That night was the worst yet. Some people say that dreams are symbolic, but what exactly would a lion sinking its teeth into my flesh represent?

The beast ripped into my left shoulder, just above my heart, covering the ground with steaming blood. I was able to break free but the lion readily crouched, its black eyes full of hunger. I tried to stand but the weight around my neck held me firm on my knees. The fish still dangled below my throat. I slowly lifted my arms behind my neck and released my ties with the Christian carving. I saw that the lion's eyes followed the fish as it fell from my neck, its intent no longer upon me. "Is this what you want?" I picked up the necklace from the sticky, wet grass where it had fallen. I tossed it away from me and watched the lion pounce and rip into it.

When I awoke, my whole body ached as though I had really been attacked by a dangerously fierce creature. I moaned as I sat up and tried to shake off the disturbing feeling. The wooden gift bounced against my skin as I rubbed my eyes. I quickly tore it from my neck, not taking the time to untie the knot and threw it in my waste basket. It was nothing but trouble, and its maker was truly out of my life now.

The moment had come for me to move on, but not until I made a quick check on Bryan Evans. The mental recordings of him plunging the glass into his stomach were too much for me to overcome. I had to see him again in order to move past it all.

I quickly got dressed in time to catch a ride to the hospital with my mom.

"Don't look so worried, Addy. I'm going to be fine and will be able to return to school in a few weeks, which is really good. I freaked out when I thought I might not be able to graduate on time. I don't want to stay in Ledo any longer than I have to." Bryan adjusted himself on his hospital bed.

"That's what you are worried about?" I laughed, thankful there was no blame in his voice.

"Well, yeah. I'm pretty embarrassed too. Quite the show I put on, I imagine." He had an awkward smile on his face. "Thanks for… you know, stopping me."

I nodded. "You look like you are still in pain."

"I am. This headache is worse than anything I have ever experienced. And they even have me on all sorts of stuff for the pain."

"I'm really sorry, Bryan."

"I know you are."

I sat and talked with him for several minutes before he informed that Pastor Morris and the Tuckers were on their way. I decided it was time for me to make my leave.

I had a feeling that the strange events of last night were a memory neither of us would soon forget. The sounds, the smells, and worst of all, the sights. A memory that kept my actions in check from then on.

That next week I returned to ignoring my friends, but I soon felt free of the inner struggle and tug-of-war that fought for my heart and soul. I was almost glad to be moving on from living my double life and in no time I would be reunited with my father.

Bloodstains removed and a new sound technician found, our play continued the following weekend without interruption. Off stage, Ben and Olivia didn't even try to speak to me, which made things simpler, although a twinge of pain struck the cords of my heart as I realized they had given up on me.

The sun was soon shining again as was the possibilities of my future when I received my acceptance letter to Princeton. Not the direction I would have chosen for myself but perhaps that was only because I wouldn't have been able to even consider it without the Roth's generosity. James and I would begin growing a whole new branch of the tree, another coven to live in the truth of our ancestors. But in the meantime I had to worry about keeping up my grades until graduation.

It was the middle of April when some disappointing news was brought to me.

"The night of your Commitment Ceremony has been chosen," Charles informed me.

Our coven sat in the basement of the library. Everyone became quiet as Charles spoke.

"May 17. A night of a full moon is always selected for initiation rituals. This is the last one before graduation. The perfect time." He smiled but I reserved my excitement.

It wouldn't have been a problem except for one thing. It extinguished my last ember of connection with Benjamin. May 17 was the night of junior/senior prom.

"Can I choose another night?"

James frowned. "What for? This is the right night for it, Adelaide. Trust us."

"But this is *my* initiation, and I have the choice to do things my way, right?" I had been waiting anxiously for the day of my ceremony to come, but I hated to break my promise; and besides, it would be a shame to let my gorgeous dress go unworn.

This argument lasted several minutes, but I was adamant and despite their displeasure they couldn't deny that I had the right to decide for myself. It was settled but not exactly agreed upon that I could attend prom with Benjamin, as long as this was my absolute last interaction with him. James was quite bitter but as a group they seemed to understand my need to keep my promise. I would have to wait another month for a full moon and May 17 supposedly was chosen for me by divine spiritual seeking but no matter how long we discussed the issue we still ended on the truth that it was ultimately my choice.

James was truly disapproving of my brave and firm stance, but he was feeling more secure in my devotions, as was I. After the nightmare with the lion, my dreams just ceased, leaving me with the feeling that I had finally done the right thing, eliminated the enemy. Perhaps it was my subconscious torturing me as I allowed doubt and troubling influences into my life or perhaps it was shunning Yahweh completely out of my life that brought relief.

Enough time had gone by that I felt Benjamin was safe and one last evening should bring him no harm. The only question was, did Ben still want me as his date? In retrospect, I had not been a good friend to him, and I couldn't blame him if he wanted nothing to do with me.

I didn't get up the courage to talk to him until two weeks before the big day.

I waited for drama class when we would have more time to talk. So close to graduation, Mrs. Buchannon decided to turn the remainder of our classes into a work period as we studied for finals and worked on essays but mostly just talked and goofed around, the excitement nearly uncontainable among the seniors in the class.

I took an empty seat next to Benjamin who was laughing and talking with the highly entertaining Jake Stockton.

"Excuse me, Ben. Can I talk to you?" I said quietly.

Ben and Jake both stared at me, attempting, but failing to hide their shock. It was likely just my imagination but the lively room seemed to pause for a moment as I spoke my first words to Ben since the last performance. I hadn't really spoken to anyone in the class since then either, so I could see how this may have grabbed their attention.

"Okay," Ben said, still unrecovered from his surprise.

I looked around at everyone, mentally telling them to mind their own business. When they quickly went back to whatever they were doing, I turned to Benjamin.

"Prom is coming up." My heart pounded with the possible fear of his rejection.

"Yeah." He frowned slightly.

I forced a hopeful smile. "A promise is a promise." I gave him the phrase I had said many times before regarding our May date.

Ben's brows furrowed. "You still want to go with me?" He had dipped every word into a bucket of confusion before pulling it out for me to hear.

I clenched my teeth together and nodded.

His lip twitched with a hidden desire to smile. "I don't get it."

"It wasn't nice of me to ignore you again, I know, but we could spend one last evening together before we go off to college." My voice was beginning to sound desperate.

"Where are you going?" His face was still cold with doubt.

"What?"

"College. Where are you going?" he questioned again.

"Princeton, I think. What about you?" I answered, slightly annoyed at the rabbit trail that we had taken.

Ben's eyes widened at my answer, but he didn't comment. "Washington University. Calvin went there for a few years."

He wasn't warming up to me yet.

"That's great." I took a breath in and tried again. "So how about it?"

"You *really* want to go with me?" He was having a hard time accepting it. "Did something happen? Are you still…" He thought for a second, brows furrowed once again. "Can we talk again?"

I looked down at my nicely manicured fingernails. "No, nothing has changed, it's just…well, the honest truth, Ben, is that I am supposed to have an important ceremony that same night, and I am willing to put it off if you still want to go to prom with me. But no more than that, everything else remains the same. I know I don't have any right to ask that of you, I know you've given up on me—"

Ben quickly cut me off. "I haven't given up on you!" The hard lines of his face melted. "Sure, I'm not happy with you, but we all still love you, Addy. We pray for you all the time. We haven't given up, just…backed off. You're really stubborn." He laughed. "I think God is the only one who can get through to you."

I smiled.

"Okay, Addy, I'll go to prom with you, especially if that means more time for…well, for God to work in your heart."

"Well, I'm not sure about your reasoning, but I'm glad you accept."

"So, I guess I'll pick you up at seven, two weeks from tomorrow."

"Okay." A simple word but there was great gratitude in my voice. Not the way I had pictured it, but I really wanted to go to prom. And I really wanted to go with him.

"So, no more talking until then?" Ben asked skeptically.

"That's right," I whispered as I flipped open my notebook.

I tried studying for the remainder of class, but my mind wandered in daydreams instead. The unimportant dream of a silly little girl that was buried deep within was bubbling up with excitement.

Exactly two weeks and one day later, my mom was pulling curlers out of my hair and drenching the silky swirls in hair spray. We were both bouncing with excitement. My grandpa waited patiently in the living room with his newly purchased disposable camera as my mother artistically applied my makeup after I had slipped into my starry blue gown.

"You are breathtaking, my sweet baby girl, absolutely breathtaking," my mom said, stepping back to examine her work.

I could hear the faint sound of knocking and my grandpa shouted, "He's here!"

I held my breath and my mom gasped in excitement. I was sure this would be a night to remember, but I had no idea it would be the most important night of my entire life—a night to trump all others.

21

Prom

I ran to the living room where Benjamin was greeting my grandfather with a handshake. Ben turned to stare at me, his mouth slightly parted in a look of awe. "Wow, Adelaide, you look incredible." He slowly walked over to me.

"Thanks, Ben, you look great too." I smiled kindly at him, trying very hard to keep my heart rate down as he pulled my arm up and slipped a lovely white orchid corsage over my wrist.

"I know how you like your orchids." He winked at me, still holding my arm. The first time Ben and I had ever met I had shoved a pot of planted orchids into his face, so I could see the sweet humor in this.

Grandpa stood behind Ben, generously snapping pictures of the moment. In all the excitement I had overlooked a very small yet important detail to my ensemble. I probably wouldn't have remembered if Ben hadn't brought it to my attention as it was suddenly brought to his.

His left hand remained, clutching to my arm, as he brought his other hand up to trace a purposeful scar upon my bare forearm. His eyes slowly pulled up and locked into mine. He didn't speak, just looked at me with unnecessary sorrow lining the features of his face.

I was quickly aware of my mother standing behind me and the dangerous visual proximity of our white-haired photographer.

"I forgot my gloves!" I held my arm and ran down the hallway past my mom, wondering if she had already noticed.

"And your heels!" My mom laughed as I turned into my bedroom.

Gloved and shoed, Benjamin and I were able to leave after another twenty or so photos were snapped. He assisted me into his heated truck, and we had a very strange and tense drive together. Ben tried to get me talking, but things were so different between us I wasn't sure how to act.

White columns welcomed us in through the front door as we pushed through a sea of silver stars and balloons floating about our heads. The prom theme this year was "A Moment in Time." The high school gymnasium was creatively decorated accordingly with old light posts and large, old, analog clocks set to the midnight hour. Whitish blue fabric was draped about in a decorative fashion with a bluish light resting softly throughout the dim dance floor.

"This is awesome!" I said excitedly, taking in this special moment in *my* time.

"Adelaide!" Ollie skipped over to me, pulling Cody along behind her. "You look great!"

"Thanks, Ollie, you too." It felt strange to be talking again, but I tried to act as though nothing had ever come between us.

"Well, should we all wander over to the drink table?" Cody suggested, looking very sharp in his black suit, a touch of lavender in his tie and vest to match his date.

My date was also dressed to match. We hadn't discussed it so assumed Olivia had filled him in. He wore a nicely fitting black tux and dress shirt with a dark blue vest. He looked so handsome, flawless in my eyes. He was like the handsome prince that every girl dreams of but usually never finds and here he was, at my side, watching me with adoration. This life was full of cruel tricks.

Everyone agreed to the drinks and we kicked our way through a balloon covered floor until we reached the designated table. Juniors and seniors excitedly greeted us, every girl making the necessary complement to each other's dresses.

Fifteen minutes later, Ben was able to pull me onto the dance floor for our first dance of the night. Benjamin was his usual easygoing self, and he made every moment fun and enjoyable. I had feared things would remain awkward between us, but it really wasn't, at least not once I was mentally able to overcome my own concerns that it would be.

"It seems like forever ago that I asked you to be my date to this thing," Ben said, the touch of his arms around me leaving my crumbled, stone heart feeling dangerously oowey goowey.

"It does, doesn't it?" I studied his face, wondering why I let myself do this. Was a fun night at prom worth the pain of ripping myself away from him again?

He smiled down at me—yes, yes, it was worth it.

"Are you okay?"

"Yeah, I'm good," I replied.

The song came to its end, forcing us to take a step back from each other.

"How about a snack?" Ben shouted as a rowdy song blasted over the speakers.

I nodded and was guided through a well-dressed crowd. Ben had me take a seat as he retrieved a plate of food for us to share.

"They really went all out on the food." Benjamin sat down beside me in a plastic blue chair.

"I can see that." The plate mainly consisted of pretzels, potato chips, and celery sticks.

After a few bites, Ben revived the conversation. "Are you having fun?"

"Oh, yeah, loads of fun," I answered honestly.

"What was your ceremony going to be for?" Ben's words made a big splash into the still waters of my mind.

"My final commitment ceremony." I looked at him, surprised that he wanted to talk about it.

"Like an initiation?" He raised his voice above the noise.

"Yeah, exactly." We were easily talking about this as though we were discussing homework, it didn't seem right to me.

"Are you happy about that decision?" There was no judgment in his voice.

"Yes." My voice, however, was full of skepticism. Was there a sermon to follow this conversation?

Ben rested a rough hand against my soft cheek. "You were meant for great things, Addy, I'm sure of it."

Words caught in my throat. What do you say to that? I wasn't even sure what he meant by it. A simple complement or was he implying that what I was doing was not great and I needed to get on the right track?

I shook it off when he lowered his hand. "Thanks, Ben."

"And I think, right now, that great thing would be to do the chicken dance with me." Smiling, he stood up and took my hand while the corresponding music played.

"Oh no. How about I just watch you do it?" I tried pulling my hand back.

Ben smiled mischievously. "Are you too chicken?"

A short exhale of laughter burst out of me. "Fine."

Head held high, I made my way to the dance floor to participate in one of the most humiliating party rituals.

After a few hysterical minutes of quaking, flapping, and shaking tail feathers, Ben and I fell into each other's arms for another slow dance, trying desperately to stifle our laughter. We twirled slowly and joyfully across the dance floor wishing that this night would never have to end. Cheek to cheek, we swayed as Ben quietly talked to me.

"I told myself that I wouldn't bring this up tonight." Ben sighed. I couldn't see his face but he held me a little tighter. "I wish that you could just take my word for it, I wish that you could know that I'm telling you the truth, I wish you could see it in my life. I don't go to sleep at night in fear. Can you say that?"

I gently tried to pull away in rejection of his words but he arms remained firm.

"My God fills me with joy and peace. What are you filled with, Addy?" His words were soft in my ear. "Life is still hard sometimes, but my Lord loves me and is always there to help me. He loves you so much too. I wish you could see that."

I could hear Benjamin still whispering in my ear, but his words blurred together while another voice dominated my focus. The shrill hissing of the spirit realm demanding my attention; it began with the simple whispers of my name. I tried to ignore it as my date danced me around in his treacherous words. "Adelaide." The invisible messengers clawed their way into my mind. "Adelaide."

"No, not now!" I whimpered as my eyes darted around.

"Okay, I'm sorry. I'm done," Ben apologized to my misdirected complaint.

"Not you, Ben, I…" I winced as the voices got louder and more demanding.

"Come to us, Adelaide. Now is the time. Now!"

I pushed out of Benjamin's arms. His mouth was moving but the words sounded as though they were pushed through water; the music also drowning in its waves. The words in my head were overpowering the tangible and physical world that most ignorantly lived in, never aware of the depths of reality.

"I'm going to the bathroom. I'll be right back, I promise!" I yelled at him through the ocean between us.

I intended to keep that promise too, but as I stumbled into the dark hallway of the school, the torturous whispers had overcome my mental clarity and sane reasoning. They knew what they wanted, and they wouldn't stop until it was theirs—until I belonged to them, belonged to Donar. This night was chosen for me and despite my arguments there was no escaping it. My "Moment in Time" had come to an abrupt end.

I picked up the bottom of my dress and ran down that dirt road beside the school as fast as my high heels would take me. I didn't know what I would do when I reached my destination, I had already denied this full moon of its purpose, but I really had no choice in the matter. The screeching and moaning drove me through that dark forest. I wasn't considering my direction or location as my feet carried me away, but I soon broke from the trees and into a clearing.

"I can offer more than life, Adelaide, just take a bite of my power, sink your teeth into my knowledge. Give yourself to me and you will be free! There's no turning back, now, you already belong to me, just make the commitment, make the sacrifice…" A strong voice echoed behind me, pushing me into the meadow.

"Right on time, Miss Dawson." Adam's emotionless voice was nearly a relief as the other voices finally backed down; their battle was won.

"I'm glad you changed your mind." James walked over to me. He, Sasha, and Adam appeared to be the only ones in the sacred field.

I grabbed James's arm, trying to catch my breath. "You were right, James, it has to be tonight." I could feel my body trembling with exhaustion and fear.

"I'm glad you are seeing things clearly." He wrapped his arm around mine and led me over to a blanket displaying the tools for our ritual. "We should get started. We should have a good ten or fifteen minutes before everyone shows up."

"Everyone? But how did they know that I would be here?" My fear rose as I considered the incomprehensible power of this god, my god.

"We had a good feeling about it. Sasha has already begun casting our circle. I would like for you to prepare and sprinkle the salt." James kneeled down on the blanket and unfolded a white cloth that was softly embracing a golden dagger.

I was familiar with every object on the blanket and had used each of them in the past. I had also been involved in enough circle casting to know what I was doing, only this time I had this strange feeling that I was digging my own grave.

I pulled off my flower and gloves and let them fall carelessly to the ground before I knelt down beside James and took a small bowl of cleansed salt and mixed in purified water. James passed me the dagger to stir the ingredients. Once finished, I took the bowl to the circle outlined in blood across the ground and lightly sprinkled the concoction atop the blood to sanctify the area.

"Salt and water by casting thee, no spell nor evil purpose be, except in true unity with me, and as my will, so it must be," I mumbled, unenthusiastically as I walked clockwise around the ring.

Sasha fallowed behind holding burning sticks of sage above her head. The thick, gray smoke purified and cleansed the circle of unwanted energies and spirits.

With the frightening voices I was beginning to feel the power of our work with a shudder of excitement at the possibilities. My spirits were picking up yet they couldn't fight passed the prickly feeling of unease.

Adam had lit the large fire pits that surrounded the meadow as our company of white-clothed supporters came trickling out of the forest of trees. I recognized nearly every face, including several adults.

Observing our united covens, I whispered to James, "I'm not wearing white."

James smiled. "That's okay. We choose to wear white because it is a combination of all light frequencies. This reflects energy and light. It is traditional for these rituals, but since this is your night you are allowed to make little adjustments. And besides, I think you look wonderful." He eyed my figure wrapped in flowing silk and lace. "Are you ready for this?"

I swallowed hard and nodded. I was ready to dedicate myself, ready to take the next step to talking with my dad again. I was ready. Absolutely no doubt. One hundred percent ready…okay, honestly, it was more like a steadily decreasing forty, thirty, twenty percent.

The circle soon became a round, white wall as I took my place between Charles and James, connecting our union. Viktor Roth stood in front of me, staring straight into my soul as he lightly bound my wrists with a thick white cord.

It had felt like this day would never come and now it was here, and I was spiraling into inner turmoil. I had truly believed that I was ready for this. Maybe it was all nerves, maybe I would feel better once I had made my commitment and all the attention was off of me.

My lines had been perfectly memorized and were sitting on the cliff of recollection waiting for me to push it off. "Donar, I do summon, stir and call you now, to bless this night and guard this circle. Spirits that surround me, I welcome your powers, caress me, carry me, and hold me safe as I journey between the worlds." I tried to make my words sound firm and confident. Closing my eyes and lifting my hands, I slowly continued, trying to focus on who I was addressing. "I am one with the spirits and align myself with Donar. I am here tonight to consecrate myself in his name."

This was it. I would soon be a true child of Donar just like my father. "I vow to honor the Way of the Craft and of my Coven. I vow to walk the path of the witch in honor and courage." My knees buckled beneath the invisible weight of that familiar darkness. My heart stumbled in doubt. *Don't chicken out, Addy!* I screamed at myself inside my head. *Chicken.* I smiled remembering the image of Benjamin flapping his black, cotton wings. Oh, dear God, what if Ben was right! Would a loving god really terrify me so much? Would I feel so twisted inside if I were to follow Jesus Christ?

The unexpected thoughts of doubt quickly sent my body into a full panic mode. Tormenting voices crept back into my mind, trying to frighten me into their grasp. Sadly, it worked.

"I Adelaide, solemnly swear, and in the presence of the Universe, of my own free will, that I will abide by the law and spirit of the Craft." Was it really my own free will? Because it sure didn't feel like it. My voice was shaking as I closed my eyes more tightly, afraid to look around at my witnesses. *Oh God, oh God, oh God!* my heart cried out as my words continued, "To harm none without reason and to hold in shadow our ancient secrets." *Please God, help me!* I pleaded, hoping the right God would hear me. *Donar, if you love me, take away this uncontrollable fear! Jesus...if you love me, please save me!'* There was no way I was getting out of this and the fear did not subside. Wishing with all my might that I didn't have to say these words, I continued, "From this day forth, I shall be a child of Donar."

It felt as though the loose bonds were tightened around my wrist, painfully signifying that I was enslaved to him—the lion, the serpent. Did I do the right thing, or had I just sold my soul to the devil? I exhaled deeply, feeling sick to my stomach.

Viktor slowly unwound my restraints as he spoke, his voice deep and raspy. "The circle is cast. We are between the worlds, beyond the bounds of time and space where night and day, birth and death, joy and sorrow come together as one."

A hissing ached in my ears as I cringed with the feeling of something moving across my skin.

Jesus, I'm...I'm sorry. If You truly are who You say you are...I'm sorry. If you are more powerful than their god, than these dark spirits, then please help me, help me out of this mess! I prayed in desperation, a small feeling of certainty rising up in me, confirming my mistake. I think the spirits, demons, whatever they were, knew my thoughts. My mind had invited their great enemy and attacked me for it. My body shook from the inside as bursts of pain struck my back as though claws were tearing deep into my soft flesh. I wanted to collapse, but I knew that I had to stay strong. I feared the spiteful darkness, but I also feared its followers and I had yet to figure a way out.

"It's too late!" a voice growled in my mind, warning me to forget my hopes for an escape.

James handed me the small wooden bowl that contained an unknown liquid.

"Just taste it, little one. One drink. I can give you more than you can imagine. Just drink!" The enticing whispers and sounds flapped in the cages of my personal thoughts, swaying my mind in a dizzy spell.

I was lying in a bed of snakes, surrounded by a hungry lions—alone and utterly hopeless! One wrong move and there would be a feast on my soul.

I raised the dish above my head with quivering hands and forcefully vomited out the words, "I am a child of Donar. I offer myself to him." *No I don't, no I don't, no I don't!* I cowardly thought to myself as I drank the elixir. The liquid was cool across my lips and tongue but tasted of burnt ashes.

I took a few shaky steps into the moonlit circle and faced the stone alter. Eyes wide, I stared regretfully at my defenseless victim that struggled in its restraints. Its cries had been haunting me through the whole ceremony. A poor innocent lamb lay across the smooth rock, bound with ropes and bleating desperately. The sound sucked my subconscious into the memory of an old nightmare. Wasn't it I that lay dying upon this alter until a poor lamb sacrificed its life for my own? For the first time I was recognizing the symbolism of the disturbing, nonexistent event. Jesus Chris, the Lamb of God, had died for me, to save me. *I believe. I believe that You died on the cross for me. I don't deserve for You to listen to me after all I have done, but I beg you, forgive me, please!* Several tears ran down my tense face as I lifted the dagger that rested beside the white lamb.

What horribly poetic irony.

"This is my sacrifice...and show of loyalty," I spoke softly without a drop of confidence.

I lifted my head and met the threatening gaze of Viktor's dark, knowing eyes. I had no choice. It was me or the lamb. I had to do it.

With that resolve, I held my breath and slid the blade down quickly into the heart of my blood sacrifice.

The creature gave a long and agonizing death cry, synchronizing with the cry of my heart. I felt as though I had pierced the flesh of God himself, that I had personally nailed him to that wooden cross. I was ready to drop to the ground and break into tears. What had I done?!

I felt the drugging effects of the mysterious liquid that I had drank as I watched Charles and Derek pull the lamb off the altar, leaving behind a thin layer of steaming blood.

"And we are your witnesses," the circle recited as one. "Walk with us in spirit, in soul."

Walk? I would rather run, run far away from here.

A warm wind gently kissed my face as I heard a new voice enter my obviously non-restricted thoughts. "I will never leave you or forsake you." The words were comforting as I kicked off my heels and lay down atop the wet stone; a disturbing chant building up around me.

22

The Battle

The stars in the sky blurred together as I lay petrified like a dead fish against the cold stone. The drug felt similar to the cider I had drunk during the winter celebration except in a much higher concentration.

I slowly tilted my head and observed the seated, worshipping wanderers of the unconscious realm. I didn't belong with them, I knew that now, but I didn't see how I had any options. What if the rumors were true, was this an *all or nothing* commitment? Did Satan really want my soul *one way or another*?

I thought back over my past, over every discarded memory that contained the truth of the One True God. Mom had told me several times how to ask Jesus into my heart, and Ben had said that through Him all things are possible. I suppose if He can overcome death, maybe there is a chance He can save me from this circle of hell. With this in mind I prayed once more, as those around me "prayed" to another god. *God, I know that you are a good and powerful God, and I'm sorry for hating You and blaming You for my dad leaving me. Please forgive me of all the awful things I have done and terrible thoughts I have had…please forgive me of…of my sin. I hope it isn't too late. I want You to live in my heart and in my life, even though it will be a pathetic place for You to be right now. Please change that, give me strength and courage and most of all, Jesus, I need a way out. I don't know what to do, please save me, I'm so scared!* Warmth spread over me as I spoke honestly with my new God. Love, safety, and freedom—feelings I had desperately craved to posses now wove themselves into my being. I squirmed slightly, pulling my skin away from the sticky blood upon the rock. I was literally *washed in the blood of the lamb*. I smiled at that thought and realized what I was doing. How could I be smiling at time like this? My life was on the line…but thankfully my soul was not.

A summer breeze rustled through my dark waves of hair bringing with it gentle commands. "Find me, Addy. Find me."

But I thought I already did. The faint words had confused me.

"Find me!" the voice urged, reminding me, once again, of words spoken in distant dreams.

The meadow was filled with the haunting sounds of Germanic mumblings. Nearly twenty dangerous witches sat on the grass surrounding me. Like the stars in the sky, their bodies were blurring together, and I was seeing things that were not there before, hallucinations perhaps. The drink was meant to open you up to the other realm, to allow yourself to be one with the spirits. Dark smoke was weaving between each white figure, encircling it in bondage like a mighty snake constricting its prey. I could hear its evil hissings and whispers taunting me and threatening me to stay where I was. I knew they spoke to individuals of the coven. It was possible that they would communicate my betrayal toward them. Would they make me their next blood sacrifice?

I tried to tell myself to be realistic, but I had personally felt the hate and power emanating from several of these people. I couldn't be sure what they were capable of but my instincts were telling me that I was in great danger. I certainly couldn't just ask to go home now; in fact, I was feeling so incapacitated from the drink I wasn't sure I would be able to walk away even if I wanted to.

"Find me…," The loving voice of Yahweh insisted again.

I pushed myself up to a sitting position, leaning on my blood-soaked hands and looked around. The wall of white, the smoke, the pits of fire; it was all one directionless blur. I didn't know which way was which. *Where are you, Lord?*

I was just about to let myself fall back onto the hard stone when I saw a bright shining cross at the tree line. It must have been the glow of the full moon illuminating a tree but to me, I had just *found Him.*

Okay, now what? They are going to see me, God. What do you want me to do!? My answer came immediately. "Follow me, Addy."

I considered the great possibility of my legs not functioning and falling right on top of Viktor Roth. Doubt and fear consumed my mind until truthful and encouraging words swirled around me, "I will set your feet upon a rock, I will establish your goings." The familiar words that had brought me safely to the sandy beach upon my slippery fall from the icy cliff; Yahweh would protect me as he always has.

I took a deep breath and held it in as I stepped lightly from the alter, the blood-soaked grass squishing between my toes.

I walked lightly across the ground between a literal rock and hard place, the wall that separated me from safety; a wall that formed the ring of my personal little hell, complete with blood, fire, and smoke. I stopped in front of Luke where the swirling smoke seemed to thin out, a weak spot.

Every eye was still closed, and I desperately prayed that it would stay that way. *God protect me!* I carefully scooped up the bottom of my dress and draped it across my arm as I slowly stepped between Luke and Danny, breaking the circle. My wobbly knee lightly bumped against Luke's arm, and I could feel him move but instead of waiting around for his response I obeyed God and followed him, running straight toward the hazy cross.

"You cannot escape me!" hissed an angry voice behind me.

I stumbled passed a fire pit and grabbed onto the first tree I came to. My mind was spinning in-between consciousness, every movement a great physical effort. Clutching my arms around the rough bark of a pine, I turned back to see the dark smoke slithering chaotically disrupting the white shapes. Voices and shouting told me I had to keep moving.

Stumbling across twigs and rocks that broke through the tender skin of my feet, I forced my shaking legs to continue as the yelling came closer and closer. I started to worry when I never came across the dirt road; I was lost in the woods closely followed by a furious tribe of witches, likely with my blood on their minds.

"There is no hope little one! You are mine!" The sudden sharp words in my ear interrupted my momentum, causing me to trip across a tree root and fall hard to the forest floor. I stayed still for a moment, sobbing in fear and pain. I could hear my hunters spread about through the forest, calling my name with such hatred I didn't want to ever move again.

Jesus, I'm lost, I need you. What can I do? I whispered aloud into the darkness.

"Dance with me, Addy," I heard the voice loud and clear.

Dance? Oh, God, this doesn't make any sense to me! Tell me what to do! Tell me which way to go! Please, God, please! I pleaded in my mind.

"Dance with me!" The voice echoed through the trees, startling me. Could the others hear these voices as well?!

I lay quietly for a moment feeling a strange mushy substance beneath my arm. A rotten apple. I could feel several lumps of apples beneath my body, distracting me for just a moment when someone nearby screamed.

"She's over here!"

I dug my hands into a bed of moss and pine needles and pushed myself back on my feet and ran. *Oh God, which way?!* A new sound was intermixed with yelling and hollering that pierced between worlds; demons and humans alike breaking the silence of the forest. But this new noise was an answer to prayer. It was music! You need music to dance! *Thank you, God!* "Run to me, Addy, run!" the command was thickly laced with warning as I turned toward the faint music.

I picked up my speed, pushing past branches and stumbling over my own feet until I broke free from the forest of a betrayed enemy. I was across the street from the school, so without looking back or thinking twice about a plan, I dropped my gown and ran as fast as my poor little injured feet would take me; across the rough pavement and the cold cement. If I could just get to Benjamin, he would know what to do!

ROOTED IN EVIL

Breathing heavily, I burst through the double doors of the gymnasium, abruptly pulling the focus of the room onto myself. I could just imagine my appearance—covered in blood and disheveled with pine needles and twigs sticking from my hair, but I didn't care.

I walked past several classmates, thankful that their faces were too blurry to make out their disapproving and horrified expressions. "Benjamin!" I screamed between breathes. "Ben!"

Head spinning and legs heavy, I collapsed to my knees and cried. "Ben," I whimpered through my sobs as I placed both hands on the cool gym floor trying to hold the world still for a second.

"Adelaide?" I think it was Mark who knelt down beside me. "Oh my gosh, what happened to you?!"

"Benjamin!" I pleaded in response.

"I'll go get him." He bounced up. "Stay here."

Yeah, like that was even an option any more. I let my head hang as I closed my eyes and tried to ignore the harsh suggestions of my peers.

"Look at all that blood?!"

"Do you think she killed someone?" a girl gasped in horror.

"Maybe it's part of one of those crazy witchcraft rituals."

"What if she's hurt? Should we call an ambulance?"

"Witches can heal themselves, don't you know that?" Someone laughed right above me.

"Honey! Where were you?" Ben pushed through the crowd of critical onlookers and gasped at the sight of me. "Oh, Addy, what happened? Are you okay?" He fell on his knees.

I grabbed at the front of his shirt to pull myself into his arms. "They're coming, Ben!" I whimpered.

"But...why?" He held me tightly.

"You were right, Ben, I'm sorry. I was so wrong. I should have believed you! Jesus loves me, I know that now."

Ben's chest moved out as he took a deep breath in. "That's great, Addy."

"Is it too late? They are coming for me, Ben!"

"Sshh, it's never too late, but we should get you out of here." Ben scooped me up into his arms, glowing like a knight in shining armor...literally, he seemed to be letting off this warming light, as did several others scattered throughout the room. I greatly preferred this over the menacing smoke and darkness that surrounded my pursuers.

"Get Cody and Ollie and meet us at the church right away!" Ben ordered Mark.

People continued to conjure up insulting conclusions, some of which were actually not too off base.

We ignored them all as I was swept out of the school and into Ben's old pickup. I stared at him in all his shining glory and wondered if I possessed a glow now, as well. I could feel the distance separating me from the evil darkness that wished to devour me. I had stopped crying and my fear was replaced with a comfortable feeling of safety, despite the high speeds at which we were traveling.

"Are you hurt at all?" Ben questioned.

"Not badly..." I pulled my knees up to my chest and scrunched back the hem of my dress to examine my feet. Distracted by what seemed to be my most important thought I immediately looked back up to Benjamin's face. "Am I glowing, Ben?" I smiled excitedly like an innocent little girl hoping to be told she was truly a princess.

"Glowing? No, but you are beautiful, if that's what you mean... and you smell like apples." He was quiet for a second and then asked, "Are you...drugged?"

I nodded, closing my eyes again. The colors flying by were causing my stomach to clench and turn.

"We're here." Ben quickly hopped out of the cab and pulled me out after him, scooping me into his arms again. "Come on my little, apple pie." He ran toward the brick building

"Do you think...they will...follow us...here?" My words fluctuated with each jogging bounce.

"Yeah, I do." He paused right outside the church door. "There's something I haven't told you, honey. Something I've had to keep from you. I didn't want to. You'll find out soon, but I just don't want you to be mad at me."

I lifted my hand and set it over his shimmering face. "I won't be mad, not at you. I love you Benjamin." I smiled carelessly and tucked my hand back down into my cradled body; my words an embarrassment I would be very slow to realize.

A surprised laugh came out of Ben before he pushed through the doors and made his way to the sanctuary.

I tilted my head to see the glowing figures that filled the room. A hush fell over the crowd as my hero carried me right down the aisle and up to the stage. He gently laid me down on my side with a view of the angelically bright rows of people. I squinted at the fuzzy, mumbling, church attending light bulbs while Ben spoke to the man on stage, presumably Pastor Morris.

The pastor then spoke quickly to the congregation about my sticky situation and told everyone to gather by the stage and start praying. He called it "spiritual warfare." What a perfect description; that's exactly what this was, a spiritual battle with fleshly dangers.

A man knelt down in front of me and touched my shoulder as the comforting sound of prayers filled the church. When my eyes adjusted to his sunshine-like gleam that seemed to be seeping from his heart, I realized that I knew the man. It was the face of a man unseen for many years; a face I had no hopes of seeing again except from the promises of my deceptive enemy. It was the kind face of my father.

"No, no! I'm not supposed to be seeing you!" I shouted at him, horrified to have any part of the devils trickery.

"It's me, baby, your father. I'm sorry I wasn't there for you, but I'm here now." The apparition, hallucination, or whatever he was kissed my forehead, the sensation so wonderfully real upon my skin.

I wanted to embrace him, but I knew this couldn't be reality so I covered my face and prayed.

"It's okay, Adders, nothing bad will happen to you now, I promise." His voice seemed to fade away as I shook my head, praying even harder. I heard the thud of a book flip open against the wooden pulpit beside me and Pastor Morris read aloud, "Be strong in the Lord and in the power of His might. Put on the whole armor of God, that you may be able to stand against the wiles of the devil. For we do not wrestle against flesh and blood, but against principalities, against powers, against the rulers of the darkness of this age, against spiritual hosts of wickedness in the heavenly places…"

The pastor paused his reading when the church doors opened. My heart stopped and I opened my eyes. The vision of my dad had vanished and two of the three newcomers were glimmering brightly. I lifted my head and looked around for Ben, feeling alone and vulnerable on the stage floor.

Ben must have noticed my searching because he was quickly at my side, pulling me to a sitting position and into the safety of his arms. "Don't worry. It's just Mark, Cody, and Olivia."

"What are we going to do, Ben?"

"Do you believe that there is one God, Addy?"

"Yes," I answered with wholehearted conviction.

"Good. You should know that even the demons believe and tremble. God is mightier than Satan and all his followers. He can protect us. In fact, He already has provided us with a surprise blessing."

"What's that?"

"You know Bryan has an uncle in law enforcement, I'm pretty sure he has full jurisdiction throughout the country. You know what that means, Addy?" Ben held me from behind, talking into my ear. "It means that if anyone tries to lay a hand on you, he can have them arrested, even if it's the sheriff of Ledo. He's got us covered in the physical sense and God is here with us, ready for war. It's going to be—"

Ben stopped talking as the door opened once more, bringing a hush over the room.

I heard some people yelling to the intruder but there was no fear when, despite the cloudy waters of my mind, I saw the boy's face. "It's Luke!" There was no glow about him, but I knew he meant me no harm.

"Adelaide! You need to get out of here!" Luke panted, supporting himself against the back pew. "They are going to be here any second."

I could hear Mark yelling for him to get lost, followed up with accusations of his snitch-like behavior.

"No, Ben, help him. They'll hurt him too." I reached an arm in the direction of the shy sophomore, scared for his life; here and eternal.

"You can stay here, with us, Luke," Ben yelled across the room.

"Here? You need to get out of here! Get *her* out of here!" Luke was reasonably frantic.

Someone approached Luke and led him closer to the stage. I was glad to see him welcomed with open arms before the fervent prayers enveloped the room in warmth and light once more. I soon found myself shutting my eyes as the glow seemed to spread and brighten like a shining star reaching its peak before bursting into a super nova.

My eyes quickly flipped back open. My skin felt prickly as I watched the darkness seep into the room spreading around the light like oil around water, never intermixing, just consuming every opening.

"They're here, Ben," I whispered to him. The threatening sound of doors slamming immediately confirmed my statement.

Suddenly the room appeared to be swallowed in darkness while my enemy stood at the back of the sanctuary, some mumbling in German while others demanded that the church give me up. I screamed horrified and shocked that my light was gone though I could still feel its lingering warmth around me. "Go away!" I yelled, more at the thick, intruding darkness than at the covens that awaited my surrender. "My God is greater. My God is greater. My God is greater," I mumbled.

"Yes, He is, Addy," Ben said, confidently in my right ear.

"Things don't need to get out of hand here." The hissing voice seemed to come straight from the heart of the darkness, but I knew it was Viktor speaking. "Maybe we could even come to an agreement. You need money to add on to this precious little sanctuary, Morris, you know very well I can make that happen. And you, Tucker, your wife has a very important message for you. You can speak to her again, all we ask is that you let Miss Dawson go. We won't hurt her, you have my word."

"Take your temptations elsewhere, Viktor!" the pastor shouted, standing right above me.

"Your word means nothing. My wife is basking in the glory of our God in heaven!" I could hear Ben's dad shout from beneath the blanket of darkness.

"In heaven?" The mocking voice of Derek echoed against the walls. "Well, that's too bad because you might be needing him down here on earth right now." He laughed; the kind of deeply disturbing sound that turns your blood and stiffens every fiber of your being.

I clutched tightly onto Ben's hands. "It's so dark, Ben," I said quietly, wondering if everyone else could see the power of the enemy covering our heads.

My heart pounded as more powerful and moving words burst through the shell of heavy darkness, pouring out light like a shining sword splitting through a velvet curtain. "God is light and in Him is no darkness at all," Ben said firmly, his words were a response to my concerned whispers but also a stabbing wound to the enemy.

"If we walk in the light as He is in the light, we have fellowship with one another, and the blood of Jesus Christ His Son cleanses us from all sin!" someone else yelled the quoted words of the Bible without a trace of fear upon their voice.

Shrieks and screams filled the back of the room as they shouted back louder, their own commands to the spirits and begging Donar to show his power.

"Donar, we invoke thee. Come to us. Give us the power to do your will. We call upon the spirits of the earth. We call upon the spirits of the moon and sky. Come and empower us. We are your willing servants. Let your children not be separated. We are bonded by blood, let us not be broken. We give you our lives, we are your vessels. Give us the power to complete your work!"

"Holy, holy, holy is the Lord God Almighty!" someone boldly shouted back.

"You cannot escape him!" James yelled at me. "He will not allow this. It's too late for you, Adelaide! You already committed yourself to him! You belong to him!"

"All of you who have turned your back on our god, you shall suffer! He will have you one way or another!" My uncle's voice shook in desperation. I assumed he was talking about Luke and I. The threat must have hit Luke hard with fear; I could hear him break down and sob beneath the shelter of growing light.

Someone near to me defended our side with passion, as though the threat were linked to him. "The Lord is my light and my salvation. Whom shall I fear? The Lord is the strength of my life, of whom shall I be afraid?!" The voice sounded like the distantly familiar voice of my father. If only it could be him! If only he had believed that; if only he had chosen God before it was too late! A tear streamed down my face as this reality hit me for the first time.

"Hide me under the shadow of Your wings, from the wicked who oppress me, from my deadly enemies who surround me," Ben whispered for only me and God to hear.

The verses that once hung heavily around my neck in the form of a wooden fish now lifted my soul; words that were permanently etched into my mind floated onto my tongue "If you say, 'The *Lord* is my refuge,' and you make the Most High your dwelling, no harm will overtake you, no disaster will come near your tent For he will command his angels concerning you, to guard you in all your ways." I could hear all of the Tuckers and several others repeat the verse with me. "They will lift you up in their hands, so that you will not strike your foot against a stone. You will tread on the lion and the cobra; you will trample the great lion and the serpent. 'Because he loves me,' says the LORD, 'I will rescue him; I will protect him, for he acknowledges my name. He will call on me, and I will answer him; I will be with him in trouble, I will deliver him and honor him. With long life I will satisfy him and show him my salvation.'"

"This is your destiny, you cannot run from this!" Viktor's voice boomed above the crowd.

"Come spirits, come darkness, come shadows. We awaken your power. Fill us this night!" the covens chanted repeatedly as they slowly moved in closer to the stage.

Alight with anger and sorrow, I fought against my long flowing gown and struggled to my feet with the help of a surprised Benjamin.

My soul ached for their hearts that were so sunken in a sticky swamp of deception. If they could just know the truth as I do! "Jesus came into the world as a light, so that no one who believes in him should stay in darkness," I repeated the words that God had once spoken to me as I wondered in my own darkness. "He is the light of the world, whoever follows Him will never walk in darkness but will have the light of life!" I yelled into the blur that was the room, filled with the battle of light and dark, wishing that they wouldn't reject those words as I had. I could have been saved a lot of pain if I only had recognized the Truth sooner.

A strange silence fell across the soldiers of good and evil, and for a split second, I was hopeful that they had climbed up the rope of God's words and out of that dangerous pit.

"He'll have you one way or another!" Viktor yelled as his entire tribe circled the stage, continuing their chants and threats. Within the commotion, someone had scooped me up and retreated farther back against the stage. I watched Ben as he oversaw my departure. Who had taken me? Had I been rescued or kidnapped? I struggled to get a look at the man's face.

23

Sword to Flame

I had been swept off, separated from the crowd, and there was no doubt of the man who had taken me.

"Dad!" How does a hallucination manage to carry you away?

"I gotcha, baby. I won't let anyone touch you." He cradled me tightly.

I examined his face trying to see past the brightness that surrounded him and the blurriness of my eyes. It was the familiar face of the assumed-to-be homeless man who no longer hid under a salt-and-pepper beard and scruff. Clean-shaven and his hair cut away from his face, it was clear that those brown eyes and crooked smile belonged to my father. I didn't understand how he was alive and why he was here and how I could have not recognized him sooner, and I didn't have time to bombard him with those questions now as he was already being bombarded with threats from his brother and nephew who had stepped passed their boundary and onto the stage.

"So this is where you disappeared off to, Stefen? We haven't seen you around for a few weeks."

"Why don't you just let us walk away, Henri?" My father's rough voice rushed my mind with old memories and then it hit me; this was the man who found my Bible. How incredible! God used me as He led my father out of darkness. That Bible I had dropped gave my dad the strength to break the bonds of Satan and to change his life.

"We've already let you walk away once before. You know that you and your daughter belong to us. You of all people should know that you can't escape Donar. It didn't work out so well for you last time, Stefen." My uncle's voice raised unsteadily above the noise.

"We had an agreement, Henri, and you broke it! I only came back so you and your 'god' would leave my daughter alone! Your promises were broken. You lied. The deal is off, and now I have the only real God on my side, there is nothing you can do to separate us from His love."

Henri and Charles stared back at us before Viktor found his way to their side.

"How could you betray us for our enemy? The very one who tortured you when your wife brought him into her life and into your home?" Viktor snarled.

All of the Tuckers and the pastor were suddenly beside us, supporting my dad as he stood up for his new faith.

"It was Satan who was torturing me, giving me nightmares and tormenting my thoughts, driving me to madness and he never stopped until Yahweh, your mighty enemy, filled my life with his strength and power. Satan will do anything to keep us from the truth, from God. But, Viktor, the god you serve will only lead you into suffering and darkness. You are deceived by the devil himself, I see that now, it is all so clear. I wish you could see it too." I could hear that same sorrow in my dad's voice that I had felt.

There was fear and confusion surrounding Charles, sadness covering Henri, and pure, fiery hatred that flamed from Viktor.

"Stefen, how could you?" His brother seemed genuinely hurt by the betrayal.

"I had to give up my wife and daughter! My life was nothing but misery. But I thought it was for the best. I didn't want my little girl caught in our mess. And you ask how could I! How could you, Henri? How could you bring her to this town and offer her these dangerous lies!"

"I was only doing as Donar told me. We swore ourselves to him long ago, I had no choice, you know that." There was remorse behind Henri's words.

"Give us your daughter, Stefen, and we will let you be!" Viktor loudly brought the conversation back to point.

"Not a chance, Viktor. And if you lay one hand on her—" My dad's potential threat was interrupted but also assisted by a man I did not recognize.

"Viktor. I have been hearing a lot about you." The man slid his jacket around his hip, revealing a holstered gun and badge. "I've seen enough here tonight to cuff you all right now. Threatening this entire church and attempted kidnapping and who knows what kind of blood this kid has got all over him." He waved his hand in front of Charles.

I knew the blood was only from the lamb that I had slaughtered, but the idea still seemed to scare Charles. His eyes widened, and he stepped away from Viktor.

"And don't think for one second that your little sheriff buddy can get you out of this mess. He won't be the sheriff when I'm done with him. This is highly inappropriate—"

Viktor laughed heavily, amused and slightly crazed by the man's suggestions. "Do you have any idea who I am? We have connections that far exceed your high positioning. You don't scare us at all, isn't that right, Henri?"

Henri's eyes darted from Viktor to me and to a spot on the wall.

"Like Stefen here was saying, if you lay one hand on her…on anyone of us, I won't hesitate…" The man, whom I assumed was Bryan's uncle, patted his gun.

"We don't need to lay a hand on anyone to get what we came for." Derek Adler had made it through the crowd to support Viktor. "Let us summon the spirits to help us, Viktor, let them deal with her, let them reveal the power of our god against theirs. Donar has his mark upon these wanderers. He will *not* let them stray without consequence." Derek carefully pulled Viktor back and down the stage.

"We shall see who serves a mightier god, Stefen! You better hope that you chose right, there shall be no mercy for you this second time around," Viktor hissed as he walked away, glaring daggers at Luke as he went.

The frightened young sophomore scurried up the other side of the stage to stand between my dad and the pastor. As weird and new as it was, I was certain that my father and I could withstand the attacks of our spiritual enemy, but Luke was another story. He was sitting on the fence, rooting for our side but not playing for the team. He could easily fall into the wrong ballpark.

The lost and angry Children of Donar slowly returned to the back of the sanctuary, mumbling in German as they prepared their curse, spell, or summoning—whatever evil plot they had conspired against us.

"We need to pray. They worship a false god, but the enemy is still very real. We need to put on the full armor of God. They said they would not touch us physically, well, let's not let them touch us spiritually either. Darkness cannot dwell where the light is!" Morris motioned for everyone to gather onto the stage. There was an overflow onto the floor and into the first pew as we all knelt down and prayed more fervently than before.

"He has delivered us from the power of darkness and conveyed us into the kingdom of the Son of His love..." Morris quoted scripture, encouraging the troops and using what he called "the sword of the spirit," which is the word of God to fight the powers unseen.

I tilted my head away from my father's soft shirt and saw Viktor holding up the white cord that had earlier bound my wrists as I gave myself to their "god." The large group of white chanted together as Viktor slowly tied a single knot into the cord before every sentence was spoken.

"By knot of one, this spell has begun. By knot of two, He calls to you. By knot of three, you shall never be free. By knot of four, your protection shall be no more." The darkness came against the light again, trying to force it down, seeking openings to dive in and attack. "By knot of five, you shall be His, dead or alive..." They continued their chant as my father set me down to kneel beside him in prayer. I could feel the heaviness of darkness over me, but the strength of the Lord was holding me up.

"By knot of eight, we have sealed your fate. By knot nine, your life is mine!" Viktor tied the last knot into the thick cord.

"At the name of Jesus every knee should bow, of those in heaven and of those on earth, and of those UNDER THE EARTH, and that every tongue should confess that JESUS CHRIST is LORD, to the glory of God the Father!" Mr. Tucker shouted loudly, expanding the literal shining glory of God above us.

I tried to shut my eyes, but I couldn't take my eyes off the knotted bondage that was held high as Derek lit a match beneath it. "In Donar's name we bind Adelaide to the flame, may you bring upon her death or pain, unless she renounces the enemy's name…" I tuned out their frightening curses as the rope burned and the pressure above me gained, collapsing my back, I leaned forward supporting myself up with my hands. I could feel the burning fires pressing into my forearm, like the traumatic memory of the hot iron brand against my flesh. My scar was glowing red like a hot ember. "You have no power over me," I cried. "I am a child of the one true God now. I don't belong to you!" Instantaneously the burning pressure stopped as a warmth spread across my skin. Tears fell freely from eyes, splashing onto my trembling hands that clutched to the blue carpet. What a mistake I had made! The love I felt was overwhelming; His power greater than any. "Thank you," I sniffled.

My dad gently put a hand on my back as others gathered closer to me.

"Submit to God. Resist the devil, and he will flee from you," Ben whispered beside me, setting his hand atop of my salty, wet one.

"Jesus said, 'Behold I give you the authority to trample on serpents and scorpions, and over all the power of the enemy, and nothing shall by any means hurt you,'" someone within our group said firmly.

I could hear sobbing as someone fell heavily to their knees in front of me. "Addy… Addy," Luke whimpered. "You have to help me, tell me what you did to escape his voice!" He clutched his head and shook it back and forth as he cried.

My body shook as I forced myself up. "Ben told me earlier that God is light and in him there is no darkness. You need to ask God to forgive you and to live in your heart, Luke."

"'The night is far spent, and the day is at hand.'" Pastor Morris put a kind hand on Luke's shoulder. "'Therefore let us cast off the works of darkness, and let us put on the armor of light.' That is from chapter thirteen of the book of Romans, Luke, in the Bible. And in chapter ten of that book it says 'that if you confess with your mouth the Lord Jesus and believe in your heart that God has raised him from the dead, you WILL be saved.'"

"Do you believe that, Luke?" I asked, feeling the strength of love and joy as I watched my friend nod sincerely.

"I have been so deceived, and I am so sorry! I believe that Jesus Christ is Lord!" Luke shouted, turning his head in the enemy's direction. He bowed his head and was quiet for a moment as he prayed.

Our light was growing so brightly that I put both hands over my eyes but the light still streamed between the cracks of my fingers. Glowing brighter and brighter, it was like being inside a star as it was ready to explode. "Jesus, Jesus, Jesus," I whispered over and over.

"Glory to God!" someone yelled, sending out a charge of light, pushing back the forces of darkness that pressed against us.

"Holy, holy holy is the Lord God Almighty, who Was and Is and Is to come!"

Cradling my head between my arms I bent over, resting atop the black lace against my knees to shelter my eyes from the bursting light that banished all darkness from our presence; a supernova that silenced the covens.

Like the ringing silence after a loud explosion the room went quiet. The twenty or so people who stood by the back wall were stunned, baffled by their suppression of power.

I didn't move from my cradled position as I listened to the sound of a conquering army standing to their feet.

Several witches panicked and begged to leave. Viktor's booming voice shouted at their early surrender until the distant noise of police sirens sent the whole clan into a rushed frenzy.

"Addy?" Ben touched my shoulder. "Are you all right?"

I made a sleepy gargled noise in my throat, exhausted with no will to move.

"You said she had taken a drug?" my father asked, crouching down beside me.

"Yes, sir," Ben replied.

The slamming of doors was a comforting reassurance that the fight was over, at least for now.

"I'm sure she's not feeling good. After a couple hours of its hallucinogenic and relaxing-type effects, it hits you hard. She'll probably be in a dead sleep until late tomorrow morning." My dad carefully picked me up and pulled me close to him. "I'm so sorry, baby, you should have never had to go through that. It's my fault. I wanted to be there for you but…my mind was so weak. I had nearly lost my sanity over the years. I wanted to talk to you, to save you from this, but it was too early. I would have been dragged down again. When I saw you on the sidewalk that night I was so…so enraged. And I'm ashamed to say, I was too afraid to confront you; afraid of the spirits and voices that haunted me every day. Please forgive me, Adelaide, please."

"Henri…" I tried to lift my ten pounds of eyelids to see his face. "He said you were dead." I wanted to jump up and down with delight over my dad's return but I was like dead weight in his arms.

"Oh, sugar! I am so sorry. I only wanted to protect you. I didn't think there was any other way. I didn't think that there was any escape from…from Satan." His voice cracked.

My mind flew through the words that I could say to make him feel better but all that came out was a simple, "I love you."

He kissed my forehead and slowly walked down the stairs; the silk and lace of my gown tickled the sides of my feet as it swooshed back and forth.

I could see blue and red lights flashing through the window, but I was asleep before we made it through the doors, ending the worst and best day of my life.

That night my sleep was restful with no nightmares or lingering fear. Just like the marvelous nap I took in Olivia's bedroom, I awoke with a smile and feeling of well-being. Not a trace of doubt in my mind.

I was on the right track in life. My mother would be so happy, and my dad...my dad!

I popped out of my lavender sheets and ran out of my room in search of my father.

I went tumbling out of the hallway to see not only my father grinning shyly at my smiling and teary-eyed mother in the kitchen but a living room full of chatter. My grandfather sat at our table talking to Mr. Tucker and Pastor Morris. Ollie was giggling loudly between Cody and Calvin on our couch and of course there was Benjamin, smiling and listening to his brother's animated retelling or the previous night.

"You're awake!" My dad had spotted me and ran over to pull me into a bear hug.

"Daddy, you're here!"

"He's *home*," my mom said, joining the hug.

The overwhelming and joyful emotions tried to drip from my eyes, but I quickly caught them and held them in for later.

I held on to my father for another good five minutes as we talked and listened to my mom fuss over my life-threatening night.

"Well, you're father is helping me make lunch for everyone. You should go say hello to your friends. We can talk more later, sweetie." My mom tugged at my dad's arm.

"Lunch?" I asked, surprised.

"It's almost two o'clock, Adders," my grandpa explained, overhearing the conversation.

I walked over and kissed his bearded cheek. "I guess I was pretty out of it."

"I'd say so," he replied. All three men at the table smiled at me.

I turned to the young crowd; Ben was grinning at me as he scooted over in his overstuffed love seat, patting the empty cushion. Ignoring my fluff of hair and dirty face, I plopped down beside him. "Good morn—afternoon, Benjamin."

"How are you feeling?"

"Great. I don't think I could ever be any better! I'm safe, my dad is home, and I'm sitting with my best friend." I smiled at him.

"Friends!" Ollie corrected, butting into the conversation.

"Of course, Ollie." My cheeks warmed as I thought of how awful I had treated my friends. "I need to apologize to you all. I should have listened to you and I should have been nicer…"

"Well, now you know to listen to me from now on." Olivia shook her finger at me, giggles seeping from her serious tone of voice.

"We're just thrilled that you're okay," Calvin said.

"Was anyone arrested last night?" I tried to think back.

"Everyone was gone when the cops pulled up except for your uncle. He was collapsed in the lawn outside, crying. You don't remember that? Your dad talked to him for a while. Pastor Morris even prayed with him and Charles. It was amazing. Marshall Evans said that he would lose his job as sheriff, but I think Henri was okay with that. He doesn't want any part of his past."

My jaw dropped; I couldn't believe it.

"It was a very powerful experience last night," Cody added. "I think Mark realized for the first time just how real God is."

Ollie leaned forward on the couch. "I'm not sure what will happen to all your old friends, but you're going to be just fine, Addy. Satan had his hooks in you, though, and he will never stop trying to get that back. He attacks everyone differently. You need to be watchful and strong in your faith. The spiritual battle never ceases, it's around us all the time. Pray and read God's word. Keep up your defenses."

"It might be pretty rough for a while, but you have all of us," Calvin continued. "God calls us to love our enemies, even pray for them, and that's what we will continue to do. I'm sure your dad will be keeping a close eye on you now, too."

I smiled and sat back, thinking on that last phrase. I quietly observed my father and mother interacting in the kitchen. My mom was attempting to spread mustard onto a sandwich, but my dad continued to sweep her into his arms and whisper into her ear. What he said I wasn't sure, but my mother giggled like a little girl.

My smile was deeply embedded into my face. All was well within my home and family for the first time in so many years. All was well within my heart also, for the first time in my life.

"I'm glad to see you back to your old self again." Ben grinned, watching my happy expression.

"Better than my old self." I exhaled a sigh of contentment.

"Did Calvin tell you that he is going back to college next year?" Ollie snuck back into our conversation. "I'm going to be brother-less!" She stuck out her bottom lip in a pout.

Calvin shook his head at her and looked at me. "Where are you going, Addy?"

My eyes grew big as I realized that I only had a few weeks left before graduation and my college plan was no longer plausible…or desirable. "I…oh my gosh, I have no idea!"

Calvin laughed and looked at Ben who was grinning widely.

"What?" I said confused by their lack of concern for me.

Ben pulled a folded envelope from his jean pocket. "No pressure. Your mom and I thought you might want some more options, so we applied for you. I hope that's okay."

Shocked, I opened the envelope and read my acceptance letter to Whitworth University. "This is where you two are going next year?" I said excitedly.

"Yup." Ben laughed at my enthusiasm. "But like I said, no pressure. It is your choice, but I would really love if you were there with me."

I examined his incredible features. He was too handsome to let loose in a big school without me; selfish reasoning, but by the way he was looking at me, I was sure he didn't care. "Thank you. I don't know what I would have done…"

"So that's a yes?" Ben's eyes lit up.

I nodded.

He was quiet for a minute and then a mischievous grin spread across his face. "How much do you remember about last night?"

"Everything, I think, at least until I fell asleep." My voice became skeptic as I saw the look in his eyes. "Why?"

"So do you remember what you said to me just before we entered the church?"

My cheeks filled with warmth as my humiliating words came back to me. "I said…I love you," I replied sheepishly. "But in my defense…I was heavily drugged!"

"Are you saying that you didn't mean it?" Fake pain lined his face.

I glared at him as I quickly tried to think of a response that wouldn't be a lie.

He chuckled. "I didn't mean to make you so flustered. I guess what I am asking is…was that your way of saying you want me to be your boyfriend?"

I couldn't tell if he was teasing me, but I was stunned and embarrassed by his accusation. "What! No, that's not…No!"

Ben raised both eyebrows. "Hmm, well, about that…"

"As you have therefore received Christ Jesus the Lord, so walk in Him, rooted and built up in Him and established in the faith, as you have been taught, abounding in it with thanksgiving. Beware lest anyone cheat you through philosophy and empty deceit, according to the tradition of men, according to the basic principles of the world, and not according to Christ." (Colossians 2:6–8)

Truth

- *White witches* is a term covering all that practice witchcraft but claim to do no harm.
- These witches accept other religions but are offended by Christianity, the one truth.
- Most modern witchcraft is a religion based in nature.
- Wicca, one of the most popular forms of ancient witchcraft, is an official religion in the USA.
- In 2001, there were an estimated 134,000 Wiccans, 140,000 pagans, and 33,000 druids in America.
- The number of those practicing witchcraft is rapidly growing. Estimated to have reached 342,000 Americans identifying themselves as Wiccans by 2008.
- Judges have ruled that witches must be allowed to lead prayers at local government meetings.
- In 2006, there were an estimated 1,800 active-duty service members that identified themselves as Wiccans.
- Paganism includes all religions that discount the God of the Bible. Paganism accounts for 50% of all religions.
- Most witches believe in a deity as god and goddess and worship mother earth and the Horned One.
- Witches claim their religion has nothing to do with the devil and that he is only a notion created by fearful Christians. Wiccans believe in no evil entity.
- Their symbol is the pentagram. The five points are earth, air, fire, water, and spirit.

- Xtianity is the religions of witches that believe they follow Christianity, so-called "Christian Witches." There are many references to witchcraft in the Bible. Never can it coincide with Christianity. Never is it acceptable to worship anyone or anything but God himself.
- Many practicing witchcraft avoid sacrificial and sexual rituals, but these rituals are highly important and common among many.
- In 1960, there were groups of witches in East Germany who hunted deer to use for "blood-drinking rite."
- Witchcraft is said to be the fastest growing religious belief in the U.S. Making it the second or third largest religion in the U.S. Witchcraft numbers passed Buddhism in 2005 and Hinduism in 2007, passed Islam in 2008, and passed Judaism in March of 2009.
- The traditions, beliefs, views, and rituals vary within each cult/coven.
- Rituals are practiced within a circle. This is said to be their gateway between worlds, a time to communicate with spirits. A witch is never to step outside the circle during a ritual unless a doorway has been prepared. A circle is highly powerful and important to a witch.
- A hereditary witch is one who was taught by a relative and can trace back the practicing of the craft back through their family tree.
- The legendary Donar's Oak was sacred to the Germanic tribe of the Chattii. Donar was their god of thunder that wields a hammer.
- Most witches would say that Jesus may have been a real man, but he was not the son of any god. They believe the Bible to be false.
- The truth is, the Bible is the Word of God, the one-true-God, who is the same yesterday, today and forever. There is freedom in this truth.

God's Truth
- 1 Timothy 4:1
- Deuteronomy 18:9–15
- Hebrews 9:27
- Galatians 5:19
- Psalm 106:36–41
- Leviticus 19:31
- Genesis 3:5
- Deuteronomy 12:31
- Psalm 24:1
- Leviticus 20:6
- 1 John 4:1–6
- Daniel 2:1–27
- Deuteronomy 4:19
- Revelations 9:20
- Exodus 7:10–9:8
- Acts 4:12

About the Author

Natalie Joy Andrews resides in her beautiful home town in the Rocky Mountains of Montana where she can indulge in her love for exploring nature and discovering new adventures. She spends most of her time working with midwifes at the local hospital and studying for her degree in crisis counseling psychology.

She has had a love for writing since she was a young girl fed by years of exchanging stories through the mail with her grandmother.

CPSIA information can be obtained at www.ICGtesting.com
Printed in the USA
LVOW08s2321160716

496614LV00001B/356/P